When it comes to love . . .

With his dashing good looks and looming bankruptcy, Nathan Cantrell is Sir Harlan's answer to one of his three problems: three unwed daughters. And he's not above a little blackmail to bring about a satisfying end to his dilemma. So Nathan must choose between ruin—or marriage to Violet, the willowy widow, Sophy, the high-spirited schoolgirl . . . or Abigail, the bookworm. Nathan despairs of his options—until a morning swim finds him besotted by the captivating beauty of a most unlikely water nymph . . .

. . . Experience is the best teacher

Certainly Abigail had no idea the Adonis she encountered in the pond would turn out to be her father's guest, whose knowing eyes and sensual smile make her weak. Nonetheless, she has more important things to attend to beind closed doors—for Abigail lives a secret life as London's premier author of Gothic romance. Surely the woman who lives vicariously through romance in her novels has no need for the real thing. Then again, research is always beneficial, especially since happy endings are the most crucial aspect of any good love story . . .

HIS CHOSEN BRIDE

Alexandra Bassett

ZEBRA BOOKS
Kensington Publishing Corp.

ZEBRA BOOKS are published by

Kensington Publishing Corp.
850 Third Avenue
New York, NY 10022

ISBN 0-7394-5555-9

Printed in the United States of America

For Elena

Chapter One

Up the rocky hillside galloped the dark-cloaked figure, his hat set against the wild wind whipping around the grounds of Raffizzi castle. The black steed's hooves stirred a pounding, pounding echo that seemed to announce, "I approach! I approach! Beware . . . Miss Abigail!"

—The Prisoner of Raffizzi

"Miss Abigail!"

Abigail Wingate blinked down at the page before her. *Abigail?* The heroine of her story was named Clara. Yet for some reason she'd actually written her own name, as if it had been spoken to her.

After gaping in surprise at her handwriting, she realized her name *had* been spoken—by Peabody, the Wingates' butler—and that the pounding, pounding echo was actually him banging on the closed door to her study.

She flipped over her papers and tried to appear absorbed in the book in front of her, a history of ancient Rome. "Yes?"

Peabody bustled into the room. "Miss Abigail! I've been knocking for a full minute!"

"I'm sorry, Peabody."

"How you do get lost in your reading!"

The butler, slight of build except for a slightly bulging pot for a belly that pushed against his immaculate waistcoat, looked irritated. But Peabody was always perturbed about something. After his last position at the elegant Duke of Stafford's—whose early demise from the measles

Peabody still mourned with genuine tears—his situation at Peacock Hall was seen as a bitter comedown in life. He bore his reduced circumstances like a man trying, though not always succeeding, to bear the flag of British civilization bravely through a populace of heathens.

He slicked a hand over the thinning hairs on his head. "I'm sure I don't know how you can sit calmly reading when the entire house is at sixes and sevens. I've never seen such a fuss since I left the Duke's employ, though of course at the Duke's I was never in mortal peril."

"Mortal peril?" The novelist in Abigail had to admire a man who could reap so much drama from a job as butler in a rather drab household in Yorkshire.

He mopped his brow with a handkerchief starched within an inch of its life. "The turtle, miss."

"Turtle?" She didn't know what the man could be talking about. But of course she had been hiding herself in her little study for the express purpose of avoiding the chaos that reigned in the household before events such as the dinner to be held there tonight.

"For the soup. Cook sent to London for a turtle and it only just arrived." Peabody frowned. "Though part of me wishes the vile reptile had been kidnapped on the road. The creature nearly took my hand off!"

The poor man did appear more traumatized than usual. As if working for the Wingates weren't bane enough for Peabody under normal circumstances. "There, there, Peabody," Abigail said in an attempt to soothe him. "The soup pot will be your vengeance on the beast." She closed her book, carefully placing it over her papers. "Was there some reason in particular you wanted to see me?"

"Oh!" Peabody, who had apparently been reliving his near-escape from the jaws of the soup turtle, came to attention. "Your father, miss! He's asked to see you and your sisters in the library right away."

And of course while she had been absorbed in the tale of Peabody's turtle attack, *right away* had probably come and gone. Abigail jumped up. Sir Harlan was not a man to be kept waiting.

She hurried to her father's library. The room, which despite its name contained only a smattering of volumes, was decorated precisely to Sir Harlan's taste. It was thoroughly masculine. Antlers stood sentry on either side of the door. The walls were wainscoted in oak, and heavy drapes of forest green brocade drooped gloomily around the windows. The crush of furniture was of the good, sturdy English variety, so at odds with the rest of the house, which had been decorated by their late mother, who had a taste for the French mode. That woman's portrait, by Gainsborough, graced one side of the room. The opposite wall was occupied by an even larger painting of Sir Harlan's other great love—his peacocks, Garrick and Mrs. Siddons— done in vibrant oils by an artist of slightly lesser repute.

"About time!" her father bellowed from behind his desk as she scooted into a chair between her two sisters, Violet and Sophy, who were already seated.

Violet, who hated to be kept waiting as much as their father (but who never hesitated to keep others dangling if it suited her whim), cut her eyes toward Abigail in irritation, while Sophy, high-spirited even for a girl of seventeen, reached over and pinched her elbow. Clearly, something was afoot . . . and Abigail could only guess that it had to do with the guest for their sumptuous dinner, whose identity Sir Harlan had heretofore kept secret from them.

They all turned back to their father expectantly.

At first glance, Sir Harlan Wingate did not cut an impressive figure. Short and stout, with a mop of dark hair peppered with gray and large blue eyes that bulged over a decidedly bulbous nose, he had a distinctly froglike appearance. Yet upon closer inspection one could see that his clothes, though in the country fashion, were nevertheless cut from a London tailor of the first stare. Though Sir Harlan had made his fortune in trade and earned his social prominence through marriage to a baronet's daughter, he never let it be forgotten that the Wingates had been among the first families of Yorkshire long before he had bought his knighthood from the perennially strapped Prince of Wales five years earlier.

"I beg your pardon for taking so long, Father," Abigail said breathlessly as she folded her ink-stained hands in her lap. "I was only—"

"Scribbling, I'll be bound!" her father croaked.

"I told you she'd be at her diary," Sophy piped up. Her lively dark blue eyes danced with humor. If there was anything Sophy could not understand, it was a person wanting to spend her time in pursuits that had nothing to do with the pursuit of men.

"Damme if I know what a girl of four and twenty who hasn't left the county in three years could possibly have to record about her life," Sir Harlan said. "It's a lot of nonsense, if you want my opinion."

"Yes, Father," Abigail said obediently. She had never kept a diary in her life, but if that was what her family wanted to believe, she was happy not to disabuse them of that notion.

"I always told your mama we'd live to regret sending you girls to that expensive school." He looked up at the portrait of his late wife as if he were continuing a long argument they'd had throughout their married life. "But no, she wanted you to be elegantly educated—and look at the result! I've been saddled with literate, useless females! You should be married with homes of your own."

Violet's fashionably pale cheeks flushed with indignation. "But father, I *was* married—to the heir of a marquess, no less!"

Sir Harlan harrumphed. "To a namby-pamby who died of influenza before you'd been off my hands two winters. And what've you been up to since then, I'd like to know. No husband on the horizon that I can see."

Abigail's older sister bristled. "Father, when one has been the wife of an heir to a marquess, one is obliged to be selective when considering a second marriage."

"She means it's an earl or better, or nothing," Sophy said with a snicker.

Their father chortled heartily along with his youngest as Violet's pallor turned to pink. "It's very hard to hear my bereaved state referred to in such a coarse, jocular manner," she said heatedly.

Sophy nearly doubled over. "Oh, Violet! The only thing you've ever grieved is the fact that you weren't born to the aristocracy."

Violet stiffened like an animal under attack from two sides. "You shouldn't let this child talk to me so disrespectfully, Father!"

"I'm not a child, I'm seventeen," Sophy said, sobering quickly. "I've finished school."

Sir Harlan barked mirthfully at that bit of braggadocio. "Your school nearly finished us, you mean! Miss Pargeter's Academy for Young Ladies, by gad! I should have demanded the school be renamed in my honor after that Pargeter creature put the final squeeze on me."

Sophy bridled prettily. "Oh, Father!"

"Though I can't say it might not have been better to park you there a while longer and damn the cost," he said as he scratched his chin. "Considering all the trouble you've stirred up since you've been home. Gossip seems to sprout up about you like dandelions!"

Sophy, who was still living down a recent shame after having been discovered with a certain handsome young groom in Sir Harlan's gun room, fell wisely and uncharacteristically silent.

"Father." Abigail was still impatient to know why he had summoned them for this conference. She wanted to get back to her scribbling, as her father would have phrased it. "What did you wish to speak to us about?"

Too excited to sit, Sophy hopped out of her chair. "Yes, do tell us, Father. I'm sure it has something to do with the dinner this evening!"

Even Violet was suddenly rigid with interest. "Is the earl coming to dine with us?"

The Earl of Clatsop, a contemporary of Sir Harlan, was of particular interest to Violet. It didn't seem to matter to her that the earl was elderly, balding, and more interested in ornithology than flirtation. He was a bachelor, and titled. Ever since her father had developed a passing acquaintance with the earl, it had become Violet's dream (and Peabody's) to see herself installed as the mistress of Clatsop Castle, whose ancient walls she had never seen, but the magnificence of which she was never in doubt.

"No, the earl is not coming," Sir Harlan said dismissively, dashing poor Violet's hopes, "but yes, I wanted to speak to you of our dinner guest, Mr. Cantrell."

Abigail frowned at the name. Old Mr. Cantrell, of the nearby estate called The Willows, had died a year ago. Sir Harlan had to be speaking of one of the two sons.

Her hunch was confirmed by Violet's reaction. "*Not* Nathan Cantrell!" she exclaimed in disgust.

"I thought he was in the army." In fact, Abigail knew he was. That's why so few in the neighborhood knew him. He had been sent off to school, and then to the war on the Continent. His younger brother, Freddy, she had encountered a few times. An apparent budding aspirant to the dandy set, the last time she'd seen him.

Sophy clapped her hands delightedly. "A soldier! How delicious! Is he handsome?"

Violet let out an unbecoming snort. "Neither of you would remember him, but *I* do. A more ill-mannered beast there never was. One dance with the man practically crippled me!"

"He's recently left the army," Sir Harlan informed them. "And you won't be dancing tonight, Violet, so you needn't worry over your slippers." Sir Harlan rapped his knuckles on his desk. "I want the three of you to be on your best behavior tonight." His keen dark eyes homed in on Sophy. "Which means, miss, stifle your giggling. And no winking at the serving boy."

"Patrick serves now," Sophy reminded him. Patrick was seventy, and so frail that he always appeared in imminent danger of toppling under the weight of the food platters. But he had replaced a younger man, Stevens, who one memorable moonlit evening broke into the cook's sherry and was caught singing a rather bawdy song outside Sophy's room.

Sir Harlan laughed. "Well for heaven's sake, don't wink at

Patrick. The man might pass out in the pudding." He turned next to his oldest. "And *you,* Violet, try not to put on airs. A man who's served with honor on the field of battle doesn't need to be under fire at home by a top-lofty chit."

Violet recoiled in offense. "Why, you make it sound as if I'm a snob!"

Abigail coughed into her hand to cover a laugh. Violet was the most snobbish person living at Peacock Hall—except for, of course, Peabody. Concerning the social hierarchy, and the need to climb it at all costs, woman and butler were in complete sympathy.

Unfortunately, the small gesture of her ink-stained hand drew attention to herself. As he regarded her, Sir Harlan's expression showed, if possible, more exasperation than he'd aimed at either Sophy or Violet. "And you, Abigail, for once in your life put on something other than those dowdy brown drapes you call dresses! Good heavens, the way these London modistes drain my coffers every year, you would think my daughter wouldn't have to run around looking like an unsightly bluestocking. And scrub your hands until you get the ink off your fingers—stop your scribbling for the day if you must. And your hair—" He lifted his hands and made fluttering motions around his own short locks. "Curl it or whatever females are doing these days to seem fashionable. Just try to make yourself look less like a damn schoolmistress."

On that note of paternal devotion, they were all dismissed.

The sisters left the room in starkly contrasting moods. Sophy, who was jubilant, practically danced on her toes down the hallway. "Did you hear? A war hero is coming to dinner! Maybe the very man whose bullet felled Napoleon!"

Abigail shook her head. "Napoleon is still alive," she informed her sister, who had managed to absorb the fact that the war had ended but left the details for others to sort out. "He's in exile now, on Elba."

"Oh!" Sophy pouted in confusion. "Then I suppose Mr. Cantrell mustn't have shot him—or else didn't do a very good job of it. Is Mr. Cantrell handsome, Violet?" She didn't wait for an answer. "Oh, he must be—and at the very least, he's young." She frowned. "Well, leastwise he ain't old, like all the men around here."

Violet rounded on her in vexation. "And whose fault is that? If you didn't flirt with every servant in sight, Sophy, our staff wouldn't make Peacock Hall resemble a pensioner's home. And as for Mr. Cantrell's being handsome—not in the least! As I recall, he was a spotty boy of nineteen, with lumpy features and ill-fitting clothes. A true rustic."

Though Abigail was still stinging from her father's harsh words, she smiled at Violet. "I suppose, since we *are* from the same neighborhood, then we are also rustics?"

Violet lifted her chin and posed proudly, showing off her slim stature and fine bones to perfect effect. "Don't be ridiculous. Our mother was a baronet's daughter, while the Cantrells are of no consequence whatsoever—they only managed to be at all acceptable socially because the women in their family always managed to marry titles."

Which, Abigail might have pointed out, was no worse than buying yourself one, as their father had done.

"Father just wants us to be kind to him out of respect to his father's memory," Violet continued, "but everyone knows those Cantrells don't have two pence to rub together. They haven't had a female for three generations. And there's no hope of Nathan Cantrell marrying well. A more unpromising match I couldn't imagine!"

Abigail knew little of the younger Cantrells, so she couldn't contradict her sister. Certainly old Mr. Cantrell hadn't been one to turn the ladies' heads, but what did that signify? Who would have guessed that Sir Harlan would produce such a fair, statuesque beauty as Violet?

"Oh, fiddle!" Sophy looked deflated in her disappointment. "I was so hoping he would be dashing. Of course, he *is* a soldier, so he'll be in uniform, I suppose."

Violet sneered. "I thought the only uniform that attracted you was livery."

At the reminder of Sophy's recent encounter with the groom in the gun room, Abigail cut off the conversation. "Violet, enough!" There was ample talk about that unfor-

tunate incident in the neighborhood already; she didn't
want the servants to hear them discussing it. Although Violet was correct. Thanks to Sophy most of their servants
required ear trumpets to hear anything at all.

"Father is absolutely right," Abigail said, though it
pained her to say so. Fancy dress? Curl her hair? What a
bother! "Naturally we should make every effort to be
everything agreeable to our returning neighbor. Which
should include not sniping amongst ourselves."

Violet rolled her eyes in disdain. "Well, I would think
you *would* want to make yourself attractive to the fubsy-
faced Mr. Cantrell, since I'm sure you will have few
chances to meet more promising men cooped up in Peacock Hall as you always are. You'd be wise to try to impress whatever comes your way, given your advancing
years. Why, you're twenty-four and haven't so much as received a proposal."

Sophy sucked in her breath. "You shouldn't speak to her
that way!" she cried, rushing to Abigail's defense. "Abigail
can't help it that she's a hopeless old maid. She has a frail
constitution, and hasn't had the opportunities you have
had."

"Frail or not," Violet twitted Abigail, "I would think
you'd be in a frenzy at the prospect of moldering on the
shelf."

Had she not just lectured her sisters on the need to com-
port themselves like ladies, Abigail might have followed
through with her impulse to reach over and twist her sister's twiggy arm. "There are other goals in life besides
catching a husband," she pointed out heatedly.

Violet blinked. "I can't think what those might be."

Sophy seemed likewise perplexed. "I can't either. How
strange you sound sometimes, Abigail! One would almost
think you *want* to be a spinster." She shuddered, then
placed a reassuring hand on Abigail's sleeve. "But of
course we all know it's just your unfortunate circumstance
that makes you say such things."

After her meeting with her father and her discussion
with her sisters, Abigail was no longer in the mood for

writing. The clock in the hall struck eleven—eleven, and it already felt warm in the house. She decided to slip out for a long walk to the pond.

Once out in the sunshine, she found herself huffing along faster than she was wont to do around her family, who lived under the belief that she was invalidish. This misconception was owed to the fact that, before her first Season, she had contracted mumps just a week before she was to go to London. Her Aunt Augusta, who was to sponsor her, had felt so sorry for her that she had sent Abigail a whole trunkload of books to read during her recovery. They were mostly Gothic novels of the rather lurid, romantic variety. Aunt Augusta would be shocked to know what an antidote her present had proved for Abigail. She so enjoyed reading the books that she tried her hand at penning one herself. Pleased with her effort, on a lark she had sent the manuscript to a publisher under a pseudonym, Georgianna Harcourt. To her amazement, it had been accepted and published.

Thus had begun her double life. The next season, she was late getting *The Scarlet Veil* to her publisher, so she had developed a spurious putrid sore throat and was again kept in the country to recuperate under Sir Harlan's negligent eye. The large amount of outgoing mail to one H.P. Black she explained as correspondence and reading matter for an unfortunate old school friend who was bedridden.

After three years of such deception, and three successful novels published in secret, her family had ceased to make the effort to bring her out. This capitulation had been a triumph for Abigail, who wasn't attracted to the social whirl. Her London finery from her earlier aborted trips was packed in camphor, and now her Seasons were marked with intrigues completely of her own making. Her "scribbling" had earned her six hundred pounds. In addition to the pleasure of writing, she spent many enjoyable hours planning on ways to spend her income. So far she was unable to decide whether she wanted to be a seasoned traveler or a generous philanthropist—maybe a mix of the two would be best. And in the meantime, she had to say

she much preferred penning sweeping dramas of kidnap-
pings and other sinister goings-on to presenting herself on
the marriage mart, where she doubted her prospects for
success in any case.

That was why her father's admonition to trick herself up
like Sophy and Violet so dismayed her. No amount of fuss
and feathers could make her match the beauty of her sisters, and she felt foolish even trying. If Violet was blond
and striking, and Sophy dark-haired and red-cheeked with
health, then Abigail inhabited a no-man's land between the
two. She had brown eyes and much duller brown hair than
Sophy's. She possessed neither her older sister's splendid
height and bearing nor her younger sister's petite, pistol-
like vitality. Violet looked elegant in any gown she wore
(though of course she never appeared anything less than
fashionably turned out), while Sophy was always girlish
and fresh. Finery didn't suit Abigail. She preferred dresses
she could work and breathe in. Besides being comfortable,
her dowdy dresses fed the illusion of poor health since
their drab colors were unflattering to Abigail's complexion.

By the time she reached the pond, she realized that she
had worked herself into a state of nerves over this evening.
What a nuisance! She was beginning to dislike fubsy-
faced Nathan Cantrell almost as much as Violet did. Also,
she was hot. She looked out over all the cool blue water of
the pond with longing. When she was a girl she'd thought
nothing of peeling off her dress and hopping into the water
on a sweltering July day.

But now that she was supposed to be a lady . . .

A spinster . . .

An invalid . . .

A wicked, rebellious smile spread across her face and
she hurried to the shade of a willow tree and shucked the
brown muslin frock her father had found so offensive. She
didn't even bother to delicately wade into the water but
plunged right in. Her hair uncoiled from its bun, but she
didn't care. There would be plenty of time for her hair to

dry before dinner—and for her to try to tame it into some sort of acceptable style.

She stroked across the cold pond twice, feeling reinvigorated. Banished were thoughts of hated dresses, angry turtles, and Violet's insults. She floated and gazed up at the clear blue sky and thought about nothing but six hundred pounds and sea voyages and the Baron of Raffizzi, who was the dark hero of the novel she was just beginning. *The Prisoner of Raffizzi* would be her best book yet. Which, considering her modest view of her talents, wasn't being overly effusive. But at the start of each story she always had high hopes, and enjoyed the prospect of several months of living the exotic, eventful life of her heroine. In this case, it was Clara, a penniless governness to an English couple in Italy who becomes drawn into Rudolpho Raffizzi's misguided scheme of vengeance against her employer, the woman he had loved and lost.

Floating in the shade of the willow, Abigail missed the sound of a horse's hooves until they were nearly upon her.

A flush mounted in her cheeks at the idea of someone finding her floating in the pond in her shift. Pray God let it be Sophy on one of her afternoon rides—although her family would be aghast, and suspicious, to discover "frail" Abigail bathing in the open air.

It was too late to make a dash for her clothing, so she scooted beneath a willow branch overhanging the water. Moments later a rider came over the hill within sight of the pond. Alas, it was not Sophy. The man, who rode a large roan, reined in his horse next to the pond and dismounted. For a few seemingly endless moments he stared at the water in contemplation, leaving a panicked Abigail to scrutinize him. He was a large man in high boots and buckskin breeches. Beneath his navy wool coat he wore a snowy white shirt. He doffed his hat to reveal a head of thick, dark blond hair.

Ride on, Abigail silently commanded him. *Oh, please, get back on your horse and ride on.*

Her plea went unheeded. The man unbuttoned his coat, shed it, and tore off his shirt. Finding herself gazing at a beautifully muscled torso, Abigail swallowed a gasp. Good Lord! She hadn't expected the man to strip to bare skin!

Then, to her dismay, the man unbuttoned his breeches. Her eyes bugged as she caught flashes of buttock, sculpted thighs, and that part of the male anatomy known only to her from artistic renderings. Though no artist or sculptor she had yet encountered had ever used *this* generously endowed man as a model.

By the time he was pulling off his boots, a beet-faced Abigail had slithered as far beneath her willow branch as humanly possible. Would that she were a fish and could dart *beneath* the water! All she could do was wait, pray she would remain undiscovered, and listen to the splashing as the man frolicked in the water as she had done.

And watch. Try as she might to avert her eyes, the sight of the man's chest drew her gaze again and again. His broad, lightly haired torso glistened as water droplets cascaded over it.

Her fascination was purely that of an author, she assured herself to assuage a guilty conscience. For though she had written in detail about the impressive physiques of her heroes, she had never had an opportunity to study the male form so closely. Excepting, of course, those artistic renderings. She had seen quite a bit of statuary during her one museum trip in London.

But she now realized at once that there was a vast difference between statuary and a flesh-and-blood male. A statue never made her pulse race quite like hers was racing now. A fine statue existed to arouse lofty thoughts—this flesh-and-blood torso brought a more animalistic appreciation. Even pictures of the beautiful statue of David, with its splendid, thorough anatomical detail of the male form, had never brought heat to her cheeks.

The swimmer came dangerously near the willow, then dunked his head under the water. Abigail frowned for a moment, wondering what on earth had happened to the man. She waited, shivering, for him to emerge again.

And waited.

Just when she was becoming concerned that he would

drown, he erupted out of the deep, breaking the surface with an exuberant whoop. The tidal wave of water resulting from his movement smacked Abigail square in the face.

She gasped and found herself gulping and trying not to cough up the water she had inadvertently swallowed. But it was a futile effort. She had been detected.

The man turned in shock, and through tearing eyes and willow leaves she got a closer view of his face. Lord, he was a handsome creature! Thick, waving hair. Piercing green eyes. A wide mouth with red, full lips.

Right now that mouth was hanging open in surprise.

"You startled me!" he exclaimed.

Abigail coughed.

His dark brows drew together. "Are you all right?" He began to glide towards her.

She slapped her palm on the water, trying to recover her voice. "Do not . . ." She coughed again. ". . . come closer!"

He stopped, frowning. "But you're choking."

"No, I—" She sputtered and hacked for a few seconds.

"Allow me." In two strokes he had crossed to her. He held her arm with one hand while the other pounded on her back.

Mortified, Abigail gagged up the last of the water and then heard herself release a loud, unladylike belch. Despite heat flaming in her cheeks, she was shivering now with cold, and was thoroughly discomposed. Gooseflesh rose on the arm he held. She could not look the man in the eye even after her respiratory functions were somewhat back to normal. Her heart was beating like a hummingbird's wings. What was she doing standing in nothing but her wet shift with a naked man? If anyone were to see them, the scandal would outdo even Sophy's most foolish escapade.

"There!" he exclaimed, revealing none of her mental frenzy. "Better?"

She finally managed to look up at him and nod. He had fine bones, and a strong jaw that was finished off with a slightly cleft chin. And those eyes—they were so green, the color of new spring foliage. She'd never seen their like.

And she'd never felt a grip like the one he had on her arm.

"Sure?" he asked, his wide mouth curving up into a smile.

Moments earlier she had been certain that she couldn't feel any more hot and flustered; but she'd been wrong. That smile and the questioning spark in his green eyes made her feel fiery all over. Yet at the same time, she shivered. "Qu-quite sure," she replied through chattering teeth. She gave her arm a subtle tug that he apparently chose to ignore. "I just wasn't expecting to get a faceful of water when you rose from the depths like Neptune."

A low chuckle rumbled out of his chest. "I wouldn't have done so had I known there was a water sprite hovering in the bushes. Why didn't you make yourself known?"

Could he not see that she was mortified? Had he no sense of propriety?

She quivered in irritation. "Sir, I was—*am*—in no position to receive company!"

Her exclamation brought another low laugh. "Nor am I—though I certainly wouldn't have shucked all my clothes if I'd known the pond was already occupied by a lovely nymph."

As if he had to remind her that he was standing before her as bare as Adam! And did he have to keep calling her a water sprite? And *lovely?* That was doing it too brown. "Since you *do* know I'm here now . . ." She tugged again at her arm.

Finally, he let her go, if only so he could cross his arms over his wide, muscled chest and laugh. "I see! You're vexed that I swam over to you. But surely you aren't such a chucklehead that you'd prefer choking to death to a little embarrassment."

Her mouth flopped open. No one, not even her father, had ever called her a chucklehead.

"You needn't look so out of countenance," he went on. "You're perfectly covered in that . . ." He nodded towards the shift that floated up above her shoulders. The only part of her body poking out of the water was her head from her chin up. ". . . bathing costume."

Far be it from her to tell him that she was standing before him in her undergarments. "But *you* are not!"

He looked down at his broad-shouldered, muscled torso, then returned her red-faced gaze with a devilish smile. "No, I prefer to be unencumbered when I bathe."

"And I prefer to be undisturbed!"

"I couldn't very well allow you to choke," he reminded her.

"I'm sure you've been most heroic," she said. "I thank you. But now I really must ask you to go."

His eyes widened. "But I just arrived."

"But—" She was brought up short by his reply. The man could be no gentleman if he didn't feel the necessity to withdraw. *Who was he?*

"I had planned to linger a while," he explained.

She stiffened. "But you *must* go."

"Why?"

Why, indeed? This pond was not on Sir Harlan's property, so she could stake no claim of ownership. In fact, she could only think of one rather lame response. "Because I was here first!"

"Yes, and now look at you." To her dismay, he lifted her hand from the water and turned her palm over. He *tsk*ed at her. "You're wrinkled like a prune—a sure sign that *you* should go and I should stay."

She yanked her hand free and shook with anger. "I cannot get out of the water while you are in it," she insisted stubbornly.

He seemed genuinely puzzled. "Why ever not?"

"Because I—" She gulped. "I am scantily clothed!"

To her utter dismay, he tossed back his head and chortled. "You needn't tease yourself over that. I will be a perfect gentleman and avert my eyes."

Beneath the water, her hands fisted at her sides. "I find it hard to trust that your behavior under any circumstances could be labeled gentlemanly!"

"But, my dear girl, what is the alternative? I am, as you

say, even more scantily clad than you. By allowing you to take your leave first, I hope to spare your maiden eyes from seeing that which they should not see."

"Never mind my maiden eyes," she said tartly, growing weary of his taunting.

His brows arched. "If you're a girl of delicate sensibilities . . ."

Could a man be so utterly dense? "*I've* already seen *you!*" she exclaimed. Then, as a wicked smile spread across his face, revealing the wolfish white gleam of his teeth, she slapped a prune-fingered hand over her mouth in horror.

"And you worry that *I* will not turn my head in modesty," he said delightedly. "Why, you're a regular peeping Tom!"

Her mouth opened and closed like a beached fish as she cast about for some reasonable excuse for her voyeurism. "But I couldn't help . . . I was so taken aback that I . . ."

"Do not bother to explain. I believe we have settled who is the more trustworthy of the two of us." He turned his back to her, clearly indicating that he was dismissing her. When she did not move, he darted a glance back at her. "If you don't mind? This Neptune would like a few more turns around the pond."

She gasped in shock. She'd never met a man with such a lack of manners! No doubt this fellow worked for Lord Overmeer, who was notoriously lax in checking the references of his staff. Last year one of his footmen had run away to Gretna Green with the curate's daughter.

Her tormentor laughed. "Of course, if you would rather stay and watch me some more . . ."

Quickly she also turned away so that her back was to his. "No thank you." She began to slog clumsily out of the water. What choice did she have? The man wouldn't budge. With her dripping wet shift sticking to her form like an awkward second skin—and a frightfully transparent one at that—she scrambled up the embankment and lunged for her dress. She had it over her head in nothing flat. Safely covered, she stepped into her slippers. "Pray enjoy your swim."

He turned, grinning. "I will. Your vacating the pond shall not have been in vain."

"I did not vacate. I was evicted!"

"You make me sound like an ogre. Is that the thanks I get for saving your life?"

She twisted her lips in dismay at the wicked twinkle in his eye. "I am all gratefulness."

"You are all sarcasm," he replied. "And as to your earlier hesitation to leave the pond before me, let me assure you that a woman with such a lovely form as yours has no need for embarrassment."

Her jaw dropped. "You swine, you peeked!"

He laughed delightedly. "What is the expression? Turnabout is fair play?"

Earning six hundred pounds by her pen helped Abigail not one straw when she needed to come up with words to answer this vulgarian. Instead, gathering her tattered pride about her, she decided she wouldn't deign to respond at all. She hurried away, her soggy feet squishing in her shoes, and pretended not to hear when he called after her.

"Farewell, sprite!"

Likewise, as she heard the splashes behind her, she pretended not to envision exactly what her handsome tormentor looked like as his impressive male form cut across the clear blue water.

Chapter Two

There was nothing the least hesitant in the way the stranger strode across the glistening wet cobblestones. He planted his boots on the threshold that provided but feeble shelter from the driving storm and knocked authoritatively, as if the castle were his still. As if the woman inside were his still. The old butler gasped and bowed at the sight of the large dark man with the jagged slash of a scar on his cheek.

"Baron!" The feeble retainer's gnarled hands reached out in a gesture that could have been that of a man thanking God . . . or pleading for mercy.

"Si, Tomaso," Raffizzi growled as he pulled off his long black cape in a single sweeping gesture. "I have returned!"

—The Prisoner of Raffizzi

"Thank goodness you have finally arrived!" The Wingates' butler sent Nathan a look of thinly veiled irritation as he practically tugged him over the threshold. "But you should have used the back entrance!"

Nathan stared at the man uncomfortably for a moment. "That's odd. I'm in the habit of gaining access to houses by way of the *front* door."

At Nathan's casual tone, the man froze. Doubt overcame impatience in his round face. "Aren't you here about the shrubbery?"

Nathan stared at him. "Shrubbery?"

The small pot-bellied man twiddled his white-gloved

hands, and his Adam's apple bobbed erratically for a moment before he gulped and spoke in a voice that was nearly a squeak. "The terrace shrubbery?"

"My name is Nathan Cantrell."

As the name registered, the butler's look of uncertainty transformed to one of deep mortification. "A thousand pardons, sir! Sir Harlan is waiting for you in the library." The butler motioned for Nathan to follow him and bustled ahead, yet couldn't help pivoting to explain his blunder. "There's been rather a quake here today, sir, and with our own gardener out with rheumatism—he's quite elderly, you see—and . . . well . . ."

"I understand," Nathan assured him.

"And as to your arrival, I was led to expect—"

The words were cut off quickly, but the butler's fleeting glance from Nathan's damp hair to his hastily polished boots spoke for him. He had been led to expect someone of importance . . . not a man in a coat several years out of fashion and a cravat that was wilted, if not positively damp.

Nathan smiled. "I suppose I've been mistaken for worse things than a horticulturist."

He shouldn't have stopped by that pond. But the stress of the past week, when he'd discovered just what a mess his father had left the estate in, made him feel a need for a physical outlet. Thinking of the debt he owed Sir Harlan and the impossibility of paying the mortgages on his family's property, which Sir Harlan held, had worn his nerves down to nubbins. He had left the army thinking that he was coming home to manage The Willows. To take his place as head of the Cantrell family . . . what remained of it.

But after today, he supposed, he would be known as the Cantrell who lost The Willows, an estate begun by a land grant from Queen Elizabeth.

Distressed by the thought of having to see Sir Harlan, he had stopped by the pond on the way and taken a plunge. Meeting the feisty water sprite had lifted his gloomy spirits—at least temporarily. During their banter, he'd managed to forget his worries. Who was the girl in that awful brown rag of a dress? A ladies' maid hereabouts? An escaped governess? He wished he could find her and offer her some word of thanks for giving him the first carefree moments, the first crack at a laugh, he'd had in a full week.

Just the memory of her brought a smile to his face now, as he marched ahead to face what would surely be the most difficult conversation of his life.

The butler opened a heavy oak door and gestured for Nathan to enter.

"Major Nathan Cantrell," the man announced, his voice still carrying an undertone of astonishment.

Nathan found himself in a dark study festooned with mounted animal parts and a large painting of two peacocks. His father had always said Sir Harlan was a bit over-enthusiastic when it came to his birds.

Startled by Nathan's entrance, Sir Harlan slammed the top drawer of the desk where he was sitting, jamming his coat in the process. After extricating himself, he hopped up and came around to pump Nathan's hand amiably.

"Nathan, my boy!"

Nathan drew back in surprise. He hadn't expected so warm a welcome.

Sir Harlan's eyes narrowed. "I hope you don't mind the familiarity. Your dear father—so missed!—spoke of you often, you know. And everyone is so proud of you, almost as if you had sent Napoleon to Elba single-handed."

"Hardly."

Sir Harlan clapped him on the shoulder. "Too modest by half!" He then stepped back and frowned as he gave Nathan's appearance a quick inspection. "I must say, I expected you to be decked out in full military regalia."

"I have put away my uniform," he replied. "I resigned my commission."

He didn't add that his resignation had turned out to be unhappily premature from a financial standpoint. He had harbored plans that seemed impossible now.

"Ah! Like the old song. What was it, eh? You know the thing . . ." His hands raised like a conductor's and his voice croaked out a tuneless phrase. " 'Oh, I wish no more to be a soldier-o!'" He laughed, then punched Nathan playfully on the arm. "My Sophy'll be disappointed to see you turned out like a normal gentleman, but oh, well. Have a Madeira?"

Nathan blinked. "No, thank you." He was a bit confused. He had been steeled to have a fiercely unpleasant conversation about financial matters. Which is why he had supposed Sir Harlan had invited him here the very afternoon before they were to have dinner—to give him a few hours to contemplate his utter ruin before plying him with a consolation dinner. Yet so far the man did not show a countenance for a sober discussion about money.

"This younger generation doesn't care for Madeira, I suppose. When I was a sapling we drank buckets of the stuff."

"Sir Harlan, I—"

"Snuff?"

Nathan shook his head. "Sir Harlan, I assume you have rather serious business to discuss with me."

Sir Harlan's brows rose, then he bellowed, "Upon my soul, I do like a man who doesn't beat about the bush! Have a seat, have a seat." He put a paternal arm about Nathan's shoulders and practically inserted him bodily into a deep-cushioned chair.

Even though this man held him in a vise of debt, Nathan couldn't dislike him. He waited till Sir Harlan had circled back around to his own chair before speaking. "I have spoken to my family's solicitor, Mr. Arbogast, and he has revealed all about the mortgages, sir."

Sir Harlan raised his hands in a dismissive gesture. "The mortgages, yes! Yes! We'll have plenty of time to discuss that little matter."

Nathan was astounded. What could be more pressing to speak of now than the mortgages? "The matter weighs very heavily on my mind."

"No doubt!" Sir Harlan leaned back and folded his chubby hands over his considerable paunch. The man was amazingly egglike through the torso. "I am very sensitive to your position, Cantrell. You might look at me and see only a man fairly flush in the pockets, but let me assure you that was not always the case. When I inherited this estate from my uncle it was practically a ruin. It was just a pile of stones for a house and a yard full of peacocks that were pecking the pantries bare.

"But I do pride myself upon being one who knows how to seize opportunity. So back in eighty-two, when the Duchess of Devonshire made peacock fans all the crack, I plucked my birds bald supplyin' the ton with plumes. Then, just before I judged the whole trend had topped out, I sold practically the whole flock, saving only my favorites." He gestured to the painting on the wall. "Garrick and Mrs. Siddons. I've got their offspring out in the yard now."

"Yes, I saw them as I rode in." Nathan smiled politely. He was beginning to see what his father had meant about Sir Harlan's bird mania.

"What I mean to say, Cantrell, is that I knew a good thing when it came around. In the end, with wise investment, those peacock feathers made me a tidy sum. Helped get me a beautiful wife, too." Almost as an afterthought, he nodded towards the portrait of a woman of spectacular beauty on the wall opposite the peacocks. "An estimable woman—baronet's daughter, you know. I was lucky she would have me."

There was a pause as Sir Harlan looked at him expectantly. Though for the life of him Nathan couldn't think of anything appropriate to say.

Sir Harlan shot a meaningful look at Nathan. "D'you see?"

Nathan fired his brain to try to make some connection between the peacocks, the late Lady Wingate, and his mortgages, but the task brought him up short. "Sir Harlan, Mr. Arbogast said that the entire estate is entail—"

"Ah!" Sir Harlan interrupted. "I understand. You wish to talk about the mortgages."

Nathan practically sagged with relief. "As I said, sir, it's been very much on my mind."

"Naturally! It's not every day a man comes home from

war to discover his father's left him completely rolled up. Damned unpleasant situation."

"Yes, sir."

"I can't say I relish my position in this business, either." Sir Harlan's shaggy brows beetled oddly. "Unless you raise a fortune in the next month, I will take possession of your house, your land, everything."

"That's what Mr. Arbogast led me to understand," Nathan said tightly.

The lines in Sir Harlan's face creased mournfully. "I told your father when he found himself on the rocks that a mortgaged estate would be a shabby thing to leave a son, but your father . . . well, you know."

Nathan felt something close to agony. To have to defend his spendthrift father was hard, yet he felt himself obligated to try . . . "I am certain he intended to pay the mortgages, and would have, had he lived." Which was stretching credulity, to say the least.

Yet it was a stretch Sir Harlan happily made. "Naturally! Poor man—he was my friend, you know. Much missed! Never a feather to fly with, of course, but quite the devil at whist when his luck was good."

Which, neither of them felt compelled to add, was almost never.

Sir Harlan let out a nostalgic sigh, then shook his head. "Of course you must be feeling the pinch in the most dashed way."

"Yes." There was nothing else to add to that. He and his family, what was left of it, were ruined.

"You had hoped to improve on the estate and pass it on to a son, I expect."

Even spoken in the kindest tone, the words were like a knife twisting in Nathan's gut. "Actually I did have a plan for improving the estate. I was hoping that we could discuss my plan and perhaps come to an arrangement. As to passing it on to a son, I am a bachelor and have not planned that far ahead."

The old man's bushy brows drew together sternly. "You should! Time passes quickly, or like a thief, or whatever it is those poet Johnnies put so well, you know. Do you care for poetry, Cantrell?"

"Not particularly, sir."

Sir Harlan registered his approval. "Lot of blither, mostly. I like a good story, myself. Sir Walter, and Georgi—" He cleared his throat. "Ahh-hmm, and so forth."

Nathan hardly felt in the mood for a literary discussion.

"What I mean to say," Sir Harlan droned on, "is that those long-winded versifiers are quite right when they warn that a man gets old and starts to wonder what his life has been about. Take me, for instance. Been a busy fellow all my life—accumulated wealth, raised a family, and so forth. Yet here I am with no grandchildren to see reap the rewards of my life's work. Which is precisely why I want you to marry one of my daughters."

Nathan, who had been nodding blandly through the speech, wondering if they would ever come back around to the subject of the mortgages, was brought up short by the last sentence. "I beg your pardon?"

Surely he hadn't heard correctly. It sounded like Sir Harlan had said he wanted him to marry one of his daughters.

Sir Harlan repeated, "I want you to marry one of my daughters."

Nathan went stone still.

The older man laughed. "Knocked you quite out of the box, have I?"

Utterly befogged, Nathan shook his head and nodded. Was this a joke, then?

"I would like a male heir," Sir Harlan explained. "A continuation of my legacy."

Nathan was still flabbergasted. "Well, sir, if you want more offspring, I'm sure you're not too old . . ."

"Ha! A fine husband I'd make shadowing in on sixty. No, no." He nodded up at the portrait. "Lady Wingate was my wife. Can't imagine another in her place. And my daughters—well, one of them needs to get married, but I'm afraid none of them will. One's rather finicky and another's keen on flirtation. By the time any of 'em settle down to the business of creating their own flock I'll probably be resting my bones in the great hereafter. They want prodding on a bit." Those bug eyes pierced Nathan with a determined stare. "And I've decided you shall be my prod."

Nathan was astonished beyond words. Why would Sir Harlan want him to be father to his grandchildren? He was in no position to provide for a wife, and he held no title that would make up for his lack of financial wherewithal. Nor could he imagine that there was any inclination on Sir Harlan's daughters' parts. The eldest Miss Wingate he remembered from his youth as a most unpleasant, shrill kind of girl. They danced once, he believed, and afterwards she complained loud and long about the state of her slippers. He knew Sir Harlan had two other daughters as well, but he hadn't seen the younger ones since before he had entered the army. They had both still been just girls, and he had no real memory of either of them, couldn't even recall their names. He did remember hearing something recently about the youngest daughter from gossip at the vicar's. Nathan had only been half-listening at the time but as he recalled, it involved a groomsman named Dick, and that a gun room featured prominently in the torrid tale.

"Cat got your tongue?" Sir Harlan asked. "You look like a man who's had a cannonball lobbed at him." Another laugh blasted out of his host. "By Jupiter, though, that's a good description of getting engaged, ain't it? Like having a cannonball lobbed at you. Ha, ha! I'll have to remember that the next time I'm at my club."

Nathan wasn't sure what he was expected to say at this juncture. "Sir Harlan, forgive me for not joining in your mirth, but I'm quite taken aback. I cannot credit this . . . this . . . proposition, if that's what it is."

"And why not? I'm giving you a golden opportunity— think of it as your own personal peacock fan windfall."

Good heavens! "Do I take it to mean that if I marry one of your daughters you will tear up the mortgages?"

"Just so!" Sir Harlan threaded his fingers together and

leaned forward, indicating that they were settling down to business. "And I will settle twenty thousand pounds upon my daughter."

"Twenty thousand!" Nathan repeated in amazement.

"Furthermore, the moment the blessed union produces a son, I will rewrite my will to make him heir to all my property—minus substantial settlements on my other two daughters, of course."

"That is most generous." Generous to the point of madness, Nathan might have added.

"Nothing would make me happier!" Sir Harlan assured him. "And you're a man at the right age to marry. Surely you've considered it."

"No." Nathan had never met a woman he wanted to marry. Most of the women he'd known in the army had been of the lightskirt variety, but this morning's encounter with his water nymph had been more tantalizing than any liaison with a camp follower. A brief flash of how she'd appeared getting out of the water came to him. Her hair had flowed down her back, her legs were long and shapely, and her figure was that of a veritable Venus. He'd been staggered by his physical reaction to a mere wet girl in a shift. Especially given that the water was so cold.

And that was another amazing thing about the woman—paddling about in the frigid waters in the open and arguing with naked men. Very bold behavior! He was afraid he would never find such spirit in the women who were considered suitable candidates for his wife.

Of course, if in the unlikely event he could find a woman who possessed the qualities he required—beauty, spirit, wit, a kind heart—he *would* be tempted to marry. But in any case he wouldn't be in a position to make an offer. Not now.

Sir Harlan obviously did not see the flaws in his plan, which were so many Nathan didn't know how to start enumerating them. "I believe you have overlooked several small problems. And one in particular that is not so small."

Sir Harlan frowned. "What's that?"

"Your daughters."

The bushy brows arched. "What about 'em?"

"I don't know them."

His host banged his hand on the table. "That's precisely why I invited you to dinner tonight. You can meet them. Nothing very taxing in picking a wife, once you get down to business. Why, I knew I wanted to marry Lady Wingate within ten minutes of clapping eyes on her."

"Sir Harlan," Nathan said, trying to absorb the man's meaning. "Is it your intention that I choose one of your daughters *tonight?* After dinner?"

"Why not?"

"It sounds terribly casual. Like choosing an after-dinner cigar."

Sir Harlan leaned back and considered. "Of course you would not *have* to choose right away. Take a few weeks if you like."

A few weeks? Nathan heard himself sputtering, "B-but your daughters, sir! Wouldn't they perhaps have reservations . . . ?"

"Ah, the girls!" Sir Harlan's mouth puckered in thought. "Naturally, I wouldn't expect a girl to marry against her will. We're not barbarians, after all, to drag a girl off by her hair to the marriage bed."

"I should say not."

"It's up to you, Cantrell, to woo and win the girl yourself. And after all, you've got a month till the mortgages come to term."

The mortgages. Which Sir Harlan conveniently held.

Nathan froze.

Suddenly, what Sir Harlan was doing became clearer. Sir Harlan wasn't an avuncular figure trying to get him to marry for his own good. This wasn't a friendly chat. This was something more sinister.

"And if I refuse your generous offer?"

The question was met with a fatherly shake of the head. "Think of your future, man. You're facing ruin."

Indignation rose in him. "This is an outrage! It's blackmail, pure and simple."

"No doubt." Sir Harlan shrugged. "I've found it takes

initiative to get what you want in this world. Sometimes one is forced to be cunning to make a fortune, or secure a son-in-law. I *do* like you, Cantrell, or else I wouldn't be putting this offer to you. And if you are willing and the girl is too . . . well, where's the harm in a plan that benefits both parties?"

It was wrong because Nathan could not bear the idea of bargaining his bachelorhood for financial solvency. It made him feel cheap.

On the other hand, there were those mortgages, and the future of The Willows to consider. Not to mention the many improvements he had in mind for the place. That was *not* cheap. And when you figured in a dowry of twenty thousand pounds . . .

If the girl was willing.

Nathan found himself becoming a little indignant on behalf of Sir Harlan's daughters. The man obviously thought he had to dangle ruin in front of a man to marry them off. Which, now that he thought about it, didn't speak well for the daughters. What kind of girls were they? Nathan's gaze homed in on Sir Harlan's bug eyes and bulbous nose; he suppressed a shudder.

"Why on earth would one of your daughters consent to this scheme? Everyone must know the Cantrells are done for. Nor do I have a title to compensate for my lack of wealth."

"The girls will know they will have their own wealth," Sir Harlan said. "And as for the rest, you're too modest! Everyone knows the Cantrells are related to scads of titles. Few more respectable names in England. Besides, you're a war hero, and I'll be bound you cut a handsome figure with the ladies."

"Didn't I hear that Miss Wingate had married?"

"Violet?" Sir Harlan nodded. "She's Mrs. Treacher now. The poor girl's been widowed these three years."

Unless Violet's tart personality had altered in the intervening years, he could well imagine what had hastened Mr. Treacher's demise.

"But the girl's heart isn't in the grave," Sir Harlan

hurriedly added. "And besides, there are the other two, you know. Violet's the oldest, you'll remember her, I daresay. Then there's also Sophy, the youngest—only seventeen but quite the beauty, and lively in the bargain. Life would never be dull. Ha, ha!"

Nathan was now certain that Sophy, the youngest, must have been the one found in the gun room with the unfortunate Dick. "And your middle daughter?"

Sir Harlan's laughter died. "Ah! Well! Abigail." He coughed. "Wonderful girl, of course! Has a bit more of a serious nature than her sisters, but that could be because of her frail constitution. But she's very sensible. Very. I imagine she'd make an altogether *worthy* sort of wife."

Good Lord! The girl must be an antidote. Or else a dead bore. Which essentially boiled his choices down to the shrill widow or the rattle-brained, groom-chasing infant. On one of these females his entire future hung?

It was simply unthinkable.

Resolutely, Nathan stood. "I'm sorry, sir. With all due respect, I find this very distasteful."

"I'm sorry to hear that." Sir Harlan frowned. "I believe Abigail's also quite a hand at needlework, if that sways you."

"I'm not speaking of Miss Wingate, but rather the whole scheme. I cannot be a party to something I find disagreeable in the extreme."

"But the mortgages."

"Hang the mortgages!" Nathan said, pride welling up in him with a vengeance. "Between my schooling and soldiering I've barely lived at The Willows. As far as I'm concerned, you're welcome to it."

"You're being very rash."

Nathan knew he was tossing away twenty thousand pounds and all his dreams that were tied to his home. He felt like a drowning man purposefully swimming away from a lifeline. But Sir Harlan's offer was against every principle he believed in. "I'm sorry."

"Oh, my boy," Wingate said mournfully. His big sad

eyes locked with Nathan's, startling them both. It was almost as if he regretted ever making the offer.

But in the blink of an eye a strange expression flashed across Sir Harlan's features; he waggled his eyebrows oddly. Nathan wondered if he had some sort of an itch. With a strange and not altogether convincing menace in his voice Wingate declared, "You'd do well to think carefully before turning down my offer. We can talk further tonight."

Tonight! And have the three daughters lined up before him like fillies at auction? "I'm not sure I will be able—"

With another lightning change of expression, Sir Harlan cut him off and was perfectly jovial again. "Nonsense! 'Course you can come. We're having turtle soup, you know, and Cook does a wonderful mutton." Sir Harlan slapped him on the back, like an actor too well pleased with the role he had just performed. "Things always seem clearer with a good feast resting in the old pudding box, eh?"

As if the situation could be any clearer, Nathan thought gloomily. He was clearly in a fix.

Abigail frowned in displeasure at a line she had written.

The old butler gasped and bowed at the sight of the large dark man with the jagged slash of a . . .

Rudolpho was too ordinary. He needed some singular characteristic, something in addition to his jagged scar, which was a rather humdrum thing, now that she thought about it. All her heroes seemed to have scars somewhere or another. The one time she'd tried to create a hero without the subtle deformity, in *The Scarlet Veil*, she had not been at all pleased with the result.

But Rudolpho . . . he needed something besides the usual facial disfigurement. She taxed her brain for a moment before crossing out the line and writing over it neatly: *The sight of the man with the singular, startlingly green eyes . . . as well as the unforgettable jagged scar on his cheek . . . made the old butler gasp in recognition.*

She scowled at the new line. Green eyes? Good heavens! She'd never attempted a green-eyed hero. Green eyes were altogether inappropriate for Rudolpho. He was supposed to be brooding, yet dashing. Green eyes would indicate a light complexion, which would never do.

And yet . . . the man at the pond today had had green eyes. And his skin had seemed rather bronzed . . .

She let out a bleat of dismay. Oh, that foul creature! First he had ruined her morning reverie, and now he was worming his way into her literary efforts. She dipped her pen to blot out those horrid green eyes—if only she could blot them out of her memory as easily!—when her hand fell still over the page.

Her mind replayed the sight of her Neptune diving into the clear water, muscles tight. Warmth spread through her, and a smile played at her lips.

Perhaps green eyes *would* be a change of pace, if she handled them correctly. It might be a change for her readers, as a matter of fact, as they were surely accustomed to her penning dark-eyed heroes exclusively. She didn't want to wear her audience out with darkness, after all. Her last book, *Count Orsino's Betrothal*, had walked a fine edge there.

Green eyes might add a whole new dimension to this story.

In any case, she never did get the opportunity to blot out the line, because at that moment the door was thrown wide and in flew Sophy in a whirl of her usual giddy spirits.

"Abigail, he was here!"

In a gesture so practiced it was second nature, Abigail pulled open the desk drawer and slid her manuscript into it. Then she folded her arms in front of her and faced her sister calmly. "Who was here?"

"Mr. Cantrell!" Sophy's cheeks were bright with color. "I just heard Peabody say that the new groom, Old Hal, pulled his back out bringing up Mr. Cantrell's horse! Isn't that peculiar?"

"Not when you consider that Old Hal is almost seventy." Frankly, Abigail was surprised that Sir Harlan had hired such an elderly man for a position in the stables. Except, of course, that Sophy was particularly fond of riding, and they needed *someone*. And preferably someone who would not be prone to serenading his daughter and plotting secret trysts in the hayloft. By those criteria, Sir Harlan had found an altogether perfect groom. Old Hal was susceptible to sciatica, but not to Sophy.

Sophy rocked on her heels and rolled her eyes. "I didn't mean Old Hal pulling his back, I was referring to Mr. Cantrell. He was *leaving*, don't you see?"

Abigail finally caught up with her sister's scattershot train of thought. "That *is* peculiar. Why would he pay Father a visit when he will be here tonight?"

Sophy bit her plump lower lip. "Maybe he feels ill and wanted to turn down the invitation."

"If he felt ill, he would have sent a servant."

"Maybe he doesn't have a servant," Sophy said. "Violet said the family is terribly, well, pinched right now. Can you imagine a man's being so poverty-stricken he can't even retain a servant?"

"I hardly think—"

"Poor Mr. Cantrell!" Sophy exclaimed, carried away by this new vision of their neighbor living in romantic poverty. "One longs to comfort such a tragic figure, don't you think? Especially if he's a handsome man in uniform?"

Abigail didn't want to encourage this line of thinking. The trouble with Sophy was, she lacked any type of discernment. Heaven only knew how they would restrain her when her first Season in London began. Sophy and an entire metropolis of strapping young men! The prospect made Abigail shudder with dread.

"In any case, I doubt he came here for your comforting. I think it far more likely that Mr. Cantrell was here because he had some business with Father."

"But why not wait until tonight?" Sophy asked.

Abigail shrugged her shoulders, willing to dismiss the matter as one of life's unanswerables, when the door again opened and in Violet floated. She always looked so beautiful, almost ethereal. But then she would spoil the effect by speaking.

"Abigail, this hideous room! I don't understand how you can spend so much time here!"

It was true. The room was not appealing. Formally it was called the peacock room, because after the fashion for peacock fans had waned, their father had used the overflow of unsold feathers to line the walls. To stand in the middle of the room was to be engulfed in plumage. It had the distinction now of being the least popular room in the house, which is why it suited Abigail's needs perfectly.

"I stay here because I can *usually* depend upon a certain amount of privacy."

Violet's face twisted in disgust. "I half suspect these walls molt occasionally. To be shut away in this room so much cannot help your constitution."

Belatedly, Abigail coughed delicately.

Sophy clutched her arm. "Poor Abigail! What a sad little life you lead. Maybe you shouldn't come down to dinner tonight."

Dinner, it seemed, was the reason Violet was here. "Would that we could all beg off! I saw Mr. Cantrell through an upper window not two hours ago, and I regret to inform you that the man is little improved."

Sophy gasped. "You *saw* him? Why did you not come get me?"

"I am sure you will see quite enough of him at dinner. Peabody assures me that he is coming back." Violet laughed. "Poor Peabody! He mistook Mr. Cantrell for a gardener! *That* should give you some indication of the man's appearance."

Sophy's face screwed up in puzzlement. "Are gardeners wearing uniforms now, too?"

Violet sent her sister a quelling look. "He wasn't wearing his uniform. Just shabby buckskins and riding boots and an outmoded coat of blue superfine."

"That doesn't sound like what a gardener would wear, either," Abigail said.

"I know. Poor Peabody!" Violet sighed. "He's not himself today. If you could have seen the anguish on his face when he told me that all of this fuss and bother today is taking place for the benefit of a man one could mistake for a laborer! It was heartbreaking, and frankly I felt a little embarrassed for the Wingate family. One is so often judged by the company one keeps."

Eager to get back to her work, Abigail felt more than usually impatient with her older sister's snobbery. "I am sure we will be able to live down the shame of having a neighbor to dinner. Eventually."

Her sarcasm sailed cleanly past Violet. "I hope so. Though I was so sorry for Peabody, I felt compelled to promise him that when I marry the earl, I will take him with me. He is accustomed to waiting on families of only the highest ton."

"Oh, Violet!" Sophy exclaimed. "Has the earl spoken to Father about you? Do you really think he's going to make an offer?"

Violet lifted her chin a little defensively. "I am certain he will soon. He never fails to speak to me whenever he visits."

Abigail laughed. "Perhaps because you never fail to corner him."

The Earl of Clatsop visited Peacock Hall occasionally because he was a friend of Sir Harlan, and having a noted expertise in ornithology, he enjoyed viewing Sir Harlan's prized specimens of peafowl. But no one could convince Violet that the earl's peacock enthusiasm was not simply a subterfuge that allowed him to spend more time in her company.

"The last time he was here he told me that I was looking quite lovely," Violet said.

"Small wonder!" Abigail exclaimed. "When you heard

that he was coming you spent a full three hours at your looking glass preparing for the occasion."

Violet frowned as her sisters fell into whoops at her expense. "Laugh all you like," she said, lifting her chin proudly. "I promise not to hold it against you when I am the mistress of Clatsop Castle. It shall never occur to me to remind you of your derision and of how wrong you were. I shall be able to afford to be forgiving."

Sophy's giggling came to an abrupt stop when she glanced over at the peacock-shaped carved oak clock and gasped dramatically. "Look at the time! I'd better hurry if Tillie is going to have time to do my hair. I saw a style in *The Gallery of Fashion* that I want her to copy exactly!"

She charged out the door. Obviously concurring with her youngest sister that it was time to begin to manicure herself for the evening, even if it was just for dinner with a neighbor who resembled a gardener, Violet followed, drifting back out of the room without acknowledging Abigail.

Abigail looked down worriedly at her wrinkled brown dress; there wasn't much time left for her to continue with *The Prisoner of Raffizzi*. She had not written nearly as much as she'd planned for this afternoon. What was wrong with her today?

But of course she knew. It was Neptune wreaking havoc on her life again. She must really fix Rudolpho's ride up to the castle . . . and then there was the quandary over whether he should have green eyes.

What a mess. And now, thanks to this dinner and their guest, she was pressed for time. For once in agreement with Violet, Abigail found herself wishing the inconvenient Mr. Cantrell at Jericho.

Chapter Three

Orsino's black brows drew together in thunderous anger, almost blotting out the jagged scar marring that high expanse of forehead that broke at the line of his thick dark locks. "Marry one of your daughters, Prince Lorenzo? Never!"

"I could tell tales about your late wife's fate, Orsino. Most of the villagers think someone might have tampered with her carriage wheel. A word from me and you could spend the rest of your life in a dungeon."

"You broke that wheel, fiend!" Orsino growled.

"Who would the villagers believe? Or the law?" The prince grinned wickedly. "What is it to be, Orsino—the altar or the jail?"

The scheme was blackmail, no less! Did the prince believe him a knave that he could use him thus? Onyx eyes flashed. He would teach the prince to misjudge Count Orsino!

—Count Orsino's Betrothal

It was impossible. Unthinkable. He simply wasn't going to do it.

As he pounded his roan toward The Willows, Nathan released a snort of defiance. Marry one of Wingate's impossible daughters? No, thank you. He knew Violet Wingate well enough to understand that a man who'd tasted his fill of war had best shy away from her. The youngest girl sounded like she had one foot still in the schoolroom (and the other in the stables). And the other . . . well, considering the way her own father hemmed and hawed over her, perhaps the unfortunate creature was best left stowed in the attic, or wherever the Wingates hid her away.

He had just been shackled to the army, for heaven's sake. He didn't want to be shackled now to some unwilling, witless, or unsightly female.

As he rode up the overgrown drive to The Willows, the stately brick pile tugged at his conscience. Damn, but it was a beautiful—or it might have been, had his father not allowed the grounds to fall into neglect. Rhododendrons hulked around the grounds like giants. Hollies, which in his mother's lifetime were pruned within an inch of their lives, now grew to the size of oaks. And the house! Crumbling stone. Peeling paint. Shutters askew. Drafty, moldering rooms that bespoke years of abandonment. His father had apparently lived in three rooms and shut the rest off—his one bow to economy.

How could his father have left The Willows, and him, in such straights? It was criminal, it was . . .

Nathan gritted his teeth. It was too late to do anything about his father's negligence. He felt no compulsion, however, to sacrifice his own happiness just to keep a damn house in the family. Granted, he had had happy days here as a child, before school, but that was years ago.

And his mother had loved the place. He could still see her strolling with her basket, collecting roses, with his little brother toddling after her on chubby legs.

He shook his head. Dwelling on sentiment now would do him no good.

He stabled his horse—the groomsmen having long set off for greener stables—and entered the house in a state of rigid determination. Not only would he not marry one of the Wingate sisters, he would not attend Sir Harlan's soiree. What would be the point? The man intended to ruin him. Nathan was not going to allow himself to have turtle soup poured down his gullet just to assuage Sir Harlan's conscience at snatching The Willows at the first opportunity.

Nathan thought of losing his home and felt a stab as fierce as that of a bayonet to his pride.

Well, so be it. Losing The Willows would be a black mark on the Cantrell name, and he had had plans for the place. Thinking of those plans caused him another pang of regret. These past years he had spent plotting out a scheme for when he returned. He had sought out the advice of fellow officers who had some knowledge or skill about the business he was concerned with, and he had hoped to enlist their help when the battles were over and the men who returned home found themselves idle and in need of paying work. That grand scheme now seemed to have all the substance of a castle in the air. He could barely eke out pay for the two servants left on the property.

He didn't know what he would do now. Perhaps he could always take a position somewhere, maybe India, and make his fortune. Or he would go to the Continent—now that the little blackguard had been packed off to Elba, there was probably plenty of opportunity there for a man of character and ambition.

He hurried through the drafty old house, seeking comfort and a brandy. He found the morning room open, with the covers off the furniture, and tidied. The work of Mrs. Willoughby, no doubt. The old family retainer and her husband were all that was keeping The Willows together at this point. He crossed to the liquor cabinet.

"Bone dry, old man."

Nathan jumped about two feet out of his boots. He turned in surprise to find himself staring into the mischievous face of his little brother, Freddy.

Freddy wasn't so little anymore, however. Long gone was the toddler of the chubby legs. Freddy was twenty and tall as a beanpole, which was emphasized when the young man stood up in all his dandified glory, wiping plum juice from his mouth with an apple green silk kerchief.

"Good Lord!" Nathan exclaimed, taking in his brother's eye-poppingly bright jacket and ridiculously high boots lined with fur at the tops. "Where did you come from? Part of you looks to have escaped from a carnival, the other part from the tsar's cavalry."

Freddy laughed. "Either would be so much more exciting than the truth. Pity me, brother—I've only escaped from Brighton."

"That's right, I forgot you'd be between terms at Cambridge."

His brother pursed his lips. "Yes, I had hoped to spend the summer in Brighton, but it got devilishly expensive there, especially since I'd already been on the town in London for a few weeks before. So I decided to spend a few weeks rusticating—horrible word!" He cast a distasteful glance about the room. "But rather appropriate in this case, unfortunately. Every time I come back here, I'm more struck by how backward this place is. Damned inconvenient for Father to have lost the London house like he did. Hard to believe a man could be so blasted unlucky at faro. Tell me, now that you are master of The Willows, mightn't you spring for some new furnishings? I know we should be proud of our Elizabethan pile, but must we be always perching on the same chairs Good Queen Bess favored, too?"

Nathan felt a headache coming on. Minutes ago, when he had been so rashly thinking of giving up the property and dashing off to the Continent to make his fortune, he had not taken Freddy into consideration. Freddy, who, like a chip off the old block that he was, went through money like water through a sieve.

Freddy, who was now his sole responsibility.

When his father died, Nathan had known he had responsibilities here, but there had also been a war to fight, so he had not made it home until a year after the funeral. Here he'd thought Freddy well accounted for, packed off at Cambridge. He forgot that his brother couldn't be expected to spend all of his time there. Lord only knew what kind of debts he had managed to rack up in town. He hoped he didn't suffer from their father's weakness for cards!

Nathan found himself in the uncomfortable position of

having to listen to his brother's financial woes with ears that were unfamiliarly *in loco parentis*. "What happened in London and Brighton?"

"Oh, you know, the usual. We managed to amuse ourselves tolerably."

"We?"

"Lord Fothersby and I. Excellent fellow, Fothersby. Likes to tear it up."

"Mm." That didn't sound good. Please don't let him have discovered a love of faro, Nathan silently begged.

Freddy, unaware of Nathan's worry, went on. "Fothersby insisted nothing would do but I accompany him to London to enjoy what was left of the Season. I must say, it helps a chap to get to town regularly in order to keep up with the latest fashions. We had quite a time at his tailor's." He twisted to show his bright blue, severely swallow-tailed coat at its best angle. "Fothersby has a man of the first rank do all his coats. He assured me this was all the crack."

"And those boots? Surely *they* aren't all the crack!" Nathan hadn't been out of London *that* long.

His brother looked put out. "They're lined in Turkish gray."

"Gray what?"

"Rabbit."

"Dear Lord!"

"Quite," Freddy replied, sniffing. "Dashed hot in this summer weather."

Nathan didn't care a hang about his brother's comfort; he was more concerned with the cost of all this imported rodent fur. "I didn't even know the Turks had rabbits."

" 'Course they do," Freddy said. "Though apparently not too many. Otherwise I can't think what would make the cost of their hides so dear."

The more he heard about his brother's shopping spree, the more his spirits sank. "For heaven's sake, Freddy. Not that I begrudge you a pair of boots, but couldn't you have bought a pair lined with sturdy English rabbits?"

"Didn't see any." Freddy frowned. "Anyhow, I'm not

sure English rabbits rank as stylish just now. It's the allure of the foreign, you know."

Nathan shook his head. "You might want to think twice before being taken in so, Freddy."

"Well, as you said, I needed boots."

"Creditors have to be paid, you know."

Freddy blinked at him. "Are you quite all right? You seem blue-deviled."

"I have a headache." It wasn't lessened by thinking about Freddy's bills.

Freddy eyed him pityingly. "It's no wonder your head hurts, given the state of your hair." The young man patted his luxuriously pomaded curls. "Need to layer more off the top. You could pop down to town and see Fothersby's man. He would see you in a jot if I recommend you."

Nathan groaned. How to tell his brother that he might have to give up his titled friends and take up a trade was beyond him. A few minutes ago, when he'd been dreaming of running off to destinations foreign, he had forgotten his brother completely, except as the sweet little boy of memory. Now, confronted with Freddy and his fopperies, his self-indulgences, he found himself in an entirely different position. The tailors, not to mention Cambridge, would have to be paid. His character also needed attending to, somehow. Though Nathan doubted his own fitness for molding a young mind.

What was he to do now? Running off to the Continent grew more appealing by the minute, but to leave a line of angry creditors . . .

To pull Freddy from Cambridge . . .

He looked at his brother, trying to think of what was to become of him. It would do him a world of good to face up to the hard facts of life, of course. But somehow, looking into those dark, dewy brown eyes befuddled Nathan's mind. He wanted to be stern, but in the back of his mind his dear mother's voice was echoing her endearment for her younger son, Freddy-weddy, in her lilting sing-song . . .

And what could he recommend? The army was the only life he knew, and yet he doubted whether Freddy would distinguish himself as a soldier. It was difficult to think what Freddy would be fit for. He could hardly pack off a giggling young man in rabbit-fur boots to learn to be a clerk, or a cheesemonger.

"Where have you been this afternoon?" Freddy asked him. "I got here hours ago. Had to resort to playing a game of chess with Willoughby. Old man skunked me eight times." His lips pursed thoughtfully. "Seemed all too happy to do so, too."

"I had to visit our neighbors," Nathan said.

"Lord Overmeer? I thought he spent all his time in London now."

"I was at Peacock Hall, talking to Sir Harlan Wingate."

His brother looked horrified. "Good lord! That fat, froggy fellow who was bosom bows with Father?"

Nathan nodded. Should he explain now that the fat, froggy fellow would soon be rousting them from their home?

If he could just figure out a way to save the place . . .

He thought fleetingly, and greedily, of the generous settlement Sir Harlan was offering for his daughters. Twenty thousand pounds would save his home. Freddy could continue at Cambridge. The Cantrells wouldn't be shamed. He could make The Willows more productive than it had been in its entire history. Not to mention, the business he had hoped to start here would provide work to many of the returning soldiers from the Continent now that they had achieved peace.

"What could you be talking to that fellow about half the day?" Freddy's question was just the opening Nathan needed to discuss the straits their father had left them in.

"I wasn't there all day," Nathan replied. Unbidden, as if a balm to his troubled mind, he remembered his encounter with the feisty girl at the pond. A pang of longing returned as he recalled how he'd felt as he'd watched his tart-tongued Venus slogging her way out of that pond, her wet shift clinging to her with unwitting seductiveness . . .

Nathan groaned. He was losing his mind. Maybe he *should* be looking for a rich wife . . . he obviously had women on the brain. But Sir Harlan's daughters were not tempting.

And yet what other prospect was there for gaining a fortune in less than the month allotted by Sir Harlan?

Maybe Violet had changed, he thought feverishly. Maybe the youngest had grown up since the gun room incident. Maybe the middle one wasn't a bulbous-nosed madwoman.

He lifted his head abruptly and looked straight into his brother's worried eyes. "I'm sorry I'll have to leave you, Freddy. I am dining out tonight."

"There are people to dine out with here? But I thought Lord Overmeer—"

"Not with Lord Overmeer," Nathan said. "I'm sorry to abandon you, but we can go hunting tomorrow if you like."

Freddy recoiled in horror. "You mean get up with the birds and trudge about the countryside shooting at things?"

"That's usually what one does when hunting."

His brother yawned. "I believe I'll need to stay late in bed tomorrow. Had quite a week, you know. London can take it out of a fellow."

Nathan shook his head disapprovingly. "As you wish. See that you're complimentary of the dinner Mrs. Willoughby prepares for you tonight," he warned. "We can't afford to lose any more servants here."

The trouble was, if Nathan didn't come up with a plan, they wouldn't be able to afford to keep the two servants they had left.

He hurried upstairs to dress for Sir Harlan's feast, trying to reconcile himself to a blackmail marriage. After all, it wasn't as if his heart were already engaged. And he was the oldest son. Carrying on the Cantrell name wouldn't be an entirely bad idea. And if it would save The Willows, and keep Freddy in Cambridge, then what would be the downside to such a plan?

Unfortunately, the answer came to him instantly. *Those daughters!*

* * *

A heavy knock at the front of the house startled both mistress and maid.

"Oh, miss!" Tillie fretted as she took in Abigail's appearance.

Abigail looked in the mirror and . . . trembled. True, her best gown was very pretty—a muslin dress with gauze overskirt, the bodice trimmed in plaited green satin. But it had just been brought out of camphor and hastily pressed by Tillie, and the result was not at all what the London modiste who had designed it had in mind, Abigail feared. The dress, fitted for her when she was twenty—the last year she had bothered going through the motions of ordering a wardrobe for another of her missed Seasons—was a tight squeeze four years later. For the most part, the gauze partially covering the underdress concealed its snug fit. But there was no masking the expanse of bosom spilling from the once modest neckline. Abigail never realized she had been such a late bloomer.

"At least most of the smell is gone," Tillie said doubtfully.

That was another of her ensemble's flaws; it smelled faintly of camphor. Since she'd never had occasion to wear it, Abigail had naturally tucked the fine dress away. An afternoon's airing hadn't completely eradicated the odor. Abigail was grateful that she was to be seated in relative isolation next to Violet and well away from their dinner guest.

And her hair! It had dried in clumps after her swim in the pond, and she had not left herself enough time to wash it this afternoon. The only thing to be done was to gather the mass into tight braids, which roped towards the crown of her head, secured by an ivory comb that was sticking out in the most peculiar fashion. And to top it all off, she had tried to curl her bangs and they had simply frizzed.

"Your color is very good, miss," Tillie remarked in a last-ditch attempt to give her courage.

"Because I'm scarlet with embarrassment," Abigail moaned inconsolably. "What can I do now? That was surely Mr. Cantrell at the door. There's no time to fix me!"

"I couldn't think of a way to fix you anyhow, miss."

Realizing how her words sounded—how unfortunately true—Tillie clapped a hand over her mouth. "Beg pardon! I only meant that . . . that . . ."

Abigail sighed. "Never mind, Tillie." She looked longingly at her wardrobe closet. "Don't you think I'd do better just to wear my gray evening gown? It's clean, and isn't too heavy."

Tillie's head shook violently at the notion of such a comedown in fashion. "Maybe with some rose water . . . and if you'll just let me adjust the comb *just a bit* . . ."

For five minutes more they frantically attempted to set Abigail to rights, to little avail. Although the smell was improved, the hair remained a problem, and there was simply no way for her to suck in her bust.

"I'll put on my gray wool," Abigail declared, just as her little sister flew through the door.

"Thank heavens you're ready! Don't you look—" Sophy eyes traveled from Abigail's hair to her neckline, whereupon her words died. "—*Interesting!*"

That did it. Abigail charged towards the wardrobe. "I was just about to change."

Sophy caught her by the sleeve. "There's no time! Father is as mad as a hornet. Says you're taking longer than Violet—and you know what a thunderclap he is with her when she's late!"

Abigail couldn't stifle a moan of despair. "But I can't go down now—not as I am. Our guest will think me most odd!"

Sophy shook her head excitedly. "Oh, no. Mr. Cantrell is not one to leap to conclusions, I'm sure. And he's far more handsome than Violet led us to believe, really quite the gentleman!"

"Oh mercy." It was hard to remember when she'd felt so dispirited.

"Bah! It's not like you to worry how you look, Abigail. Is it, Tillie?"

The maid's face formed a perfectly neutral expression, as if she wanted nothing more than to be left out of this discussion.

"In any event," Abigail said, "it's not simply how I look that's troubling me, as much as the odor."

Sophy stepped close and sniffed Abigail's sleeve. "It *is* a bit . . ." Then she brightened. "Marvelous! My head has felt stuffy for days, but it's all cleared up now."

Being a cure for stuffy heads was cold comfort to Abigail as she was propelled towards the door by her sister. Sophy practically had to yank her down the stairs and towards the saloon where the men and Violet awaited them. As Sophy pulled her across the threshold, Abigail nearly tripped into the room.

"Upon my word!" their father cried. "Abigail, you're looking in the pink!" Her father obviously was too relieved that she was wearing any color besides brown or gray to notice the details. Although he did cough a bit as he was hit with the wave of her *eau d'rose-camphor*. "Well, shall we go in to dinner?"

Violet sent both her father and Abigail a glance of restrained exasperation. Despite her father's admonition to be on her most pleasant behavior, Violet was taking no pains to hide what a waste of her time this evening was. "Father," she said impatiently, "I believe an introduction is in order. Abigail has not met our guest."

Abigail felt as if there were a rock in her stomach. She wondered whether she was about to be the object of pity or contempt and couldn't decide which would be worse. Steeling herself, she hazarded a glance towards their guest.

Sophy was right. Violet's description hadn't done Nathan Cantrell justice at all. He was extremely handsome, with dark blond hair and an impressive build clad in a dark green dress coat with a black velvet collar. Unfortunately, he was staring at the carpet at her feet, looking as miserable as she'd ever seen a dinner guest appear. His face was almost contorted in pain, as if he were compelled against his will to eat turtle soup at Peacock Hall. Most unnerving of all, he seemed to be studiously avoiding looking her in the eye, as if expecting something horribly unpleasant.

Abigail was afraid she met his low expectation all too well.

"Mr. Cantrell, this is my daughter Abigail," Sir Harlan said hastily.

Nathan Cantrell looked up, straight into her face. Abigail felt as if every last drop of blood were being drained out of her. *Oh, Lord! It was Neptune!* The green-eyed devil who had been ruining her book this afternoon. She hadn't recognized him on dry land . . . and clothed. But there was no mistaking those eyes.

She felt dizzy with embarrassment as she met their green gleam. And to think she had fussed so over how to dress herself—all for the benefit of a man who had seen her in practically nothing at all!

If only . . . Oh, it was only a faint hope, she knew, but perhaps he would not recognize her.

A wide smile spread across Nathan's face, and Abigail's slim hope was dashed. She felt chilled and feverish at once. "Did you say Abigail?" he asked in aside to Sir Harlan. "Or Venus?"

Abigail's knees nearly buckled as she dipped him a curtsy.

"Abigail," Sir Harlan said. "Easy enough name to remember, I would think."

Sophy giggled. "Venus! What an odd name that would be, Mr. Cantrell! Who would ever name a girl after a planet?"

Humor danced in Nathan's eyes.

How Abigail was supposed to calmly sip soup with that smirk facing her she couldn't imagine. How was she going to endure this?

Although she knew her father must be ravenous at having the meal put back to seven, Sir Harlan had a peculiarly satisfied, almost gloating, expression on his face as he exclaimed, "Fine! Now that we have done the pretty, we can go in to dinner."

Violet stood at attention, ready to take Nathan Cantrell's arm, but the man's gaze was still pinned on Abigail. He seemed in no hurry to go while there was fun to be had at her expense. "Haven't we met before?"

Gone was any hope that he would be a gentleman and not allude further to their earlier encounter. But of course, she should have known from his pond-hogging behavior of that afternoon that his manners were hardly gallant.

Before she could stammer out a fib for the benefit of her family, Sophy saved her by laughing breezily. "Met Abigail? I should think not! My sister never meets anyone, Mr. Cantrell. Because of her sickly constitution, she rarely even leaves the grounds, poor dear!"

The brows above those green eyes lifted in surprise. "*Never?*"

"Well, almost never. You do take constitutionals, don't you, Abigail?"

Feeling more wretched by the minute, Abigail nodded.

Her discomfort only seemed to amuse their guest. "Constitutionals are fine and good, but I always say a good swim is just the thing to perk a body up," Nathan said.

Abigail shot Nathan a glare.

"A swim? That's a most unusual way to treat a weak constitution, I must say!" Sir Harlan commented.

"And most improper for a lady," Violet added with bristly primness. She seemed vexed that the parade into dinner was being delayed by this discussion of Abigail's health.

"Unusual it may be," their guest said, never taking his eyes off Abigail, "but I confess I enjoy a swim above all things."

"I suppose that would make you an odd duck," Sir Harlan said. "Or should I say an odd *fish*?" He guffawed lustily, but alone, at his little joke.

Abigail began to seethe under the man's mocking gaze. "I suppose it is convenient to know the peculiarities of one's neighbors. One would hate to come upon a swimmer unawares. It would be so rude."

"Only place to swim around here is Overmeer's pond," Sir Harlan said. "Used to go there myself as a boy."

"You wouldn't have to worry about running into Mr.

Cantrell there, Abigail," Sophy informed her helpfully. "It's miles away."

"Much too far a hike for an invalidish young miss," Nathan agreed with a sly look toward Abigail.

Violet stamped her foot impatiently. "It is rather pointless for us all to be standing around talking about ponds when dinner is ready."

"Quite right," Sir Harlan said. Taking the bull by the horns, he grabbed Violet's elbow and tugged her towards the dining room. Though she had been mocking their guest as a rustic mere hours before, the young widow hardly hid her annoyance at being escorted by her father.

Nathan was still smiling down at Abigail.

Happily, Sophy took advantage of her father's breach of etiquette by performing a breach herself. She hooked her arm through Nathan's. "Coming, Abigail?"

Nathan offered his other arm to Abigail. With an air of extravagant concern, he asked, "Is the walk to the dining room too much for you, Miss Abigail? I know how invalids are. It will be my pleasure to take the slowest of steps."

Sophy laughed. "Oh, Mr. Cantrell, I can assure you Abigail will make it to dinner just fine. My sister is simply rather independent and peculiar sometimes."

The annoying man refused to walk ahead. "One worries about leaving such a delicate creature behind."

"You needn't worry about me at all," Abigail assured him through gritted teeth.

"Indeed, no," Sophy agreed impatiently. "You shouldn't pay the least attention to Abigail and her peculiarities. None of the rest of us do."

She unceremoniously yanked their guest towards the dining room.

Nathan could barely credit what he was seeing. He felt like an imprisoned man who had been expecting the hangman's noose and instead had found himself receiving laurels. He had never expected to meet the water sprite again, and yet here she was—one of Sir Harlan's detestable daughters!

Suddenly, the prospect of being a blackmailed bridegroom was much less grim.

Of course, he wasn't in much of a position to talk to Abigail, seated as he was next to Sophy, who was bent on monopolizing both the conversation and him. And then Violet kept scowling at him, as if he were some sort of toad who had happened to hop up to their dining table. Sir Harlan simply ignored them all and gobbled down his dinner, and occasionally came out with a bellowed remark about the hunting or fishing in the area.

For the most part, Abigail kept her eyes trained on the mutton and turnips on her plate. Though occasionally her eyes would stray to Nathan's face, her cheeks would pinken, and then she would look away again.

What sort of double life was she leading here? The vision of Wingate's invalidish daughter that afternoon, rising gloriously from the water, her wet shift clinging to her well-shaped form, was seared into his brain. Certainly she was no wraith, but instead strong-limbed and plump with health. Hardly the sickly antidote he'd anticipated.

Nathan regretted the lack of opportunity for speech with her. All the conversation round the table seemed rather disjointed. Her oldest sister spoke exclusively of titled people she knew—even titled people her butler knew. And as the ancient serving men quavered around the table, their rheumatic limbs clumsily refilling glasses, Sophy spoke of how dull the country was, how lucky Nathan was to have been on the Continent for so long, and how she couldn't wait for her first Season.

"It should have been this year, but Father kept me at my dreadful school an extra six months, even though I told him I couldn't wait to be in London."

Sir Harlan grumbled. "I just thought London might need some time to prepare itself. As if for a siege."

Sophy laughed. "Oh, Father! You make it sound like I'm Napoleon." She gasped. "But I'm sure Major Cantrell knows all about sieges after spending all that time in Sweden fighting the French."

Nathan coughed into his napkin. "Actually, it was in Spain where I saw the most action."

She frowned at him. "What on earth were you doing there?"

"Fighting Napoleon."

"Good heavens! Was he *there*, too?"

Abigail darted a glance at him. Mischief danced in her eyes. "Those six extra months at Miss Pargeter's Academy made *much* improvement."

Nathan sputtered into his wine glass, nearly choking. But before he could reply to Miss Abigail directly, she was staring at her turnips again.

"I know Napoleon is a treacherous villain, but I have *always* admired the way he crops his hair," Sophy declared. "The French always seem to manage their hair so well."

"Would they could manage their tyrants half so well," Nathan said agreeably.

Violet cleared her throat. "The French have a stylishness we would do well to imitate. That's why I think we are so fortunate so many of their aristocrats settled here."

Sir Harlan let out a gruff roar. "Bosh! Back in my day we had good sturdy wigs, and quite handy they were, too. None of this bothering with barbers all the time. A lot of flummery, if you ask me. Wish those Frenchy aristocrats had stayed put and left our hair alone. Give me a good powdered wig any day!"

Nathan frowned. "I'm not certain that the French are entirely to blame for our hair woes."

"Well they certainly haven't helped any," Sir Harlan declared. "But then they never do, do they?"

Sir Harlan went on at length about the many crimes, social and political, caused by the French. The monologue was peppered with observations from Sophy on the relative handsomeness of various men dating from Charlemagne to the present. From Violet came pronouncements of the fitness of the same men's fortunes and their bloodlines. But from Abigail there was only amused silence.

After cake and fruit the women were gruffly dismissed by Sir Harlan, who, no matter what his feelings towards the French as a people, was fond of his smuggled French brandy. As Abigail looked uncertainly back at them from the doorway, Nathan sent her a broad wink. With a barely audible yelp of dismay, she whirled through the doorway to catch up with her sisters.

Sir Harlan might enjoy his after-dinner libations, but tonight Nathan was going to see that they were kept to a minimum. He was too eager to get back to his sprite, his Venus, the young lady who had apparently been living a deception in her own home . . . and who was now counting on him not to betray her.

And to think, he had come here thinking he was completely at Sir Harlan's mercy. Now it appeared Abigail would be at his. Nathan felt his lips turn up in a smile as he sipped the brandy. This could be fun.

Sir Harlan grunted at his happy expression, which he attributed to his liquor. "Satisfying, isn't it?"

"Very," Nathan agreed.

Chapter Four

*Clara crept down the long dark staircase, covering
her candle as closely as her cupped hand could bear.
She did not want to be spied just yet. Her madly beating heart sounded so loud to her own ears that she
feared the whole castle could hear it. She could
hardly credit the news just delivered to her by
Tomaso. Rudolpho, the stranger of whom she had
heard so much. . . . here . . .*

—The Prisoner of Raffizzi

Abigail peeked through the potted palm towards the
door and nearly lost her concentration. She was not giving
Mr. Haydn his due. But how could she, knowing that her
father was closeted with a man who had seen her in practically nothing? Her heart fluttered like her poor belea-
guered heroine Clara's every time she thought of that
afternoon.

Now she understood why matrons in town scolded their
father for not providing an older woman of unimpeachable
character for his daughters. And occasionally Sir Harlan did
call on their cousin Henrietta to serve as a chaperone. But
Henrietta—though certainly of unimpeachable character—
was hardly the stern figure the locals had in mind to rein in
Sophy. Henrietta was a little too nervous to be an able min-
der, and she tended to create more problems than she solved.
The last time she had been to Peacock Hall for dinner, she
had knocked over a porcelain peacock lamp Sir Harlan had
been particularly fond of. She had not been back since.

Abigail had always considered such close surveillance and cosseting of females aggravating in the extreme. But if there had been some finger-wagging woman watching over her, would she have shucked all her clothes and hopped into a pond with a naked man? No.

Of course, in her defense, she hadn't known the man *would* be naked, or for that matter that there would even be a man jumping in the pond with her at all.

Her sweaty fingers slipped on the keys and Violet flicked an annoyed glance her way. "Your playing tonight is very erratic."

Sophy, who was on pins and needles waiting for the men to rejoin them, jumped to her defense. "Don't criticize poor Abigail. I think she's doing very well, considering how awful she looks tonight. It must be the heat bothering her."

As if Abigail weren't self-conscious enough, Sophy's wincing gaze focused steadily on her hair.

"Nonsense," Violet said. "Her ill looks are more attributable to overheated curling tongs than the weather. Abigail, that frizz dangling above your eyebrows is most unbecoming."

Abigail felt that enough had been said on her appearance and answered back defensively, "I regret that I lost track of the time and didn't make the grand toilette that you seem to think this evening requires."

"In any event, I like hearing music, even poorly played," Sophy said, holding her skirts and whirling dreamily. "It makes me think of all the fun I'm going to have in London."

As always when that subject arose, Violet and Abigail exchanged anxious glances, for once united in their feelings. God help them when that time came. For sojourns in London, Sir Harlan usually packed them off to stay with their aunt, but Aunt Augusta sometimes seemed to need a stern chaperone herself. She could be rather whimsical in her attention to the proprieties, according to Violet, who had lived with her for an entire Season before she landed the heir to the marquess. A combination of Sophy and Augusta would likely land the Wingate name in the scandal sheets.

Abigail turned her attention back to the pianoforte and tried to train her thoughts on more productive matters. Most of the time she was able to use this time after dinner to concentrate on her story. In fact, she was often scolded for being so lost in thought. Alas, her latest Gothic epic was no match for the irritations of the evening, and the most annoying part of the evening was Nathan Cantrell.

What was he doing here? She flicked a worried glance towards the door leading to the hall. Across that hall, Nathan was talking to her father. About what?

Dear heaven, let it not be about her.

Moments later, the sound of Sir Harlan's croaking laugh preceded the men into the room, giving Abigail a little time to scoot over so that she was better concealed by the potted palm . . . and was closer to an open window, which was all for the best considering that there was still a mild lingering aroma of camphor attached to her. The maneuver positioned her at the treble end of the instrument, making playing Haydn a bit more awkward, but it gave her a much better vantage point for observing their guest.

Sophy, who had been fidgety ever since being banished from the dining room, pounced on him almost as soon as he came through the door. "Do you like to dance, Mr. Cantrell?"

Sir Harlan chuckled. "Quite a coincidence that you should mention dancing, Sophy. I was just saying that we ought to have a party here at Peacock Hall."

Even Violet gasped. "We haven't had any kind of gathering like that here since my wedding!"

Sir Harlan winked at their guest.

Abigail caught the subtle exchange between the two men and narrowed her eyes at the music sheet in front of her.

"Just because we haven't, doesn't mean we can't, eh?" Sir Harlan remarked, chuckling. "A man mustn't get too set in his ways, I always say. A little fun never hurt anyone. All work and no play . . ."

Abigail listened to her father spouting clichés like water from the mouth of a fish at a fountain and began to wonder. Odd that Sir Harlan would suddenly volunteer to have a social event here after all these years. Of course, Sophy was forever begging him to have people over, but he was more fond of going out to seek pleasure without the company of his daughters. Balls he always pronounced noisy affairs that were nothing more than elaborate excuses for women to waste money.

Maybe welcoming Nathan back home to the neighborhood in style was simply her father's way of honoring Mr. Cantrell, Senior. There was no doubt Sir Harlan missed his old friend. He had seemed broody since the man's death, and had taken to shutting himself away in his library more often than usual.

"I've heard all soldiers are wonderful dancers," Sophy said. "Is it true?"

It was obvious to those who knew her that Sophy was angling for an invitation to dance, but to Abigail's amusement, Nathan seemed to tackle her question from a strictly scientific viewpoint. "All soldiers?" He tapped his chin. "Let me see . . . that would encompass quite a few men. I would think it unlikely that *all* of them would have mastered the art of dance to your satisfaction. And then, how could we know that the number who did actually differed from the proportion of, say, tailors who danced well? Or even bootblacks? You might be applying your enthusiasm to the wrong profession entirely."

Though clearly exasperated, Sophy persisted. "But surely *you* like to dance."

"At the appropriate time." He turned, green eyes still twinkling with laughter, and caught Abigail's eye. "And with an excellent partner."

As his gaze lingered on her, Abigail felt a flush move from the roots of her hair to the tips of her uncomfortable shoes. He made it sound as if *she* would be an excellent partner, and the way his eyes settled on her lips, she had to rein herself in from imagining them whirling around a candlelit terrace. The fanciful image startled her.

What was it about this man? He seemed able to invade her thoughts at will. There was a spellbinding power in those green eyes. But why would he aim all this sorcery at her, when her sisters were so much more worthy of flirtation?

Though perhaps he wasn't flirting with her. Perhaps, after their encounter of that afternoon, his wicked smile was only meant to tease her.

"Do you *always* hover behind foliage, Miss Abigail?"

The question, calling up the memory of shivering behind the willow this afternoon, confirmed her suspicion that he was simply trying to torment her. And how well he succeeded! Her hands slipped off the keys and she was hard pressed to pick up her place again. "Greenery is very soothing," she said, and was aware of hoping that the smell of camphor was being drawn out the window. "And it also allows a certain privacy . . . unless someone is bent on purposefully intruding on that privacy, of course."

He laughed. "You mean it gives you good cover for peeking at people. Another hobby of yours, I'll be bound."

Unaccustomed to being ignored, Violet seemed unusually stiff-backed on the other side of the room. "Abigail's chief hobby is writing in her diary, which I think a very dull occupation."

Sophy, still intent on dancing, also appeared impatient with his attention to Abigail.

"One *would* like dull things if one felt sick all the time, as she does. Poor thing."

"Oh, yes, how could I forget?" At the reminder of Abigail's frail health, Nathan's eyes twinkled with humor. His expression became so overly solicitous that even at the risk of betraying her falsehood, Abigail was hard pressed not to laugh. Especially when he swooped over to the piano and hovered over her worriedly. "How are you feeling right now, Miss Abigail? Are you sure you're strong enough to keep punching away at those keys? I fear you must be utterly fatigued."

She flashed a warning at him with her eyes. "I am fine."

He clucked over her. "But it must be so taxing for you."

In spite of herself, she bit back a smile. "I assure you, I can play an hour at a stretch without fainting over the instrument."

He sagged with exaggerated relief. "You have no idea how that eases my mind," he said. "I would feel terrible if you were wearing yourself out just for my benefit."

Sir Harlan coughed and scurried over to take Nathan's arm. "No, no. Nothing of the sort. Abigail plays often—no need to worry about her in the least."

"Play a dance tune," Sophy begged her. "I'm sure Mr. Cantrell is dying to dance."

"More likely *you* are, Sophy," Violet said.

"Well!" Sir Harlan said, intervening. "Dancing. Yes. That would certainly be amusing."

"I thought there would be no dancing," Violet said, tossing an arch glance at them all. "Otherwise I would have worn different slippers!"

Sir Harlan had forgotten the discussion earlier of Violet's history of crushed toes when dancing with their guest. He angled a glance at her feet and pronounced her shoes very sound. "Those would do fine, I imagine."

Violet looked commandingly at Nathan. "I think I would prefer a turn around the room."

"Would you?" Nathan paused a moment to allow Violet to begin to preen herself to appear at her best advantage. Then he grinned and took Sophy's hand. "I think I would like a dance, myself."

Gratified by the way he was tweaking her older sister, Abigail obliged Sophy by playing a quick country dance. Out of the corner of her eye she saw that Nathan was indeed a very competent dancer. And Sophy was looking at him as if he were top-of-the-trees.

Violet, on the other hand, had gone rigid at his slight. The woman fairly trembled with anger.

Sir Harlan seemed anxious, as well. After the dance had ended he hurried over to Nathan and practically dragged the man to Violet's side. "Violet is a most accomplished dancer . . . perhaps the best of all my daughters."

"Father!" Sophy exclaimed.

He wagged a finger at her. "Now, now. Youth has its advantages, but Violet can bring to the dance the grace of experience."

Violet looked as if she had sucked on a lemon. "*Experience?*"

Sophy laughed. "Father, you make Violet sound like an antique!"

Sir Harlan flapped his hands in front of him. "No, no, not at all! She's just twenty-six," he told Nathan. "Still a spring—"

"*Father!*" Violet warned.

Abigail feared she would dissolve into whoops. She had never seen her father behave so oddly—so nervously! At least not since a noted bird specialist had come to examine the offspring of Garrick and Mrs. Siddons for purchase.

Sir Harlan's words faded under the blast of Violet's icy stare. "Well! Why don't you two dance?"

Both Nathan and Violet's lips pursed in distaste. Yet at his host's urging, Nathan forced a bow and asked her if she would do him the honor.

"Certainly," Violet said, offering her hand with a final flick of irritation at her father. "At my advanced age one longs to demonstrate the fruits of *experience.*"

Smiling wickedly as she watched them facing off like two mad cats, Abigail considered being kind and playing a dance that would allow them to keep their distance. But she was afraid it just wasn't in her nature to pass up such an opportunity for amusement. She started playing a passionate waltz. Both dancers hesitated.

"Go on," said Sir Harlan, gesturing them to assume the appropriate close embrace. In fact, if the movements of his hands were any indication, he seemed to be hoping for a violent collision. (Which was not at all out of the realm of possibility, Abigail decided, glancing at them.)

"No need to worry about my disapproval, Cantrell," Sir Harlan assured him. "I like to watch the waltz above all things."

Nathan shot Abigail a long-suffering look and took the stiff body of his partner into his arms. The romantic song was completely undone by the unhappy performance of the dancers. It was all Abigail could do not to double over laughing—especially when the music ended, and before the dancers could spring apart, Sir Harlan urged an encore.

After her ordeal was over, Violet fled to the other side of the room and pulled at the bell to have the servants bring in the tea tray. She looked completely put out.

"*I* would like to waltz!" Sophy exclaimed.

Sir Harlan chuckled. "Let the man catch his breath."

Sophy fell onto a sofa in a huff.

Nathan rushed to Abigail, a grudging respect in his eyes for her waltz maneuver. "Very nicely played."

She hid a smile. "I thought you would enjoy it."

"Enjoy is too mild a word, I'm afraid," he said, coughing subtly.

"Is it? I know *I* enjoyed watching you, Mr. Cantrell."

"Indeed? Watching me seems to be a habit with you. I am flattered."

She glowered warningly, hoping to keep him from bringing up the subject of the pond again.

Happily, Nathan took her hint. "You seem to know all the latest music for someone who is reported to live retired from society," he said.

"No man is an island—especially when one has sisters. They bring me all the current music."

"But how do you dance, if you are always playing for others?"

"I don't dance often, as a rule." She fanned herself with a glove. "It can be so tiring."

"Oh, yes," he said, barely suppressing a chuckle. "Especially after one has been gadding about all day. But naturally you wouldn't know about such things . . ."

She smiled stiffly. "Do you intend to make your home in the neighborhood, Mr. Cantrell?"

His brows rose in amusement and he spoke in a low tone, almost a purr. "Are you afraid that I mean to hog all the best afternoons at the swimming pond? You sound as if you would like fair warning."

"Nonsense." But of course that is exactly what she wanted. If he stayed in the neighborhood, she would be certain to keep herself more secluded than usual. And she certainly wasn't going to risk another encounter like the one of this afternoon.

"To be honest, whether I stay depends on . . ." She could swear she caught him shooting a glance at Sir Harlan. ". . . On how well I like it here. At present, The Willows is not as welcoming as it once was."

She frowned, remembering his recent loss. "Oh, I'm sorry. I didn't mean to be unfeeling. I suppose the house holds painful memories for you."

"No, happy ones, mostly," he said. "I'm afraid I was speaking, selfishly, of my own comfort. The house is in a bit of disrepair."

Sir Harlan had heard this part of their speech and grunted. "You'll need money to fix it."

She detected a cloud cross Nathan's expression. "A good deal of money, I'm afraid."

"Houses are such a bother," Sophy said with a sigh of commiseration, "but I suppose they're necessary."

After this curious comment, it took the others a moment to regroup and think of how to start the conversation again.

When Sir Harlan commenced, he had reverted to a former topic. "Yes, I believe a ball will be just the thing," he said, thinking aloud. "I will leave the preparations for it in the girls' capable hands, of course."

Sophy clapped, and seemed to come to life again. "This is so exciting. A real party!"

"But whom shall we invite?" Violet asked, envisioning clouds where her sister saw only rainbows. "There are hardly enough people here to make a fashionable squeeze for a ball."

"There is a town full of people," Abigail reminded her.

Violet looked uncomfortably at Nathan before upbraiding her sister for such a foolish remark. "But people we'd actually want to socialize with," she clarified. Then, as a pleasurable thought struck her, she clasped her hands together and turned to Sir Harlan. "Father, you'll have to ask the Earl of Clatsop!" She lifted her chin as she explained to Nathan, "The Earl of Clatsop is a frequent visitor to

Peacock Hall. I am sure he would want to come, Father. He could even stop a few days here."

Sir Harlan thought for a moment. "I'll bet the old boy would enjoy it at that."

"You will ask him, won't you?" she begged.

"Of course, of course."

Suddenly, Violet was ebullient. She seemed more like Sophy in her girlish enthusiasm than herself. "A ball. What a wonderful thing to look forward to!"

Abigail smiled. "Another waltz, Violet?"

In such a dreamy frame of mind, it took only a little coaxing from Sir Harlan for Violet to twirl once again in the arms of their visitor, no doubt dreaming of herself in the slightly palsied embrace of her imagined partner, the earl.

Nathan shot peevish glances at the piano player all the while. Abgail was enjoying his discomfort too much to care, however. And for that matter, she was enjoying herself too much to take note of how oddly pleased her father looked, seeing his eldest daughter fairly beaming in the arms of their young neighbor.

Unfortunately, it was that pleased look in Sir Harlan's eye that lingered in Nathan's mind later that evening as he sat in front of a fire with a glass of his father's finest wine. Say one thing for his father, the house might have been falling around his ears, but his wine cellar still contained some excellent vintages—if you knew where to look for them. His father had obviously feared incursions from Freddy, so that the wine cellar was actually in what had been the cheese room in his mother's day. As he swirled the burgundy in the crystal goblet, he idly wondered what happened to the cheeses these days . . . .

But that was neither here nor there. He had no business thinking about cheese when he was facing one of the most important decisions of his life. To marry or not to marry, that was the question.

As he had ridden over to dinner, Nathan had come to the

decision that he was going to have to give Sir Harlan a polite refusal of his very obliging offer. He had decided they
could either come to terms over the mortgage, or he and
Freddy would just have to fend for themselves some way.

But that was before he'd espied Abigail and realized that
she was one of his choices.

Abigail . . . he smiled as he pictured her slogging away
from him in the pond this afternoon. As he remembered
the body that was encased in the dripping shift, he thought
it would not be at all hard to find himself caught in the par-
son's mousetrap with her. It wasn't only that she possessed
an attractive body; she had shown wonderful spirit and wit
as well during their conversations, which might more aptly
be called sparring matches.

"Where did you unearth that wine?"

Nathan looked up to find Freddy standing next to him
with a look of outrage on his face. But the most noticeable
thing about his brother was the sartorial effect achieved
with his very puce dressing grown decorated with bright
green and yellow dragons and finished off with a pink cravat folded negligently around Freddy's long neck.

Freddy continued with his grievance. "I have been per-
ishing of thirst since I arrived, and here you lounge, tip-
pling back the fruit of the vine. Mrs. Willoughby actually
served me a glass of milk with my dinner this evening! I
haven't had milk with my dinner since I was in short
coats!"

"I hope you didn't do anything to offend the Willough-
bys, Freddy. They are quite overworked and undercom-
pensated as it is."

"Damme, I don't see how they are the ones who could
be offended—they weren't stuck trying to wash down that
leathery mutton with lukewarm milk!"

Nathan couldn't suppress a guffaw at the thought of his
elegant brother sitting down to mutton and milk.

"Well you may laugh, but on top of it all, I think the
stuff was going off," Freddy announced with an injured air.

As a peace offering, Nathan indicated the decanter on
the side table. "Help yourself."

Freddy poured himself a generous glass and took a swallow—or rather gulped it like a man who has just crawled out of a desert might slurp down water. After he had downed one glass and poured himself another, he obviously was feeling sociable once again.

"So how did the dinner party go at *chez* Wingate?"

"It was fine." Nathan certainly didn't want to go into the details of his current muddle with Freddy. "We had turtle soup."

"Fancy! Where does one procure a turtle hereabouts?"

"The turtle had to be sent for all the way from London, apparently." As Sir Harlan had prosed on during dinner about the turtle's pedigree, Nathan had never dreamed he would have an opportunity of repeating it.

"Sir Harlan sets a good table?"

"Oh yes." He served up soup and meat as readily as he served up blackmail . . .

Freddy's eyes were moist with longing. "Several courses, no doubt, with lots of removes?"

"Several," Nathan confirmed.

"My goodness, they quite killed the fatted calf for you, didn't they? Well, there's nothing like a hero back from the wars. You know you just might mention that you have your younger brother staying with you the next time they invite you to dinner. I am sure that Sir Harlan keeps a fine cellar if that big red nose of his is any indication—and it usually is a sign, I think you'll find."

"Been making a scientific study of it, have you, Freddy?" Nathan asked with a smile.

"Not precisely scientific, but I keep my eyes open, don't you know. Well, if you don't mind, I may head for the feather tick—always feel devilishly sleepy in the country. Must be all the fresh air and that milk I had for dinner. See you tomorrow."

"Good night, Freddy."

After he left, Nathan sank down further in his chair. How on earth would Freddy get on if Nathan didn't come to terms with Sir Harlan somehow? And what leverage did he have to bargain with Sir Harlan? He was going to have to seriously consider the offer of marrying one of the Wingate girls.

Of course, when he thought of the Wingate girls, there was no choice. Violet and Sophy were out of the question. No, only with Abigail could he imagine developing the sort of relationship that could lead to a happy marriage. In fact, he believed that even without Sir Harlan's encouragement he would have found her worth pursuing. He could hardly wait to learn more about her, particularly why she seemed to encourage her family into thinking she was a fragile flower. All you had to do was observe that peachy complexion and look at her beautiful smile and you knew that she was in perfect health.

As he continued to contemplate Abigail's smile he wondered if he was just using Freddy's foibles as an excuse to allow him to do exactly as he wished—to pursue the delightful acquaintance of Miss Abigail Wingate.

Abigail sat at her dressing table with a cup of hot milk—so beneficial for invalids—that, untouched, was quickly growing cool. Trying to brush through the mess that had passed that evening for her hair was proving a struggle. It was in parts frizzy where her maid had so injudiciously applied the hot curling tongs and then sticky from whatever was floating in the pond water.

The negative repercussions from that afternoon's swim seemed never-ending, Abigail huffed as she once again caught her brush on a snarl. She remembered her embarrassment in the water, then the even greater humiliation of her appearance and Nathan's taunting words every time he got her alone. Would she never live down the afternoon, or was she doomed to shave her head and to go into hiding from her neighbor? And if that wasn't possible, could she trust him to keep his mouth closed about the unorthodox situation of their first meeting?

That was what made her mind race frantically. The way he had ribbed her before and after dinner had come far too close to revealing the secret of their meeting that afternoon for her peace of mind. If her family discovered that she was well enough to be splashing about in a cold pond miles from home, they might start wondering if she was lying about her health. In fact, all it would take would be for one of her family to take a close look at her, and they would realize she was far from an invalid. For years she had been flourishing in their studied disinterest. Now that there was a stranger among them, they might look at her through fresh eyes.

Of course, she could resolve this dilemma by making a full confession. All she had to do was tell them that she was a published authoress, and these worries over maintaining her secret would be over. There was nothing that shameful in it, after all. Other ladies wrote books and were not ousted from their families. It's not like she printed under the family name, after all.

Yes. All she had to do was stand up and say, "Father, I have an announcement. I am Georgianna Harcourt."

To which her father would no doubt reply, "Who?"

She sighed. That was the trouble. If she were a fabulously successful authoress, perhaps her father would approve. He might even feel he had something to boast about. But her novels were rather . . . well, lurid. She blushed to think of her father reading some of the scenes she had written. What if her family sneered at her efforts? Her publisher had been very kind, and forwarded positive comments from the public, but in her seclusion she had been as shielded from harsh criticism as those flowers that needed to be shielded from the hot sun.

There might even be a scandal. Look what had happened to Lord Overmeer's younger daughter. That learned young lady had returned from school and announced that she would be a poetess, which Lord Overmeer encouraged by setting her up in a London apartment with a chaperone. In six months, Olivia Overmeer had produced nothing but extravagant bills from dressmakers and furnishers, a scandal involving one of Lady Jersey's footmen, and mad rafts of rather shocking verse detailing her unrequited passion for the Duke of Wellington. Even Lord Overmeer, whom

Sir Harlan always pronounced a lax, permissive parent, was shocked. Olivia Overmeer had been promptly divested of her apartment and her quills and removed to a convent in Ireland.

After that incident, Abigail feared if she confessed she would be packed off to Ireland straightaway.

No, confessing would only be done as a last resort, she decided as she put down the brush and turned towards her bed. Her life served her right now quite well. She longed to go somewhere else, of course—to London, or a picturesque seaswept cottage somewhere—but she wanted just a little more money in reserve before she took such a drastic step. If necessary to keep up her subterfuge, she would have to redouble her efforts to seem frail and retiring, a prospect that only made her more irritated with Nathan Cantrell.

What was he doing here? She belatedly caught some of Sophy's curiosity from that afternoon. Why would the man come to Peacock Hall twice in one day? Was there some business he had with their father?

She couldn't deny that their father had seemed unusually attentive to Mr. Cantrell, and altogether more keyed up than was typical of him, even when they had company. Something was afoot and it looked like it would behoove her to keep a very close watch on Mr. Cantrell.

At the thought of watching over him, the forbidden image of Nathan's gleaming torso popped into Abigail's head. She had to admit that Nathan was handsome. She had never been put in the way of seeing so glorious a specimen of undressed male anatomy before. She also remembered the thrill that she had experienced when Nathan had taken her hand in the water, the warmth that had seemed to suffuse her entire body, despite the cold. As he had caressed and examined her fingers, the sensations she had experienced were like tiny lightning bolts of pleasure.

Of course, she sighed to herself as she snuffed out the candle on her nightstand, then he had pronounced her "wrinkled like a prune," which had quite dampened those electric sensations.

Chapter Five

*Clara trembled on the last stair. She dreaded entering
the study where the savage-faced nobleman awaited
news of his fiancée. Would it be left to her to tell
Rudolpho the woman he sought had left with another? That his long-sought revenge would not be
taken today? The object of his desires had left for . . .*
　　　　　　　　　　　　—The Prisoner of Raffizzi

Abigail looked out the window and let out a lengthy
sigh. Although the rain had let up for a bit, it was still very
dark outside. You would think all this eerie weather would
be conducive to her writing, but since Nathan Cantrell's
appearance in her life, Abigail had done very little. Poor
Clara was still hovering with her candle on the blasted
stairway. The fearsome Rudolpho had been stuck twid-
dling his thumbs in front of a roaring fire in the study for
almost a week since the dinner party with Mr. Cantrell.
Abigail had eked out only two measly sentences in all that
time.

She stood up from her desk. Perhaps stretching her legs
would help spur her creative juices, which now seemed in
peril of congealing. In any case, she needed to consult a
map to research where Rudolpho's faithless lover could
have fled. She marched down the hall to her father's study,
where the door was slightly ajar. Cautiously, she peeked
inside, not wanting to risk a confrontation with her father
and an explanation of why she wanted to consult his atlas.
But instead of finding Sir Harlan, her gaze fell on Sophy

and Nathan standing together on the stepladder, locked in an embrace.

Abigail blinked at the couple in surprise, but remained speechless. Her instinct was to retreat, but her feet felt leaden. Nor could her eyes, which didn't seem to want to believe what they were seeing, yank themselves away from the entwined pair.

Abigail sucked in her breath and suddenly her sister looked up. Sophy's dark eyes were round and lit with merriment. (Though Abigail was relieved to see that she at least had the decency to blush.) Nathan turned also, his face a mask of surprise. His reaction made Abigail indignant. *Could he have actually thought he would not be discovered?*

He stumbled off the ladder and started fumbling for words. "Abigail! I didn't hear footsteps . . ."

Her lips pursed. "Were you listening for them?" She imagined him with a guilty ear cocked towards the door.

Sophy slipped down from her perch. "You look as stern as a judge, Abigail."

Abigail crossed her arms; she wasn't certain with whom she was more vexed. Sophy deserved a sharp pinch for such shocking behavior . . . but Nathan! She didn't doubt that he was as much a contributor to this situation as Sophy was. Certainly his behavior at the pond hadn't been passive by any stretch of the imagination. In fact, he had been very forward. And now this!

Sophy scurried by her. "You see, Abby, I was just getting a book."

That statement alone was suspect. Abigail's brows arched.

"I have been so bored for the past week that I decided to try reading," Sophy explained. "Naturally, it *never* occurred to me that Nathan would be in the library, all alone, just when I needed to be there, too. But he very kindly offered to help me reach my selection . . ."

Abigail shot the man a withering look. "And naturally to reach this volume he was forced to have you climb the ladder before him and wrap his arms around your person."

Nathan took a step toward her. "I didn't . . . that wasn't how . . . I mean to say . . ."

She shook her head. "Such acrobatics are wasted in a library, Mr. Cantrell. You could offer your talents to Astley's circus and profit handsomely, I'm sure."

Sophy tittered. "Oh, Abigail, you are so funny. But you shouldn't scold our guest!"

Guest. Heaven help them. In the past week the man's presence had become as ubiquitous at Peacock Hall as stray feathers, but of course Abigail doubted he would be idling about much longer if their father got wind of episodes like this one. First they were deprived of servants who could function. What next? Would they only be able to receive visitors of a certain age, as well?

"You won't tell, will you, Abigail?" Sophy asked.

"I . . ." Abigail didn't know how to answer. Part of her *wanted* to run and tattle to their father immediately. She would then be a very definite one up on Mr. Cantrell.

"Abigail would never tattle to her father of *another's* impropriety, would you, Abigail?" said Nathan, reminding her that he had a story he could tell her father too.

But would he?

She narrowed her eyes, studying him, and came to the conclusion that he would. Gleefully.

She lifted her chin. "*I* wouldn't."

Sophy fell on her in gratitude. "Thank you!" Before flitting out of the library, she turned and trilled her fingers at Nathan. "Good day, Mr. Cantrell."

Nathan blinked after her. He was still standing next to the ladder, holding a book, and seemed nonplussed by Sophy. "That was not what you think."

Abigail tilted her head skeptically. "What was it?"

"Well, as she said, I was just helping her reach a book . . ."

"And you just accidentally swept her up into a tight, lover-like embrace?" Abigail finished for him. "Mr. Cantrell, I am well aware that my sister can be a bit, shall we say, high-spirited, but I'm sure she wouldn't be able to trap a man in her arms unless the man were a somewhat willing partner."

"But I wasn't, I assure you."

She laughed. "You mean that my sister attacked you on that ladder, and you, a poor defenseless ex-soldier, were helpless against her superior strength?"

He looked utterly bewildered as he replayed the event in his mind. Indeed, he seemed as if he honestly didn't know what hit him. "I simply climbed the ladder to find her a book, and then . . ." His words trailed off into confusion before he could pick back up again. "In any event, it was *you* I was hoping to see."

"I'm sure you couldn't have confused me with Sophy."

Nathan shot a wicked glance up and down her body and stated, "Absolutely not."

She started backing towards the door, forgetting all about her atlas. Being near this man made her uncomfortable. Her body seemed to go feverish on her when he was around. And she couldn't deny that bad things tended to happen. A soothing swim turned into a mortifying experience. An attempt to dress for dinner—disaster. And every time she was near him she had to endure his smirking, pointed barbs, meant to torment her in front of the rest of her family. Was she now supposed to be pleased that he had been seeking her out and only accidentally found himself fondling her sister?

"I am very busy at the moment, Mr. Cantrell. I can ring for Peabody, who will find my father or Violet for you if you are desperate for company."

He hurried towards her. "No, please. What I would like most of all is to be alone with you."

That bald statement made her jump. Finding herself alone with Nathan, just inadvertently, was disconcerting. She had seen far too much of him already, and she meant that literally. She had no intention of placing herself in his exclusive company if she could help it. After seeing him *alone* with Sophy, she feared the man was somewhat of an animal. "Mr. Cantrell, you have been to Peacock Hall four times in a week. What exactly are you doing here?"

He was looking into her eyes, and seemed startled to discover that she had spoken to him. "Hm?"

She sighed with impatience. "Peacock Hall seems to have become a favorite haunt of yours since your return from the Continent. I wonder why that is."

"Why do you think that is?"

"If I had a melodramatic turn of mind—" Of course, Mr. Cantrell had no way of knowing that was exactly what she did have. "—I would consider the possibility that you had some hold over my father."

"Not the other way around?" He smiled. And in her current frame of mind, it was easy for her to believe that the smile was rather . . . sinister.

"My father? Oh, no."

"In fact, your father has been very kind to me since my return."

"Yes, and you seem to be repaying that kindness by molesting his daughters."

He grinned. "Come now, I did not molest you at the pond."

She nearly quaked at the memory. "No, I escaped, thank God. But you have been intent on vexing me ever since, it seems. Every time I turn around, there you are."

His brows drew together. "Strange. You have been vexing me, as well. You pop up at odd moments, and yet when I want to speak to you, you retreat into that shell of yours as fast as a turtle."

"How bizarre that I should do so, when you ladle out such handsome compliments! I don't know the last time I was compared to a leathery old reptile."

He laughed. "You added the old and leathery part yourself."

"No doubt you were thinking of a nimble young turtle."

He took a step closer towards her, a simple gesture that made her stomach perform an uneasy flip. "Actually, I was thinking how much I would like to know about you. For instance, what kind of ruse are you playing with your family? I seem to be the only person at Peacock Hall who knows you are as fit as a soldier."

He was smiling, but his ribbing her about her health was no laughing matter to her. "And I seem to be the only one here who would question why a man so recently returned to the area has suddenly become inescapable!" she volleyed back.

He reached out to her. "Abigail——"

She backed out of range of his grasp, then nearly found herself flattened when Sir Harlan roared through the door, Violet at his side.

"There you are!" he exclaimed to Nathan.

"I was just speaking to Miss Wingate," Nathan said.

The two of them stood, stiffly, several feet apart. No one who was not privy to the racing of Abigail's pulse would ever guess that he had been reaching out for her. In any event, she had been acting with her family for so long that she was confident it appeared as if they had merely been having an impersonal chat in the library.

Sir Harlan threw his middle daughter a weary glance, as if he considered it bad form for her to be monopolizing their guest's time. "Yes, Abigail often comes in and out of this room. Mustn't mind that."

"Indeed, I didn't mind a bit," he said, smiling so brightly that Abigail felt herself blush just from the warmth of that gaze.

Sir Harlan took Nathan's arm. "Thing is, I've discovered that Violet needs to go to town—some dressmaking business. You know how the ladies are!" He coughed. "And I noted that you rode over in your carriage . . ."

Violet interrupted. "At the urging of my father, I have decided to grant you the privilege of driving me into town."

"Well!" Nathan seemed filled with dread. "I am speechless."

Abigail couldn't help beaming a malicious smile at him. Clearly, a drive to town with Violet was something he looked forward to as much as she herself would. "Speechless? This must be a first!"

Ignoring Abigail, Sir Harlan hustled Violet to Nathan's side. "There now! Don't hurry on my account, Cantrell. I know how young people will lollygag on a nice summer day."

Abigail looked out the window, where she saw blue-black clouds gathering on the horizon. "But it looks as if it might start raining again," she pointed out.

Sir Harlan coughed at her in irritation. "Well! Yes! Might clear up, though. In which case you'll no doubt want to stop and stare at flowers and birds and whatnot. Make good use of your time."

Abigail frowned in puzzlement. Since when would her father have considered staring at a flower good use of one's time? And the image of Violet picking posies was almost enough to make her laugh out loud, if this entire situation weren't so peculiar.

Nathan, who was being herded towards the door, threw a panicky glance back at her. "Are you sure we shouldn't bring Miss Wingate with us as well?"

"No call for that!" Sir Harlan inserted quickly. He was already pushing the pair down the front hall. "Violet's been married, you know, she doesn't need Abigail to play chaperone."

As if the only reason she would be invited was a *chaperone*? Abigail recoiled as if she had been slapped. Is that what her family thought of her? No doubt soon they would dispense with the services of her poor cousin Henrietta altogether!

"I couldn't possibly go out in this weather," she said icily.

Peabody scurried towards Violet with her cape and bonnet, a more than usually worried look on his face. Especially when he caught sight of the uneven crease on Nathan's breeches. "Do be careful, ma'am."

"Yes, do," Abigail called after them. "Stay away from ladders, by all means. Mr. Cantrell is very unpredictable on them!"

Peabody looked more alarmed than ever, while Violet only appeared confused.

Sir Harlan flicked Abigail an annoyed glance. "Ladders? There are no ladders on the way to town."

Nathan was barely able to look back once at Abigail,

and when he did, she laughed and trilled her fingers much as Sophy had done earlier. *"Arrivederci*—Mr. Cantrell!"

The door had closed before she realized that she had nearly called him Rudolpho.

"This is quite an old carriage, isn't it, Mr. Cantrell?" Violet asked, after they had bumped along the road to town in stiff silence for a good quarter of an hour.

Nathan had to bite his tongue. Though his eyes had been trained on the road, he had felt her staring him down in distaste. "Old, but serviceable." Actually, it was a relic. The leather of the hood was dried and cracked, and the wheels felt so loose he feared they might actually come off, stranding them. God forbid. He hoped to get this errand over with as quickly as he could.

"Mm. From your grandparents' day, no doubt."

"I beg your pardon, Mrs. Treacher. I did not think you would mind being driven in it, considering that we are not in London, or anywhere in the vicinity of anyone who has a better mode of transportation than this."

"That is not accurate." She sighed. "Father has a beautiful phaeton just two years old, but he is so stingy with his horses. And of course it would require work for the grooms, and he is loath to ask them to do any sort of work."

Nathan shook his head over this. "Your father has a kind heart."

She laughed in a brittle manner, tilting a sidewise glance at him. "His kind heart has little to do with it. Although he seems to have developed a penchant for taking in strays just lately."

Nathan frowned. He knew that was meant as a barely veiled insult, just one of many she had planned for the afternoon, he was sure. Perhaps it would be best if he steered the conversation away from his family . . . a depressing subject to him at the moment. He turned his mind to a far more fascinating one. "Your sister Abigail also seems very kind, like your father."

Violet laughed. "Abigail? She and Father are as similar as chalk and cheese!"

"But I would think she has a good heart?"

"I suppose she does," Violet answered, actually seeming to give the matter thought. "I believe it is her lungs that give her trouble from time to time . . . or some ailment of that kind. I have a hard time sorting it all out."

Obviously. The entire family seemed particularly vague on this matter. "I meant good as in *kind* heart."

"Oh!" She frowned. "Yes, I suppose so. If you care about that sort of thing."

"What could be more important than kindness?"

She considered. "For some people, I am sure it is a very important trait indeed. You certainly want poor people to be kind and respectful, or else there would be anarchy in the land. But as for the aristocracy and those of superior breeding, matters are very different. Naturally you can't expect the same rules of behavior to apply to everyone. A little condescension from someone of breeding is becoming, I'm sure, but too much makes them seem foolish. They should have pride."

"I suppose you are one of those who consider it necessary to have pride?"

"My late husband was the heir to a marquess."

"I am sorry for your loss."

"Oh, so am I! Especially since Percy had such a wretch for a younger brother. No sooner was my dear husband lowered into his grave than I was informed by his family that I was being sent back to my father! I consider myself very ill-treated."

"And the family left you with no source of financial support?"

"Only a very small pittance—barely enough for my upkeep—and a small property." She huffed. "In Cornwall!"

"That is beautiful country."

She rounded on him in horror. "Cornwall? It's the end of the earth!"

"No, just the end of England."

"Practically Wales!" she moaned. "I have heard that it is

full of outlaws and smugglers and people of no consequence whatsoever!"

He couldn't tell which she considered worse: lawbreakers or nobodies.

"Is it a nice property?"

Her face twisted into a look that told him he must be mad. "I've never been to see it, of course. Since my brother-in-law gave it to me, I assume it must be a hovel. A stingier man you never knew."

He could see that Violet considered herself ill-used in every way. "I am surprised you don't live in London."

"Would that I could! But I have so little money. We have an aunt, Aunt Augusta, who lives off Grosvenor Square, but hers is a small house. Father absolutely refuses to pay for a house of our own in London, though perhaps I will be able to cajole him into opening his purse when Sophy is in Society. I do not think we can leave Sophy's social tutelage to my Aunt Augusta. She needs a more sterling example of gentlewomanly conduct." She let out a long-suffering sigh. "I suppose *I* will accompany her, and act as chaperone, a job that is sure to be mortifying."

For once he could sympathize with her. If what he had endured on that ladder this morning was a true example of the girl's "high spirits," being responsible for Sophy's behavior would be an unenviable position for anyone.

"What about Abigail?"

Violet practically snorted at the very idea. "We've given up on her ever having a Season, or ever showing her face in London. The poor thing used to take ill every time it was time to pack her bags to go to the city."

"Ah, I see . . ."

"So Sophy's care will probably be left entirely on my shoulders, naturally. I always seem to be bearing the burdens of the Wingates. But at least I will have an excuse to be in London."

"Dear, dear," he said, clucking sarcastically. "You seem to be staring down a vast maw of doom."

She heaved a heavy sigh. "Doom? No. But I will admit my prospects are all challenging ones."

"You do have prospects, then?"

Some poor victim lined up, perhaps.

"That is a very impertinent question, Mr. Cantrell."

"I beg your pardon," he said. "I hoped you might look upon me as an old friend."

She smirked. "No doubt."

He frowned. "What does that mean?"

"Nothing."

"I sensed more than the usual dose of sarcasm in your tone. Why?"

"Well—I believe it is obvious that you have singled me out as a prospect for yourself. Which makes me glad we have this opportunity to talk, so you will never be able to assert that I misled you later on. I wouldn't want you to entertain false hopes."

False hopes? At first he had to strain to understand to what the woman could be referring. And then the answer dawned on him like a lightning bolt of absurdity. She was referring to hopes that he might have for *her*. "You think that I . . ."

"Why else would you have jumped at the opportunity of escorting me?"

He practically dropped the reins. "Jumped at the opportunity!"

She lifted her shoulders in a shrug, as if it were obvious. "Mr. Cantrell, please do not be upset. Believe me, I am accustomed to such attentions from locals. Indeed, I am flattered."

"By heavens, I meant no flattery!"

She only smiled. "As you say, Mr. Cantrell. But believe me, you are not the first man here who has aspired for my hand in vain."

Of all the . . .

He tried to keep his temper. The woman deserved to have her ears boxed, and he was sorely tempted to do it. In fact, he would have dearly loved to dump her out in the mud. Even though he could not actually set her down in the elements, at least the joy of imagining doing so made the rest of the drive into town bearable.

He left Violet at the dressmaker's, promising to pick her up in an hour. In the meantime, he ambled towards the old Frog and Fiddle Inn. He had not meant to, but after his drive he felt the need to sit and think. And seethe.

What an impossible, exasperating woman! How could she possibly imagine that he was in love with her? She was about as lovable as a razor strop, and a great deal less useful.

In the taproom of the Frog and Fiddle, he was greeted with a bracing slap on the back by the innkeeper, Barlow, who insisted on serving him a pint on the house.

"For your dear old father, God bless him! He lost more money at that table yonder than any man in the county."

That, unfortunately, was not an exaggeration. Nathan turned to look at the empty table, which at this early hour looked as if it had been vacated in memoriam. He wondered just how many of his troubles were a direct result of the misfortunes of the card games that had taken place there.

"We all miss your father, Major," Barlow said. "Indeed we do."

"Thank you."

"We are all proud of you, though. Sent that little Frenchie devil on his way single-handed, I'll wager."

Nathan shook his head. He understood the feeling of jubilation everyone felt now that the conflict was finally over, yet he felt awkward taking much credit for a war that was much harder on others. Five young men from town had lost their lives. "I had help."

"Your modesty becomes you, Major," Barlow said with a wink. "Your father was always singing your praises."

He wondered what his father would think of him now that he was considering marrying a Wingate daughter to rescue the family from debt. Not much to be proud of there!

Then again, it was foolish to feel embarrassed by what his father might think of such a move, since it was his father who put him in such a damned awkward spot, Nathan thought bitterly.

While Barlow tended to cleaning the floor, Nathan slowly worked on his pint. One moment he would think he was absolutely going to tell Sir Harlan to forget his foolish scheme, and then the next he would remember Abigail. Pretty, intriguing Abigail, who had such an aura of mystery about her. And her family was so unappreciative of her! It seemed they hardly knew her at all. Marrying her wouldn't seem like a compromise, would it? Not if there was real fondness between them, and why couldn't there be? Such an arrangement would benefit them both. She would be a married woman, in her own house, and he . . . he would be fulfilling his familial obligations.

What was the point of him spending the last years of his life risking himself to preserve his and his country's way of life in England, if he lost his home to Wingate?

The minutes ticked by, and out of the one dirty window he could see rain begin. Lovely. He finally had to get up and fetch Violet . . . much as he would have enjoyed making her slog home in the damp.

Barlow held the door for him and grinned. "I see you drove Mrs. Treacher."

Oh good Lord. Nathan hadn't considered the possibility of gossip, but there was a gleeful glint in the innkeeper's eye.

"A beautiful woman, is Mrs. Treacher."

Nathan nodded noncommittally. "I brought her as a favor to Mr. Wingate. He didn't want to bother his groom with the horses, or some such thing."

"Aye, that's right. All the men at that house are stooped old fellows now, on account of Miss Sophy."

"Miss Sophy?" Nathan asked.

"Aye. Too many of the young'uns took a shine to her. Or her to them . . ."

Oh good heavens. His experience on the ladder hadn't been a singular occurrence then, but part of an epidemic. No wonder Sir Harlan despaired over his daughters.

"I hear Mrs. Treacher has money and property of her own, too," Barlow said with a meaningful look towards Nathan.

Nathan bid him good day, knowing that by the end of an hour the entire town would believe he was courting Violet for her money.

He ambled across the street to the dressmaker. He was standing outside the door, when it opened and he was suddenly pulled inside. Mrs. Henchey, the seamstress, fussed over him. "Why Major! We've seen so little of you!"

Violet smirked at him. "That's odd. We have seen quite a bit of him at Peacock Hall."

Mrs. Henchey's gaze flitted from his face to Violet's and back again. She smiled knowingly. "Is that so? But I suppose it's natural, you being neighbors."

"Actually, I have some business with Sir Harlan . . ."

Mrs. Henchey winked at him. " 'Course you have."

He managed to pull Violet from the building and get her back into the carriage in short order.

She turned to him with a wry smirk. "I saw that you went directly to the Frog and Fiddle. I am sorry if I drove you to drink."

This again! "You had nothing to do with it. I went to pay my respects to Barlow."

She chuckled.

The sound grated on him. "I am not upset that you think I am unsuited to you, Violet. In fact, I glory—indeed, I revel—in the fact that you have another man in your sights."

"And yet now you are calling me Violet, when I certainly did not give you permission."

He rolled his eyes. "It just slipped off my tongue."

"Indeed—as if you had been thinking of me quite a bit."

He slapped the reins over the horses' rumps, hoping to reach Peacock Hall as soon as possible. Even seconds could make the difference between whether he strangled Violet or not.

"Have I angered you, Mr. Cantrell?"

"No," he bit out.

She folded her hands in her lap with excruciating primness. "I see that I have."

"*Mrs. Treacher,*" he began, turning to her so that she

might see his disinterest clearly. "I do hate to be the one to disabuse you of the notion that you are irresistible, but I am quite able to retain my good sense around you and see you for exactly what you are—a spoiled, top-lofty, ill-mannered termagant."

As he spoke, her jaw began to wobble and then slowly fall, until her entire face looked as if it had fallen slack. Two angry bolts of red flashed across her cheeks. "Stop this carriage at once!"

"Don't be ridiculous."

"Stop or I will jump!" she warned. "I have never been so insulted in my life! I refuse to sit here and hear myself abused by one such as you for a moment more."

He laughed. "I am fresh out of abuse. Besides, it looks as if another downpour is imminent."

"I don't care! You might think it is a matter of fun to insult a lady, Mr. Cantrell, but others will think differently. I would not be surprised that, if the Earl of Clatsop heard of your ill treatment of me, he called you out."

Nathan frowned. "Clatsop? That doddering old fellow I used to see about my father's club in London with his nose in a science book?"

"He is a man of impeccable breeding and excellent character—which is more than I can say for you!"

Suddenly, Nathan understood. He slowed the horses and gaped at her. "Clatsop is your idea of a prospect?"

She seemed uncertain how to respond. "So?"

"Nothing—only aren't you setting the bar rather low?"

"On the contrary, Mr. Cantrell. I find the earl to be a fascinating man."

"With a fascinating title, I have no doubt. Only I would think, after your bad luck with the heir of a marquess, you would want to find someone a little more robust this time around."

"That is quite enough!"

He couldn't help it. He laughed.

"I refuse to be insulted!" she cried. "I would rather walk the rest of the way to Peacock Hall!"

Which, by the by, they were only a hundred yards away from now.

"Don't be a ninny," he said.

She yelped, and to his utter shock, she pushed herself up and made as if to hop down. Quickly, he scooted over and held her arm.

"Let me go," she demanded, with one foot on the carriage's step.

"Get back in. You are almost home."

"Then I would prefer to walk!"

"I won't let you."

"You are an ill-bred, ill-mannered beast! I cannot believe my father ever invited you into our home, knowing what a wastrel your father was!"

He recoiled, and anger filled the spot where there was previously merely exasperation. He let go of her arm just as she gave one final tug to free herself. As a result he had the pleasure of seeing her fly backwards to the ground, skirts flapping around her, and with a dramatic splash, land flat on her behind in a mud puddle.

To Abigail it seemed the unthinkable had happened: she was actually jealous of Violet.

Ridiculous, of course. She had lived all her life in Violet's shadow, and never felt envious of her looks or her position as the oldest daughter. Of course, while growing up Violet had been altogether more companionable than she was now. It had not been hard to like her when she was younger and her sense of propriety and yearning to be in Society had not yet hardened into a rigid snobbery. It was only as grown women that the two sisters had grown distant, like two magnetized objects compelled to move farther apart.

But in the early years, she had been proud of her sister and happy for her triumphs. She had certainly lived very comfortably with the idea that her sister was the wife to the heir of a marquess, and had stood very happily at her sister's side during the wedding, since it seemed to be a perfect match for

Violet. Some sisters might have harbored envy—especially since Violet rarely endured success in silence—but Abigail had truly felt none.

But now she felt as if something was physically gnawing away at her. Nathan and Violet had been away for two hours.

It wasn't that *she* wished she were with Nathan. Oh, no. She certainly wanted no part of his sneering and smirking.

The trouble was, she couldn't explain what it was she did want. Or why she cared how long Nathan and Violet had been gone together in that carriage . . . alone . . .

Abigail, Sophy, and their father were gathered in Sir Harlan's study. Sir Harlan was busily drawing up a guest list for the coming ball, a task that he had surprisingly commandeered from Violet at breakfast. He was uncommonly eager to send out invitations. Sophy was on the sofa fitfully perusing a ladies' magazine she had been through twenty times at least, and Abigail was sitting with a forgotten book in her lap and staring out the window. At the road. This, of course, was part of the reason Abigail had felt drawn to the study in the first place; it afforded Peacock Hall's best view of the drive.

Not for the first time since Violet and Nathan had left, Sophy sighed. "I wish someone would have told me Mr. Cantrell was taking Violet into town. I would have liked to have gone."

"There was no time, dear," Sir Harlan said. "Violet seemed rather in a hurry. Both of them did. Eager, you might even say."

Abigail felt her brow pinching. *Had they looked eager?* At the time, she had thought Nathan had appeared rather queasy at the prospect. Had her eyes deceived her?

Sophy flopped back on the sofa in a huff. "Everyone is always rushing about, never thinking of me."

Ignoring his youngest daughter's woes, Sir Harlan tapped his quill on his chin and said, "I suppose we'll have to ask your Aunt Augusta, though I don't suppose she'll come . . ."

Sophy then launched into one of her favorite indoor

pastimes, the "I never get to have any fun" monologue, which, if unimpeded by appeals to reason, could run half an hour or more. As the youngest, she had no end of examples of slights, oversights, and rank unfairness to back up her arguments. People had been going places without her since the days when she had been confined to her cradle and Abigail and Violet had been frolicking in the garden. During their nursery days, the older girls' French lessons she had viewed as a means to talk about things she couldn't understand. And let us not speak (or, rather, let us speak incessantly) of the horrors Sophy underwent being locked away at Miss Pargeter's whilst Violet was off in London, dancing her feet off. Even Violet's marriage and subsequent bereavement Sophy saw as a mark of injustice towards herself. Why was all this romance and excitement allotted to Violet? Life was passing Sophy by, and no one but she seemed to care!

On this day, Abigail and Sir Harlan couldn't have done a better job affirming her fears if they had actually conspired to do so. Neither was actually listening to Sophy's lament, although they didn't particularly need to since both had heard the details innumerable times. It wasn't even that they didn't care. It was simply that there was such a peculiar scene occurring out the window—a window Sophy could not see because she was draped across the sofa with her arm flung over her eyes to best illustrate her dejection and despair.

Abigail had been so intent on the road that she was actually startled when the carriage she had been waiting for all these hours finally made the curve at the bottom of the hill and began its ascent up the drive.

Would Nathan be coming in? she wondered. Not that she wanted him to, the pesky beast. And yet she was determined that if she were to find herself alone with him again . . . accidentally . . . that she would not let him off so easily as before. She had asked him what he was doing in her house, and he had denied her an answer. She would not be denied again.

Then, still down the hill from the house, the carriage stopped.

Abigail frowned. There was quite a bit of rain coming down, so she didn't believe that Nathan and Violet could have stopped to pick daisies, or whatever Sir Harlan had instructed them to do. Indeed, she could only faintly make out their figures in the distance, but Nathan seemed to be holding Violet's arm, as if to keep her from alighting from the carriage.

Violet . . . want to walk in the rain? Impossible!

Abigail gave up all pretense of being interested in her book and craned towards the window for a clearer view. Yes, Violet *did* appear to be trying to get out of the carriage . . . and Nathan was trying to prevent her. Why did the man not just pull the carriage up to the house? Was there something wrong with his wheel?

Violet half stood, then was pulled down. Abigail's face twisted in confusion at the tug-of-war that ensued, with Violet's arm as the rope. The carriage wobbled from side to side during the conflict. Abigail lifted a hand to her throat.

Good Lord! What was happening?

"Good Lord!" Sir Harlan exclaimed as Violet went flying off the carriage and fell to the ground on her backside. The guest list fell out of his hand and fluttered to the floor.

Abigail had been so absorbed in the scene that she had not noticed that her father was also a spectator.

"What's happening?" Sophy said, sitting up and rubbing her eyes, as though her litany of complaint had put her in a trance.

Abigail was on her feet. "It's Violet!"

Violet was now trying to extract herself from a mud puddle as Nathan scurried around the carriage to her side.

"She's up!" Harlan said, just as Nathan approached Violet and she went flying backwards again. "No, damme, she's down again."

"Father!" Abigail cried. "Shouldn't we help?"

He looked surprised, almost as if she had suggested breaking up a boxing match. "Why?"

Abigail could only sputter, "B-because—something terrible seems to be happening!"

"The girl simply fell in the mud," her father pointed out. "Nathan is there to help her."

Sophy was at their side in a blink. "Violet is *in the mud*?"

She was. Still. And from looking at the pair, it would seem that Nathan was somehow impeding her attempts to jump to her feet. The offer of his hand she steadfastly refused.

"Don't want to stop a man from doing his Sir Galahad bit, you know," Sir Harlan said, chuckling.

"But—"

"Ooop! She's up again!" Sir Harlan cried.

"She's . . . she's . . . *running*!" Sophy exclaimed with a surprised squeak.

They all three could only stare in amazement at this. Abigail couldn't remember the last time she had seen Violet *running*. It had to have been sometime before she was ten. Yet here she was, streaking towards the house, bonnet askew, her skirts plastered to her long legs, her feet flying beneath her and tossing up mud like a racehorse on a track.

Meanwhile, Nathan had followed her halfway up the lane and then stopped. He watched her as she fled towards the house.

So much for Sir Galahad, Abigail thought with a silent smirk. What on earth could have transpired between those two?

They did not have long to wait before Violet burst through the door, breathing in great gulping gasps and dripping rain. She practically fell on the bell pull to call Peabody. As she wobbled across the room to the sofa Sophy had so recently vacated, a large clump of mud dropped off her backside and onto the carpet. She groaned.

Abigail ran to her. She had never seen her sister in such a state. In fact, she was shocked that Violet would even allow herself to appear this way and hadn't run directly up to her room. "What happened?"

Violet fanned herself violently with her filthy glove. "I was attacked!"

Abigail gasped. "What did he do?"

Her sister looked like she might faint. "Oh, it was horrible! The wretch spent the entirety of the drive back from town declaring his love for me. Apparently the poor man has been obsessed with me since that dance so long ago, when I rejected him. I was never so embarrassed, though of course I retained perfect composure. But then, just as we were approaching Peacock Hall, he stopped the coach and declared that I *would* be his. We fought—"

Abigail nodded. She had seen all of this. Though of course she had not known of Nathan's pressing his suit to Violet so boldly!

"I tried to jump out of the carriage—truly, I didn't feel safe in the same vehicle with the man. But he was no longer a man, he was a beast!"

"Good heavens!" Outrage began to swell in Abigail's breast.

"Did he take you into his arms?" Sophy asked eagerly. "Violently?"

Violet shuddered. "Everything about him seemed violent. I feared for my person, I truly did! Heaven only knows how I managed to escape!"

Abigail glanced outside. Nathan was gone. Naturally. He wouldn't want to stay knowing that they would all be aware of his shameful behavior. And to think that just minutes before, Abigail had *envied* Violet her carriage ride with Nathan—a ride that had turned into a perilous wrestling match.

Abigail crossed her arms. Her breath was coming in heaves. "Father!"

Her father was looking a bit non-plussed. "Attacking you in the mud! That's going a bit heavy, I would say."

"A *bit*?" Abigail asked. "He might have . . . well, there's no telling!"

Sir Harlan chuckled. "Well, you know . . . it's spring. A man is bound to be carried away in the presence of a lovely girl."

Abigail couldn't believe her ears. "Father, this man has insulted us all! Just this morning I found him attacking Sophy in this very room—on a ladder!"

Everyone's gaze swiveled to Sophy, whose eyes widened.

"Is this true?" Sir Harlan asked her. "Did Nathan attack you?"

"Oh!" Sophy squirmed. "Not . . . well, that is to say . . . yes. He has such strong arms, too!"

Violet lifted herself up. "Why did you not tell me this? I would never have gotten into a carriage with that madman, no matter how badly my dress needed alterations!"

Guilt overwhelmed Abigail. She *should* have said something. "You see, Father? He's not to be trusted. I don't understand why he has made himself such a presence here anyway. I certainly don't think you should be as welcoming in the future."

"Not welcome the son of my greatest friend?" Sir Harlan asked, more shocked by that statement than from the fact that the same man had just attacked two of his daughters in one morning. "Nonsense! I'm fond of the boy."

Abigail was astounded. "But—"

Sophy interrupted her. "What did Nathan do to you, Abigail?"

"I beg your pardon?"

"You said that he had insulted us all," Sophy said.

All eyes were pinned on her. "Oh!" She cast about for a reasonable answer. She certainly could not confess to having swum naked with Nathan. "He . . . er . . . I only meant that an attack on one sister's honor—not to mention two in one day!—is an attack on us all, is it not?"

"You're so right!" Violet exclaimed. "I agree that the man should not allowed to set foot in this house again."

Just then, Peabody rushed into the room. His gaze fell on his mistress, whom at first he didn't recognize. When he did realize who the bedraggled woman on the sofa was, he rushed to her side and nearly wept. "Oh, madame, whatever has happened?"

Finally receiving the wholehearted sympathy she

craved, Violet patted his back comfortingly. "There, there. Everything will be all right, Peabody."

She sniffed bravely and they staggered to their feet.

"But your best white poplin is mud-stained!" he exclaimed, taking out his handkerchief. He used it to blow his nose.

"I was thinking of dying it blue in any case."

Peabody's brow wrinkled crookedly. "Light blue?"

"No, more of an indigo . . ."

For heaven's sake! Abigail thought with irritation. Was she the only one in the house who truly cared about what had just happened? After Violet and Peabody had left the room, she turned to her father again. "If Nathan comes back to the house, Father, I think you should have a word with him."

He cleared his throat and looked serious for a moment. "Indeed I will."

"I find this all most disturbing," Abigail said. "I don't know why Nathan should think he can treat the Wingate women so insultingly, so I assume it can only come from talk in the neighborhood."

They both looked pointedly at Sophy. "What?" she asked innocently.

"I think we should ask Cousin Henrietta to come stay with us," Abigail said. "To be a chaperone."

To keep me from wanting to be alone with Nathan myself, and seeing if his arms are as strong as Sophy says . . .

Both Sir Harlan and Sophy let out startled sounds. "Cousin Hen!" Sophy groaned. "Oh, no! Must we?"

Sir Harlan, no doubt remembering the tragedy of his peacock lamp, seemed less enthusiastic even than his youngest daughter. "I don't think that's necessary. I always say, there are enough hens about Peacock Hall without adding another!" He laughed at his (oft-repeated) joke. "Besides, you girls are all old enough now not to need a lady like that hanging about . . ."

Abigail couldn't believe it. "But *Father!*"

"Father's right," Sophy declared. "Why would any of us need a chaperone?"

She was a living reason herself, but Sir Harlan seemed in perfect agreement with her. Abigail was too stunned to speak. She wondered what Nathan Cantrell would have to do to be expelled from Peacock Hall. Nothing short of ax murder, apparently.

What hold did the man have over them all?

Chapter Six

Count Orsino stared grimly at the young princess. How could he have such a drab young chit as this be forced upon him while the magnificent, cunning Isabella awaited his return to the island? It was impossible! He would not stand for it.

Yet he needs must contend with the prince—the fiend, the architect of Orsino's misfortune. Orsino had not yet decided how best to dispense with him . . . or the girl.

—Count Orsino's Betrothal

"Quite a pair, aren't they?" Sir Harlan asked.

It was another overcast and warm day, and Nathan mopped his neck with a kerchief as he took in the large colorful birds before him. For their parts, Garrick and Mrs. Siddons gazed back disinterestedly.

"Finest specimens in the land," Sir Harlan boasted.

As birds went, they seemed nice enough. But Nathan wasn't enough of an aficionado to know whether Sir Harlan's boasts were true, or just the natural remarks of a proud peafowl owner, so he merely dabbed at his brow and nodded. Lord only knew why Sir Harlan had dragged him out here to stare at the birds, but he'd seemed very keen on paying a visit to the part of the grounds where they tended to be. There was a small pool of water nearby for them. Nathan only wished it were large enough for him to jump into.

The thought reminded him of the afternoon he'd first seen Abigail. Where was she? He had seen no one except

Sir Harlan since coming to Peacock Hall today. He wanted to speak to her, so that she wouldn't be left with the negative impression he might have created by inadvertently clasping Sophy to his bosom on the ladder and then allowing Violet to fall into the mud on the same day. The woman might get the idea he was some sort of brute.

Not that Abigail wouldn't be able to hold her own against a brute. While reserved, Abigail looked like she would give as good as she got. Nathan smiled, momentarily imagining that it was Abigail he'd been with on that ladder. A very different—and much pleasanter—experience that would have been!

"Are you interested in birds?" Sir Harlan asked.

"Hm?" Lost in his own thoughts, Nathan had to drag his attention back to the peacocks. He didn't want to appear too bored, although he was beginning to wonder if Sir Harlan registered boredom in others. The man seemed to have an endless capacity to drone on about things ornithological with absolutely no encouragement.

Fortunately, Nathan decided this was an opening to broach a different subject. "Actually, I have been thinking more about sheep."

"Sheep!" Sir Harlan exclaimed, as if this were an altogether strange idea. "Enjoy a good rack of lamb, do you?"

"It's actually the wool I am interested in . . ."

Sir Harlan appeared nonplussed by the disclosure. "Upon my word."

Nathan underwent a moment of doubt. It seemed foolish now to be talking about his old scheme, never truly fleshed out, when he was completely rolled up financially.

But once started, he couldn't seem to help himself, any more than Sir Harlan could stop himself from repeating his peacock's bloodlines to anyone in possession of an ear. "You see, when I was in the army, it seemed that what was needed was a lighter-weight wool. I observed a small place in France making such a cloth. Very fine. But there is no reason why such a product couldn't be made here and produced in larger quantities."

Sir Harlan's eyebrows shot up. "You mean a kind of factory? In this area?"

"Yes, outside our very own village," Nathan replied.

"Isn't that the type of thing best left to the towns?"

"I don't think so. We lose some of our finest young people to the bigger cities. Why? Why not give them a reason to stay here? Also, with the end of the war with France, there is an even larger pool of unemployed men seeking work."

Sir Harlan beamed. "I like that kind of thinking! That's just the sort of ambition that reminds me of. . . . Well, I don't mean to brag, but reminds me of myself when I was a younger fellow."

"Thank you, sir," he replied, knowing that the man intended a comparison to himself to be the highest compliment. He slapped an insect on his neck and looked longingly towards the house. He would dearly love to be out of the way of birds and bugs.

"Come to think of it," Sir Harlan went on, "I have a book on sheep husbandry . . . by Bennington. Read that one?"

Nathan eyed Sir Harlan warily—he was exhibiting more excitement for the subject of sheep than even he himself would. "No, I don't believe I have."

"Be happy to lend it to you," Sir Harlan said. "I'll get it now."

"I'll go with you."

Sir Harlan turned, practically running backwards now, and waved him off. "No, no, stay right here and enjoy the beautiful weather—just be a moment. I wouldn't want you to cut short your visit with Garrick and Mrs. Siddons."

Nathan stood in stifling despair as his host disappeared. Visiting with two birds? What was he supposed to do? He stared into the cold beady eyes of one—Garrick, he supposed, since he possessed fancy plumage—and was fairly certain the peacocks didn't especially desire his company.

Nevertheless, he continued to wait for Sir Harlan. And wait. Even his legs began to ache; it was like standing on parade. "I don't think he's coming back," he muttered.

Garrick tilted his head and peered at him.

Nathan stared right back. "You're a nasty-smelling beast, aren't you?"

To his shock, the bird let out a yowling, almost human-sounding cry that pierced his ears and nearly made him jump out of his skin. A wind blew up, almost as if in answer to the peacock's cry, and was moments later followed by another force of nature. Nathan looked up to see Violet puffing towards him, carrying a pail that seemed in danger of slipping through her fingers. When she caught his gaze, she stopped short and streaks of red appeared in her pale cheeks.

"*You!*" she exclaimed. Wind blew the tight curls framing her face.

He smiled ruefully. "I'm afraid so."

She said nothing in reply.

"You're looking a great deal tidier than the last time we met, Mrs. Treacher. In fact you cleaned up quite nicely." He made a show of looking around them. "Couldn't be that there's an earl skulking about the place?"

She glared at him and started flinging meal to the ground in choppy gestures. "Would that there were! It would be a vast improvement over the society we have been getting here lately."

He laughed. "I have never met a lady I get along with less than you, Mrs. Treacher. We seem to have a souring effect on each other."

"So you say, and yet I am constantly in your company."

His mirth turned to a groan. "I believe we have been over this already."

"Yet here we are again, and not by *my* design," she said. "It is certainly not a usual part of my daily routine to feed these wretched creatures. I wonder how you persuaded my father to set up such a 'chance' meeting."

Nathan shook his head. "Once again I find myself in the awkward position of trying to convince you that I don't long to make love to you."

"Nothing would relieve me more than to believe that!"

He smiled stiffly. "How gratifying that I can ease your mind, then."

She stared at him, as if she couldn't decide whether to believe him. She seemed to have no clue that his interest in her had all been a figment of her imagination. "Could you please take my pail?" she said. "I find this activity exhausting. Especially in this heat!" She made a great show of fanning herself as Nathan took the bucket from her.

He tossed the meal on the ground. "I would think your family had servants for feeding the birds."

"We do, even though they're all practically decrepit," Violet said. "In a pinch, it's usually Abigail doing this sort of thing. She's much better at . . ." Here, Violet shuddered. ". . . *chores.*"

His brows rose. He knew, of course, why Violet had been sent out to feed the peacocks—Sir Harlan was doing a little matchmaking. Sir Harlan had no way of knowing how much more promising his odds for success would have been had he sent Abigail. "Surely, this is no task for a woman who is invalidish?"

Violet snorted. "Abigail's complaint doesn't normally preclude her from such daily tasks. Unfortunately, these days everything seems to fall on *my* shoulders."

"You are to be pitied," Nathan agreed. *The way one pities any useless, spoiled princess*, he thought.

She looked at him as if she didn't want his pity—or anything to do with him, for that matter. "I'm going inside."

"I think I'll join you."

"Of course you will." Violet sighed in saintly resignation.

The hundred yards to the house might have been a hundred miles. They walked far apart, in stiff, awkward silence. Her manservant appeared at the front door, his face drawn in concern. That concern doubled when he caught sight of Nathan.

"Oh, Mrs. Treacher!" He dashed over to her, as if his person could perform a protective wall between herself and Nathan.

Nathan was uncomfortable under the man's glare—he was staring at him almost as if he were a criminal.

At her servant's acknowledgment of her travails, Violet nodded her head in appreciation. "Father sent me out to feed those revolting birds."

The butler gasped. "If I had only known! I would rather perform the deed myself than see you so demeaned." He again glared at Nathan.

Nathan was unsure which Peabody considered more demeaning for Violet—performing manual labor or enduring Nathan's company.

She smiled gratefully. "Thank you, Peabody."

The man bowed deeply, then fussed and clucked as he whisked his ill-used mistress back into the house, leaving Nathan standing alone in the now deserted front hall. Although he had been here often (too often) in the past week, he didn't feel quite at home here and was unsure of what to do next. So when he spotted a housemaid, he smiled charmingly at her, but her eyes flew open in alarm and she scurried towards the nearest hallway.

He frowned. What went on here?

It would seem he was a pariah today.

Suddenly uneasy, he decided to find Sir Harlan and tell him that he had to leave. He hesitated at the library door, which was ajar, but, hearing a shuffling sound from within, he pushed it open further and peered inside. He was surprised to see Abigail, not Sir Harlan, sitting behind the desk. And even more startling was the sight of her attacking one of the drawers of her father's desk with a letter opener.

"What are you doing?" he asked, stepping inside and closing the door behind him.

She jumped, and her guilty gaze swung to his. The letter opener dropped from her hands and clattered to the floor.

What was he *doing here?*
And how had Nathan come in without her hearing him?

The man must move as quickly and quietly as a cat. Not long ago she had seen him with her own eyes standing out among the peacocks with her father!

He would have to come upon her right now, at this moment. His steady, half-amused gaze discomfited her. Especially since she had been caught red-handed as she was trying to break into her father's desk.

This was all his fault. The only reason she would have ever attempted such a devious act was because of him. The man had some kind of hold over her father, and she wanted to discover what it was. No other person that she could remember had ever had such open access to the house or had ever wreaked such havoc in the house without rousing Sir Harlan's ire. Why, one unfortunate servant had lost his job for singing to Sophy. This man had manhandled her on a ladder, and their father had brushed the incident off with a chuckle. It did not add up.

She sensed a blackmail scheme of some sort. Of course, it helped that she had invented quite a few blackmail schemes herself . . . for the benefit of fictional characters, it was true. But she did have a sense of how these things worked.

One of the surer signs of nefarious goings-on was the locked drawer. And here she had one right in her own father's library. She silently cursed Nathan for walking in just as she had been about to discover the secret hidden inside it . . .

Though more likely she had been on the verge of finding out how sturdy the locks on this old desk were. Apparently this one would require a battle-ax to get it open.

"Looking for something?" Nathan asked.

His smile had such a wolfish quality! Or perhaps she was just projecting that characteristic on it, after seeing evidence of his wolfish nature in his behavior with her sisters.

"I had run out of ink . . ." she muttered, then yanked helplessly on the drawer. "Unfortunately, this drawer is locked . . ."

He crossed his arms as if he didn't believe her, which made her wonder if he knew what was in the drawer.

"You seem nervous," he observed.

She lifted her head. "And why shouldn't I be?"

"I don't know . . . why?" His eyebrows drew together. "Quite a few people seem unaccountably jittery around me today. I just encountered a housemaid who ran from me like I was a hound from hell."

She let rip an unladylike snort. "Your reputation has preceded you, Mr. Cantrell."

"If you are going to insinuate bad things about my character, I wish you would call me Nathan. It seems less formal, and more appropriate for casting aspersions."

"Yes, it would seem that we will have to be on less formal footing with you, since you gad about the place with as little thought as I do now. My father seems to have adopted you into the family."

He stepped forward, a delighted grin on his face. "Oh, but I entreat you not to think on me as a brother, Abigail."

Her heart gave an uneasy flutter. Indeed, it felt as if he were flirting with her.

Which would have been more gratifying had she not known that he seemed to flirt with anything in a skirt that moved.

"Now please tell me," he said, "what it is that I have reputedly done that you malign me so?"

"I am only reacting to what I saw with my own eyes."

"What?" he asked. "With Sophy on the ladder . . . ? I thought I had explained that."

"And so you had. I was almost beginning to believe your wild story of contortions in the innocent pursuit of reading matter. But then I saw you attacking my older sister."

He looked appalled. "Attacking Violet? When?"

"In your carriage. I saw you out this very room's window."

He laughed. "I'll admit that Violet and I did have an altercation, but I was under the impression that *I* was the one who had been under attack."

"Ah!" she exclaimed. "You said something similar about your encounter with Sophy on the ladder. You seem to have the misfortune to be always the hapless victim of women!"

"Violet was trying to convince me that she was irresistible."

She crossed her arms. This was too much! "And you tried to prove her wrong by assaulting her?"

His jaw dropped. "I would hardly call her jumping out of my carriage an assault!"

"I saw you throw her in the mud with my own eyes."

"You saw no such thing," he said firmly.

"She came in seconds later covered in mud!"

"I will admit that your sister fell into a puddle. I deny responsibility for such a fall. It was her own fault that she leapt out of the carriage. I tried to prevent her."

"Violet would contradict that statement. In fact, she was wild when she came back to the house."

"Wildly frustrated to have found a man who doesn't want to kiss the hems of her garments, I'll be bound."

Abigail choked back a laugh. He sounded very sincere in his antipathy towards her older sister.

Of course, this antipathy may not have sprung up until after he'd been rejected by Violet. Maybe this was just him putting on a brave face, as Violet would certainly claim.

Though if he were recovering from a rebuff, why would he have come back the next day?

For that matter, if he had attacked Violet, why would he return to the scene of the crime?

And yet it had looked to Abigail like Violet was trying to escape from Nathan. Who to believe?

"Perhaps it would set your mind at ease if I told you that I have just seen Violet, and she seems no worse off for having endured another encounter with me."

"You were with her again?" From Violet's words yesterday, she would have thought her sister would have done anything to avoid seeing him! And how could he have just been with Violet? "I saw you walking with my father."

He smiled. "Did you?"

"Yes. Just a little while ago. You were standing out on the lawn, with Garrick and Mrs. Siddons. The two of you seemed very involved in conversation."

He seemed delighted. "Are you always peeking out from

behind curtains and following people's movements, or is it just when I am about?"

Her lips flattened. "I heard a horse . . . so naturally, I looked out . . ."

He tilted his head and came a few steps closer to her. "Or perhaps your spying had nothing to do with me. Perhaps you were more interested in watching your father's movements, so that you could creep in here and discover what is hidden in that drawer."

She gasped. "I told you I was looking for ink—why would you think I'm spying on Father?" *And how would Nathan know?*

He chuckled. "Maybe it's because this inkwell appears to be half full." Nathan pointed to a silver one in the shape of a peacock standing on the corner of the desk. "And perhaps because the first time I came here to speak to your father, he tossed something into that drawer and locked it, which certainly aroused my own curiosity. I would also be tempted to break into it . . . had I that few scruples."

She was about to bite out a retort when he nodded to an old cabinet in the corner. "That is locked also. Or have you checked it already?"

She swung around to the indicated piece of furniture. True, its doors had always been closed in her presence, but she had never given it much thought. "That is just where Father keeps his decanters."

Nathan shook his head and pointed to another, larger cabinet. "If that is the case, then why did he offer me Madeira from *there*?"

Abigail frowned at the offending cabinet. Here she was trying to solve the mystery surrounding Nathan's presence, and he compounded her questions! She was almost as vexed as she was impressed. "You seem to have noticed a great deal."

He lifted his shoulders. "My years in the army. I always found it useful to try to keep one's eyes open."

She leaned forward and asked in a low voice, "Were you a spy?"

He laughed. "You would like that, wouldn't you? You seem to have a keen interest in drama."

She drew back with a start. That was a little too close to the truth for her comfort. "What nonsense!"

He leaned against the desk. "Is it? From where I stand, your whole life seems to be a puzzle. It's always said the person who has the most secrets is the first to see subterfuge in others."

She eyed him sharply. "I merely want to know what kind of hold you have over my father."

"And if I answered none at all, would you believe me?"

She swallowed. "No."

He leaned closer. "And if I said my only interest in coming here today was to try to find a moment alone with you. . . ." His low voice sent a thrill through her. He was standing so close. "What would you say to that, Abigail?"

She looked up in his face fearlessly. "I would say it was nonsense!"

But what beautiful nonsense! Her eyes were caught by his as if by a snare. She shifted her gaze to his lips, red and full. What would such lips feel like against her own? Her youthful experimentation in kissing had left her uneager for further research, but now she found herself desperately wanting to test Nathan's osculatory skill. Her very blood seemed to cry out for her to inch just a bit forward, to encourage him to take her into his arms . . . just as he had Sophy . . .

Oh heavens!

She straightened, and laughed nervously. She was becoming as bad as Sophy. Swooning at the first utterance of a false compliment. Naturally he would compliment her, now that she had declared that she was onto his game—whatever his game was.

She took a deep breath. "I would also say that you are a silver-tongued sneak!"

His eyes widened. "A sneak?"

"Yes! To try to throw me off the scent of this mystery with a few flimsy compliments!" she exclaimed, letting out a derisive laugh directed more toward herself than him. After all, it had almost worked. "Pray tell me why, if you were here solely to have a meeting with me, did you not simply ask for me? Why go strolling about looking at peacocks, and seeking out Violet first?"

"I did not seek out Violet."

Her brows darted up. "She sought you out then?"

His mouth went through a series of contortions; the poor man looked flummoxed. One would think if he were going to speak such outrageous lies, he would at least be prepared to back them up.

"Abigail . . . I wish I could tell you all . . ."

Before he could finish this intriguing sentence, Sir Harlan bustled through the door. "There you are!" Belatedly, he noticed Abigail. "Oh!" His gaze returned to Nathan. "I thought you were with Violet."

Nathan straightened, clearing his throat. "Violet grew tired of feeding birds."

Sir Harlan chuckled amiably. "I'm sorry—I forgot all about you. I was going to look for that animal husbandry book, wasn't I?"

"Yes."

"Probably why you made your way to the library," Sir Harlan said, turning to his shelves. He found the book he was looking for in short order.

Meanwhile, Abigail glared at Nathan. *Animal husbandry?* And he had been trying to make her believe that he had sought her out on purpose!

And she had wanted to believe him!

"Here we are!" Sir Harlan said, bustling over with a large tome. It was twice as big as her book on Rome. "It's quite the last word on sheep, I think."

Nathan ducked his head slightly as he took the book from him. "Thank you."

"Well!" Abigail said, feeling blood pounding in her head. "Now that you have what you were looking for, Mr. Cantrell, I will be on my way."

She dropped a half-hearted curtsy and steamed out of the

room, furious at herself. At him. To think that she not only ranked behind Violet and Sophy—but also behind *sheep!*

Old Thomas Caruth Cantrell glowered his disapproval at Nathan.

Or perhaps he was just imagining that his ancestor disapproved, Nathan thought, staring back at the picture. Right now the picture gallery at The Willows seemed full of long-gone Cantrells *tsk*ing at him through their still, painted lips. Old Clementine Cantrell, his great, great grandmother, who had been a duke's niece, seemed especially dour today and beamed her disapproval down at him. *Look how you're letting the place go!* she scolded.

Nathan gulped down the rest of his glass of whiskey— his sixth of the evening—and retorted, "What am I to do? Her only interest in me is why I am at her house. And I suspect the moment she finds out, I am well and truly done for."

He had been on the verge of confessing it to her today. He didn't mind keeping up the subterfuge that he was just Sir Harlan's visitor around Sophy and Violet. He could not have cared less what they thought and he had no intention of making either of them a marriage offer. But Abigail . . . it seemed wrong to be lying to her. Even if it was just a lie by omission.

The trouble was she was the only sister he had the least amount of interest in. Yet he suspected that she would be the most offended by Sir Harlan's scheme. She had pride and also good sense. No sane woman would want to be bartered away for money.

He looked around the hall, at all the women who had once been daughters who had been taken in marriage by various Cantrells through the ages. How many had married for love? Very few, he imagined. Or, at least, very few of the male faces in the portrait gallery seemed capable of inspiring love in a woman's breast. But perhaps he simply had a difficult time seeing past all the wigs and fussy clothes. (The outfits people used to wear never ceased to amaze him.) What were the other reasons for all those alliances that produced a succession of people culminating, unspectacularly, in just himself and Freddy? Surely some married for money. It was practically required in the old days, he believed.

"It's not shameful," he muttered, tipping his glass back again before he remembered it was empty. He sucked on nothing but air, and released a slight belch. He desired another drink. In fact he desired several more drinks that would release him from thinking about this marriage coil. "Nothing wrong with money." He mumbled. "Everybody needs it."

Some more than others.

"I'll say!" Freddy exclaimed.

Nathan spun in surprise. His head continued to reel long after he had stopped moving. This was, no doubt, mostly a result of all the alcohol he had consumed, and yet he couldn't help thinking that perhaps a little of the spinning in his head was the result of the startling green of Freddy's velvet waistcoat, and his eye-popping pink silk cravat.

"For instance, I myself am a trifle cucumberish now. If you have a few quid to spare, brother . . ."

Freddy looked more closely at his brother and frowned. "Hello! What's that in your hand?"

Nathan had to look down to check. It was the glass. Surely his brother had seen one before? "S'empty," he slurred.

His brother sniffed the air like a hound on a rabbit's scent. "That's *whiskey* you've been drinking—you're practically boiled!" He laughed, as young men do at the thought of anyone imbibing beyond his limit. "Well I'm relieved, I must say."

"Why?" Nathan asked.

"Because I've been standing here watching you talk to these paintings, thinking you must have gone barmy on me."

"Talking to paintings?" Nathan asked, stiffening.

Freddy chuckled. "Saying the craziest things—all about love and marriage and money."

His head began to throb. "Oh."

Freddy's face fell. "Say, you haven't gone and fallen in love, have you?"

"Well, no. I wouldn't say that." He hadn't had a chance.

"Because that would be a great nuisance," Freddy said. "Having another woman besides Mrs. Willoughby fretting about the place, telling us what our business should be. I should find that most irritating."

Little did his brother know that having a woman about the place was their only hope of salvation. In a month, if there was no woman, there would be no place. Or there would be, but he and Freddy would be elsewhere. They would be evicted, and Freddy would be the world's most disastrous fishmonger's apprentice.

"Oh Freddy!" he exclaimed, suddenly overcome with contrition. "I am sorry."

Freddy drew back, surprised by the outburst. He then stepped over and found the half-empty bottle of whiskey on the table. "Nothing to be sorry for, except not sharing."

Though, glancing anxiously at Nathan, he made no move to take a glass for himself. In fact, he secured the cork and pushed the bottle back on the table.

Nathan sank back onto a striped fainting couch. "But there is. I have not been honest with you. You say you are banging against the rocks financially. But the truth is, we both are."

"What?" Freddy asked with raised brows. "Been gambling, have you?"

"No."

"Do you have a mistress then?" he asked. "I don't mean to sound insulting, but it can't be that you are spending all your money on clothes."

Nathan shook his head. "There is no money. For either of us. We are—that is, the Cantrells are—entirely rolled up."

Freddy goggled at him. In fact he required a few moments to allow the startling words to settle in his brain. "But that is impossible."

"It's entirely possible. Father left debts."

"Oh, is that all!" Freddy sagged with relief, as if he had been holding his breath. "Debt! The thing I've learned about debt is, you just wait and pay when you can. These merchant chappies all pretend to be in dire need of your money, but the truth is, if they needed money so badly, how could they be in business in the first place?"

Nathan frowned. "What?"

"What I mean to say is, they're obviously paying rent and buying materials. It takes money to stay in business. How hard up could they be?"

"Freddy . . ." He shook his head, not sure where to begin to counter that argument. He decided to skip it altogether. "Look, it's not just a few bills. It's the house, the very land we're on. Father mortgaged the property, all of it, to our neighbor, Sir Harlan Wingate."

His brother's eyes flew open. "Mortgaged it? What does that mean?"

"It means that in a month it will not be ours, unless we can find a way to pay the mortgages."

"But that's ridiculous. Do you mean to tell me that The Willows could be taken away from us?"

"Yes, exactly."

"That fiend!" Freddy exclaimed. "Who does that Sir Harlan Wingate think he is, diddling our home away from Father? I should call him out."

Nathan tried not to laugh, but the idea of Freddy and Sir Harlan in a duel was too much for him.

Freddy stiffened. "Do you think I wouldn't?"

"I don't doubt you would, you fool. But Sir Harlan has offered us a way out. In fact, he has made an offer that will enrich our coffers considerably."

"Well then!" Freddy said. "I think we should take him up on it, whatever it is."

"He wants me to marry one of his daughters."

Freddy gasped. "Oh no!"

"Yes."

"But that's blackmail!"

"Yes indeed. But it's also a solution to our problems."

Freddy decided to hit the bottle after all. He poured himself a drink, whereupon Nathan took his bottle back. No sense in both of them getting shot in the neck.

"Oh—my poor brother!" Freddy exclaimed. "Have you met his daughters? I haven't seen them in ages. They seemed fetching enough as children, I suppose, though I don't recall many particulars . . . except that the oldest one boxed my ears once."

"She hasn't changed."

"And the others? We all know how cute little nippers can grow into the most appalling adults. And I can't help but think that those father's features on a female are not what one would wish to look at across the breakfast table every morning."

Nathan grunted.

Freddy shook his head. "All like Sir Harlan?"

"No, they are all unlike him physically . . . and yet there are other problems . . ."

Freddy sank down on the fainting couch Nathan had just vacated. "No wonder you have been such miserable company lately. Married in a month!" He shuddered.

"There are worse things than marriage, you know."

His brother gaped at him. "I can't think what!"

"Well, being poor, for one. Having to go find menial work. If we don't find a way out of this situation, Freddy, you will not be able to continue at Cambridge."

Freddy gasped as this frightful possibility struck him full force. "But what shall I do?"

"I have been thinking that perhaps, if I spoke to some of the government men I met during my army days, we might be able to find you a civil service post."

"Service!" Nathan exclaimed. "You mean—sit at a desk all day, write things down all neat and tidy, then file it away?"

Nathan nodded.

Freddy looked close to weeping. "I would be nothing but a clerk. How will I face my friends? Fothersby would never understand!"

"Yes. It seems an unfortunate part of human nature to want to avoid those who have sunk in circumstances."

"But there has to be a way!" Freddy exclaimed. "Our whole future can't depend on Sir Harlan and his daughters."

"I'm afraid it does."

The two men sipped at their whiskey in silence for a moment.

"And these daughters . . . none of them seem promising?"

Nathan lifted and dropped his shoulders. "One. But she is stubborn."

"What?" Freddy asked, his voice looping up in outrage. "She doesn't want to marry you?"

"Freddy, we haven't discussed marriage. We barely know each other."

Freddy sank back down again. "I suppose it does take time to woo and win a girl."

"Yes."

Freddy slugged down the rest of his whiskey.

"Easy there," Nathan told him. "At least you're not the one facing matrimony."

"But that's just the trouble," Freddy said. "I feel so damnably useless! There has to be some way I can get us out of this coil!"

"If you think of one, let me know as soon as possible."

Freddy stood. "I will," he said. "And I *will* find a way, I promise you that. You might think I am a dandy and a no-hoper, but I will surprise you." He tapped his head. "I will not rest my noggin until I have discovered a way to save The Willows."

At his brother's sincere determination, Nathan felt his eyes well. Or maybe it was the glare of that waistcoat again. Nevertheless, the fact that his little brother was going to try to pull himself together and work to find a solution to their problem was gratifying. In fact, for a long time after Freddy had retired to his room, Nathan wondered if he could remember anything more noble than the sight of his little brother marching off in pink and green to find a way to save their home.

Chapter Seven

The man was a fool if he thought he would get the best of Count Orsino. "I will not fall prey to your vile scheme," Orsino growled.

The old prince eyed him steadily, the way a cat might stare at his prey. "How might you avoid it?"

"There is a way," Orsino declared, "And by heaven, I will find it. You shall have your pieces of gold, but not my soul."

The prince threw his head back and the cackle of his laughter sent a chill down Orsino's spine. "Nay, Orsino, I shall have both!"

—Count Orsino's Betrothal

Nathan rode most of the way to Peacock Hall at a gallop, even though his whiskey jag of the night before made each clop of the horse's hooves feel like cannon fire in his head. In the middle of the night, an answer to his problems had occurred to him.

In fact, the solution to his financial woes became so obvious that he marveled he had not thought of it before. He had forced himself to sit through breakfast with Freddy before riding over to confer with Sir Harlan—a delay in deference to the impropriety of making a too-early morning call and to the fact that Nathan couldn't remember the last time Freddy had appeared downstairs before noon.

Not that his brother had proved a felicitous companion at table. On a morning when Nathan could have used a little of Freddy's chatter to pass the time and take his mind off the aching in his temples, his brother had remained silent, stoically so. Subdued, even. Fear of poverty had knocked the stuffing out of him; even a gold and puce checkered dressing gown, accented with a jaunty purple silk scarf, could not disguise the fact that his spirits were spectacularly low.

Nathan had wanted to reassure him that all would be well and that their problems would soon be resolved. But just on the off chance that his hunch was wrong, he didn't want to get Freddy's hopes up. So he endured the breakfast punctuated by his brother's morose chewing of dry toast, the languid slurping up of a bowl of strawberries and cream, and interminable sighs.

"I am going to Sir Harlan's this morning," Nathan had informed his brother at the end of the meal.

Sad eyes looked up at him. "Pursuing one of those dreadful women?"

"They're not all dreadful. One is quite nice."

Freddy looked on the verge of tears. "That you should be reduced to accepting such a scheme!"

"I believe it might turn out all right."

Freddy sighed. "I tossed and turned all night trying to think of something I might do. I doubt I got seven hours of sleep altogether!"

"What are you going to do this morning?" Nathan asked.

"I am going to continue cudgeling my brains," he said listlessly. "Perhaps I shall take a walk."

Freddy, thinking? Taking exercise? All at once Nathan understood how seriously Freddy had been affected by their conversation the night before. Which made him all the more eager to get to his conference with Sir Harlan.

The barn at Peacock Hall appeared deserted when Nathan arrived there. No groom in sight, as usual. The man who was in charge of the stables and had thrown his back out assisting Nathan on his first visit evidently was still out of commission. Nathan led Thor into a stall, tossed in some fresh hay, and turned to find himself face to face with Sophy, who had stepped on the first rung of the stall gate and was swinging on it lightly. She was wearing a blue velvet riding costume, dainty riding boots, and a hat Nathan was certain wouldn't hold up to a trot.

When he jumped back in surprise, she let out a laugh. "Did I startle you?"

The girl had the uncanny ability to catch him unawares. "Actually no, it was the large black beetle I saw crawling across the gate."

She let out a shriek, but before he could bask in his successful payback, she had hopped right off the gate and into his arms.

He stared down into her eyes, which were both bright and dewy. An uncommonly pretty girl she undoubtedly was; with uncommonly little sense, alas. "There was no beetle," he informed her.

She sagged in his arms. Really, it was as if she had fallen in his lap, only he was standing. He couldn't quite see how she managed it.

"You shouldn't scare me like that!" she exclaimed, tilting her lips up towards him.

He frowned. This scenario was all too reminiscent of their encounter on the library ladder. He quickly set the girl on her feet.

Sophy straightened her habit and tilted Nathan a flirtatious glance. "Wouldn't you like to go riding with me?"

"No, I must speak to your father on a matter of business."

Her eyes widened. "Why would you want to waste this lovely morning in a library talking about boring business?"

"It is bad taste on my part, I know, but I am rather interested in boring business."

"You won't tell him about having to save me from the beetle, will you?"

Nathan shook his head. What a skitterbrained girl she was! "No, of course not."

"Oh, thank heavens! I would hate for him to think I was being forward with you. He might then ban you from the premises. Just like poor Dickie."

"Who?"

"He was just one of our former groomsmen, our last young one, actually."

Her partner in crime from the gun room, no doubt. "If you are worried about your reputation, you should be more careful on ladders and gates."

"I know I should be," she said, "but it's so difficult! Next year I'm going to have my first London Season, but what am I to do until then? It's so dull here!"

"Perhaps you should take up a hobby until the Season begins. My mother always did needlework, for instance."

She sighed as she swatted a fly with her riding crop. "I did try taking up cards, but Father says I haven't the head for them and will end up ruining us all."

"That's very good advice." Would that his own father had played with Sophy and not Sir Harlan!

"Everyone's always giving me good advice," Sophy said with a pout. "I detest good advice. It always seems to be regarding propriety. I think propriety is awfully boring."

"Dull is better than dangerous."

She sighed again, reminding him not a little of Freddy. "Oh well. I suppose I will go riding now. All there is to do is ride, and yet there isn't even a groom to saddle my horse."

"May I offer my assistance?"

She brightened. "Would you?"

He supposed it was the least he could do, since he did seem to be indirectly responsible for the Wingates' lack of groom. But the long and the short of it was that it took another ten minutes for him to saddle Sophy's horse and send her on her way. By the time he found Sir Harlan, the man was very curious about what had been going on in the barn. He looked up at Nathan from a sea of crude drawings of various fauna on his desk in which he seemed thoroughly involved.

Sir Harlan held up a sample drawing.

Nathan eyed it warily. "That's a nice drawing of a . . . a . . . peacock?"

Freddy could have done better when he was six.

"The spitting image of Garrick, if I do say so myself," Sir Harlan said. "I'm thinking of ordering an ice sculpture in his image."

"I beg your pardon?"

"For the ball!" Sir Harlan boomed. "Not far off now, you know." His eyes squinted at the drawing. "At first the cost seemed prohibitive, but then I thought this is certainly an occasion for a splurge. Of course, it looks like I'll have to send for it from Scotland, and it seems there's no guarantee that carting the thing down all that way won't melt it. I thought about having Cook do a meringue instead, but she seemed a little miffed when I suggested it to her. The toast was positively charred black this morning at breakfast— always a bad sign when Cook starts burning the toast. Should have waited until after I'd eaten before approaching her about it, what?"

"No doubt, sir." Nathan cleared his throat. He wasn't sure what more to say. With the news that his engagement was to be inaugurated by a giant, melting ice peacock, he felt even more attached to his bachelorhood.

Sir Harlan smiled. "Well! Where have you been? I saw you ride up some time ago."

"Yes, I know. I was pressed into service by your youngest daughter."

His eyes twinkled. "Delightful creature, isn't she?"

"She seems to find the country lacking in stimulation."

"Oh, but all young girls crave city life. She'll get over that. I say, if you are going to choose Sophy, that will save me the cost of her Season." Sir Harlan was much struck by this thought. "In that case, we must certainly have the ice sculpture!"

"You must do as you think best, sir, but I wouldn't want you to order it with the assumption that I am going to marry Sophy," Nathan said.

Sir Harlan let out a chuckle. " Aha! I thought you had your heart set on Violet."

Nathan gaped at the man. *His heart set on Violet?* "No, my heart is set on no one."

"Well, you must set it, then! The ball will be here before you know it."

"Sir Harlan—"

"Ah, look, there goes Abigail." Sir Harlan barked, "Abigail!"

Abigail had passed as a shadow across the library doors, then doubled back when she heard her name. She stood in the doorway. Her eyes met Nathan's briefly, after which she pinned her gaze on Sir Harlan. "Yes, Father?"

"Where is Violet?"

"In bed. She says she has a stuffy nose from getting caught in the rain a few days ago." She tilted her head and glanced pointedly at Nathan for a moment, then looked back at her father. "She fears coming down with pneumonia before the ball."

"Oh dear! But don't you think a walk would do her good? Nathan is here."

Nathan detected a smirk on Abigail's lips. "I believe her last outing with Nathan accounts for her current complaint."

"Well!" Sir Harlan huffed. "It was raining that day. Not today. Today's quite fine. Where's Sophy?"

"Riding," Nathan reminded him.

"Oh." The man seemed dispirited. "Well."

"Where are you going?" Nathan asked Abigail, noting that she was wearing a brown bonnet that almost matched her drab brown dress.

"To town. Violet wanted me to pick up some new ribbon. She's having her maid trim a hat."

"If you could wait until I've finished my business with your father, I would be pleased to escort you," Nathan offered.

Abigail reacted as if he had made her a dubious proposition. "No, thank you, I would not want to put you out."

"It would be my pleasure."

"But I noted that you did not bring your carriage today."
He chuckled. "Peeping from behind curtains again?"

Sir Harlan narrowed his eyes. "What's this about?"

"Your middle daughter is a spy."

Though it was a joke, Sir Harlan reacted with alarm. "Is she? How?"

"Always watching people through windows," Nathan said, enjoying the color staining Abigail's cheeks.

"I will leave you two to your business," she said. Looking at Nathan reproachfully and somehow suspiciously at the same time, she turned on her heel and left.

When she had disappeared, Sir Harlan shook his head. "Odd one, she is. We're so different, it sometimes seems hard to believe we're flesh and blood. Well now, my boy, where were we—am I to wish you and Violet happy?"

"Actually, I came to speak to you about some other business. Not about the marriage," he said, growing more anxious, "but about another scheme entirely."

Sir Harlan's head snapped up with interest, causing a slight jiggling of his jowls. "Scheme? What kind of scheme? Does this have something to do with your idea about a woolen factory that we discussed the other afternoon?"

"Yes. I must confess to you that I was not telling you the truth when I told you that I had no plans after I left the army," he said. "That is, I had plans, but by the time I spoke to you, they were obviously as impossible as . . . well, as my sprouting wings and flying to the moon."

Sir Harlan's eyebrows beetled. "I'm not sure I follow you."

"Well, the truth is, during my years in the army, while my father was alive, I always assumed I would return to The Willows. I was very interested in being a good landlord to my tenants."

"You'll need a lot more of the ready to realize that wish."

"True. But before I had seen that my father let our lands fall to ruin, I didn't realize that cash would be such a problem. I assumed that I would be a landlord of a considerable property, and so when I came back and saw the place's condition I was bitterly disappointed. But I see now that I was merely arrogant. My family has no money, and now Freddy and I must earn our way. That much is clear."

Sir Harlan's brows rose. "But that is why I am suggesting—"

"Exactly. And it is a very generous proposition, but I have a counteroffer. With all respect, I am offering myself to you, Sir Harlan, not as a son-in-law, but as a bailiff."

The muscles in Sir Harlan's face went slack. "Bailiff!"

"I could oversee the breeding of the sheep as your employee in addition to performing other bailiff duties. There would be some satisfaction in doing the work myself. Once we have the right herd, we can start the factory. Do you see?"

"I am not sure that I do, son."

"What I am proposing, Sir Harlan, is that you let me stay on at The Willows as manager, and that I should follow my original scheme of woolen production—with a small investment of capital from wise investors—and that you would therefore reap the majority of the profits. Then slowly, after I have a chance to get the factory going, and if all goes well, I can buy back The Willows from you."

"So what you're saying is that you want me to bankroll your sheep scheme."

Nathan swallowed nervously. "In a word, yes."

"But I have no interest in sheep."

"Yes, but—"

"It's a grandchild I want, not a passel of lambs."

"Yes, I know, sir."

They stared at each other.

"Then you're simply saying no?" Nathan asked.

"Well . . ." Sir Harlan looked stricken. In fact, for a moment his wrinkles melted away and he appeared baby-faced and hurt, as if Nathan had impugned his character. Then, just as quickly, his bushy brows waggled, his countenance changed, and he aimed a stern look at Nathan. "As a matter of fact, I am. Nay, I must!"

Nay? Nathan looked closely at the man, who now was almost a caricature of a forbidding old gentleman.

"You would not play whist with a man and switch to faro midgame, would you?" Sir Harlan bellowed.

Nathan shook his head, which was beginning to pound again. "No, certainly not."

"You would not invite a man for dinner and present him with nothing but tea cakes, either, I assume."

He was having a hard time following Sir Harlan's logic. "Indeed, no."

"Then you cannot one day tell me that you want to marry one of my daughters and present me with grandchildren, and the next say that all you can offer me is mutton on the hoof!"

Listening to him, you would think that Sir Harlan believed that the whole marriage scheme had been Nathan's from the start. That Nathan had actually knocked on the door and suggested that it would be a good idea if he married one of Sir Harlan's daughters. Sir Harlan was completely innocent in the matter; he had never *heard* of blackmail.

"But . . ."

"Now I don't want to hear any more about your sheep for the moment. It's time we get back to my plans. Which of my daughters shall it be?"

"Sir Harlan, I hate to disappoint you—"

"Then don't. You've got exactly two weeks to make up your mind. Oh, that reminds me! I was going to ask you whether you had appropriate clothes."

"For . . . ?"

"The ball, the ball! Good heavens, you seem distracted this morning." He laughed, then gave Nathan an avuncular clap on the shoulder. "I know you are a soldier just returned and mayn't have acquired proper evening clothes. Wouldn't surprise me to hear that you hadn't a stitch for the ball."

"No, *that's* not the problem." *Not having a fiancée might be more of a coil . . .*

"Well! Good. I was going to offer you the use of my tailor in town. Samuel's his name. Good fellow."

Obviously the subject of his plans for The Willows was closed, Nathan thought bitterly. He might just as well have accompanied Abigail to town rather than waste his breath with her ball-obsessed father. With that thought, Nathan backed towards the door, hoping to catch Abigail on her way back from her shopping expedition. "Excuse me, Sir Harlan, I think I'll just follow after Miss Wingate, and see if she needs my help carrying back her packages."

"Oh, she won't want help," Sir Harlan grumbled, looking back down at his drawing of his beloved peacock, and essentially dismissing his prospective son-in-law. "Never wants anyone's help."

Nathan cleared the door and broke into a run.

Abigail's footsteps hurried forward and her eyes trained on the road ahead as she returned to Peacock Hall. She had not wished for Mr. Cantrell's company . . . so why had she felt disappointed when he had stated that he was remaining behind to talk business with her father?

This contradiction bothered her. For the past few years, she had been such a focused person. Now, more and more, she found herself wanting two things at once. She wanted Nathan gone; she wanted him to stay. She wished he wouldn't speak to her, but she was driven to distraction thinking of others enjoying his company. She tried to banish the vision of him and Sophy on that ladder from her mind; yet she visualized *herself* in Sophy's place.

Clearly, she was going mad.

She had heard of this happening. When she was five, her governess had warned her that bad things happened to girls with too much imagination, and now look. She was on the verge of losing her mind. If Nathan hung about Peacock Hall much longer, no doubt she would end up being locked in a dark room, or packed off to Ireland to live with nuns.

The bright side of finally going mad was that, if she were shipped off to Ireland, perhaps she would be able to get some work done. She was making no progress on *The Prisoner of Raffizzi* here, unfortunately. Her mind kept wandering back to the situation between Nathan and her family—her poor heroine Clara was more likely to die a spinster than suffer any harm from the villainous Baron Rudolpho.

It was not only her writing that she had neglected. She hadn't even been successful in searching her father's library. Abigail thought bitterly of the times her stupid heroines had pried open various types of locks with letter openers, hair and hat pins, and other common ladylike accessories. One had even managed to undo the manacles imprisoning her in a dungeon with a knitting needle she just happened to have on her person! Yet Abigail couldn't manage to break into a measly Queen Anne cabinet.

It just showed how wildly improbable her plots were.

Thinking of this and how her father and Nathan were closeted together right then in the library renewed her determination to get to the heart of their mystery. She knew it had something to do with the ball about which her father was so enthusiastic. Said ball was in two weeks, so that didn't leave her much time for investigating.

As she neared the crest of a hill, she suddenly heard the sound of rapid footsteps on the other side. Just when she'd given up looking for him! Her heartbeat sped, but she schooled her expression to calmness. She knew it was him. Knew it in her bones. It was as if there were a powerful force connecting them—the same as there was between the hero and heroine in her books.

Just then she caught sight of Nathan coming towards her. "I was hurrying to catch you before you returned," he said.

She did not halt as she came abreast of him, but he turned and fell into step beside her. She turned her head, forcing her knees not to buckle when she looked into those green eyes. She was amazed to see that he was barely breathing hard, even though he had been moving fast, from the sound of the footsteps she had heard. He'd hardly broken a sweat!

He was smiling at her. At first she returned the expression, but then she forced herself to appear disinterested. He was *always* smiling at her, throwing her off the scent of whatever it was that kept him hanging about Peacock Hall. She lifted her brows. "Why were you in a hurry?"

"Why, to help you carry back your packages, of course." When Abigail looked at him skeptically, Nathan added, "Also, I thought this might be a good opportunity for us to talk."

"I'm surprised you could tear yourself away to find me. You seem never to tire of loitering about Peacock Hall these days."

"I had something important to discuss with your father."

Her ears pricked. This was the closest hint he had made about what kept him about their home. "Was this personal business?" she asked.

"Of a kind," he said, hedging. "Your father and I have been in . . . negotiations."

"On the matter of . . . ?"

His mouth snapped shut, and he looked off into the distance for a moment before turning back to her somberly. "I'm not at liberty to say, unfortunately. I give you my word, Abigail, that if I could say something of the nature of our business, you would be the very person I would want to tell."

"I'm so flattered at your statement of trust. But since you choose not to confide in me, it rings rather hollow."

He had the grace to appear discomfited and then nodded. "Yes, I suppose it is difficult to have faith in me."

She narrowed her eyes at him. Maybe specific questions could prod him into giving her answers, like that parlor game they used to play in school. "Does your business have to do with those drawings that I saw on his desk?"

"Indirectly, I suppose."

"Is it something about Violet or Sophy?"

"Not specifically."

"All of us?" she asked.

He looked torn and then shook his head. "It's difficult to explain."

"But you have explained nothing!" she said in frustration.

"True." He laughed. "In any case, I will say that what I came to talk to Sir Harlan about today was my business exclusively, and it was all about sheep."

He sighed. Apparently the discussion had not left him satisfied.

She squinted at him. "Sheep?"

"Yes, my plan was to improve the herds in this area and to start a factory one day. I was hoping Sir Harlan might help."

"But he refused you?"

"Yes, he did."

That was most strange. In general Sir Harlan was quite generous with people in the neighborhood who needed help.

"Outside of his dinner plate, Father knows very little about sheep, I would guess," she said, trying to conjecture why Sir Harlan would be so tight-fisted with Nathan. "And it's been some years since he had anything to do with manufacturing." Could this business proposition really be all that there was between her father and Nathan? She was burning with curiosity.

Too much curiosity was another vice her governess had warned her against, once upon a time.

Nathan sighed again. "He refused to help, for which I certainly cannot blame him. Nevertheless, I shall not press him for aid again."

"I am not certain you should give up so easily. My father has never shown much interest in livestock outside of peafowl," she continued, glancing again at her companion. "But he has never shown much interest in parties, either. And yet now he is throwing himself into the preparations for this ball."

Nathan nodded. "He seems keen on the decorations."

"The decorations, the menu, the music—he has hired professional musicians from York. He even went with Violet to pick out the invitations, and overruled her on the matter of the script!" She shook her head in wonder. "I cannot understand it. Father is more involved in this ball than the one he had for Violet's engagement." Nathan tripped, and she stared at him sharply. He was not the tripping kind. "I don't know why, but I suspect you are the cause for his current attitude," she said.

"I?" he asked, all innocence. "I am merely going to be a guest."

Yet she detected a certain tension in his manner. He wasn't telling her all.

"If I were possessed of a wild imagination," Abigail said, "I would envision my father stepping forward at the stroke of midnight to declare you his long-lost stepbrother, or his ward."

He looked amused. "That is outlandish."

"No more so than my father consulting with Peabody over flower arrangements, Mr. Cantrell."

"I wish you would call me Nathan."

"I should be delighted to, of course," she said.

"Good!"

"As soon as you inform me what scheme you have going with my father."

He chuckled. "I attempted to tell you earlier."

"Sheep?" she asked. "I don't believe it. I believe you were simply trying to explain and evade at the same time."

"I can assure you that the only scheme with your father *I* am interested in instigating simply involves sheep and wool production." He then reached out and touched the fabric on her skirt. "You might benefit in taking an interest in textiles, if I might say so. This material does not do you justice, though no dress could be anything less than lovely on such a model as you."

She dropped a sarcastic curtsy. "I'm blushing! No one has insulted me quite so prettily before."

"I only meant that the cloth seems to have strayed from a sacking material warehouse."

While secretly agreeing with him, Abigail forced herself to be stern. "Very amusing, *Mr. Cantrell.* So, you chased me down in order to tell me I am lacking in fashion sense."

"Ah! Then you noticed."

"Noticed what?"

"That I was chasing you."

His eyes twinkled, and when he smiled at her she had to look away, as you would have to look away from the sun. She cleared her throat and stared forcefully at the road in front of her. He was *flirting* with her. She didn't trust that.

"You needn't lose sleep over my choice of garments, at

least as it concerns this party you and Father have cooked up. I am having a new dress made in town. Of silk."

"I am glad. I hope I will have the honor of being the first man to dance with that dress."

"I rarely dance," she said.

"Oh, yes, your health," he remembered. "Odd that a frail young lady would shy from dancing when she can practically sprint the three miles into town and back."

"I am nowhere close to sprinting."

He grinned. "Are you not? Perhaps I am breathless simply from your presence."

Her cheeks flamed in spite of herself. The man was too charming by half! Every instinct was screaming at her to be wary. She attempted to turn the subject from the personal. "I cannot wait till this ball is over! It has been nothing but a distraction for two weeks. Two weeks wasted with gown fittings, invitation writing, and bother!"

"What has it been distracting you from?"

She blinked at him. "What?"

He was suddenly dead serious. "Your time seems very valuable to you. I was wondering what it is that the party has distracted you from that distresses you so."

Unbelievable! Here she had been trying to probe him for information, but he was much better at finessing secrets out of her than she was of him. She shook her head. Probably that was the reason for his flirtation; he was trying to loosen her tongue. She had used this device herself countless times. In her books, at least. So far she hadn't had the courage to use this strategy on her aggravating neighbor.

"No one likes to do what they find less than enjoyable, don't you agree?" she answered with what she hoped was successful evasiveness.

"I have never met a young lady who wasn't over the moon at the idea of a ball."

She stopped and turned, extending her hand to him.

He appeared startled, but he took her hand all the same.

"Allow me to introduce myself," she said. "I am Abigail, whose feet are quite squarely still on the earth even at the idea of this particular ball."

He laughed. "How do you do? I am Nathan, who is determined that it will be one evening that you shall never forget."

He bent over her hand, as if to kiss it, but at the last moment he turned her hand and placed his lips on the pulse on her wrist just above the line of her glove. Abigail admonished her knees to remain locked.

"You talk as if this ball is the key to your future happiness," she said, breathlessly. Nathan still had hold of her wrist and was staring deeply into her eyes.

"Perhaps it is," he said.

Just as she took a deep breath to steady herself, Nathan leaned closer, so close that she could almost feel the whisper of his breath. Their eyes remained locked—five seconds, maybe ten—and in those moments all thoughts of balls, sisters, and even locked cabinets flew from her mind. They were dangerous moments, moments in which the smart hare would have hopped safely away from the hunter. Yet she remained motionless, captivated by those eyes staring at her that had appeared so often in her dreams. The difference was that in her dreams Nathan had seemed teasing, or leeringly seductive; yet now she felt the tug of sadness in his gaze, of wanting something that he feared he could not have. It was almost as if she were looking into his soul and seeing a reflection of her own.

She should have averted her eyes. She should have stepped away.

She didn't.

He bent and brushed his lips to hers, gently at first. And though she had sensed he was about to kiss her, it still came as an exquisite surprise to feel the warmth of his mouth against hers. His arms wrapped around her waist, pulling her yet closer to him.

She should have resisted. She should have protested at his forwardness.

She didn't.

She was too busy reveling in the physical sensations of this kiss. She could tell by the ginger manner in which his lips explored hers that he was giving her just the merest sampling of what a kiss could be. Yet she felt desire pooling inside her as surely as if he were ravishing her in the manner of one of her heroes. Feeling the sensations swirling inside her, she understood what would cause one of her heroines to swoon.

Fortunately before her legs had quite turned to jelly, Nathan ended the kiss. He stepped back, studying her.

Her senses returned to her, until it felt as if she were blazing beneath the heat of his gaze. She couldn't think of what to say. Her hands balled into nervous fists at her side. Part of her wanted to put off having to think of the consequences of what she had done by throwing herself at him again and losing herself in his kiss for a while longer. But another part of her was beginning to take in details of her surroundings: they were at the bottom of the hill leading up to the house. Anyone could have been looking out the window and seen them, just as she had seen Violet's altercation with Nathan days before.

That memory sent a steadying jolt through her. She crossed her arms.

Nathan obviously absorbed her change in mood. "What is wrong?"

"I just remember that this is the very spot where I witnessed you attacking my sister," she said.

Aggravation registered on his face, and he rolled his eyes. "I did not attack her."

A few minutes ago, Abigail had been inclined to believe him, but now she wasn't so sure. Nothing the man did seemed without ulterior motive. And now the sly fox had managed to divert her attention from investigating his presence at Peacock Hall so successfully that he'd had her swooning in his arms!

"That's right—it was an accident, just as the incident on the library ladder with Sophy was an accident."

"Kissing you just now was not an accident, however," he said.

He spoke very convincingly, with just enough purr in his voice to make her heart begin to pound irregularly. She braced herself against the tug of desire that pulled at her when he took a step towards her. "Are you making a hobby of forcing yourself on all the Wingate women?" she asked him.

He shook his head. "You know I did not force myself on you."

He was correct. But she certainly had not imagined herself kissing the man in broad daylight on a public road. That wasn't like her at all. The man must have bewitched her in some way to make her start behaving so wantonly. No telling what he had done to Violet to make her desperate enough to leap into the mud!

"Nevertheless, your behavior has not been gentlemanly. I would call it very boorish, in fact. And you have never been able to explain to my satisfaction why you have come so often to Peacock Hall."

His eyes seemed to darken as he looked at her. "Would you believe, to see you?"

The delicate ice structure that she had been attempting to surround her heart with threatened to melt all at once. *Her?* Oh God. It was shameful how much she wanted to believe him.

But yet she couldn't. Wouldn't. "I would certainly not believe it."

"And yet it is true."

"Was it true when you pushed Violet out of the carriage?"

"Once and for all, I did not do your sister any harm."

"I saw it with my own eyes."

"Your eyes were deceived."

"I don't believe you," she said.

She *wanted* to believe him. But what she had seen with her own eyes belied his words. And if she believed he was telling the truth about Violet, would she also have to believe his honeyed words about coming to Peacock Hall just to visit her? Would she have to accept the amazing yet seemingly unreal idea that a man had seen Sophy and Violet and yet had chosen *her*?

He leaned closer. "What can I do to convince you?"

Kiss me, she thought, practically fainting.

Then her mind screamed in protest. He was simply bam-

boozling her, seducing her with the warmth of his words
and kisses for his own ends.

She needed to get away from those soulful eyes, and those
lips. She needed to flee the lure of those muscular arms.

And this time, she did.

I wandered lonely as a . . .

No, that had been done.

Freddy sighed and lowered himself down onto the cool
ground on a hill by a jutting rock. He didn't worry about getting his breeches dirty, since they weren't his anyway. After
breakfast—just after Nathan had left for Peacock Hall—
Freddy had raided his brother's closet and procured for himself buckskin breeches and a loose white shirt of cambric.

Now that he was going to be poor, he had decided, he
would need a new wardrobe. None of his clothes were ap-
propriately plebeian, so he had put on his brother's clothes
and set off on a contemplative walk, which was far more
exhausting than he had anticipated. Being depressed was
very tiring work all around, in fact.

And yet, as he had walked he had a startling epiphany.
Heretofore, he had always been concerned with worldly, if
rather fanciful matters, and suddenly he was aware of a more
mournful side of himself. It was rather stimulating, actually.
Maybe it was the loose clothing, but suddenly he was having quite high-flown thoughts. He was at one with nature
and part of the earth, part of the teeming, struggling mass of
animal life all around him. And by God, there were really
elegant phrases buzzing around in his brain, too!

Oh, cruel fate that would hand me poverty in my prime!

Poverty in my prime was a catchy sort of phrase, he
thought. It was poetry—which was nothing he ever thought
he had a knack for. But maybe he did. He reviewed the line
again, falling in love with its rhythm. And look how he had
just instinctively come up with *poverty* and *prime.* There was
even a word for that kind of thing, though he couldn't put his

finger on it just at the moment. But he was pretty sure this indicated a natural gift on his part.

A fantastic idea struck him. Maybe he really could do this. He would save his home and rescue Nathan from marrying against his will.

He could pen a few verses and become the rage, like that Byron fellow. *He* wasn't starving for bread or affection.

As Freddy lay collapsed against his rock, it seemed more and more appealing, this business of poetry. And why not? He had been to school. All that studying of words should be worth *something*.

Now all he had to do was string a few phrases together and make a name for himself.

He stared up at the clouds overhead. All that came to him were bits of Wordsworth.

He wondered if anyone would notice if he pinched a few of old William's phrases here and there . . .

As if in answer to this plagiaristic impulse, the very earth beneath him began to shake. Freddy straightened, alarmed that his guilt should be punished even before he had set one borrowed word to paper. Then, he saw the reason for the quake beneath him. A rider.

A beautiful dark young lady in a flowing blue velvet habit was thundering down the road quite close. She had a heart-shaped face, full lips, and dark blue eyes fixed on the road in front of her. Her bonnet had fallen off and was trailing behind her, lost in a riot of thick brown hair streaming in the wind. Her cheeks were red and almost disgustingly healthy. She seemed, every inch of her, youthful and invigorating and vital.

And so beautiful it was almost painful to look at her.

Freddy scurried on top of a rock, both to protect himself from flying debris being kicked up by her gray steed's hooves and to better stare at the marvelous creature before him. (The young lady, not the gray steed.) A spirited, determined girl.

And then, just as she pulled abreast of him on his perch, she looked him directly in the eyes and laughed—such a melodious, joyful sound that it made his heart almost ring in response.

Before he could call out to her, however, she was gone, pounding across the field.

Looking at her had made his pulse leap and his heart race. It was like standing beneath a dark sky as thunder clapped.

More poetry!

By heavens, he *really* had a flair for this. Excitement built in him. He was bound to make a go of it. He would be famous, the newest toast of the town.

As his young lady in blue continued into the distance, becoming a speck on the horizon, he began to concoct a future for himself. For both of them. He would pen poetry about her—his blue lady—and earn money and fame. And then he would find her and confess that she was his inspiration.

Or maybe he would confess before. Earning money and fame could take a deuced long time.

Oh, but what did it matter? He had a purpose in life now. He wanted to run home and set to work. Only he couldn't run because he had a blister on his heel from his new boots. He was going to have to get other footgear if he was going to do all this wandering the moors for inspiration. Maybe there was an extra pair of boots in Nathan's closet, Freddy thought hopefully.

But for now he would limp home and get to work just the same.

Byron walked with a limp, he had heard.

They had a lot in common, he and Byron.

Chapter Eight

*Would that he had never laid eyes on Fiona! After
their embrace on the windswept rocks, Orsino felt
done for. How could he have allowed a mere slip of a
girl to affect him so? It seemed impossible that the
daughter of his bitter enemy could have charmed her
way into his heart and bewitched his very soul.
Ah, but she had.*

—Count Orsino's Betrothal

There was something different in the house that disturbed his already troubled mind. At first, Nathan couldn't
put his finger on the exact source of this new uneasiness,
except that there was a faint smell of smoke in the air.
Probably the result of some sort of accident in the kitchen.

And then Nathan remembered something that gave him
pause. Freddy. He had passed Freddy's room, and he
wasn't taking his usual predinner nap. Nor was he lounging in the parlor. And apart from sleeping or lounging, he
hadn't seen Freddy do much of anything lately. He hoped
his brother hadn't wandered out and gotten into mischief
while on his walk.

But what mischief could involve smoke? Freddy was
too old to set fire to things.

Wasn't he?

In the hall, Nathan stopped Mrs. Willoughby, who was
bustling towards the kitchen. The woman was always
bustling. One would have thought she had a palace full of

people to care for, instead of a mostly closed up house with two lone men rattling around in it.

Of course, since there were only two servants on the entire property, that was probably one explanation for why the woman always appeared busy.

"Have you seen my brother, Mrs. Willoughby?"

As always when he mentioned his brother, the woman's lips pulled into a tight line. "Master Frederick is in *the study*." She pronounced these words with the greatest distaste.

"The study?" Nathan asked, confused. There had not been a pressing need for a study at The Willows during the last generation. His father had not been what you would call a studious man, unless one were to count the diligent and yet fruitless study of whist.

"That means the billiards room," the good woman translated for him.

Nathan frowned. He could not remember entering the billiards room since before he was in the army. It used to be the place his father would retire to with his cronies after dinner. But that had been in the old days, before his father's cronies had become his creditors.

"I see. Well, I'll just—"

Mrs. Willoughby marched right over his words. "Master Frederick came back from his walk and asked Mr. Willoughby to build a fire there, and he insisted we call it the study! Naturally Mr. Willoughby does not mind taking pains for the young master, but that room has been the billiards room as far back as I can remember."

Her face was so tense her chin wobbled, as if being requested to rename a room were an act of the greatest presumption.

"I'm sorry, I'll—"

"Then the chimney started smoking!" she interrupted. Apparently her litany of complaints was not yet exhausted. "An old sparrow's nest, my John said."

"Oh, dear. Well—"

"But Master Frederick wouldn't hear of clearing out. Oh,

no. Not him! He said he liked the smell of smoke—that it made him feel as though he were in a French garret!"

"Thank you for taking such pains, Mrs. Willoughby."

"There weren't no pains taken, Major. Not on my part. Master Frederick wouldn't allow me to dust, just let me take the covers off the furniture."

"Well. Thank you just the same."

The old head bobbed loftily. "You're welcome, I'm sure. Only I don't like to have my housekeeping compared to an unkempt hole in some foreign place! The only reason the room was in such a state was because old Mr. Cantrell ordered the room closed after he sold the billiards table. I haven't got time to keep up with all the closed-up rooms in this great barracks of a place," she said, stiff with defensiveness. "Mind you, if anyone had said they wanted that particular room cleaned, I certainly would have done it."

"Of course."

"Cleaned it within an inch of its life, I would have done!"

"Indubitably."

"No one's ever called a room in The Willows a garret in my time!"

"I'm sure he meant it in a positive sense, Mrs. Willoughby."

The good woman let out a skeptical harrumph and steamed on her way towards the kitchen.

Nathan followed the trail of smoke and finally found himself staring at a most peculiar sight. The room, with its oak-paneled walls graced only by shadows where pictures used to hang, felt cavernous and empty. Yet on the side with the fireplace—a massive stone structure that boasted a shoulder-height mantle and was clearly built with the room's northern exposure in mind—a toasty fire roared. The sparrow's nest must have burned to a cinder, because the chimney was drawing fine now. Facing the hearth, on a sofa covered in faded mustard silk with maroon piping, draped his brother in a flowing white linen shirt with no neckcloth. He was balancing a ladies' writing desk—their mother's—on his lap, and held a preposterously large plume in his right hand.

"Freddy! What are you doing?"

At first Freddy showed no sign of having heard him.

"Freddy!"

His brother's head snapped up. "Good Lord! You scared me. I was in the thrall of my muse."

"Your what?"

"My muse. You know, one of those Greek bits of muslin that appear when one is spilling over with creative juices."

"With *what*?"

"Oh yes, I forgot." His brother's lips turned up in a half-pitying, half-condescending smile. "Being an army fellow, perhaps you wouldn't understand the lure of poesy."

Nathan shook his head. Clearly, his brother had gone mad. He should have known to break the news of their reduced financial state gently. This is what came of hitting the bottle. If Nathan hadn't been soused last night, Freddy might still be in ignorance of their precarious state and in reasonable control of his senses.

Not to mention, his own head might have been a damn sight better off. He might not have gone galloping first after Sir Harlan, then after Abigail. As far as he could tell, neither encounter had done him much good, aside from the wonderful but ultimately frustrating experience of tasting Abigail's sweet lips.

He would have enjoyed dwelling a little longer on that memory, but forced himself back to the matter at hand. He gave his brother's outfit a closer inspection. "Where did you get those clothes?"

"From you. I borrowed them from your room this morning. Very nice shirt, I think, although I think my tailor could spiff it up a bit."

"It does not need spiffing," Nathan fumed. "At least not when it is being worn by its rightful owner."

"Oh, rightful . . . yes. I'm all for rights—Tom Paine, John Stewart Mill, and all those fellows. They're right up my alley now."

Nathan rolled his eyes. "What are you talking about?

Freddy, I wish you would use plain English and stop speaking in riddles."

"I'm sorry," he apologized. "I forget that when last you saw me I had not been transformed."

"You had not yet raided my clothes press, you mean."

Freddy inspected the paper in front of him, then reluctantly handed it to Nathan, as if this would explain all. Nathan took the paper and perused it warily. It seemed to be a poem of some sort, though it was hard to make out. Freddy's handwriting was a slanted maze of curlicues.

> *O! Thunderous beauty!*
> *O! Breathless day that first ere I saw your face*
> * gallop by*
> *Whilst by my rock like Icarus I lay lashed,*
> *Wandering lonely as a wind-buffeted leaf.*

Nathan squinted at the words, trying to make sense of them.

"What do you think?" his brother asked, practically clambering over the back of the sofa like a dog desiring a pat on the head.

Nathan hesitated. "It's . . ." He frowned. "*You* wrote this?"

Freddy nodded.

Good Lord!

"What's the matter?" Freddy asked.

Nathan felt beads of sweat popping out on his brow. It was hard to know where to begin. "Well . . . it's rather . . . *flowery*, isn't it?"

"What?" Freddy looked alarmed, and a little offended. "There's not a mention of a flower in the whole thing! I made sure of that. There's just a bare mention of a leaf. A little nature is all the crack these days when you're in the poetry line."

"I only meant flowery in its style . . . it's rather high-flown."

"Oh! Well, that's all the thing now, too. Ask anyone in the verse game. Can't have a poem these days without a few O's and references to all sorts of Greek chaps strewn in. Of course, you might not know that, not being a literary type yourself."

"Yes, but, this Greek you mention. Icarus."

Freddy broke into a grin. "Do you like that? I thought that was a stroke of genius, myself."

"But wasn't it Prometheus who was lashed to a rock?"

Freddy's eyes flew wide open. "Damme, was it?"

"Icarus was the man who strapped on wax wings and flew too close to the sun."

His brother slapped his forehead. "I *knew* there was something that wasn't right. Pythagorus, you say?"

"*Prometheus.*"

He snapped his fingers and snatched back the paper. "Right! I'll just make a quick change . . ."

As he scribbled, Nathan leaned over him. "And while I know that these four lines are just a draft, you might take note that one cannot be lashed to a boulder and at the same moment be blowing around like a leaf, or whatever you said . . ."

"*Wandering lonely as a wind-buffeted leaf . . .*"

Nathan's nose wrinkled. "That has a familiar ring—I think you stole that line."

"I borrowed it, merely."

His brother seemed to be happily borrowing from all over, Nathan thought, eyeing his own shirt draping in folds around the younger man's slender shoulders. "Isn't that Wordsworth?"

"No!" Freddy exclaimed. "That is, it is an *allusion* to Wordsworth, certainly, but not . . ." He sighed in exasperation. "Well, I can't expect a *soldier* to understand all the ins and outs of this business. You'll just have to trust me."

"Trust you to what? What are you up to?" He gestured around the room, and then towards his pilfered outfit. "Freddy, I am glad if you have discovered a hobby—"

Freddy brayed with indignation. "Hobby! Ha! My hobby is going to make us rich."

He frowned. "How?"

"Behold the strength of my pen, brother. And before you laugh, you might remember that they all laughed at Lord Byron. And now look at him."

Nathan frowned. "Lord Byron!"

"I'll bet *his* house isn't mortgaged."

"Yes, but he's—" *Talented* was the word that almost slipped out of Nathan's mouth. Instead he finished, "—well-connected. He is a peer."

"Ah! But I have Fothersby. As soon as I send him a few of my efforts, I am sure he will want to be my patron. And I already have a muse, so I would say I'm ahead of the game."

"Muse? Who?"

"That is a secret!" Freddy, however, couldn't help adding, "A ravishing dark lady. I will tell you no more."

As far as Nathan knew, Freddy hadn't seen a female except Mrs. Willoughby since being sent down from university. And worthy though she was, no one would call that woman, with her ruddy cheeks and gray hair, dark or ravishing. Unless Freddy had drunk a bit more of that whiskey last night than Nathan had realized . . .

His brother flopped back on the couch, lips curling up dreamily. "She will be my own Caro Lamb . . . only one hopes she will not go insane, as that lady did." He sighed. "But of course, when one is world-famous in the arts, one has to expect that the occasional lady will react to one by losing her wits. It's very hard for women to handle brilliance. Like moths who flutter towards the flickering flame . . ."

"Mm." Somehow Nathan couldn't imagine too many women bashing themselves to death against Freddy. "Where did you find this woman?"

"My muse found me. And that's all I'll tell you about her. It's supposed to be a mystery, like the dark lady that what's-his-name had."

"Could the name you are searching for be Shake-speare?"

Freddy snapped his fingers. "Exactly! That's just the chappie I was thinking about."

"Good God, Freddy, I'd hardly refer to Shakespeare as a *chappie*."

"I don't know, from what you read of him, he seems to have been bursting with the old *joi de vivre*. Quite a jolly mate, in fact. If one is a writer, one has to pattern oneself on someone . . ."

"You have chosen quite a model."

"I was going to concentrate on writing an epic, since they're currently the rage," Freddy thought aloud. "But then I thought maybe I should start with something shorter. A collection of those what-you-call'ems . . ."

"Sonnets?" Nathan prompted.

Freddy clapped his hands. "Sonnets! Exactly. That's just what I've set my mind to. I don't expect I could have finished an epic before the end of the month, whereas I daresay I can dash off a whole book of sonnets in no time."

"The month! You mean you think you can save The Willows with a few poems?"

"The pen is mightier than the gambling vowel," Freddy said, poking his plume at Nathan for emphasis.

"I believe it is said to be mightier than the sword."

"Swords are your line, brother. You toddle along wooing heiresses, and I will keep writing. We'll see who manages to save the old manse."

For a moment, Nathan stared into the fire, remembering the stubborn look on Abigail's face as she insisted he was a plague to all Wingate women. And this was *after* she had fallen into his arms.

The prospects for saving The Willows seemed to rest on shakier ground than ever. His romancing versus Freddy's versifying.

God help them.

There was no question of getting any work done before dinner. Every time Abigail sat still, her mind latched onto the memory of Nathan's lips against hers. She had relived the moment a hundred times this afternoon, and it never failed to send her off into a fugue.

What really set her mind awhirl was the stark contrast between how she had felt entwined in the warmth of Nathan's arms, and then merely standing before him. In his arms, the world had seemed startlingly clear—there was just the two of them, and the desire that seemed to encircle them like a cocoon, shutting out all troubles, all the doubts she had harbored about him in her mind. The idea of nestling forever inside that cocoon, of tasting the full sample of bliss of which Nathan was offering her the merest sample, was very alluring.

But the full force of her doubt had returned the moment she stepped outside that circle. In some ways they had been compounded. No man had ever flirted with her so outrageously, or gone so far as to steal a kiss from her on a public road. Nor had she ever dreamed she would let such a thing happen! So why had this man done so, and why had she let him?

Her heart wanted to believe that he had simply found her irresistible, but her head remembered the scores of men she had met in her lifetime who had very ably managed to resist her. Her heart wanted to believe that this man was merely different—that she had found her soul mate. Yet never had she imagined her soul mate would be a former soldier who talked of sheep and different grades of wool. Her heart wanted to believe that love was not bounded by professional inclination . . . and yet she had always dreamed of finding a man who shared her passion for words.

On the face of things, all Nathan truly seemed to have a passion for—and an indiscriminate passion, at that—was creating scenes, public and otherwise, with herself and her sisters. This baffled Abigail. And it was what stopped her heart and its foolish yearnings cold. There was something about Nathan she simply did not trust.

In that light, as she relived their kiss again, she squirmed. How could she have been so lost to all sense of propriety as to engage in kissing a man on a public road? This was conduct more befitting Sophy than her own sensible self. And it was probably at about that very stretch of the road that Violet had begun her struggle with Nathan that had landed her in a mud puddle.

Naturally, Nathan would tell her that she couldn't believe what she had seen with her own eyes. He simply wished she *hadn't* seen it.

Then again . . . in retrospect she had to admit that the violent encounter Violet described did not square with her own experience. The disparity puzzled her. To Abigail, Nathan had always been teasing. His smile had been wolfish, but his arms had been gentle, coaxing. In her presence he had never behaved like the passion-driven maniac Violet had described.

But perhaps his passion towards Violet was more outrageous because his passion for her was more violent. That thought caused Abigail's throat to catch. Yet she had to accept that she knew very little about Nathan except the behavior she had witnessed these past few days. And that behavior, by any measure, was odd.

One thing was certain, the next time she met Mr. Cantrell, she was not going to fall so easily into his arms. He was going to have to make a clean breast of it about all these shenanigans with her sisters and secret meetings with Sir Harlan.

Upon this resolution, Abigail made her way to Violet's room in order to deliver the ribbons purchased in town. The task would take but a moment, but Abigail hoped to linger a while with Violet. Having now experienced her own encounter with Nathan, she wondered if she might elicit more details from her sister about hers.

Unfortunately, Violet was not in a good humor today. She was never at her best when ill, and though Abigail could not detect a concrete symptom of what was ailing her sister, it was obvious that even the slight chance of being incapacitated for the ball, still two weeks off, was causing Violet no small amount of stress. She sat up in bed, fanning herself. A glass of barley water rested on her nightstand.

When she saw Abigail enter her room, she greeted her like a patient might greet a nurse the morning after a long, dark night of suffering. "Oh, Abigail! Thank heavens you are back. Why am I so hot? Feel my forehead! Do you think I have a fever?"

"Your color is good," she pointed out.

Violet picked up the mirror on the side table and inspected herself so that Abigail could not touch her forehead. "Yes! I do look quite well for someone detestably ill."

"In what way do you feel ill?"

"It's my throat!" Violet exclaimed in despair. "I felt a definite scratch in it this morning. That is always the first sign of serious illness, everyone knows that. If I am too sick to attend the ball, what will the earl think? Surely if there is anything I can offer him—since he is too noble to be concerned with mere worldly wealth—it is my youth. But what draw will that be if I develop a wasting sickness?"

Abigail settled gently at the foot of the bed. "You have other traits to recommend you, Violet."

"What, pray?"

"You have good taste and beauty."

Violet rolled her eyes. "Of course. That goes without being said. But a fat lot of good being pretty's going to do me if, during the ball, I am sallow from weeks of illness."

"Has your throat bothered you since this morning?" Abigail asked her.

"Of course! I have thought of little else."

"But has the scratchiness been repeated?"

Violet pursed her lips. "No, but I am not taking any chances. I am not leaving my bed except for my dress fitting."

"You cannot sit in bed for two weeks for no reason."

"No reason!" Violet's jaw dropped. "Betrothal to a peer is hardly what I would call no reason!"

Abigail sighed. "I only meant that in this fine weather, a few constitutionals would do you all the good in the world."

Violet clucked unhappily. "Fine weather, indeed! It was all that rain that caused all my problems. If I had not gone out with that odious Mr. Cantrell while it was wet, I'm sure I would not be in the perilous condition I am in now."

Abigail leapt at the reference to Nathan. "That *was* a terrible day," she commiserated. "All the more so since Mr. Cantrell behaved so abominably."

Violet, who was peering anxiously at the clear, healthy whites of her eyes in the mirror, seemed to barely register her sister's words. "What? Oh, yes, it was atrocious. My gown was quite ruined."

"In fact, if you are sick during the ball, it would be all Mr. Cantrell's fault. Wouldn't it?"

"Of course!" Violet craned her neck, searching for flaws in her complexion. Finding none, she put the mirror back down on her coverlet. "I am lucky I can still walk after I fell out of his carriage. It would be just my luck not to be able to dance!"

Abigail fell still. "After you leapt out, you mean."

Violet blinked. "Leapt out of where?"

"Out of Nathan's carriage. You said you had to leap out to escape his annoying attentions."

"Oh yes! It's hard to remember exactly."

Abigail frowned. "But you must remember. You said he forced you to throw yourself into the mud."

"Yes, there was a struggle."

"And *he* was the cause of the struggle," Abigail said. "He behaved like an animal, you said, and was raving in frustration because you thwarted him."

Violet seemed bored with the topic and was again busy examining her reflection closely. "Hmm. Yes, something like that."

Something like that? Could it be that Violet had exaggerated . . . or *lied* about the nature of their combat in the carriage?

"It's what you said," Abigail reminded her sister.

"So?"

"Violet, if what you said is untrue, then you have besmirched the man's character."

"Well, what does that signify? It's not as if I made a public accusation."

"You announced it to us all!"

"Oh, well, yes—to the *family.*" She obviously felt that this amounted to nothing. "Anyway, what Father could be thinking letting that man hang about so frequently is beyond my comprehension. Mark my words—there will be trouble with that one and Sophy, and then I shall have to pay the consequences when the Wingates become social pariahs."

Abigail groaned. Oh, if only the trouble *could* be limited to Sophy. But now Abigail was herself behaving like their flighty younger sister. And to think, she had wronged Nathan—accusing him of attacking Violet when apparently that attack had only occurred in Violet's imagination. She now owed the man an apology, but she wondered if she would have the opportunity of seeing him again.

Thinking about this possible future encounter, she couldn't help wondering if it would involve Nathan bestowing his forgiveness on her in the form of a kiss . . .

"Anyway, I can hardly worry about Mr. Cantrell now!" Violet sank against the pillows in a pout. "Not when I should be concentrating on recovering my health."

Abigail got up and headed towards the door, sighing in exasperation. She didn't know whether to pity Violet or to dump the glass of barley water over her head.

Violet looked offended. "What's the matter with you?"

"I think I have committed a wrong against an innocent person."

Violet's eyes grew wide, naturally assuming that she would be the victim. "What? Did you forget my ribbons?"

Abigail had forgotten completely about the small package in her pocket. "No, I—"

Before she could explain, Sophy burst through the door. Her cheeks were red, her bonnet trailed down her back by its ribbons, and the bottom of her dress was spattered in mud.

"Violet! What does it feel like to be in love?"

Violet and Abigail exchanged nervous glances.

"Why?" Abigail asked her.

"Oh—hello, Abigail! I don't suppose you would know

anything about it, but I was wondering if Violet knew how to tell. Because I think I am in love."

"Last month you thought you were in love with the mail coachman," Violet reminded her.

"That was just a passing fancy of mine," Sophy said dismissively. "This is entirely different. This is a gentleman."

"Who?" Violet said.

"Never mind who!" Sophy said. "If I tell you, you'll either set your cap for him yourself, or else tell Father and have the man banished from our property. And then we would have to run away together."

Abigail and Violet again exchanged glances. And Violet's glance very clearly said, *You see! I told you there would be trouble!*

Abigail's head felt as if it were spinning. How could this be? How could Nathan have walked her home, kissed her tenderly, and then ensnared Sophy's affections a mere half hour later?

Unless Sophy wasn't speaking of Nathan? She would not be so quick to leap to conclusions again. She must take a deep breath and listen to Sophy dispassionately.

"At least let us know if he is suitable," Abigail said.

"Of course!" Sophy exclaimed. "He is a gentleman."

Abigail's heart sank. There had only been one gentleman on their property recently.

"And young," Sophy went on dreamily.

That quality failed to impress Violet. "I think mature men make better husbands than young ones."

"But he's so handsome!" Sophy said. "To see him even fleetingly makes you want to weep for wanting him. Not that this is a superficient attraction on my part," she said loftily. "He is obviously not a man who prances about in finery. He is more the rugged type. And such beautiful blond hair!"

Nathan. She could only be describing Nathan.

Abigail's heart sank. Her emotions felt as if they had been set loose on a crazy swing, first reaching the tops of the trees, then free-falling to disappointment mere moments later. Nathan kissed her and her heart sang, until she remembered he had behaved the cad. Violet revealed that he perhaps was not a cad, and her hopes sprang to the skies . . . only to have Sophy announce that *she* was in love with the man.

Unless her sister was describing another man. But who would that be?

He had the gall to wink at her in church the next day. As Abigail had entered the little chapel, he had bowed to her solemnly and then given her a friendly nod and a wink. He couldn't even behave respectably in church, she thought with irritation. The vicar droned on at length about showing charity towards one's fellow man, but Abigail was having a hard time getting into the spirit of the sermon. She was certainly not feeling charitable towards Nathan Cantrell.

Especially not as Sophy, who had come with her, seemed as nervous as a young colt this morning. She twitched, she fidgeted with her gloves, and she dropped her prayer book. Their pew was second from the front, and when they kneeled, Abigail would catch Sophy attempting to cast surreptitious glances over her shoulder. Probably trying to make eye contact with Nathan. Shameful behavior! They were no doubt both making eyes at each other.

Now that Abigail considered the matter, maybe that wink had not even been meant for herself. Perhaps he had been aiming at Sophy and missed!

At one point, Abigail gave her sister a jab in the side with her elbow. Sophy squeaked in protest, but for the rest of the service managed to keep her eyes forward. Perversely, now Abigail herself wanted to turn around. Had Nathan seen her jabbing Sophy?

As Abigail reached for her hymnal she reminded herself sternly that this was not the place to be dwelling on her exasperating neighbor.

So that was that. She would put the man out of her mind. Yet when the congregation stood to begin the hymn "We Sing the Glorious Conquest," the word *conquest* naturally made her think of soldiers, which brought to mind Nathan. And a few moments later she could have sworn she heard an unfamiliar baritone booming behind her. Nathan's?

As the parishioners filed out after the service, Nathan was loitering on the path, waiting for them. Or more specifically, he was waiting for Sophy, who practically bounded up to him in delight. "Hello, Nathan! What a surprise to see you here!"

Nathan took her hand, but smiled at Abigail. "Not too much of a surprise, I hope. I have been known to darken the doors of church before."

"Naturally," Abigail said. "You've no doubt had plenty of repenting to do."

He laughed. "I see you're in fine form this morning."

"We are both doing well," Sophy said, reinserting herself into the conversation. "But Violet refuses to leave her bed until the ball."

Nathan looked surprised. "Still?"

"When it comes to catching the earl, she has amazing fortitude," Abigail said.

Nathan and Abigail fell into step down the road, but Sophy was behaving most peculiarly. Usually when a group was walking, she bounded along in front like a puppy, yet today she was dragging her feet. She kept staring back at the dispersing congregation as if looking for a different face. But they were *all* familiar. The same people they had seen on Sundays since they were children. She lagged farther behind, looking more dejected.

Abigail began to suspect that Nathan was not Sophy's mysterious gentleman. The confusion over this point kept her off balance, which Nathan took advantage of by tucking her hand in the crook of his arm as they walked along.

At the contact, she cleared her throat. But she could not bring herself to pull away. "It was a lovely service this morning, was it not?"

His eyebrows lifted and he grinned at her. "I confess that my mind was not always on the worthy reverend's homily this morning. With you sitting there in front of me, I couldn't resist reliving a certain part of our walk the other day."

"Yes, we did have lovely weather for our walk, didn't we?"

He chuckled. "Yes, lovely weather, and it was a lovely kiss."

She felt her cheeks redden and beseeched him with her eyes to keep his voice down. "I hope you don't think I make a habit of such forward behavior."

He bowed. "I am glad to hear it. It makes it all the more memorable that I was granted such a privilege. And I don't usually run around kissing people in the middle of the street either, I assure you."

She slanted a playful look at him.

"I swear it," he said.

She looked around to make sure Sophy was not following too closely. "Then you would have me believe that I am a special case. That you were walking along with me and lost your head."

"Who knows? It might happen again."

She sprang away from him in mock alarm and he laughed.

"I am not as out of control as you fear, Abigail."

"I am not so certain of that," she teased. "You have been caught in some unusual situations with my sisters for a man in control of his actions."

He grimaced. "Those were just accidents!"

Abigail decided to have pity on him. "As it happens, Violet has admitted that her fall from your carriage was more in the way of an accident than anything involving improper behavior on your part."

At first, Nathan looked relieved at the news, then his expression turned triumphant. "So you were interested in finding out the truth from Violet. I am glad that you took the trouble to exonerate me."

"It was an inadvertent exoneration," she said, attempting to depress his conceit.

He leaned towards her. "As you say, but could it be that you are relieved to find proof that your affections are not engaged by a bounder?"

"My affections, such as they are, are not engaged at all."

He laughed.

"They are not," she insisted.

"If you ogled another man as you did me at the pond, I would feel jealous. Not to mention how I would feel if you later were seen kissing the man in the middle of the road!"

He seemed so smug, she wanted to strangle him. "Since we are again in the middle of the same road with my sister not far away, I don't care to discuss this with you!"

"Dare I hope then that we can discuss those delightful encounters when we find ourselves in a more private space, Abby?"

"My name is Abigail, and Miss Wingate to you."

"Surely our acquaintance is so familiar now that we could proceed to first names? How many men know your person as intimately as I know yours?" Nathan grinned down at her.

While Abigail tried to think of a stinging setdown for this piece of impertinence, Sophy trotted back up beside them. She seemed annoyed. "I should have ridden."

Abigail shook her head. "You cannot wear your riding habit to church."

"I don't see why not," Sophy said, in a pout. "Or at the very least, I wish we could have brought the coach."

It was useless to remind her that the coach was to be used sparingly, since Old Hal had pulled his back.

"Why don't we go for a ride this afternoon?" Nathan suggested to Sophy.

Abigail put a stop to this—too fast a stop to soothe her own conscience. *I am not jealous,* she said. Someone needed to look out for Sophy, though. "I don't think it would be appropriate for you two to go riding alone."

"Oh, but I meant the invitation to include you, too. Indeed, invite your older sister and father as well. Instead of riding, why don't I send my carriage for you all? We could have a picnic on my grounds."

"Violet will not come," Abigail said.

Nathan shook his head. "That will be a disappointment!"

"And neither will Father," Sophy added. "He gets carriage-sick."

"Well! Then it shall just be the three of us." Nathan

looked at Abigail significantly. "I know of perfect *private* spot for our repast."

"I don't think . . ."

Sophy clapped her hands together. "It sounds like such fun!"

"Then it's all settled," Nathan proclaimed, not waiting for Abigail's opinion on the matter. He was already hurrying away. "I'll see you at one o'clock." With a final, triumphant smile for Abigail, he turned off on a side road that lead toward The Willows.

Sophy's eyes followed him and she sighed worshipfully. Whatever had been troubling her before seemed to have been momentarily forgotten. "Isn't he wonderful?"

Wonderful . . . and yet there was something dodgy about the man that made her uneasy. Abigail felt herself as conflicted as ever.

"It's a shame he has to be so old!" her sister said.

"Nonsense. I would guess he is not yet thirty, or not far beyond it."

"Thirty!" Sophy exclaimed, though she might have been yelling the number seventy or one hundred. So much for Nathan being Sophy's mystery man, Abigail realized. "That poor man."

Abigail shook her head and pronounced with mock gravity, "Yes, it's a wonder he manages to get about without a cane and a nurse."

Her sister shook her curls. "Only, I mean it's sad that he is so alone." She contemplated this for a moment and then brightened. "But perhaps we can find some nice mature spinster to fall in love with him. That shouldn't be too difficult."

Abigail had to bite her cheek as she resumed walking. "No, I shouldn't think we would have to look very far at all."

Chapter Nine

The lustrous bounty of jewels sparkled before inno-
cent Marguerite, causing tears to tremble in her
young eyes. Her dear mother! How precious were
these treasures that had graced that lovely woman's
neck.

But now, in the hands of her stepfather, they were
only bargaining chips.

—The Diamonds of Torrento

By the time Nathan arrived at Peacock Hall, doubts about
the picnic were piling up as quickly as the bills that formed
a small mountain of worry in his room at The Willows. It
wasn't that he didn't want to have some quiet time with Abigail, but perhaps he was rushing things a bit. It was usually
one step forward, two steps backwards with her. Yet after
church he had been so encouraged. She seemed willing to
admit that he was not the brute that she feared he was and he
had been tempted into issuing the invitation.

There was no doubt he needed to strike while the iron
was hot. He did not have a great deal of time; the date of
the ball was fast approaching, and he and Abigail still
knew relatively little about each other. A successful marriage required more than just superficial physical attraction—though Lord knew there was plenty of that.

Yet he could not help noticing that Abigail had seemed
less enticed than her younger sister by his suggestion for
this afternoon. He hoped she did not dislike picnics (or just
picnics with him).

He also worried about his house. In his mind The Willows was still the spectacular pile it had been in his mother's day. He kept forgetting that others wouldn't view it through such a rosy tint. In reality, the place was something of a wreck—not the sort of abode that might entice a prospective bride. He would only be able to show her a few rooms. Foolishly, he had felt that age-old instinct to lure a mate with a fine nest, only to remember at the last moment that his home was a sagging old pile of twigs.

And then there was Freddy, who was still acting poetic and peculiar.

And finally, there was the small matter of Mrs. Willoughby, who was far from overjoyed when Nathan had announced his intentions of having company over that very afternoon. Creating refreshments on such spur-of-the moment notice put her aprons in an uproar.

"I'm not sure there's even enough butter for cakes," she announced.

This was not what he wanted to hear. "Well . . . couldn't you find some?"

Her eyes bulged. "This isn't Windsor Castle, you know!"

As if he had to be reminded.

When Nathan's carriage, driven by a rather sullen Willoughby, pulled up in front of Peacock Hall at the appointed hour, Sir Harlan came running out the front doors.

"Magnificent idea, my boy! Now you're using your think box!" He was practically clapping his hands together in glee. "A picnic! Women love those kinds of things. Especially with plenty of sweets and cakes . . ."

Remembering Mrs. Willoughby's ominous warning about the butter supply, Nathan had to suppress a groan. "Perhaps we should delay this picnic to another day."

"No, no, this is just right. No time like the present, and all that. And what a beautiful day! A warm day, but with a pleasant cool breeze. You couldn't have ordered better!"

Nathan squinted at the sun. It was going to be the hottest part of the afternoon. If the wind died down . . .

"And you're in luck!" Sir Harlan exclaimed. "I have convinced Violet to go on the picnic."

"You did?" Nathan's heart sank to his boot heels. "But how?"

Sir Harlan fairly popped with self-satisfaction. "I told her I was going to give her my late wife's diamonds for the ball, but since she was feeling so poorly, I hesitated to pass them on to someone who might not last out the month." Sir Harlan bellowed with laughter. "The girl shot out of bed like a ball from a cannon."

More blackmail. Sir Harlan seemed to excel at it.

Nathan decided that a polite change of subject was in order before he fell under a permanent cloud of gloom. "I am sorry that you won't be joining us, sir."

"Nonsense. Wouldn't dream of missing it!"

Nathan was taken aback. He hadn't expected such a large party. Moreover, he hadn't warned Mrs. Willoughby. "But the girls said you get carriage-sickness . . ."

"That hasn't happened to me in years. I shall be right as rain." He elbowed Nathan. "Not to mention, I will be invaluable in getting the others out of your way so you and Violet can have some quiet time."

"Oh, but . . ." Nathan coughed. "Actually, I was hoping to have some time to speak to Abigail."

"She is coming along, too, I believe," Sir Harlan said. "Very nice of you to include her. Never hurts to get in good with the in-laws, boy!"

"Yes, but . . ."

Just then, Sophy flounced out of the house. "I want to ride backwards! May I? It's always such fun!"

She was wearing a pink dress and bonnet and smelled of roses. "I'm so excited! I hope there shall be cakes!"

Abigail came out next. When he saw her, Nathan's heart seemed to squeeze his chest. She had discarded her customary grays and browns for a blue muslin dress he hadn't seen on her before, and she was carrying a large basket, which she handed him. "Here's some fruit, cheese, and other things," she said. "Since there are so many of us, and you had but short notice . . ."

He could have hugged her. It was this practicality that distinguished her from the rest of her eccentric family. He smiled into her huge brown eyes, feeling himself losing a little more of his heart to her. "Thank you. That was very thoughtful of you."

As she returned his regard, a blush rose in her cheeks, and she ducked into the carriage and settled next to Sophy.

And then they waited for Violet.

And waited.

Apparently some time after shooting out of bed, she had lost momentum.

As the moments ticked by, the temperature in the carriage rose, and faces grew redder. Finally, Sophy volunteered to go after her eldest sister.

She disappeared into the house and wasn't seen again for ten minutes. Finally she appeared, dragging Violet out the door by the hand, followed by the servant Peabody. The manservant was carrying Violet's cape and parasol. As the servant was also sporting a hat, it seemed as if he had every intention of being one of the party. Nathan wanted to slap his forehead. Could this group get any larger?

"There's no more room in the carriage," Abigail told Violet as they attempted to stuff everyone inside. "Peabody must stay here."

Both mistress and servant looked offended and distressed.

"I need Peabody," Violet said, lifting her chin stubbornly. "He will assist me if I begin to feel faint."

"We are all going to feel faint if this carriage grows more crowded," Abigail said.

"Nonsense!" Sir Harlan cried in a jovial tone. "Peabody can ride above, with Nathan's driver."

At that, Peabody and Willoughby, who might have come from different universes, gaped at each other in horror.

"I will ride above," Nathan said.

"No, no!" Sir Harlan said, apparently upset by the idea of Nathan being out of Violet's company for a single second if he could prevent it. "I will ride up with Willoughby. We're old friends, he and I—and the fresh air will do me good." He breathed deeply and pounded a fist to his chest for good measure.

Nathan could just imagine Sir Harlan toppling off the seat and he glared at Violet to let her know that he disapproved of her setting her elderly father in such a position.

"All right," Violet said, capitulating. She turned reluctantly to her servant. "You had better ride with the coachman, Peabody."

Peabody looked aghast, but was too much of a good soldier to question a blunt directive. It took a full five minutes to get him up and secured to his satisfaction.

The rest of them squeezed themselves into the coach, which became a little more bearable once the vehicle was moving. At least then a breeze managed to stir up the air a bit.

During the drive, everyone in the carriage was restless, no one more so than Sophy, who struck Nathan as a girl who never liked to sit still for long. And yet there was something in her eyes that made him think that something was agitating her beyond her usual high spirits. It was the same uneasiness he had detected in her during their walk home from church. It was almost as if she were waiting for someone who hadn't arrived.

"I am too warm," Violet said.

As if they all weren't too warm at the moment.

Sir Harlan chuckled as he mopped his own brow. Come to think of it, he was looking a little green. "Just think of this as your own sweat cure."

"Father!" Violet exclaimed, obviously appalled that he would insinuate she would do anything as human as perspire.

Sir Harlan winked at Nathan. "Violet has a great sense of humor."

"I've noticed," Nathan replied dryly.

Abigail, who was wedged between Sir Harlan and Violet, aimed her gaze out the window. Her lips were flattened into a tight line, as if she were trying not to smile.

All the while, Sir Harlan exclaimed over the scenery on the way to The Willows, which his daughters had no doubt seen before, and the lovely day Nathan had chosen—as if there had been a scientific plan behind his rash invitation—and even the old carriage itself, whose dry leather seats were cracking beneath them.

"Superb craftsmanship—they don't build them this way anymore!" Sir Harlan said, looking up at the sagging ceiling of the vehicle. Sir Harlan perhaps did not notice that detail because he was looking more green with every roll of the rickety coach's wheels.

His daughters viewed the interior's details with less enthusiasm.

"And what an oak tree you have there!" Sir Harlan exclaimed, pointing out a magnificent old specimen. "You don't see fine old trees such as that very often!"

"Isn't that Lord Overmeer's property?" Violet asked.

"Yes," Nathan said, feeling almost as if he were the one who had puffed up the magnificence of the tree.

"Well!" Sir Harlan exclaimed. "Lord Overmeer is quite a fine neighbor to have, I'll be bound! Nathan, old man, you are quite a lucky devil in that respect."

As if Nathan had personally picked the old peer to live next to him.

"Father, he's our neighbor, too," Sophy pointed out.

"Ah, so he is." Sir Harlan's breathing was reduced to a few desperate gasps.

"Are you feeling all right?" Nathan asked him.

"Yes, yes," he said, waving away any concern. "I just need to breathe deeply."

But there wasn't much air to spare in the close quarters of the coach's interior. After a few moments more, Nathan had to signal for the coachman to pull over so Sir Harlan could climb out and be ill on the side of the road.

It seemed like an inauspicious beginning for his picnic.

Violet wanted to turn back, but Abigail and Sophy, concerned about their father, suggested that Sir Harlan would feel better when he got to The Willows. They were almost there.

"Of course," Sir Harlan gasped. "And look, my girls . . .

what excellent sheep Nathan has out in his meadow. Nathan is quite a man to talk to . . . about sheep."

"Those are Lord Overmeer's sheep," Nathan was forced to admit.

Nathan already felt anxious, like one of those overextended hostesses he had seen in London, who would realize halfway through a dinner party that they had perhaps been too ambitious. Just the effort of transporting his guests was proving a trial. Once they got to the house . . .

Just then, they crested a hill and The Willows came into view, in all its shoddy glory. Yet Sir Harlan lifted his head from between his knees and managed to gasp with as much awe and wonder as if he were beholding St. Peter's gate.

"What glorious stone!" he exclaimed, as if he had not seen The Willows a thousand times before.

The stone was the same variety as that used at Peacock Hall, only with two hundred years' head start in accumulating moss. Half of the house was covered in ivy, giving the place the awkward appearance of a stone snail trying to shed its leafy shell.

"Have you ever seen such camellias?" Sir Harlan exclaimed.

They hulked about like giants in an herbaceous fairy story, dwarfing even the rhododendrons, which were likewise massive.

"They want tending," Violet observed.

And she was right. Nathan felt suddenly ashamed of his greenery. In fact he briefly considered seconding the motion that they turn back—for Sir Harlan's sake—when suddenly Freddy, all in white, appeared. He looked rather ethereal as he skirted a massive pink camellia bush.

"Who is that?" Violet asked.

Everyone stared out the window with interest. Sophy gasped, and Nathan could well imagine why. His brother was quite a sight. Nathan's shirt seemed more absurdly billowy on him today, and he hadn't combed his curly hair, which jutted out in peaks, like waves on a stormy sea.

"That is my brother, Freddy."

"Your brother!" Sophy exclaimed, clearly delighted.

"He's rather at that weedy stage, isn't he?" Violet observed.

Nathan stiffened in defense. Of course what Violet said was perfectly true; it was the tone she used that gave offense. But before he could defend his little brother, Sophy leapt on the offensive. "He is tall," she said. Nathan could not recall ever hearing her speak so sharply, and apparently neither could any of the others in the coach, because they all seemed to blink at her in surprise. "I would not call that *weedy,* Violet."

"A strapping lad!" Sir Harlan exclaimed quickly to diffuse the situation. He generously ignored Freddy's uneven gait, his hair, his peculiar boots, and the way the bones could be seen poking against his clothing. One thing about Freddy's former clothes—their padded shoulders, high shirt points, and elaborate neck cloths had disguised the coltishness of his physique better than his new artistic look did.

Willoughby pulled the carriage up the drive and, finally, mercifully deposited them at the front of the house.

Nathan climbed out of the carriage and was followed closely by Sophy, who burst out of the conveyance like a shot in pink. She didn't bother taking Nathan's arm or even using the step. She simply leapt out and began looking around. "Are we to meet your brother?" she asked Nathan.

Oh, heavens. He had known the meeting of his brother and neighbors was inevitable, but he had hoped to put Freddy off until he had shaken off his poetic persona. But then he looked back at his guests and noticed Violet aiming raised brows at the still-crooked shutters he had not managed to fix to his satisfaction. Suddenly introducing them all to Freddy seemed far preferable to the house tour that he would presumably be asked to provide.

"Let me see if I can . . ."

But he did not have to see. Just then Freddy came loping unevenly around the side of the house and across the overgrown lawn. He took one look at Sophy—who, in her pink, was hard to miss—and looked as if a bolt of lightning had struck him.

After a few moments, Freddy recovered from the jolt of the first sighting of Sophy and broke into a smile. He sped up to the carriage, introduced himself to the Wingates all in the most charming fashion imaginable, and then helped Nathan extract a woozy Sir Harlan from the carriage.

"You must be the Wingate ladies I have heard so much about!" Freddy said, once they were all safely on Cantrell soil. He looked from one to the other as if he could hardly take in so much beauty at once. "Even my brother's high praise has hardly done you justice."

To Nathan's surprise, the "weedy" youth Violet had scoffed at managed to endear himself even to that woman. He bowed warmly to her and proclaimed, "I haven't seen so stylish a gown on any woman since I left London."

Violet preened under his praise. Even Peabody looked pleased.

Nathan breathed a sigh of relief. It was like having the old Freddy back.

To Abigail, who was helping Sir Harlan, Freddy offered to ease her burden and stressed how pleased he was to meet her. He crooked a shoulder under Sir Harlan's armpit and made himself into a human crutch until the older man had made it to firm ground.

But for Sophy, he positively sparkled. It was as if he were looking on a goddess. She quickly linked her arm around her father's other side and helped Freddy assist Sir Harlan inside.

In short, Freddy was being the genial host while Nathan stood by, abashed and amazed. Freddy escorted the party indoors, told Abigail where she could take the basket to give it to Mrs. Willoughby, gave Violet the best seat in the house, and ordered tea so everyone could refresh themselves before they set out on the picnic.

Nathan scooted out of the room and went to find Abigail, who had not come back yet. He found her in the portrait hall, staring up at the formidable Eugenia Cantrell.

"You have a lovely house," she said. "I've never been

inside. That seems remarkable, since we have been neighbors for so long."

"My father was not one for entertaining." He coughed into his hand. "That is, he generally entertained himself elsewhere."

"Of course. I knew your father and saw him often at Peacock Hall. I always found him an amiable, charming man." She smiled. "Much like your brother."

"Oh. Freddy." Nathan felt a pang that he was not the Cantrell she found amiable and charming.

Yet he took heart from Abigail's blue dress. Had she worn it for his benefit?

"The Willows has unfortunately been a bit neglected of late," he said. "It could use a woman's touch."

She nodded, though seemed not to take the remark to be the personal entreaty that Nathan had intended it to be. "Most places do benefit from a woman's input. Though some men, like my father, are very keen on arranging their surroundings."

"Not me." As soon as the words were out, he feared it sounded as if he were careless about such matters. A woman naturally wouldn't want to think a man indifferent to her interests. Look how Violet had practically swooned when Freddy mentioned her gown. "Not that I don't appreciate a well-turned-out room," he added as quickly as he could, "but I generally think that such things are best left to the lady of the household."

He leaned forward slightly, hopefully, as if to say, *don't you agree?*

"Perhaps you are right." She emitted a slight giggle. "I am very glad that my mother generally won her way on such matters of decoration at Peacock Hall. If it were up to my father, there would be nothing but room after room of mounted stag heads and bird paintings."

He laughed. "His study does have a very definite decorative stamp."

Her brow pinched into a frown, and she seemed to notice suddenly that they had become separated from the others. "Speaking of whom, is Father feeling better?"

"Some tea has revived him."

"Perhaps we should get back . . ."

Nathan wasn't ready to share her yet. "I was hoping to hear more about what you think should be done to The Willows."

She frowned up at him. "I wouldn't be so presumptuous . . ."

"But I wish you would be," he said, stepping closer to her.

Color rose in her cheeks, and she shifted her gaze from his. When she spoke, she swerved the conversation back onto the topic of his brother. "Freddy is very agreeable. I am surprised you have never mentioned him. How he charmed Violet!"

She attempted to step around Nathan. He blocked her.

She shot him an annoyed look. "I am surprised Violet came today," she said.

"No more surprised than I was. We owe her presence among us to your father."

She raised her brows. "Why?"

"He was keen on her coming, and apparently blackmailed her with promises of diamonds if she would attend."

Abigail's forehead tensed into lines. "Blackmailed her? With diamonds?"

"Perhaps I shouldn't have said anything . . ."

"No, but it does seem strange, doesn't it? Like a ploy from a Gothic novel."

"So I thought—not that I am overly familiar with such literature." He laughed. "Naturally one hesitates to call it that."

She recoiled, looking unaccountably startled. "What?"

"Gothic novels . . . silly writing for ladies . . . that's hardly what one would call literature, is it?"

Her surprised gaze changed to a more unreadable expression. "We should get back to the others."

"Not just yet," Nathan pleaded.

She crossed her arms. Her cheeks were red, which Nathan chalked up to her modesty. She probably worried that the others would have noticed their absence and be gossiping madly about them. "Why?" she asked. "Do you have any more literary opinions you would like to share with me?"

He chuckled. "No, we can discuss whatever you like."

"I should like to return to my father . . ."

"Freddy is doing well entertaining him, I am sure."

"Nevertheless . . ."

"He seemed especially fond of Sophy," Nathan piped up, attempting to waylay her. "Didn't you think? Of course everyone seems to be fond of Sophy. She has a winning personality."

"Yes, but I fear she will win herself some trouble if not closely watched. I should go."

He touched her arm and she practically jumped over the banister. "She will be safe with Freddy. He is very young."

"The very young are often the very foolish. They follow their hearts more than their heads."

"And what about you, Abigail, have you never followed your heart?"

"I?" She looked into his eyes and swallowed.

I should kiss her, he thought. *Spill the entire contents of my heart to her here and now.* But he had planned on wooing her gently today. He had wanted to plant ideas in her mind that might blossom into dreams they could share. Pulling her into a mad embrace might dislodge those tender feelings.

"Perhaps we *should* join the others," he said.

She swayed as if caught off balance by his change of heart on this subject.

"Of course," she said, shrugging her arm free of his hand. "My thoughts exactly."

And with those words, she steamed off ahead of him. Nathan felt as if he had lost his equilibrium, too. He wasn't sure exactly what had gone wrong, but he had the feeling that he had just handled that situation very badly. And it had seemed so promising!

As the day wore on, he regretted not taking advantage of their situation alone in the portrait gallery. He never had another chance to speak to Abigail at length. All afternoon, Sir Harlan did his best to pair Nathan off with Violet.

Violet, though she obviously did not care for Nathan's company and spent most of the time speaking in snide asides to Peabody, seemed to take it as her due that Nathan should spend most of the afternoon with her.

Freddy devoted himself exclusively to Sophy, staring up at her adoringly, and falling over himself to attend her slightest whim.

Abigail kept slightly apart, and whenever Nathan tried to include her, she seemed to be doing her best to keep her distance. He should have kissed her in that hallway. Maybe she had even expected it, because something had happened in the portrait gallery that seemed to change her feelings towards him again. Just when he thought she was warming up to him . . .

It was a discouraging state of affairs that was not resolved by the end of the day, when Freddy once more kicked into full gallop to please everyone. Upon their return to the house, he went out of his way to run and get all the ladies' wraps for them and continued to entertain them with idle chatter as they waited for Willoughby to bring the coach around again.

To Nathan's chagrin, it was Abigail who insisted that Nathan should not escort them home, but that his servant simply take them and bring the carriage back.

"There is no need for you to be inconvenienced, Mr. Cantrell," she said.

And the rest of them heartily agreed, thanking him for the pains he had taken. They all went out of their way to tell Freddy how pleased they were to make his acquaintance and to extend a heartfelt invitation to their ball.

Feeling as if he would have few more opportunities, Nathan boldly took Abigail's hand as he helped her into the carriage.

"I wish I were escorting you," Nathan said.

Her cheeks blushed prettily, though her eyes remained cool. If he wasn't mistaken, she seemed rather annoyed with him for some reason. He began wracking his brains to remember what he had said that could offend her.

"As you recall," she said, "it was very stuffy in the coach with all of us."

"Yes, but it gave me the opportunity to sit across from you."

Her hand trembled slightly, although when she spoke her voice remained even and disinterested. "No doubt we will see you at Peacock Hall in the near future."

"I would like to come to Peacock Hall to talk to you especially," he said.

Her lips flattened. "Indeed! Perhaps we could continue our discussion of literature!"

The remark was barbed in some way he couldn't quite fathom. "I would hope to speak about more intimate subjects myself."

She snorted. "Good day, Mr. Cantrell, and thank you for the outing. It was very . . . enlightening."

She then disappeared inside the coach.

Nathan watched the carriage drive away, confounded. What on earth had set her off?

Next to him, Freddy rocked on his heels. "What a day! What a day!" he exclaimed. "I am walking on air!"

No more wandering lonely as leaves or such things, Nathan guessed. "You seemed to have a rare time this afternoon."

"Why did you not tell me about Sir Harlan's daughters?" Freddy demanded spiritedly.

"What do you mean?" Nathan said. "I did tell you of them."

"Yes, but not . . ." He sighed. ". . . Sophy."

"I suppose I never thought of her especially."

His brother looked flabbergasted. "How could you not? She is exquisite! Even better standing on her feet than galloping at me full tilt."

No wonder his brother had been behaving so oddly! "Is *she* your dark lady?" Nathan asked, wanting to laugh. "The muse who is going to make us all rich?"

Freddy didn't appreciate his mirth. "I don't see what's so damned amusing."

"Only that you think she is your special inspiration, when she has besotted half the neighborhood."

Freddy crossed his arms. "There wouldn't be much point in having a muse if no one else liked her, would there? Why would that fellow have painted the Mona Lisa if he didn't think she was a popper? Do you expect Shakespeare's dark lady was an old hag, or Helen of Troy was an antidote?" As Nathan continued to laugh, Freddy stamped his foot. "Oh—never mind. It's no use trying to make you see how I feel. Anyway, I have poetry to write."

He left in high dudgeon.

Good heavens! Nathan shook his head. He had no doubt Freddy's infatuation with Sophy Wingate was just a passing fancy—like fur boots or poetry. And yet the prospect of *two* lovestruck men rattling around The Willows was not a thing he looked forward to.

"Thank heavens that is over!" Violet exclaimed as soon as the coach was pulling away from The Willows. "Feel my head, Peabody. Am I too warm?"

The manservant's brow pinched anxiously as he assessed his lady's temperature. "I believe you are fine, but we must get you back to your room with all haste."

"I'm sure I should not have spent so much time out of doors," she fretted. "Sometimes one never realizes that one has caught a chill until hours after the fact!"

Violet was now obsessed with chills. In fact, Peabody had been allowed in the carriage on the return trip because Violet insisted that he might catch a cold from the high altitude of the rider's seat, which to hear her speak of it might have been an Alpine peak. She worried that if Peabody took ill, they would never have the house in shape for the ball. Never mind that it was still warm enough outside that the wraps Violet insisted on bringing had been completely unnecessary.

Sophy sighed. "I thought it was an exquisite day!"

"Any day you run into a man under fifty is exquisite,"

Violet said. "You should have more composure around men, Sophy. Otherwise, they get ideas about your character."

"I want them to get ideas. If they didn't, I should be sorely disappointed!"

Violet rolled her eyes. "Father, *say* something to her."

Their father chuckled. "Good to see young people enjoying themselves!" Sir Harlan said, his head practically hanging out the window. When Violet's ensuing exclamation made it clear that she did not consider this a satisfactory lecture to a young lady, he winked at her. "You seemed to enjoy *Nathan's* company well enough, Violet."

Violet fanned herself. "One does one's best to be polite." She leaned toward Peabody. "Did you see those scones he offered us?"

"Stale," Peabody said, his lip curling.

"I had three!" Sir Harlan exclaimed.

The other occupants greeted this news nervously as the coach hit another pothole.

Abigail wasn't feeling too well herself. But her particular malady had nothing to do with motion sickness, or how much food she had consumed. She was simply distraught. She had to gulp in deep breaths, as if that would take away the woozy feeling she felt every time she remembered Nathan's words. She had thought he was being so courtly—so kind. It was almost as if he had planned the excursion expressly for the purpose of charming her and showing off his home.

And then came those horrible words. They still echoed in her ears.

Gothic novels . . . silly writing for ladies . . . that's hardly what one would call literature.

Well! As if *he* would know a thing about that.

Even if he didn't, his words had ruined the afternoon. She had barely been able to keep herself from exploding.

Of course, he hadn't known he was insulting her. He couldn't have. No one knew she was Georgianna Harcourt. (Nor would they ever; she would die before telling anyone now, she vowed.) He had simply revealed his own personal opinion.

His ignorant, loutish opinion.

The man was a soldier. What did he know about books? He probably hadn't read a book since he'd entered the army!

Feeling hot, she snatched Violet's fan away from her without thinking.

"You could at least say please!" Violet bleated.

"Please," Abigail said, flapping the fan angrily at herself. Violet shot her a look she hadn't seen since they both wore their hair in plaits, and Abigail had to restrain herself from sticking her tongue out at her. Such childishness! Now she was making her elder sister appear well-mannered. Perversely, she blamed Nathan, that exasperating oaf!

A corner of her conscience upbraided her. Her own heart upbraided her. He wasn't an oaf. He was really rather a sweet person . . . look how he had showed her his house, so proud . . . it had made her melt. And his younger brother, bending over backwards to impress Sophy . . . for some reason that had softened her towards Nathan, too. He was a kind man, with serious responsibilities. The spark in his eye when he had looked at her had been almost unbearable. Especially after the long carriage ride spent staring at him, or trying not to stare at him. Trying not to touch her foot against his, or bump knees, and yet of course dying to do just that. When he had come upon her in the portrait gallery, she had had the urge to throw herself into his arms.

She had hoped he would find her there. Had, in fact, deliberately separated herself from the others in the hope that he would go searching for her.

She had never behaved so foolishly over a man. Really, she was just as shameless as Violet chasing her earl, or Sophy leaving the throng of brokenhearted servants in her wake. Worse, perhaps. Because she knew she should be more sensible. She had a purpose to her life that the others did not—her own goals and aspirations. She had six hundred pounds of her own money banked. She had her own dreams to follow, and could afford to wait until she met someone she truly wanted to marry.

But was Nathan considering her as a wife? She had no idea what he was doing at Peacock Hall so frequently, but there was something in his gaze, something so seductive and tender, that she couldn't help thinking that perhaps he looked upon her as a woman with whom he wanted to share his home, his life, his bed.

That very thought—of sharing his bed—caused a fever to wash through her. As if she had caught the very chill Violet so feared. Nathan had that effect on her.

And then he had had to go and sneer at Gothic novels!

She became furious all over again, just thinking about it. Of course, his criticism was not his alone. The man had probably never read a novel of the type that he was ridiculing, or any book written by a woman. He was simply parroting what others had said.

Other ignorant souls.

Oh, not that there wasn't a little justification for criticism. She knew that her stories couldn't compare artistically to works of Byron, Wordsworth, or Scott. But she had read offerings by men that she could say this of, too. But no one dismissed those works as simply "silly writing for men" not deserving the title of literature! Abigail plied the fan even harder.

Violet shot her another annoyed look, then glanced pointedly at her property. "Really, Abigail, you are stirring up a gale force inside this carriage. You might show my fan a little mercy, after you so rudely snatched it away. It's trimmed with French lace."

Abigail ceased her hand's movement. It wasn't helping anyway.

"Here," Sir Harlan said, looking more than a little green. "I'll take that."

He put the French lace trim to work for himself.

What a state of affairs. Here she was all stirred up, and Sophy was off in her own world, and their father looked ill. Why had he come when he loathed carriage rides? Indeed, he had seemed very eager, too. It was very peculiar.

Something about the whole scenario made her uneasy.

As did Sir Harlan blackmailing Violet to go to the picnic. It was just like what old Rafferty did in her book *The Diamonds of Torrento*.

Thinking about that work reminded her of Nathan's snide remark and got her mad all over again. She could not wait to get home and put the episode, the entire afternoon, and Nathan himself out of her mind.

She was never so relieved as when the carriage pulled up to their house and deposited them at the door. Sir Harlan stumbled out, followed by Sophy, who was practically floating. Violet and Peabody got out next, leaving Abigail alone to grapple with one wrap too many. "Sophy, your cape!" she said.

Sophy turned back and took her cape, smiling at Abigail. "You thought he was nice, didn't you?"

She was asking about Freddy, of course. "A nice young man," Abigail said. *Unlike his brother!* "Very young," she repeated to Sophy. "You both are very young." She wasn't sure the words penetrated, though. Her little sister glided away as if in a trance.

Violet, who had watched the exchange, shook her head. "There will be trouble in that quarter, mark my words. As if I don't have enough to worry about!" She frowned down at the ground where the sleeve of Abigail's spencer trailed. "Truly, Abigail, you should never allow pockets to be sewn into your garments. They cause you to run about spilling things behind you."

She and Peabody exchanged amused glances, then went along inside.

Abigail looked down at the ground. There was indeed a piece of paper flapping at her feet. She couldn't recall putting anything in her pocket, but she was so absent-minded sometimes. . . .

She picked the paper up and glanced at it casually to see if she could discard it.

She had intended to go upstairs to her room and change when she got home. But what she read on that sheet stopped her in her tracks. Her face turned red as she glanced at it again. And again. Finally, her footsteps sped towards her study, where she could be alone to contemplate this in silence.

It was a poem, a very odd sort of poem. She could hardly believe the words.

> *First daffodil of spring, first dewdrop of morning,*
> *First ripple on the still waters of my heart without*
>   *warning!*
> *How you have stirred my pastoral peace.*
> *Prometheus could not know the labor it takes to hold*
>   *my tongue—*
> *Icarus cannot have known how high I have soared.*
> *Glorious muse!*
> *Do not make me wait ere long,*
> *Give me a glorious hope, a bountiful life, to work*
>   *toward!*

How had such a thing made it into her cloak?

Nathan must have slipped it into her pocket when he was helping her into the carriage. No wonder he had lingered so long with her at the carriage door.

But . . . *a poem?* Nathan?

Of course it was an abominable piece of work, obviously written by someone not well versed in poetry—or who had been exposed to just enough to get himself into trouble. Say . . . a soldier. Some of the lines caused her to giggle.

And yet the lines could be of a man who was desperate to express feelings on paper that he could not put into words. She could not help feeling flattered. It was the first time since her name had been written down in the family Bible that any words had been penned in her honor.

Once again she went through the poem, parsing every line for meaning. Did he really admire her so much? Did he really wait for her to speak so that they could work towards a glorious future? Perhaps that had been what the picnic had been set up for.

And that business about causing ripples in the still

water of his heart—an obvious allusion to when they met at the pond.

Her heart beat madly for a moment, and she imagined Nathan soaring through the skies like Icarus. She felt like she was soaring herself. *He loved her. Her.* He had seen her two beautiful sisters, and yet he was writing poetry to her.

And then she looked down at the paper again, and saw more flaws. That bit about her being his muse made no sense whatsoever. Unless he was a writer or a painter or some such person—which Nathan was most definitely not. (And what this poem achieved more than anything was to declare its author no writer at all.) And there was such sloppiness—don't make him wait *ere long.* Ere was pointless in this instance, even wrong. Whoever had written this would seem to have trouble even understanding poetry, never mind writing it.

Perhaps she was being overly particular, but she wished, if he was going to trouble himself to write poetry, he had done a more adequate job. It was hard to look at this document of affection with anything other than mixed feelings . . .

And yet—it had been an attempt!

Probably the very next day he would be over, watching her eagerly for her reaction. What a position to be in—especially after he had so insulted her own type of work.

That thought gave her pause.

And *he* had the gall to make fun of women writers? To say that Gothic novels deserved no respect? And to think—at that very moment, he had probably been standing with this poem—this blight on the name of verse—in his pocket! And he had the nerve to act the critic!

She sank into her chair, stewing. What a conundrum! To have been given a love poem of such tenderness . . . and such ineptitude.

Chapter Ten

As Clara stood in the gallery, the dark eyes of noble-blooded Raffizzis dead and gone glowered at her from the walls. You dare to think yourself worthy of our illustrious descendant, the eighth baron? *those disapproving facial orbs seemed to demand.*

Though her own father had been but a humble merchant, yet did her heart pound a resounding yes to the Raffizzi ancestors. She was as good as they. But did she dare love the baron, a man she knew to be dangerous and in love with another?

Ah! That was a different matter.

—The Prisoner of Raffizzi

An odd thing occurred the day after the picnic. Nathan failed to put in an appearance at Peacock Hall that day. Or the next.

His absence was suddenly as disturbing to Abigail as his perpetual presence had been. Where was he? What had happened to his proclaimed desire to see her very soon?

What had happened to all the impatient desire expressed in that poem?

It wasn't a bad poem, she had decided. (And she didn't have any trouble calling it to mind, since she now had it memorized.) It showed definite promise, really. Even—when she was thinking about it in tandem with brooding over Nathan's green eyes—a *flair*.

Now that he was gone and showed no sign of returning, she found herself in a more forgiving mood.

In that spirit, she had even spent an evening sewing for Violet, and another playing cards with Sophy and their father. The rest of the time, she consoled herself with her writing. *The Prisoner of Raffizzi* was beginning to absorb her interest again. Perhaps because a little of The Willows was showing up in Raffizzi castle, and poor Clara was as conflicted over the object of her desire and she herself was.

She missed her muse. Because she couldn't deny now that Nathan had become her inspiration—much more than she could be considered his, despite what he had written in the poem. That he would call her such still didn't make sense to her; the only interest he had ever expressed to her was in the manufacture of wool, and surely she didn't inspire him in that arena.

Perhaps there were other poems . . .

Or perhaps he only meant the term in a more general sense. Yet he had inspired her very specifically. He was her Rudolpho in the flesh.

She only wished her real Rudolpho would make another appearance!

Nathan had hoped that a two-day trip to Manchester, where he had arranged a meeting with a factory owner, would raise both his spirits and his prospects. But the meeting had been unproductive. He had anticipated that after telling the man of his scheme of producing small amounts of high-quality wool in Yorkshire that this gentleman would be interested in investing in the idea. Unfortunately, the man seemed more interested in trying to take Nathan on as an investor in his own faltering business. Apparently now that there was a prospect for cheaper imports after the war, the domestic business was sagging.

This discouraging news was repeated to Nathan at several banks he visited. No one seemed to be interested in investing capital in domestic schemes. Especially not to a man whose properties were all mortgaged to the hilt. More than one man of finance counseled Nathan to ask Sir Harlan for help.

Disappointment was a bitter pill. For a short while, Nathan had dreamed of returning triumphant to The Willows, with cheque in hand . . . or at least capital promised. He would be able to stop seeking a wife for any other purpose than his own happiness. Freddy could stop penning terrible sonnets, which were now littering the house like a paper plague.

Now those hopes were dashed.

If he were to save The Willows, he would have to marry. But he was unsure of Abigail's affection. And how could he win her love while this ridiculous scheme of Sir Harlan's hung over their heads? The first whiff she got of the plan, she would balk. She was proud; he would not want her if she weren't. Even if he told her that she had captured his heart, how would he ever make her believe that it was not the prospect of twenty thousand pounds that had actually captured him?

If she would just give him the slightest show of encouragement, he would not feel so tied up in knots.

When he arrived at Peacock Hall, the place seemed different. There was a shipshape sparkle to it. Preparations for the ball were in full swing. The lawn had undergone a manicure. Where once dull hedges had stood, now peacock topiaries stood watch over the grounds. New flowers had cropped up in window boxes and beds. In the foyer, brass shone, the crystal in chandeliers winked like glittering diamonds, and all the floors were polished to a blinding shine.

Nathan winced in discomfort at all the pains that had been taken. Sir Harlan had such expectations!

But they had always been false, unrealistic expectations. How could the man expect Nathan to make a woman fall in love with him in three weeks, when he had not managed such a feat in almost three decades? The chances of Sir Harlan's scheme actually working had always been slim. It was just Sir Harlan's infectious optimism that had made him think that there had been a hope.

That, and Nathan's own desperation. But now he ques-

tioned whether his desperation and his honest desire to
save his home were as important as Abigail's own wishes.

Sir Harlan's optimism hit Nathan full force when Sir
Harlan spotted him. "Nathan, my boy! So good to see
you!"

Nathan, who had been staring in a somewhat depressed
state at a maid polishing a step, reluctantly moved toward
Sir Harlan.

"Glad you could make it today," Sir Harlan boomed at
him. "Place's looking spiffing, isn't it?"

"Yes indeed." Nathan's voice couldn't help but be glum.

Not that Sir Harlan seemed to notice. "We have missed
you. Even Abigail seemed to be in a pet!"

Nathan came to attention. "Did she?"

Sir Harlan chuckled. "I suppose we have all gotten used
to your company."

"Did she mention anything specifically?"

"Lord no, and never would do," Sir Harlan replied. "But
I could tell. Violet is especially fretful as the ball ap-
proaches, I've noticed." He poked Nathan in the side.
"You're in luck! I haven't fed Garrick and Mrs. Siddons
yet. I can arrange another rendezvous for you in the bird
yard with Violet."

"I'm sure that's not necessary."

"Nonsense, it's not the least bit of trouble. Does Violet
good to be ordered about sometimes." Sir Harlan laughed
heartily. "Mind you don't forget that when you're her lord
and master."

Nathan shuddered. Heaven help him. Heaven help any
man who got saddled with that title.

"Now just you go outside," Sir Harlan said, pushing him
out the study door. "I'll have Violet there with her pail in two
shakes. You don't have long to pop the question, remember."

As if he could forget!

Nathan waited until Sir Harlan had dashed up the stairs,
presumably to Violet's room, before heading in the opposite direction of the front doors. The last thing he had
wanted today was another *tête-à-tête* with Violet amongst
the peacocks. He hung back in a hallway until he heard Sir

Harlan's steps clattering back down towards the entrance hall. Nathan then ducked into the nearest room, whose door stood slightly ajar.

He was trying to be silent, but when he turned around to see which room he had entered he barely suppressed an exclamation of surprise. The room was empty, but it felt as if a thousand eyes were staring at him from the walls. It was an octagonal room and all the walls were lined with peacock feathers. The effect was startling; he had never seen anything like it. The room managed to be both garish and gloomy at once. The light from the windows was dimmed by the presence of a linden tree next to the window, adding to the gloomy atmosphere of it all. It was the type of room that he would have avoided at all costs.

And yet it was obvious that someone spent a great deal of time here. A desk placed prominently in the center of the room was rather messy. Curious, Nathan went over to it. An ink stand and pen stood on the desktop, as did a sheaf of blank paper. A large volume was open; upon closer inspection, it turned out to be a history of Rome, which immediately fascinated him. The subject jibed with his own interest in military history, and history in general. He wondered who was reading it.

He squinted around the room again. Despite the peacock motif, this obviously wasn't Sir Harlan's haunt. There were no dead animal heads anywhere . . . just the hint of them in all the plumage. And the desk chair was a rather dainty affair; not what a man would choose for himself. On a chaise near the window someone had left another book; it looked like a novel.

So whoever spent time here was a reader. That ruled out Sophy. Probably Violet, too.

He glanced at the inkwell and suddenly understood. Could this be Abigail's lair, the place where she did all her scribbling? He looked around again, finding more interest in things he had overlooked before. A jade-handled letter opener. Was it a family piece, or had it been a gift to her? And the books she was reading . . . Roman history? He became excited at the idea of a shared interest with her.

No sooner had he started poking further into the tome on her desk than the door opened and closed, and he looked up and saw Abigail herself standing in front of him. She had apparently come halfway into the room before she had noticed his presence.

Nathan straightened, and Abigail's face went chalk white. "You are back!" she exclaimed. Then, looking down at where his hand rested on her book, she added, rushing forward, "What are you doing?"

He shrugged sheepishly. "You have caught me snooping."

Her mouth opened and she let out a yelp of outrage.

Before she could blister him with words, he raised his hands in preemptive surrender. "I know—it looks bad. You will say this is a black mark on my character. But in all honesty, I was attempting to hide from Violet. Surely you would not deny a man sanctuary?"

Her brows knit. She seemed unable to take her eyes off her history of Rome for long. "When did you come in? I only stepped out for a moment . . ."

"Just now," he assured her. "I did not even have the time to take a turn about the room."

She was reassured enough to stop darting glances first at the book and then into his eyes. Now her gaze seemed intently focused on the tree outside the window. "I wondered what had happened to you," she said. "You have been gone for ages."

It struck him as encouraging that she would refer to a few days as "ages."

"You missed me?" That was a good sign!

Her cheeks flooded with red. "I was growing used to you. In your absence it was as if the cock had stopped crowing."

He laughed. "And yet you had Hannibal to keep you company."

She frowned at him. "I beg your pardon?"

He thumped his finger on the book. "Hannibal—the Roman general. Though how you could put this down as he is just crossing the Alps is beyond my comprehension."

Her expression was a blank. It was as if she had never heard of Roman history.

"This is your book, isn't it?"

"Oh, yes, but I had just . . . well, that is to say . . . I might have opened it at random."

He tilted his head. "I see. So you don't read history."

She straightened. "I read widely. No doubt you think a bracing book like that history is more appropriate entertainment than Gothic novels."

He was at a loss to explain her churlish change in tone. "I hadn't formed an opinion on the matter, but yes, I suppose I do."

She harrumphed and flounced over to the settee. "It probably upsets you to think of your muse reading something so unworthy as a novel."

His *what*?

"Each to his own taste, is my philosophy," he said.

She sat down and blinked up at him. "It is, really?"

"Generally," he added carefully.

She tilted her head, and he could have sworn mischief sparked in her eyes. "Perhaps you are more discriminating when it comes to the subject of poetry."

"No . . ."

She smirked. "But you don't deny you enjoy a good poem."

He tried to consider this. "Well . . . yes. I suppose I do." How tired he was of thinking of that subject, though. He moved closer, hoping to coax her away from the topic. "The house seems almost ready for the party."

She rolled her eyes. "Oh, yes. No one has been talking about anything else."

He grinned. "And what have you been thinking of?"

Her gaze stared long into his, until her eyes seemed like two deep pools that he would have loved to dive into headfirst. "Need you ask?"

His heart slammed against his ribs. That sounded almost like innuendo, like flirtation. He didn't know what the hell she was talking about, but as long as she kept up that purring tone, he was willing to play along. "Tell me," he said.

"I have had much to mull over." Her gaze broke and her cheeks stained red again. "No one has ever compared me to a dewdrop before."

He had to give his head a bracing shake to make certain he had heard correctly. Dewdrop? What was she talking about? He suddenly felt like an actor who had stepped onto a stage with the wrong dialogue memorized. From her coy manner, it almost seemed that she was dropping him a hint.

Yet the hint wasn't rattling anything familiar in his brain. *Dewdrop?*

Perhaps—maybe while he had been away at war—it had become the fashion to tell women that they resembled dewdrops. Damn. He should have boned up on this type of thing.

He stood at a loss for a few moments more, before finally giving in to impulse. She *was* rather like a dewdrop, he decided—a comely, enticing dewdrop. Her lips seemed that way, at any rate. He longed to taste their sweet warmth again.

Without asking leave, he sank down next to her onto the sofa and took her hands in his. "Abigail . . . I have long wanted to speak to you of a certain matter . . ."

Her eyes fluttered and then looked directly into his. "What matter is that, Nathan?"

"It is hard to know where to begin . . ."

Her gaze oozed sensuality. "Let me guess. I have disturbed the calm waters of your life . . ."

He had been tensed in concentration, but now he looked at her in surprise. "Yes. Exactly. Much has happened in this past month . . ."

"To me, too," she said in a rush, leaning towards him.

He could hardly think when he was near her. His mind became little better than a jumble of pointless words. All that was clear to him was that he wanted to hold her in his arms again. Then they would both know that they were meant to be with each other and that nothing else mattered.

He placed his hands on her arms with more gentleness than he would have thought himself capable of in that moment. Still, she gasped, and he let out a breath, too—her arms seemed so soft, so impossibly thin and delicate. And yet he knew she had strength. He pulled her to him, tired of waiting. Tired of talking, frankly.

"Abigail, I've dreamt of kissing you again."

Instead of a protest, her eyelids fluttered, and she leaned forward and boldly planted her lips on his. Such warmth! He groaned and brought her to his chest to deepen the kiss, to taste just a little more of her.

It was like having a dream come alive. Of course this was no dream, she was flesh and blood, not specter, and he had to work to keep his soaring desire in check. But he managed it—just barely. For this one moment, he wanted to show her just how powerfully she moved him.

He had expected some resistance, but received none. Abigail kissed him, opened her lips to his as if she desired him every bit as much as he did her. As if she had been waiting for him! She allowed him to skim his hands across her breast, and shivered deliciously as he closed a hand around a soft orb. Breathlessly she whispered his name.

Restraint, he told himself.

But in his mind, in that moment, the thing was decided. She was his. And she wanted him. How often in a man's lifetime did such a miracle come along? He would have to be a saint not to savor the moment for just a bit longer.

"Oh hell," he muttered, acknowledging that he was not now, nor had he ever been, a saint.

He sank back on the chaise and pulled her on top of him. She did not seem to mind. She sucked in a breath when he unbuttoned her bodice just enough to allow him access inside. Still she did not protest. Instead, her body reacted by pressing closer to him, and moving needfully, with a hint of sweet uncertainty, against him.

Growing bolder, he pulled her up so that his lips could taste one of the sweet exposed breasts. She gasped his name again and sank against him, clearly wanting more. Her hands clenched against him, and they rocked together slowly, heat swelling between them.

He felt sweat beading his brow as desire built inside

him. Finally, he had to force himself to push away before they reached a point of no return. Even if it killed him. And for a moment it felt as if it might.

He pushed away, fearing to speak lest she could detect his panting. Yet he could not leave her in silence. "Abigail, I suppose it is no secret how I feel now?"

"No," she said, with surprising calm. Her eyes met his evenly; she hadn't even bothered to clasp her bodice properly. "Not now."

"And you feel . . . ?"

She cast her eyes down modestly. "That should be no secret, either."

Oh God, he wanted her. So many emotions rushed through him—love, desire, relief. She loved him! She must. Which meant that all his worries about offending her with his suit were over. Sir Harlan's bizarre plan might have had wisdom behind it after all.

But he swore to himself then and there that he would do everything in his power to be a good husband to her. He would make a success of his life. And up until the moment of the ball, he would work to ensure that he could tell Sir Harlan that he would not need to touch the extravagant dowry.

He stood up in resolve. There was much to do yet. "I should go."

She reached out and took his hand. "I always marveled at the connection I felt to you, Nathan. Now I understand."

He nodded. God, he wanted to kiss her again.

"We have so much in common. Even our private pursuits . . ."

Right now it was that which they did not share in common that had him stirred up. He could still see the shadow of her breast and it was damn disturbing. "You might want to tidy your dress," he suggested, "in case anyone should walk in."

She colored and then grappled with buttons.

Nathan stood. "I must go. Of course I will see you again before the ball?"

"Of course," she said. She grinned as she saw him edging

towards the door. "Are you going to leave me anything this time?"

He frowned. He felt like giving himself a solid thwack. Why hadn't he brought her flowers, or some little gift? "I'm sorry—I hadn't expected . . ."

"That's all right. I'll still cherish your words."

"Oh." He hadn't been aware of saying anything very interesting. "And I will cherish your kiss, my beautiful Abigail," he said, feeling a little awkward as he left her.

He had never been too skillful in expressing himself in matters of love.

Abigail felt as if she were soaring—just as Nathan had described. Flying as high as Icarus. Only she *would* touch the sun—and why not? What could stop her? It wasn't only in books that love could cause such elation, such power, such unrivaled bliss.

And to think that when she first saw Nathan standing in her study, her first instinct was that he had been spying on her! She laughed at herself now—that self that seemed almost like another person entirely. She had been terrified that she had been discovered. And she had been perfectly ready to throw his own bad writing in his face, but then he had looked at her with those green eyes and melted her heart. How could she have been so defensive with such a vulnerable man? Years on her own had made her prickly. But the moment he had taken her in his arms, those lonely years had melted away.

She floated up the stairs. She wanted to look into a mirror, to see if anything about her had changed. She was sure she couldn't be the same Abigail she had seen reflected as she washed her face that morning. That Abigail had been unsure, but now she felt as if something marvelous had happened. As if a force had swelled and swerved her boat onto a different current into wild, adventurous seas.

My beautiful Abigail, he had called her.

It wasn't as inventive as his poetry, but the plain and

simple words had gone straight to her heart, touching her in a way that the poem had not.

She danced up the stairs, passing Violet, who was stomping up at a much slower pace.

"Where have you been?" Violet asked petulantly. "Why am I constantly being sent out to feed birds?"

"I have no idea," Abigail said.

Violet stared at her, then shook her head. "Abigail, I realize you set a certain blue-stocking pride in being careless about your dress, but you could at least take care to button yourself properly!"

Abigail laughed. It was true; her bodice was crooked. She quickly set to righting the problem.

"Your hands are shaking," Violet said. "What's the matter with you? You don't feel a chill, do you?"

Abigail whooped. "Everything's the matter with me, and nothing! Violet—how do you know if you're in love?"

Her sister rolled her eyes. "Why does everyone ask me that question?" she asked as they reached the top of the stairs. "Love is an overestimated emotion."

"But you must have felt love when you married Percy."

Violet's mouth turned down. "I married because it was such a perfect match. That is a duty a woman owes her family and the dignity of her own person."

Abigail had to suppress a giggle. What had happened on her settee was far from dignified . . . but it was wonderful just the same. "But what about when it comes to . . . well, the physical side of things?"

Violet shivered. "One does one's duty."

"Yes, but surely if one loves one's husband. Say, if you married the earl . . ."

Violet's face turned white. As if she had never given this matter any thought. "Please do not speak of Lord Clatsop in such a way, Abigail! I find it most disrespectful."

"Oh, Violet!"

Her sister frowned at her. "What on earth is the matter with you? You're behaving like Sophy."

"I suddenly understand Sophy," she admitted.

"It's this ball," Violet said, shaking her head mournfully.

"It will be better when it's all over and I can look forward to being the lady of Clatsop Castle. Then all of these trying details of life here will not bother me so much."

She would be the Countess of Clatsop, and all would be right with the world.

And maybe I'll have my soldier, Abigail thought in rare accord with Violet. Funny, she still thought of Nathan as more of a soldier than a poet.

Chapter Eleven

*Raffizzi Castle was eerily ablaze with light, an illu-
mination that would have been breathtaking had it
not been so extreme. Instead, Clara quivered at the
sight of the light blazing through the window, which
looked almost like a conflagration. It was for his lady
love he was throwing this ball, a last attempt to win
her heart. To prove that he was not the dark villain he
pretended to be.*

"Clara."

*Clara gasped at the sound of her own name spoken
by that familiar gravelly voice. Oh, how her foolish
senses thrilled to the sound, like a spaniel to its master's voice. But Rudolpho was not her master, nor
would he ever be.*

*When she turned, however, and saw the brilliance
in those green eyes illuminated by the house he had
lit for another, she wondered if he were not already
the master of her heart. "Yes sir?"*

"I want you," he said.

Her entire being thrilled at those words.

"To see to the ladies' wraps," he finished.

—The Prisoner of Raffizzi

On the day of the ball, Peacock Hall was in such an
uproar that Abigail barely recognized the place as her
usual quiet home. All the servants, and more importantly,
all the young relatives of the servants that had been temporarily engaged in service, scurried about mopping,

polishing, dusting, and re-dusting. Abigail had thought the hall looked clean already, but apparently her standards weren't up to Peabody's.

Guests had begun to arrive; the earl had come the night before. Violet's nerves were as taut as bowstrings, but she had charmed their honored guest throughout dinner the night before and now felt sure that she would have even better success at drawing the man out during the dance.

All the activity, even though none of it was being performed by herself, heightened Abigail's own sense of anticipation. And anxiety. She had never put so much thought into a party before. But since last seeing Nathan, she had been able to think of little else besides this night, and dancing with him, and looking up into his handsome face and feeling that delicious warmth that his presence brought her. He had disappeared again, which only heightened her anticipation.

She couldn't believe she felt this way about anyone; she had never expected to. These were feelings she wrote about, not lived herself. She had never hoped to find life at Peacock Hall as exciting as that experienced by her heroines. She had never expected a soldier-poet to stride into her home and steal away her heart.

Her dress was a rose lawn, perfectly suited to her hair and her complexion. It also set off her figure very well. She was pleased with the result, and she took pains to try to train her hair into a facsimile of an elegant yet simple fashion she had found in one of Sophy's magazines. With Tillie's help, she had some measure of success.

The maid beamed at her. "I never knew you to look so beautiful!" the girl exclaimed, looking at Abigail's reflection in the mirror. Then Tillie's face colored slightly and she stammered, "That is to say . . . well! You *do* look lovely. I'm sure everyone will say so . . ."

Abigail laughed. "Thank you. I feel like a new person, so it is only right that I should look like one."

Sophy came winging in, interrupting them. Whereas it seemed only a half hour ago that Abigail had spotted her tripping about in her riding habit, her little sister was now swathed in a pale primrose silk, smelled of garde-nias, and had her tight curls arranged dramatically about her head. The effortless effect amazed Abigail. How did she manage it?

The brightness of her attire, however, for once did not match her mood. "Oh, Abigail! I just saw Henrietta down-stairs. What are—" She stopped midsentence and took in Abigail's appearance. "Don't you look nice!"

"Thank you," Abigail said, ducking her head. She wanted Nathan to notice her, of course. That was the whole point. But the fact that everyone else would also notice the pains she was taking embarrassed her. She was glad to change the subject back to their cousin. "What were you saying about Cousin Hennie?"

"I was just wondering how I was going to manage to avoid her all evening."

Abigail rolled her eyes. "Sophy! She is our cousin."

"She's a headache." At Abigail's admonishing look, Sophy squared her shoulders. "You know it's true. She al-ways makes a bumble broth of things."

Henrietta did seem very able in the muddle-making department. At their last large party she had confused Violet's then-husband with the new curate, and had but-tonholed the heir to the marquess and relentlessly railed at him on her feelings about biblical texts and the state of the chapel's stained glass. The curate, a strait-laced widower, she later regaled with some slightly ribald jokes about matrimony she had read in comic prints from a paper in Sir Harlan's study.

When she learned of her mistake, poor Henrietta had fled the scene and not shown her face in public for two solid months. If the curate had not left for a larger parish in Sussex, Abigail wondered if Henrietta would ever have come out of seclusion.

"Still, you must be kind to her." Poor Henrietta was vir-tually all alone in the world; she lived with her very aged and always infirm great-aunt, Matilda, on the other side of the village. Great-aunt Matilda was considered very pecu-liar and this, no doubt, had rubbed off on Henrietta.

Also, Abigail was secretly hoping that she might convince her cousin to keep a close eye on Sophy this night. Obviously Violet had other things on her mind right now than Sophy's behavior, and Abigail herself feared she would be less than attentive to her younger sister's comings and goings.

"I'm not being mean to her by hiding from her, am I?" Sophy said. "As long as she doesn't know I'm hiding from her, I mean."

"Well no, but . . ."

Violet rushed into the room, nearly breathless. She wore a china blue silk dress that looked absolutely stunning.

At the sight of her middle sister, Violet was impressed by how well her grooming efforts this evening had turned out. "My goodness, Abigail! I am amazed!"

"Thank you." For the first time, thought Abigail, she didn't feel that she was as appealing as an old mop next to her sisters.

"And your hair!" Violet cried. "It isn't frizzing one bit."

"A first," Abigail conceded ruefully. "Is everything all right?" There was high color in Violet's cheeks, and before she had noted Abigail's appearance, she had appeared to be on the verge of saying something important.

"Just this! I can contain my secret no longer."

"Oh, Violet!" Sophy exclaimed, clapping her hands delightedly. "Did the earl finally propose?"

"No!" Violet waited a long moment before breaking into a smile and adding, "But he's going to."

Abigail drew back in surprise. The earl had seemed attentive to Violet the night before—indeed, it would have been impossible to ignore someone who was blazing so brightly—but she had not sensed that a proposal was imminent.

Sophy was delighted. Even though she did not like the earl—Abigail had heard her refer to him as *that old horror* and *a dead bore* and she had even once called him Lord *Catslop* within his hearing—she did like it when there was news.

And this was news. Astonishing news! Their sister really would be a countess!

"How do you know?" Abigail asked.

"I saw him shut up in the library with Father."

Abigail tried not to let her skepticism show. That two older men in a houseful of young ladies would seek out solitude in the library was not necessarily an indicator of matrimonial plans. Perhaps it just meant that one of them wanted to smoke a cigar in peace. "How can you possibly know what they are discussing in there?"

"Well . . ." Here Violet looked slightly uncomfortable. "It so happens that I was walking outdoors, thinking that the earl might enjoy some company, when I spotted him headed back inside. So exasperating that I missed him! I decided to hurry after him to tell him how much I myself enjoy walking, and nature, and all that claptrap, when just inside the hallway, I saw him come upon Father. There was a maid standing near them, and I gave her a half-crown to tell me what was said between them."

"Violet!" Abigail said, surprised that her sister would stoop to paying spies.

"What did they say?" Sophy asked eagerly.

Violet's smile was so wide that her sisters knew the half-crown expenditure had been worth every penny. "The earl told Father that he had something of the utmost importance to speak to him about."

"Oh." Abigail frowned.

"The *utmost* importance," Violet repeated.

"Those few words don't seem very definitive, though, do they?" Abigail asked.

Violet stared her down. Finally she blurted in disbelief. "I have never heard of anything so petty! You obviously don't want me to be a countess."

"That is simply false," Abigail said quickly. "What I meant to say was that, were your inference true, it would be excellent news. But the snippet of conversation the maid reported seems rather vague."

Violet blinked at her, and her face turned the color of

crimson that usually indicated she was about to do some yelling.

Abigail gulped. "Don't you agree, Sophy?"

Sophy, sensing danger, started creeping towards the door.

Violet looked as if she might explode, but Abigail was relieved of her status as most-vexing relative when Henrietta appeared. Henrietta did not knock (she never did; knocking was too bold a gesture), but instead opened the door slightly and peeked her head in. She had a habit of squinting and blinking, as though she needed glasses but chose, infuriatingly, not to wear them.

"I am not disturbing you, I hope?" Henrietta asked.

A collective gathering of breaths rippled through the room, and Abigail stood to receive their cousin. "Not at all, do come in."

Their cousin slipped inside, then managed to close the door with a bang that caused them all to jump. "I'm so sorry!"

"Never mind, Hen. How nice you look!" Abigail told her.

Henrietta was wearing a peach-colored dress that was surprisingly mature in its cut. She was forever appearing in pastels and ruffles unbecoming to a woman fast approaching her fourth decade. Though, truth be told, she had never seemed like a good candidate for ruffles. Even as a girl, she had possessed an awkward look that was unsuited to flounces or overly starched bows.

"Thank you," she said, beaming. An uncomfortable silence ensued.

Abigail cast about for something to say, since Violet and Sophy had fallen stubbornly mute, and settled on asking after Henrietta's great-aunt's health. "And how is—"

"You all look beautiful!" Henrietta blurted out. "Not that there's anything remarkable about that."

Abigail couldn't help laughing.

"That is to say," Henrietta stumbled on, "you always look pretty, don't you? Well, maybe not Abigail so much, but . . . I mean . . ."

They stared at her. Even Abigail had lost enthusiasm for helping the conversation along now.

Her lips pulled into a too-bright, gummy smile. "Well! What can I say? You're a perfect trio!"

The three sisters exchanged grimly amused glances. They might love each other, but none of them relished being indelibly associated with the others.

"Sit down, Hen," Abigail said, leading her to the chair she had just vacated. Her cousin always gave the impression of being on the verge of losing her balance, as if at any moment she might turn into a storm of unintentional destruction.

Henrietta eased into the chair, straightened, and somehow knocked Abigail's silver brush off the bureau. She retrieved it from the floor, then banged her wrist putting it back on the tabletop. It was astounding, Abigail thought, how someone so gauche and uncoordinated had managed to live so long without falling off a bridge or a sea cliff.

"And how is your great-aunt?" Abigail again attempted to ask when all the articles on her dressing table had stopped wobbling and she judged the danger past.

"Aunt Matilda is fine, thank you. She sends her love and was so sorry she couldn't come."

"You mean she actually considered it?" Sophy asked, aghast.

Violet gave her a stern kick that Abigail wholly approved of. "What Sophy meant, I'm sure, is that it is wonderful that your aunt should be in such a frame of mind that she would at least consider paying us a visit."

"Oh, she never would!" Hen said artlessly. "At least, she always said she would never step foot in the house as long as Sir Harlan lives."

Great-aunt Matilda was related to them through their mother, and like most members of that side of the family, she remained firmly in the camp that believed their Isabel could have done better, matrimonially speaking.

"Of course, that is most assuredly not a view I share," Hen hastened to add.

"Obviously," Sophy said, "or you wouldn't be sitting there now."

There was something in Sophy's tone that let it be known that it was her wish that Hen *wasn't* sitting there now.

"My!" Hen said. "All this to-doing. I should have known big things were happening when I received my invitation."

"What big things?"

"Well . . . isn't someone here to be congratulated?"

They regarded her with confusion.

"On their engagement?"

Sophy, Violet, and Abigail all exchanged quizzical glances. "What can you mean?" Sophy asked.

Hen looked flustered. But then, she looked flustered half the time. Her whole life was one conversational blunder after another. "I overheard your father saying something to one of the musicians. He was instructing the man what to play after the engagement was announced."

Sophy and Abigail swerved to gape at Violet. *She had been right!* Abigail would have expected Violet to collapse with emotion, but instead she regarded her cousin with what was, under the circumstances, an impressive dose of skepticism.

"You overheard this?" she asked sharply. "You swear? He said the word engagement?"

"Oh, yes, I'm certain."

"You did not misunderstand? For instance, he did not say 'dinner'?"

Hen shook her head. "Oh no. I heard correctly, I know, because I felt hurt that no one had told me. I am a relation . . ."

"We couldn't have told you," Abigail said. "None of us knew of any engagement."

Their cousin looked flummoxed. "That is strange . . ." The implication of Abigail's statement penetrated, and Hen's eyelids fluttered with surprise. "So I am the bearer of great tidings!"

Or false ones, Abigail feared.

You might have thought Violet, after hearing that the prize so long sought was finally within her grasp, would have danced with joy, or let out a shriek of triumph. Instead, she stood very still, a faraway look in her eye, and became utterly serene. In an instant, she seemed to grow a foot before their eyes. It was as if she had already ascended to the vaunted position of the Countess of Clatsop.

"I must go," she said solemnly. She turned to Henrietta, and graciousness oozed from her pores. "It's so good that you could come, cousin. We are all very happy to have you here. It means so much, especially to dear little Sophy. We are hoping that tonight you will keep an eye on her . . ."

The look of abject horror on Sophy's face was matched only by the look of flattered willingness on Hen's. Abigail had to lift a handkerchief to her lips to hide a laugh as Violet floated out of the room on a cloud of near-nobility.

She was practically floating herself. *Maybe love makes nobles of us all*, she thought (not a bad line to put in a book, she thought, tucking away the sentiment for future remunerative reference.) Of course, she wasn't expecting to receive a proposal from Nathan. Nevertheless, her imagination was happily-ever-aftering with a vengeance.

In the past weeks, she had started imagining herself as mistress of her own home (which looked suspiciously like The Willows, only newly landscaped with fresh paint and proper shutters), and having children and a very loving husband. These were things she hadn't dreamed of since before she had failed to attend her first Season. Since that time, all her imagination had gone into her writing. Her dreams of the future, when she had so indulged herself, had been concerned with all that she could do with the money she had saved. She dreamed of travel—to Venice or Egypt—and when she settled down to domesticity she would imagine a house by the sea in Devon, or a little place in London near Aunt Augusta. She tended to be alone in these dreams, save for her pen and ink and paper.

But now she was alone no longer—not even in her writing. She imagined finally confessing her secret identity to Nathan and seeing the delighted look on his face. Both writers! Of course, he'd had a low opinion of Gothic romances when he had no idea that she wrote such books, but once he discovered she was Georgianna Harcourt, how could he help but change his mind? It was the same with his poetry. At first perusal, she had been dismissive of his effort, but now every line of his poem was blazed across her heart.

As she heard the first strains of music down below, her body hummed with anticipation. A pair of green eyes, a dance . . . who knew what the night would bring?

"We should go," she said impatiently to the others.

"Oh! Yes indeed!" Hen jumped up, and the sound of a loud rip rent the air.

When Nathan heard the first notes from a violin, his heart sank. Where was Abigail? He had greeted Sir Harlan, had received a condescending bow from a regal looking Violet, but as yet he had not laid eyes on Abigail.

And he needed to see her. Desperately. He had returned late yesterday from his latest begging trip (where he had failed a second time to find financing for his venture), and it had been too late to see Abigail. He wanted to ask for her hand, but he needed to get her alone and explain about his financial state. He was also going to tell her about her father's proposal and, if she didn't annihilate him, he was going to tell her that he refused to spend her father's money on saving The Willows. He wanted to let her know that with her by his side, he felt there were no obstacles he could not overcome eventually.

His intention to arrive early this evening had been undermined by Freddy, who had dawdled like a girl before her first trip to Almack's.

Now Freddy was looking likewise downcast, though it wasn't for lack of sighting Abigail. His clothes, so carefully chosen and the cause of Nathan's woe, consisted of a somber black jacket and pants, with only an orange silk vest giving a hint of his recent sartorial excesses. Perhaps the prospect of dire poverty had changed him for the better . . . despite his continuing poetry-writing mania.

Several nights ago, Nathan had awakened to find his brother outside, on the lawn, writing by candlelight in his nightgown and cap. He said moonlight put him in the writing mood. Nathan assumed that meant he was trying to capture the voice of one who is vision-impaired, sleep-deprived, and chilled.

"I don't see Sophy," Freddy said, shifting from one foot to the other. From his hangdog expression, you would have thought there was no one else in the ballroom to speak to or dance with.

The truth was quite the opposite. There was a throng in attendance, all unknowingly there to hear of Nathan's engagement. Nathan, who had faced pressure during battle, started to sweat as he never had before. *Where was Abigail?*

Everyone of note from the area had turned out, as had a few guests from even farther afield, such as the Earl of Clatsop. Lord Overmeer was in attendance, along with his oldest son, Henry. Many pretty faces passed before them, whom Nathan vaguely knew. The Misses Simmons and Estella Emrick, for example. Nathan considered asking one of them to dance, but couldn't work up enthusiasm. Like his brother, he wanted to save the first dance for his special lady. There was Ann Mudge across the hall, though, looking very forlorn in her spectacles and a bright green dress that overwhelmed her slight figure. Nathan was about to take pity on her, when suddenly the earl swooped in and claimed Miss Mudge for a waltz.

Sir Harlan caught his eye. It would have been hard to miss him, considering the man was practically windmilling his arms to get Nathan's attention. When their gazes met, Sir Harlan pointed to Violet, who was standing next to him, red-faced and unclaimed. Nathan took a deep breath, looked desperately around for an alternative, then saw—to his delight—Lord Overmeer approach and subsequently lead Violet onto the dance floor.

Sir Harlan frowned in irritation.

Nathan turned to Freddy. "You should be dancing."

"So should you," Freddy volleyed back. But in the next instant his face lit up. "Here she is!"

Nathan turned . . . and there she was. Not who Freddy was talking about, of course—he obviously had eyes only for Sophy—but Abigail was with her, as well as a woman Nathan recognized vaguely as a family connection of the Wingates.

For a moment, Nathan felt as if his heart had stopped. He had long thought Abigail was the most underappreciated and most attractive of the three Wingate sisters, but her appearance tonight fixed his opinion in stone. No other woman in the room could touch her for beauty. The deep rose color of her dress brought out the tawny glow in her cheeks, and made the deep brown of her hair seem lush and exotic. Her ample curves were set off by the dress's fitted bodice and loose underdress. He rushed forward.

Not as fast, however, as Henry Overmeer, who had been standing by the door. He bowed to Abigail, who looked rather astonished, and led her onto the dance floor.

She caught Nathan's gaze during a turn a few moments later; she was laughing, and her eyes seemed to catch the light prisming off the chandeliers. She waved at Nathan over Henry Overmeer's shoulder.

Nathan gritted his teeth. Next dance. He could be patient.

Freddy and he reached Sophy and Henrietta. "I worried you weren't coming down . . . that you were sick . . ."

Sophy rolled her eyes. "We were on our way ages ago, but then Cousin Hen stepped on her hem and ripped her skirt!"

Henrietta fluttered in embarrassment. "So clumsy of me! So kind of the others to wait . . ."

Sophy flicked her cousin an irritated glance that let the gentlemen know that waiting had not been her idea.

"It is fortunate for us that you were able to salvage your hem and come down to the dance."

"I'm not really here to dance," Henrietta said. "I am just here as chaperone for dear Sophy and her sisters."

Nathan smiled and nodded absently; he was looking out at the dance floor.

"I am well past the age of being a belle," Henrietta continued with modesty, "though of course I enjoy dancing."

"Do you indeed?" Nathan asked, catching Abigail laughing with Henry. His teeth clenched.

"I adore it."

When Nathan turned back to his little group, he found Sophy and Freddy staring at him impatiently, and Henrietta blinking at him in anticipation. Nathan felt a moment of panic; the waltz was ending. Surely he would be able to ask Abigail . . .

But in the next moment, he caught her agreeing to a *second* dance with Henry Overmeer. Henry—who was fat, and drank too much, and had a reputation to equal his father's!

He gritted his teeth, turned back to Henrietta, and bowed. "Would you do me the honor . . . ?"

Freddy and Sophy released their breaths, and followed Nathan out onto the dance floor.

Cousin Henrietta proved a difficult partner. Her feet seemed to have minds of their own. All her attention seemed focused on Sophy, who had disappeared into the crush of dancers.

"I am supposed to be looking out for her," Henrietta said worriedly as she stepped on Nathan's toe for the third time.

He grimaced. He needed a chaperone for his feet. "I believe, since the dance she began with my brother has not yet ended, that she is probably still with him."

"Ah!" Hen exclaimed, clearly admiring his powers of deduction. "And what kind of young man is your brother? Trustworthy, do you think?"

"Trustworthy during a waltz in a crowded room, definitely."

Certainly more trustworthy than your feet, he added silently.

The moment the dance ended, Henrietta flitted off in

search of her charge, who was darting quickly towards the opposite end of the room. Nathan hurried toward the punch bowl, where he hoped he could intercept Abigail. She, however, was stopped a few steps short of the refreshments table by a gentleman with a green coat.

Nathan couldn't believe his luck. And he was beginning to feel a little annoyed. Couldn't she refuse a dance for his sake? How was he ever going to propose to her if she kept romping away with other men?

He looked up and saw Violet sucking on a cup of punch. Her face was twisted in annoyance.

"Something wrong?" he asked.

"No," she said, then quickly sighed and said, "yes! It's the earl. Miss Mudge is completely dominating his attention. The poor man hasn't gotten a moment to take his breath, much less ask me to dance. And I'm sure he's been trying to get away from her. He has something very important to say to me."

For once, Nathan could sympathize with Violet's plight.

"I caught his eye five minutes ago as he was dancing with Miss Mudge. He seemed positively bored," Violet said.

Nathan glanced at the earl, whose head was tilted back in a laugh at something Miss Mudge had said. "He does not look bored now."

She put her cup down. "Of course he has to be polite to her. Poor thing. She is such a sad person—a sort of amateur naturalist or some such thing. Imagine a woman wasting her time that way!"

Sir Harlan appeared. "What's the matter with you two— I haven't seen you dance yet!"

Violet looked at her father as if he had lost his mind. "The earl is with Miss Mudge!"

Sir Harlan blinked. "So he is. Well! I hear she's a birder herself."

Violet snorted. "That would complete the picture!"

"I was dancing with Cousin Henrietta," Nathan told Sir Harlan.

Violet clucked in sympathy.

Sir Harlan rolled his eyes and waved his hands in front of him, as if he were playing an invisible concertina. "I meant you hadn't danced *together*."

Violet and Nathan looked up, both startled by the idea . . . and the fact that they would both look rude to refuse to do so now.

Sir Harlan poked him in the ribs and Nathan drew a deep breath. "Would you care to dance, Mrs. Treacher?"

Violet sighed. "Oh, all right."

Together, they managed to endure two sets. Both were ready to call it quits after one, but then the earl claimed Miss Mudge for the gavotte, and while Nathan was listening to Violet's outraged astonishment—to think of that little nobody so completely taking up the earl's time—another man darted in to partner Abigail. Inertia kept Violet and Nathan together, yet from the sidelines, Sir Harlan waved at them ecstatically.

Nathan vowed he would take no chances when this dance ended. So he situated himself and Violet as close to Abigail and her partner as he could, even when it meant bumping Henry Overmeer and a Miss Abernathy out of their place in the lineup.

Abigail laughed at him as the music started. "That was very bold of you."

"I intend to keep my eye on you this time," he growled at her urgently. "I must speak to you!"

The dance took them out of earshot for a while, but Nathan was able to look, entranced at the high color in Abigail's cheeks. It reminded him of that day he had first seen her at the pond.

"Isn't this fun?" she asked, laughing, as she danced by him.

He gnashed his teeth. *Fun!* He didn't have time for fun. He needed to propose.

Violet glared at him. Even though she did not want to be dancing with him, and even though her attention was as focused on the earl as his was on Abigail, she did not appreciate being ignored by her dance partner.

As the dance ended, she traced a curtsy at him. "Your

dance technique hasn't improved much in eight years," she said.

"Neither has your sunny disposition," Nathan shot back. In spite of themselves, they both laughed.

Then Abigail was suddenly in their midst—Nathan's jockeying for position had paid off. He grabbed her arm so she could not escape.

"Did I miss a joke?" Abigail asked.

"Nathan and I were just traveling down memory lane," Violet said.

"A bumpy ride," Nathan agreed.

"Oh! The earl!" Violet exclaimed. The man, for the moment, was without partner, and Violet galloped away.

"Lord Clatsop finally came free," Nathan explained to Abigail, looking at last into those brown eyes he had been seeking all evening. "And you are as elusive as the earl tonight."

"Me?" she laughed, fanning herself, though her eyes were twinkling mischievously. "I have been here all evening—since I was able to drag Henrietta down."

"Ah, yes. It would have been better for my feet had you left her upstairs."

Abigail laughed. "Poor Hen, she doesn't come to many dances. And I am sure I have never enjoyed one so much."

"And I have never enjoyed one so little, until now," Nathan said.

"Why?"

"Because I have been attempting to dance with someone who was claimed each time I turned to ask her."

Abigail smiled at him. "I am available now."

"Good—let's walk."

"Oh, no—let's dance! I'm having such a good time. I never knew dances could be such fun!"

Nathan obliged her through a country dance—not his favorite. Of course the orchestra would not be playing a waltz when he finally claimed his desired partner. And yet there was something pleasing in being able to watch her turn and pose, and to briefly have her hand in his and his arm at her waist. And the exertion made her cheeks glow.

When the dance was over, he whisked her outside.

"You are a good dancer," she said, then added with a wry smile, "better than Henry Overmeer."

"It helps to be eighty pounds lighter and not suffering the early stages of gout."

She sighed and looked dreamily up at the sky overhead as if she had never seen stars twinkling before.

"I should have asked you if you would like some punch," Nathan said, reprimanding himself. She had been dancing so much, she probably wanted refreshment.

"Oh, no," she said. "I would rather sit on this bench a moment and talk."

No need to ask him twice. He settled next to her and put his hand over hers. She smiled at him, causing his heart to stir. It was time to speak his piece. He had to, soon, before Sir Harlan came scuttling out saying that it was time to make the announcement.

He turned to her, half-expecting to plunge ahead with his proposal.

"I was reading Wordsworth today," Abigail said. Then she paused, as if this statement would have special significance to Nathan.

"Wordsworth?" Damn. That was not what he had hoped to talk about. He couldn't see a way to go nimbly from Wordsworth to marriage.

"Yes." She laughed. "You must know him."

He nodded, distractedly. "Of course . . ."

"You're practically the same person."

He squeezed her hand. "Abigail . . ."

"Come now, confess. I don't mind. It's what made me think that we are kindred souls."

His pulse kicked up. "Do you think that?" he asked.

"I'm so glad, because . . ." Something she had said penetrated his brain and pulled him up short. Wordsworth. Kindred souls. What in heaven's name was she talking about?

"Perhaps you'll think I'm very forward speaking that way," she rushed on. "But sometimes one feels one must be bold."

"Exactly," Nathan said. This was as good an opening as

any. "That is why I wanted especially to speak to you now. You see, Abigail, there is something very important on my mind."

She stared off dreamily. " 'Prometheus could not know the labor it takes to hold my tongue!' "

Nathan frowned. There was a vital connection missing in this conversation. "Abigail, if you would just let me speak . . ."

" 'Icarus cannot have known how high I have soared.' "

Suddenly it occurred to him that what she was spouting at him was not conversation, but poetry. Icarus. Prometheus. Nathan groaned. "Where is all this awful stuff coming from?"

She recoiled slightly. "I beg your pardon?"

"The craze for bad poetry is infecting the land, I think," he said, laughing. "That sounds exactly like the nonsense that Freddy has been writing."

Abigail went still. "Freddy?"

Sir Harlan's head appeared over a nearby bush and he started making *tss!* noises through his teeth. Nathan looked up and rolled his eyes. Of all the times . . .

"Excuse me for a moment, Abigail." Nathan sped over to where Sir Harlan was. "Yes?"

"My boy—the time is come. We're about to go in to supper. Shall I find Violet? She seems to have disappeared . . ."

"No, no. That is—" He cast a glance back to where Abigail was still sitting on the bench, frowning at her shoes. "My choice is not Violet. It is Abigail."

Sir Harlan drew back in surprise, and then he, too, ducked a glance around Nathan to see if they were speaking of the same person. "Are you sure? I thought you were set on Violet . . ."

"No, it's Abigail," he said. "It always has been. I love her."

Sir Harlan appeared uncomfortable with such a bold, emotional statement. Uncomfortable, but at least convinced. He nodded. "If that is your choice, then that is what matters." He clapped Nathan on the shoulder. "Congratulations. Now hurry inside. I want to make the announcement."

"Yes—if you'll just wait a moment, I just need to speak to her."

Sir Harlan laughed. "Yes, yes, but don't tarry. Just spit it out! She'll be delighted, I'm sure. I had one of the musicians practice a trumpet fanfare for the occasion."

The old man turned and hurried back inside, bits of leaves still stuck to his sleeve.

Nathan returned to the bench. It was do or die now. But he felt encouraged. He clasped Abigail's hand again. It was cold. "Are you feeling all right?"

She blinked at him, as if she hadn't noticed him rejoin her on the bench. "What?"

"Your hand is like ice."

She looked down at her hand in his as if it were a bit of foreign matter attached to the end of her arm.

"It doesn't matter."

"We will go inside soon. In fact, it is imperative that we do." He cleared his throat. "I am so glad you said what you did about our being kindred souls."

She frowned up at him. "You've never written any poetry?"

He shook his head. "Not a line. Abigail, the truth is this. Ever since I first met you . . . or no, ever since I first saw you, that day at the pond . . ."

Usually the mere mention of the pond would raise her hackles, but this time it didn't even raise an eyebrow. And her mind remained firmly, exasperatingly lodged on the subject of verse. "Then you've never considered yourself to have a muse?"

He let out a breath in frustration. "Good heavens no! That sort of crackbrained thing is what Freddy gets in his head. Sophy almost ran over him on her horse one day and he's been addle-pated ever since."

"Sophy . . ."

From inside, a trumpet blared.

Nathan jumped up. He felt beads of sweat on his brow. This was not how he imagined the night proceeding!

"Abigail, if you'll just listen. We must go inside now. Your father is making a very important announcement."

She merely shrugged her shoulders. "I know. It's the engagement announcement for Violet and the Earl of Clatsop."

Now Nathan knew he was in trouble. He hauled her to her feet, startling her out of her reverie. "Abigail, we must go in. Now. The announcement is of an engagement, but not of your sister to the earl."

She frowned up at him, bristling at his manhandling. "Then whose?"

"Yours," he said. "To me."

Chapter Twelve

Poor Fiona! She could hardly credit what was happening. Her greatest hope—to be the professed love of the man whose dark eyes made her tremble with desire—had come true in the most unwelcome fashion. She felt less like a bride than a pawn in a dangerous game. When she looked into the onyx eyes of her betrothed, she saw only a raw need to possess her. Yet Fiona did not tremble now.

—Count Orsino's Betrothal

Later Abigail would have no recollection of how she returned to the house from the garden. Did she walk of her own volition, or did Nathan have to drag her? She couldn't say. Nor could she remember specifically what he had said to her during that time. Words played through her mind, none of which seemed to make any sense. Wedding. Mortgages. Love. Wool.

Her limbs had gone dead. Her brain had gone numb.

Coming off the whirlwind feeling of joy of attending and actually enjoying herself at a party, this was quite a slap in the face. *Engagement!* Were they mad? She was still trying to wrap her mind around the fact that Nathan was not, and had apparently never been, a writer of love poems. All her little castles in the air were just that—figments of her overactive imagination. The man was not her soul mate, or even a kindred spirit. He did not care for poetry. He had never soared as high as Icarus or looked at her as an inspiration.

Indeed, he sneered at the very idea, just as he had sneered at silly Gothic novels written by women.

He cared about sheep. Woolen mills.

And then she was standing in front of everyone on the staircase leading down into the ballroom, with Sir Harlan on one side of her and Nathan on the other. Her father was beaming as he announced his great pleasure in the fact that the major had asked him for the hand of his daughter Abigail, and that he had agreed.

No mention was made of what she thought about the matter. Apparently it was assumed that she would be ecstatic.

The orchestra played a waltz, and Nathan—her betrothed, unbelievably—pulled her down the steps and began to dance with her. Eyes widened as they passed, and it seemed like the whole world was smiling, except Abigail. Her body felt as if it belonged to someone else—some other girl whom she was watching from the crowd. Some lucky girl who had just gotten engaged. Not her, surely.

She danced, though she wasn't sure how she managed to make her feet move. Her brain was completely consumed in the overwhelming task of trying to make sense of the predicament she found herself in. Which was the predicament she had dreamed of finding herself in—Nathan's betrothed. But not like this! Never like this.

Her mind raced through the events of the past few weeks. She had known that Nathan was up to something, but she had never dreamed . . .

"Abigail, please say something . . ."

The words were Nathan's. The first he had spoken since the announcement.

She forced herself to meet his eyes. "What would you have me say?"

"That you are happy."

She blinked at him. Could he be serious? Could the man actually believe that a young lady, even one who had been on the shelf for what some would call a worrisome amount of time, would be enthusiastic about being tricked into an engagement this way?

"I am not happy," she said when she finally trusted her voice not to shriek at him. "I am the very opposite of happy. Were I not so perplexed there would be no end to my anger. However did you convince my father to agree to this?"

He drew back. "But I told you—it was all your father's idea."

The words sent little pinpricks down her spine. "My father's?"

"Yes, because he has the mortgage on The Willows."

So they were back to mortgages again. Abigail wished they could stop dancing—she wasn't good enough at it to be able to dance and wrap her mind around her situation at the same time. Yet she knew the moment they stopped dancing, she would be besieged by well wishers. For the rest of the evening she would be public property, the center of attention. Something she had never wanted to be.

And now Nathan was telling her . . . well, she could hardly credit it. "You are telling me that *my father*—" A father who sometimes barely seemed to remember that she existed at all, she could have added here. "—thought you should ask me to marry you?"

"Well, yes . . . that is, not you specifically. He wanted me to marry any one of you."

Her jaw dropped.

In reaction to her look of horror, he added quickly, "But naturally there was no question in my mind. No question at all. From the moment I first met you, I knew that you were the sister I preferred."

He *preferred*?

So she was merely the best of three?

Now she remembered that odd night when Nathan was first invited to dinner. Her father had exhorted Abigail to look nice . . . but he had told them *all* to be on their best behavior. And this was why! She had gone for a walk to the pond, and then met Nathan . . . And then that night they had all been paraded before him like a line-up of yearling fillies at auction. No wonder she had come out well—she had given him a preview at the pond!

Abigail groaned.

Nathan looked uncomfortable. She suspected he would have shuffled his feet if the waltz had allowed for it. "Surely you must know how I have come to feel about you in these past weeks."

Though she had been completely lost in thought, her head snapped up now and she focused on him intently. "What I sensed was a fiction, because you have been false from the beginning. I knew you had an ulterior motive for coming to Peacock Hall so frequently, but I never guessed it was to secure a matrimonial prospect!"

"I know it *sounds* unseemly . . ."

"Unseemly!" she piped up in agreement. "Unseemly and base! Did you simply decide one day that it was time to find a wife? Did it seem handy to you that there were three unattached ladies just down the road?"

Perhaps her voice grew too heated, for a few heads turned around to peer at the couple curiously.

"Abigail . . ." Nathan said under his breath.

"For that matter, why were we the lucky house you chose? There are other single females in the county. Surely you could have chosen another house to stalk. Tell me, was it the fact that this one afforded you three females to choose from, or was it simply a matter of proximity?"

"You are angry—but quite unreasonable."

"*I* am unreasonable? And yet it is perfectly normal for a man to have an engagement announced to a lady to whom he has never even proposed?"

"I was attempting to, out in the garden," he said in his defense. "But you kept going on about poetry."

It was as if he had poked a bruise. "Oh yes! Well, I am surprised you did not simply change the subject, since poetry is so distasteful to you."

"I do not understand this sudden interest in verse," Nathan said. "That is all."

"And I do not understand your sudden mania for matrimony."

He rolled his eyes. "Abigail, if you would calm down for a moment and listen, I have been trying to explain. It all started with the mortgages."

She shook her head. These mortgages! She had never thought about things like this in her life, and now he was trying to connect them somehow to their engagement? "Why do you keep spouting off about your mortgages?"

"Because it is the reason your father cited for my need to marry."

More slowly this time, he began explaining what had happened when he returned from the war and spoke with his attorney Mr. Arbogast. Then he detailed his first meeting with Sir Harlan, the day he had met Abigail at the pond. She listened to it all intently, though every word caused her anguish.

"Do you mean to say that you were *blackmailed* into asking me to marry you?" she asked Nathan.

"Initially it seemed that way to me, but certainly I wouldn't have gone through with the plan had I not developed such a fond attachment to you."

A fond attachment born of blackmail. Abigail was less than soothed by this idea.

Her father must have gone mad! She looked over at him, and Sir Harlan grinned and waved at her. Happy with the outcome of his scheme, obviously.

Inconceivable!

She jerked her gaze back up at Nathan, who was now spluttering on about the problems of financing a wool factory.

A troubling thought scratched at the back of her mind.

Sophy came dancing up to her in Freddy's arms and tried to congratulate her.

She was, of course, ecstatic. Anyone would have thought she was the lucky little lady. But, as Abigail had remarked before, Sophy loved news of any kind. "Oh, Abigail! Why did you not tell us that this was in the works?"

Freddy, Abigail noticed, seemed to sense the tension in the air and was regarding her more somberly. He barely managed a nod and a smile for his brother. Had he known the circumstances of this happy event?

"I had no idea myself," Abigail said through gritted teeth.

"A sudden engagement!" Sophy said, tossing her head back, oblivious to any troubles. "How romantic!" She quickly reached over and pinched Abigail playfully on the arm. "I'll never feel sorry for you again!"

She danced away on a cloud of vicarious happiness.

Nathan stared down at Abigail, and though his green eyes still had the power to make her heart flutter, she had decidedly mixed feelings about his power over her now. And she couldn't get an uneasy thought out of her head. Where had her father gotten such an outrageous idea?

On one level it didn't seem outrageous to her at all. It seemed strangely familiar.

"I wish that we could start over," Nathan said. "I wish I could meet you again, like this, at a dance, and woo you the normal way. But of course that did not happen, and I am a practical enough man to realize that one cannot turn back the clock. I just know how I feel about you, and that you certainly did not seem immune to me the last time we were alone together in your little study."

Another groan escaped her. "But I didn't know what was afoot in that scheming brain of yours. That you were not flattering me from affection, but out of desperation."

"Not so," he said. "I was only desperate to kiss you." He leaned close to her ear. "As I am at this very moment."

She drew as far back as she could without injury to her neck. "Desperate to manipulate me."

He appeared exasperated. As if she were wronging *him*. "I understand your being upset at the means by which we were thrown together. But are you really so unhappy at the outcome?"

Unhappy! That was too simple a word for how she felt. She felt betrayed—a victim of an elaborate scheme to make a fool of her. It was as if she suddenly found herself one of the hapless heroines of her own silly stories—the ones Nathan found so unworthy. Suddenly, her feet stopped.

Nathan's brow clouded with lines. "What is the matter? Are you faint?"

Perhaps he thought she was about to pass out from anger.

But in fact she had gone dizzy for another reason entirely. For, like a lightning bolt, it struck her why her plight seemed so familiar. A blackmailing scheme had occurred in her last book, *Count Orsino's Betrothal.* In fact, it was similar to the point of eeriness to the situation she found herself in! Suspicion shot through her that she would not have been able to credit if it had not been for something else that had happened recently. Her father had also used one of her plot devices in blackmailing Violet to go to the picnic!

She glanced up at Sir Harlan. Could it be? Had he read *Count Orsino's Betrothal*—and decided to pattern their lives after her book?

She lifted her hand to rub her temple.

Nathan supported her at her waist. "Abigail, dearest, do you need to lie down?"

Perhaps it was the *dearest* that did her in. All her life she had wondered what it would be like to have a man call her by such an endearment and to be tenderly at her side in moments of injury. She had almost given up on the idea of having her own hero. But now here was one—very able—and she could only flinch at the sound of his whispered *dearest.* To have won a man through the device of her father's blackmail was horrible. To think that she had laid the roadmap for such a scheme—plotted her own undoing—was almost beyond comprehension.

In fact, she had to see it with her own eyes.

"I must go," she said, hurrying off.

"Abigail, wait."

Nathan trotted at her side while the guests on the dance floor parted for them like the Red Sea had parted for Moses. Murmurs followed them. She breathed a sigh of relief when she had made it to the hall leading to her father's study, but then she was stopped by Violet, who *did not* congratulate her. Her eyes were red, and she seemed more shaken than Abigail herself was.

"Why didn't you tell me!" Violet cried.

"I had no idea."

Violet was clearly not convinced. "You let me go on about the earl! And yet you probably knew the truth all along."

"I knew nothing," Abigail said.

Not that Violet was listening to her. She was too consumed by her own tragedy to take in anyone else's. "The matter of the utmost urgency the earl wanted to speak to father about was the peacocks!"

"Peacocks?" Abigail asked.

Violet nodded violently, on the verge of tears. "He offered Father money for Garrick and Mrs. Siddons!" Her lip quivered. "F-f-five hundred pounds!"

The poor woman was on the verge of a breakdown.

"Oh, where is Peabody?" Violet asked, casting her teary eyes up to the ceiling. "Why does he have to be busy tonight of all nights?"

"Why do you need Peabody?" Abigail asked.

"Because he alone would understand!"

Abigail frowned up at Nathan. "Please stay with my sister. There is something I need to see to."

Before she could turn around, she saw Violet collapse gratefully against Nathan's chest.

Abigail rushed into the library and shut the door. She simply had to know whether her suspicions were true. She ran to her father's cabinet and tugged on the door. It was locked.

She took the poker from the fireplace and ran back to the cabinet. At that moment, Nathan came in, followed by Violet. "What are you doing?"

"Investigating!" Abigail said, huffing as she tried to slip the tip of the poker underneath the small lip of the cabinet door.

"You'll break it."

She arched a glance at him. "That is precisely the point."

"But—"

Before he could stop her, Abigail slipped the poker edge in and gave it a shove that sent the antique lock flying. So much for the heirloom cabinet, she thought with a moment of regret. She opened the door and looked in amazement at what she had uncovered.

"Have you taken leave of your senses?" Nathan asked, staring with her at the row of books. "What were you looking for?"

She gestured limply toward the shelf, which contained the entire *oeuvre* of Georgianna Harcourt, as well as some better-known authors that were Abigail's inspiration. Even some of the books that Aunt Augusta had sent her all those years ago were there. She had wondered what had happened to them!

Sir Harlan burst through. "What is going on here?" he bellowed. "Why aren't you all with the guests?"

Before he could quite take in what was happening, the weeping Violet threw herself against him. "Oh, Father— I'm so unhappy! Why did you not tell me that the earl's interest was only in those smelly birds?"

"What?" Sir Harlan frowned. "*Smelly*? I'll have you know—"

"Father!" Abigail said angrily. "Why are these books hidden in this cabinet?"

Sir Harlan looked from one daughter to the other, as if he were under siege. He crossed the room as best he could with a hysterical Violet attached to him. When he got a look at his uncovered bookshelves, his expression turned sheepish. "Oh . . . those are just novels."

"Gothic novels." She glared at Nathan. "Silly women's stories."

Sir Harlan grumbled, "Some of them are quite good. Surprisingly."

"You obviously think so since you have started using them as a design for our lives."

He was taken aback that she had found him out. "I just borrowed an idea here or there . . ."

Abigail let out an exasperated huff. "Father! How could you?"

Sir Harlan shifted uncomfortably, but he didn't seem to understand the wellspring of her anger. He was still trying to justify reading Gothic novels. "Well, you see, after your mother died, I was so lonely. It seemed for years I rattled around this old house missing her. Then one day, I found a few of these books lying around, and they took my mind off my loneliness for a while. They're rather enjoyable, really."

Those books seemed to have had transformative power over many lives, Abigail thought.

"So when I read the one about the old widower prince who wants grandchildren . . ."

"*Count Orsino's Betrothal,*" Abigail said, having forgotten that the old man she had created was indeed a lonely old widower. She had only remembered that he was a conniving old prince.

"That's the one," he said, brightening. "You know it, then?"

She bit her tongue. "A little."

"Well then! I couldn't help thinking that I and that old fellow had a bit in common, you see."

"Blackmail is one thing in fiction . . . but this!"

Violet lifted her head. "Blackmail?"

Abigail hesitated to tell her sister the whole sad truth of the one moment Violet might have envied her for, but why lie? It was all bound to come out sooner or later. "Father blackmailed Nathan into asking for my hand."

"The decision to ask for Abigail was mine," Nathan declared.

Just the fact that he was having to clarify this point broke Abigail's heart.

Abigail had not been certain how her sister would react, but she was gratified to see Violet move swiftly to her side, clearly offended. "Father!" she cried, staring at him in horror.

Sir Harlan was decidedly shamefaced. "Of course, it does seem a little underhanded when Abigail puts it so bluntly . . ."

Violet shook her head and scolded, "Why did you not blackmail *the earl*?"

So much for sisterly camaraderie. Abigail let out a strangled cry. "Why should anyone be blackmailed into marriage?" she said hotly. "It's barbaric, it's insufferable, and
I won't stand for it!"

Unable to bear the sight of Nathan's face, she ran for the
door. But before she had shut it behind her, she heard her
father say, "Damme! I believe that's exactly what the girl
says in *Count Orsino*!"

Heaven only knew what they said about her absence
from the ball. Probably people assumed that the reclusive
spinster would be so overwhelmed by her good fortune
that she needed time to recover from the excitement. That
thought alone made Abigail seethe. No doubt everyone believed that tonight was Abigail's dream come true, that she
had secretly been dreaming of such a moment when she
would be swept away by a handsome gentleman . . .

And perhaps she *had* been dreaming of such a moment. Secretly. She had just never imagined the moment
unfolding—for herself, at least—in such a bizarre fashion. It was as if her dream had turned to a nightmare in
the blink of an eye.

After arriving in her room, Abigail heard from no one. Violet, absorbed in her own troubles, did not follow her to
commiserate, and of course Sophy would have to be dragged
away from a dance where there were young men present.
The music downstairs did not stop for another hour, and
after that, no one came up to wish her good night, except
Tillie, who gingerly tendered her congratulations.

"I'd like to think that the hair had something to do with
it, Miss."

Abigail nodded sadly. "I would have liked to think that,
too."

When Tillie was gone and she was alone, Abigail found
herself resenting her solitude. If only she had a confidante—
someone she could talk to. But there was no one. She wished
Aunt Augusta had shown up for the ball. If she had been
here when her father's scheme came to light, what fireworks

there would have been! Aunt Augusta would never have sanctioned such barbaric goings-on, Abigail thought heatedly.

She would like to think *someone* cared about her.

As she was preparing for bed, she heard a noise and looked down to see a piece of paper slipped under her door. She picked it up and read it cautiously. The note was from Nathan, though the handwriting was unfamiliar to her. (Naturally, since she had mistaken the handwritten poem of Freddy for his . . .)

Dearest Abigail,

Abigail harrumphed. Calling her dearest! That took cheek.

I hope you will forgive the ill-planned events of this evening and remember only the fact that I care deeply for you and hope we might yet come to an understanding.

An understanding that she wanted absolutely nothing more to do with him, perhaps.

I plan to call on you tomorrow morning to beg you to be mine, despite the bumbling manner this courtship has proceeded thus far. Until then, I am pledged to be ever yours,
Nathan

She tossed the ridiculous letter on her dressing table, circled the room once, and then picked it back up. It was imperative that she read it again, if only to confirm that its content was as outrageous as she had thought the first time around. It was.

He had very nice handwriting, though.

But a little overly tidy, she decided on second thought. There was something cold-blooded about it.

She read the short note a third time, just for good measure, then slapped it gently against her palm. So he considered himself engaged, did he? Well, she would just have to convince him that he was not engaged! Not as far as she was concerned.

Coming by tomorrow morning. How cunning of him. He probably reasoned that by tomorrow morning all her anger and hurt would have dissipated and she would be anxious to receive his addresses again. He might even think that she would have spent the night reading and rereading his silly note, being swayed by the vow of remaining ever hers.

She tossed the note in a drawer and slammed it shut.

She had a good mind not to even be here when he came sniffing around tomorrow. That would show him how swayable she was!

The trouble was, there was nowhere to go at Peacock Hall where she could not be hunted down. Her hopes sank. How could she face him?

More important, how could she refuse him to his face? It was the cowardly route, she knew, but if she could simply write him a letter—she was so much more adroit with the written word than with real life—without having the prospect of having to speak to him in person. Or look upon his face . . .

She was determined that under the circumstances she could not marry him, now or ever. The taint of blackmail would always be there between them. But she wasn't sure her determination couldn't be weakened by honeyed words purred in that gravelly voice of his, or staring up into those eyes, or a kiss bestowed at a choice moment . . .

She feared there was nowhere far enough away that she could escape the memory of his kisses.

Unless, perhaps she were to follow her dream and run away to Egypt . . . or at least London.

Her eyes were saucer-round as she stared into the dressing room mirror. London! Why not? She could pay Aunt Augusta a visit! Aunt Augusta of all people would understand what a predicament she was in, for she had heard that Aunt Augusta herself had landed in many odd romantic coils in her younger days. And perhaps Aunt Augusta could help her look into setting up her own establishment. She had hoped to put off that day until she had a little more money saved, but after last night she wasn't sure how welcome she would be in her father's house.

Her father would surely not be pleased with her for undoing what he had gone to such pains to bring about.

Besides, how *could* she stay? He had humiliated her. She had her pride, after all.

She began stacking her necessary belongings on her bed, and then dragged a portmanteau out of storage. One bag was all she could take, and even then she worried that she would have difficulty. The only transport she would find at this hour of night would be a mail coach, if she could catch it in time. But surely the driver would allow her a little leeway with the size of her bag.

After all, it helped when the mail coach driver harbored a hopeless *tendresse* for one's younger sister.

"That didn't work out too well, did it?"

Nathan looked up over his morning mail at Freddy. "What do you mean?"

His brother hesitated over his boiled egg. "Just that Abigail . . . well, she didn't seem too happy about the engagement."

"Oh," Nathan said. "That." He had been trying all night, with mixed success, to forget the look of abject horror on Abigail's face when the engagement had been announced. Sir Harlan had convinced him that it would all come out right in the end. "Of course she was a little surprised . . ."

"Why?" Freddy asked, then his face fell as understanding dawned. In fact, he looked almost as stunned as Abigail had seemed. "You mean you didn't ask her beforehand?"

Nathan let out an exasperated sigh. "No, but frankly, how could I? You spent half the evening dithering over which vest to wear, which made us unconscionably late, and then when I did get a moment alone with her, she started spouting your poetry at me."

"My poetry?" Freddy asked.

"Apparently she confused something you had written as a poem penned by me."

Freddy looked astounded, and a little offended. "How?"

"How should I know? I didn't have time to delve into that either. Before I could get a word in edgewise with

Abigail, Sir Harlan made the announcement of our engagement."

Freddy shook his head in pity. "You certainly made a muddle out of it! I'm surprised, frankly. I always thought you were so competent."

Nathan bristled. "I am more practiced on a field of battle than I am at proposing on a garden terrace. When one is a soldier, one has more familiarity with the former than the latter."

Freddy salted his egg. "That depends on which soldier one talks to, I imagine."

Nathan sighed. "Well, never fear. I'm going to clear up my mess this morning."

"How?"

"I'm going to talk to Abigail, of course," Nathan said. "She's not an unreasonable girl. When I explain everything to her, she will come around."

Freddy still looked doubtful. Moreover he seemed anguished. "This is all my fault. My spending made you feel pressured to accept Sir Harlan's offer. I should have been able to think of some alternative to your sacrificing yourself."

"It is no sacrifice, believe me," Nathan said. "And your spending—which I hope has now been drastically curtailed for good—was not the only reason. I had my own plans when I came home. I still do, and I hope to be able to instigate said plans without taking a groat from Sir Harlan."

"Then why do you still want to marry Abigail?" Freddy wondered.

"Because I am in love with her!" The admission flew from his mouth, leaving him feeling foolish and emotionally exposed.

Freddy's heavy-lidded eyes flew open. "Love! You?"

It was a bare nerve of a declaration, yet he felt better for having said it.

"Obviously you are as much a changed man as I am myself. But what good does it do us?" Freddy commiserated.

Then he shook his head. "You can see how Abigail would be upset."

At first Nathan had not been able to see it. Not logically. She cared for him, he was certain of that. Why should they not make a successful match? Desire was there, and their personalities were compatible. Abigail surely dreamed of getting married. Most young ladies did.

But then he remembered his first conversation with Sir Harlan, and how his own reaction to the scheme at first had been outrage. The plan had been entirely to his advantage . . . and yet he had felt cornered, angry, defensive.

Much as Abigail had looked last night. If only he had been given the opportunity to explain to her that her father's scheme had only brought them together. That he had every intention of supporting them on his own.

Nathan tossed his napkin down with a sigh and rose from the table. He hoped that Abigail had gotten all her stewing done with last night and would be in a more receptive mood this morning.

"Are you going to Peacock Hall?" Freddy asked him.

Nathan nodded.

"Wear your green coat," Freddy instructed. "The black makes you look like a vicar on holiday."

Nathan had intended to wear his black, but saw the wisdom in Freddy's advice.

"And try to be humble. A young lady might not be inclined to marry an ex-soldier if she thinks she will spend the rest of her life taking orders."

Nathan sighed. "Anything else?"

"Yes." Freddy eyed him anxiously. "If Abigail refuses you, what shall you do then?"

"I don't know. I sincerely hope she will not refuse me. I see no reason why she would."

"Well, there's your hair style for one thing," Freddy said. "But be that as it may, if she *does* refuse you, you don't intend to ask Sophy, do you?"

His brother seemed honestly worried about this point,

on which Nathan could whole-heartedly reassure him. "Lord no."

His brother sagged with relief.

Nathan tilted his head, suddenly worried. "Why? You don't have any crazy notions of matrimony, do you?"

"Not a bad idea," Freddy said. "Perhaps you aren't the only one who could save The Willows with a hefty dowry."

Nathan snorted as he watched his brother take another bite of his breakfast. "I wouldn't be surprised if Sir Harlan paid you double for taking that one off his hands."

It was sometimes difficult for him to tell when his brother was in jest or earnest, but this morning Nathan was taking no chances. He wore his green coat, and took particular care in combing his hair. On the ride to Peacock Hall, he rehearsed what he would say when he saw Abigail alone. Speeches of his sincere intention to love her all her days, to take care of her to the best of his ability, and to be a good provider for her and whatever children their union was fortunate enough to produce.

The mere thought of children gave him pause. There was so much ahead of them! They had only to cross this awkward hurdle and they would be on their way. He felt optimistic, really. Yes, Abigail had seemed upset. She had doubts. Perhaps the idea of marriage, at least marriage to him, had not yet crossed her mind. But a good night's sleep often made people see wisdom.

Nathan snubbed his horse in a shady bit of field and walked the rest of the way up the drive. A quick glance at the carriage house told him that the earl had already made his departure. It was almost noon, and Nathan hoped that the house was enjoying an after-breakfast calm that would afford him and Abigail some peaceful moments together.

His knock at the door received no answer for some time, and when Peabody did arrive, he looked disappointed. "Oh, it's you," he said distractedly. "Are you expected?"

Nathan nodded. "I left a note for Miss Wingate."

"Miss Abigail!" Peabody's eyes bugged, and he gulped. "Oh dear, then you haven't heard."

Nathan felt a sharp pinprick of alarm. "Heard what?"

"You had better come inside," Peabody said, ushering him in with a fatalistic wave.

Fantastic scenarios began to run through Nathan's mind. Had Abigail taken ill? Peabody wouldn't say, which only made Nathan that much more anxious. As they crossed the hall, he noticed the decorative swags on the banister of the staircase were askew. Flowers that had looked bright and cheery during the party had started to brown by the light of the day. And the bowl that had contained the expensive peacock ice sculpture now only contained a puddle of water.

He was shown into the study where he had last seen Abigail as she ran out the door the night before. Perhaps he should have followed her then and tried again to explain.

Sir Harlan entered without too much delay, and from the lines on his face, Nathan saw at once there was cause for alarm.

"Now, now—there is no reason to panic," Sir Harlan said by way of greeting.

His words, of course, had the opposite effect of their intent. "What's wrong?"

"I am sure everything will be quite all right."

"What has happened to Abigail?" Nathan blurted, surprised by the crack in his voice.

"She has left."

"Left!" Nathan bellowed.

"She left a note saying that she has gone to London to visit her Aunt Augusta."

"When?" Nathan started calculating. Perhaps he could catch up to her on the road.

"We do not know when she left. She was not discovered missing until about an hour ago."

Nathan's mouth dropped open. "She just disappeared with no one noticing?"

"She is always very quiet, you know," Sir Harlan explained. "Never calls attention to herself, usually." He frowned. "Do you think last night was too much for her?"

Suddenly, Nathan understood Abigail perfectly. As perfectly as Freddy had seemed to at breakfast this morning. Of course she had been angry! She had spent twenty-four years of her life under Sir Harlan's benign neglect, until last night. To think, no one even noticed she was missing until almost noon!

"Did she say how she expected to get to London?"

There were not too many ways of getting to London.

"We believe she took the mail coach."

Nathan was incredulous. The mail coach? What kind of desperation would drive a lady to do such a thing?

Desperation at the thought of marrying you, apparently, came the unflattering answer.

"What are you going to do?" he asked Sir Harlan.

"I was just about to sit down and write Augusta a letter."

"A letter!" Nathan sputtered. "Shouldn't someone go after her?"

Sir Harlan looked up and snapped his fingers. "I should have thought of that myself. Really I should have. When can you leave?"

Nathan blinked at him. "I? Wouldn't it be more appropriate if someone from her family . . . ?"

Sir Harlan shook his head vigorously. "No, no." He jumped up and ran over to his broken book cabinet. He removed a slim volume and crossed back to Nathan. "Here you are. *Lord Fuego's Pursuit.*"

Nathan groaned. As if these books hadn't caused trouble enough already.

"Believe me," the older man assured him, "one could do worse than patterning oneself after Lord Fuego."

"I do not want to pattern myself after anyone—especially not anyone fictional," Nathan insisted. "I just want Abigail back."

Sir Harlan nodded and gave the book a decided thump. "Then read the book, son. Everything you need to win her back is there."

Chapter Thirteen

*Colleen approached the Bride of the Emerald Isle
Cloister with an enormous sense of relief. Her journey had been long and perilous, but surely at last she
had reached sanctuary.*
*Yet a corner of her mind remained disquieted.
However far she roamed, could there ever be true
refuge from those tortured dark eyes that haunted
her?*

—The Scarlet Veil

At two o'clock, Abigail arrived at her Aunt Augusta's.
Two o'clock in the morning, unfortunately. The hired driver who brought her to her aunt's doorstep from the post-
ing inn looked doubtful as to her prospects of admittance
to the little house just off Grosvenor Square.

"I will wait, miss," he insisted.

Wait for what? Abigail wondered. If Aunt Augusta was
not at home, Abigail had no idea what her next step would
be. She would have to find lodgings for the night, and she
wasn't certain where to begin looking for them. Were ho-
tels open this late at night? Her father always put up at the
Clarendon, so she supposed she could try there first. But
she worried that the proprietors of any respectable hotel
would look askance at an unchaperoned female. Especially
one arriving in the middle of the night, bedraggled from
sitting in a coach for the better part of two days.

This, she had decided, was the flaw in running off half-
cocked with only one bag and her life savings hidden in an

old stocking. (In addition to the flaw of choosing to run away by mail coach, and a poorly ventilated one with a wheel that joggled, to boot.)

She should have developed a contingency plan during the interminable ride to London, she thought with growing hysteria. It would have been more practical than dwelling on the dilemma of her in-name-only engagement to Nathan. Now it was the dead of night, and she was a lone woman in a strange, sprawling city. *What in heaven's name had she done?*

When she left Peacock Hall, she had been thinking of the supportive aunt of her correspondence. But now that she found herself in the dark street, peering up at the house, she remembered that her aunt led a busy and unpredictable life. She might not be here at all—might be out to a party or out of town.

"Everything will be all right," she said aloud, ostensibly to reassure the cab driver.

His gaze traveled from the smallish brick house, whose windows were completely dark, then back to her face. His expression made her doubt her own powers of persuasion. "I will wait."

Come to think of it, it did make her feel a wee bit better knowing there was someone behind her as she climbed the stairs and knocked on the door. The sound of the lion's head knocker made her wince as it echoed through the quiet street and all the way back up to the square. In the unlikely event that the sound didn't manage to wake her aunt, she was certain she had succeeded in disturbing not a few nearby residents.

When no answer came, she bit her lip and steeled herself to knock again, only to have the door in front of her swing open abruptly. Abigail jumped. She had been expecting the butler, but the person on the threshold, swathed in an elegant nightdress with lace cap and carrying a candle, was none other than her aunt herself.

Abigail could have wept with relief. "Aunt Augusta!"

Augusta, not expecting a middle-of-the-night family reunion, looked startled. *"Abigail?"* She brought the candle within singeing distance of Abigail's nose. "It *is* you! What are you doing here in the middle of the night?"

"I had to come, I—"

"And making quite a racket, too! You might have wakened Butterworth," her aunt scolded.

Butterworth, Aunt Augusta's butler since time immemorial, was who Abigail had been expecting to open the door. One might have even said that it was his duty in this circumstance to have been wakened. "I'm very sorry if I startled you . . . and Butterworth."

Augusta laughed. "Well, no matter! Serve him right, the old pest. You mustn't stand out on the steps, however. Why on earth are you here?"

"Well, you see—"

"And just look—you caused me to jump so, I have spilled wax on the floor!" Augusta added, shaking her head. "Butterworth will have a fit about that."

"I'm so sorry," Abigail repeated. "It's just that—"

"How on earth did you get here?" Augusta wondered aloud.

"It's a rather long story, perhaps we could discuss it inside . . ." Abigail said, doubting her chances of being able to explain it all in between her aunt's interruptions.

Augusta peeked over her shoulder. "A cab!" she whispered excitedly. "In the middle of the night! Something is afoot, isn't it?" She leaned forward with delicious curiosity. "My dear, are you having *an intrigue*?"

"I suppose you could call it something like that," Abigail allowed doubtfully.

"Oh, this is exciting!"

Remembering that the cab was waiting on her, Abigail ran back to pay the driver and send the man on his way.

She dragged her meager bag inside the house, following Augusta's candle through the dark entrance into a salon. Augusta lit two lamps and frowned at the bag Abigail had dumped on her carpet. "Is that all you brought with you?"

"I left in rather a hurry."

"Oh—better and better still!" Augusta exclaimed, though she eyed Abigail's appearance with a hint of misgiving. Abigail didn't doubt she looked a fright. And there was no vouching for what she smelled like after a day shut in the airless mail coach with all manner of fellow traveling companions.

She certainly did not feel her appearance was up to the quality of her surroundings. Aunt Augusta's house was small, but elegantly decorated and, as always, immaculate. She had a fondness for Queen Anne furniture that had been passed to her by her parents, Abigail's maternal grandparents. In the middle of the salon, on a wall above a turquoise upholstered sofa, was a picture of Augusta herself that had been done when she was seventeen. She looked disarmingly like that portrait; the round dark eyes, small mouth, and slightly recessed chin had not changed in thirty-five years. She had merely added a little more padding. Her round cheeks contributed to her childlike appearance, as did her manner, which always seemed to project wonder at the world around her, whether she was in her familiar surroundings in London or rusticating, as she did on occasion, at Peacock Hall.

The only off note in the otherwise elegant room was a fat Prince Charles Spaniel sprawled on an Aubusson rug next to the still-warm hearth. At their entrance, he barely lifted his head, growled faintly at Abigail, rolled over, and began snoring rather loudly for such a small animal.

"Poor Lancelot has had a hard day, hasn't he, sweetie?" Augusta cooed at the beast, and indeed he didn't stir. Then she turned her attention back to her niece. "You must be ravenous after such a journey. I'll just get you a little something to eat." The older woman started walking towards the kitchen and Abigail was left to follow her.

"Thank you, but I am not sure that I really want any food, Aunt Augusta. If I could just have a little something to drink."

"Of course you may." Augusta clapped her hands. "We can have some sherry. And cake!"

The idea was almost nauseating, but Augusta threw herself into the preparation of the little repast with such gusto,

Abigail didn't have the heart to tell her that a simple glass of water would have sufficed.

"Butterworth would disapprove!" Augusta sent a mischievous grin in the general direction of the back stairs leading to the attic where her longtime manservant resided. "He's such a tyrant. He is always taking the sweet plate away before I'm finished." She cut two healthy portions of cake off a plate. "Here you are."

They settled back in the salon, balancing plates on their knees. At the smell of cake, Lancelot bestirred himself to sit at his mistress's feet, where he commenced to pant hopefully.

Once she had poured them both a glass of sherry, Augusta settled down to hear Abigail's story. Except that the moment Abigail opened her mouth to tell it, Augusta exclaimed, "I knew there would be trouble! Harlan was never fit to raise girls on his own. I have always felt guilty for not taking you dear girls more in hand, but . . ." She sighed in the way an old soldier might when remembering a siege. "Well, there were those two Seasons with Violet."

Her tone made it clear that the two had felt like five, at least. And that enduring them had taken her far beyond the call of auntly duty. "And then you have always been so ill . . ."

"But that is just it, Aunt," Abigail interjected, seizing a conversational opportunity she feared might not come around again for some time. "I have hardly been sick a day in my life."

Augusta's eyes bulged in astonishment. "But my dear, you wrote to me on several occasions, as did your father. Said you were too ill to come to town for a Season!"

Abigail had decided on the long, bumpy, sleepless trip to London—when she had plenty of time to mull over such things—that the best approach was to make a full confession to her aunt. After all, Augusta was the one who had unwittingly started her on her duplicitous life of writing.

As she had finally managed to shock her aunt into silence, she rushed forward with the whole story, starting with the fateful case of mumps and the enjoyment she got from the box of books her aunt had sent her to make up for the fact that she was missing her London come-out. She told her of devouring the stories one after another, then of her travails when trying to write her first book, and her surprise when it was actually published. Her aunt seemed just as astonished about Abigail's success as she herself had been at the time, especially when she revealed her *nom de plume.*

"Georgianna Harcourt!" Augusta's jaw dropped. "Do you mean that you are *the* Georgianna Harcourt, authoress of *The Scarlet Veil* and *Lord Fuego's Pursuit* and—oh, my heaven!—*Count Orsino's Betrothal?*"

Abigail nodded.

"But I have those books in my library!" Augusta said, as if that made invalid Abigail's claim.

"Unfortunately, so did my father," Abigail told her. "And he used them as models to blackmail a neighbor into agreeing to marry one of his daughters."

"He got that from Count Orsino's story!" Augusta proclaimed right away. As if Abigail wouldn't know this. "That was a terrible situation the poor scamp found himself in—having to choose a bride from one of Prince Lorenzo's daughters."

Abigail nodded ruefully. "And I, improbably, was the daughter Nathan chose. I have been hoisted by my own petard!"

"Nothing improbable about your being chosen," Augusta insisted staunchly. "You are quite as handsome as Violet, and I'm sure you would have to be less disagreeable in your personality. And Sophy is just a child!"

"She is seventeen."

Her aunt's eyes flew open. "Is she?"

"She'll be having her first Season next year."

These shocking revelations caused Augusta to pour herself a third glass of sherry. When she had done this (and topped off Abigail's glass, too), her face was deeply troubled. "I don't see how you could have done it," she said, shaking her head.

"Rejected Nathan, you mean?" Abigail guessed.

"No—killed off Count Orsino!" her aunt exclaimed. "He was my favorite character, and then to have him meet such a violent end . . . I was heartbroken for weeks!"

"But, Aunt, he *was* a villain," Abigail explained, forcing herself to put aside her own problems for a moment to address her aunt's fiction concerns.

"Yes I know, but he was so handsome!" Augusta sighed. "Except for that scar, of course, poor man. I always wanted to meet a man like Orsino!"

"But he had made his first wife so unhappy."

"It was a bad match," her aunt rationalized. "Not entirely the poor man's fault. And that business about the murder . . . well! Any fool could tell that it was the prince who had tampered with that carriage wheel."

"But then he leaves Fiona alone while still pursuing Isabella and her riches," Abigail pointed out.

"Of course! He is a devil, but a charming one! And he really comes to love Fiona . . . in his own way . . ."

The conversation was beginning to make Abigail wonder if it would be better if she never again put pen to paper. "People seem to be coming away from my stories with completely wrong ideas."

"You should be flattered. You created a character I could fall in love with. Believe me, I always gravitated toward dangerous men." Augusta frowned. "Come to think of it, it's lucky I never married, or else I might have ended up like that first unfortunate Countess Orsino."

"I also created an overbearing paternal figure that my own father could identify with," Abigail said ruefully.

Augusta laughed. "To think you had an enthusiastic reader under your own roof and didn't even know it!"

Abigail groaned. "Using my own plots against me."

"So amusing to think of Sir Harlan burying himself in a Gothic novel!" Augusta exclaimed. "I suppose we should be glad he hasn't been taking saws to carriage wheels."

"Aunt," Abigail said. "What am I to do?"

"*Do*?" Augusta wondered. "What is the problem?"

"Nathan!"

Her aunt blinked. "Oh, yes, the young man in the middle of all of this." She leaned forward. "Well, getting rid of unwanted fiancés is no great difficulty. I did it a half dozen times in my day!"

Abigail nodded. She had heard her father complain that Augusta had been renowned for flightiness in her youth.

"First things first," Augusta said. "Is he handsome?"

"Terribly!"

The older woman commiserated. "That is the most difficult kind of fiancé. They always put one in such a dither. A conventional-looking man is much easier to dismiss. One just has to imagine him ten or twenty years down the road, having gout and off shooting pheasants with snuff dribbling down his vest. But the *terribly* handsome ones tend to remain good-looking and devil us for years." She eyed Abigail sharply. "Are you sure you want to reject him?"

"How can I marry a man who allowed himself to be blackmailed into asking for my hand?"

"Very simple. You say, 'I will.'"

"Well, I won't. No one in this matter ever took my feelings into account."

"Hm . . ." Her aunt tapped an immaculately manicured nail against her now-empty plate. "I can see where you might not appreciate being treated like a bit of barter, like a gambling chip."

"He simply wants financial security, because his father lost the family fortune playing cards."

Augusta gasped. "And I thought *I* was unlucky at faro!"

"His father was the unluckiest man alive, apparently. And marriage to me was supposed to shore up the family finances."

"Hardly the first time such a thing has happened. My hand was once asked for by a baron who had lost all his money gambling on boxing. At least losing money at cards has a more dignified air to it—but *boxing!*"

"I do not care why the family needs the money. It is the fact that he would accede to such an arrangement without telling me that turns my stomach."

"Men are such brutes!" Augusta agreed. Her lips pursed. "I wonder what Butterworth will make of all this."

"Butterworth?"

"You know how he is," she told Abigail, who didn't. "He treats me as if I am still in the nursery. I am sure he will not trust me to clear this matter up."

Abigail was inclined to agree with Butterworth. But neither did she intend to put her faith in a butler. "Aunt, if I could just stay with you for a few days . . ."

"Of course! You must stay as long as you like." She frowned. "Though of course I leave for Bath at the end of the month."

"I will be settled by then."

"Settled?" Her aunt looked nervous, no doubt remembering those endless two Seasons with Violet under her roof.

"I hope to set up a residence of my own here in London," Abigail explained. "It will be convenient to be closer to my publisher."

"Live on your own!" Augusta exclaimed, shocked. Even though she had lived alone since her parents died, and not without scandals of her own. "My dear, how?"

"With the money I have made as Georgianna Harcourt."

"But—to live alone!" cried her aunt, distressed.

"You live alone."

"Well, yes, but . . ." She wrung her hands, obviously torn between duty and the desire for privacy. "I suppose you *could* stay here. I always intended to invite you girls to stay . . . one at a time. But I have been so busy, you see."

"I would rather have lodgings of my own."

"Well! I suppose we can speak of this in the morning."

Abigail had to admit that she was bone tired. Her aunt led her up the stairs to a room facing the street. "I hope you will be comfortable."

"I will." She kissed her aunt. "And thank you. I am sorry my arrival was so unexpected. I hope I'm not too much of an inconvenience."

"My dear, you are always welcome. And as to the rest . . .

what to do in the future . . . I'm sure Butterworth will have something to say about that in the morning." With these comforting words, her aunt floated from the room with Lancelot trailing at her heels.

When she was alone with only a candle illuminating the small room, Abigail sank her head against the pillow. She was so exhausted after her travel she had expected to fall right to sleep, but her eyes kept popping open at the sound of church bells, and the occasional echo of carriage wheels on cobblestones down nearby streets. She was in London! She wondered if anyone at Peacock Hall had even noticed she was missing yet.

They must have.

And Nathan . . . had he heard? If he had, she wondered what he thought of her sudden disappearance. The dismal thought struck her that he might give it very little thought at all. Perhaps he had moved on to another moneymaking scheme, or was planning to marry Violet in lieu of his first choice of her. Now that Violet's dreams of catching an earl were foiled, she would be free. Nathan obviously wasn't too choosy.

She sank down further beneath the covers, hurt and anger bubbling inside, with a little jealousy now thrown into the pot. Jealousy for whatever girl would eventually be duped into becoming the savior of the Cantrell fortunes!

Fatigue was obviously clouding her reasoning faculties. She didn't really envy any young lady that fate. And if she could just stop thinking about those green eyes, and that voice . . . if she could just stop dreaming about how things might have turned out differently . . .

Her eyes fluttered closed and she slept.

After what seemed like mere moments of blissful sleep, a curtain was drawn open and harsh summer sunlight came glaring through the window.

"Good morning!" her aunt chirped.

Abigail groaned. She felt as if she had drunk a sleeping

potion, like a girl in a fairy tale. She could have slept for
an age.

"My dear, wake up. The day is half gone, and there is
much to be done."

Abigail let one eye squeeze open to see her aunt looming over her with an armload of books in one hand. "First,
you must sign my Georgianna Harcourt collection," her
aunt said. "Unfortunately, I lent my copy of *The Scarlet
Veil* to my friend Jane. I must get it back from her now!"

Woozily, Abigail pushed herself up on her elbows.
"What time is it?"

"Almost eleven, dear. I was hoping you would breakfast
with me, but I suppose you were tired from so much traveling."

Her aunt spoke as if Abigail still weren't tired, when in
truth she could hardly prop her eyes open.

"A very nice luncheon is being prepared. Oh! And you
had a visitor."

Abigail's eyes opened a little wider. How could she have
had a visitor? "Who?"

"Nathan Cantrell."

The name practically lifted her out of the bed. Her heart
raced. "Nathan? But it couldn't have been. He's the——"

"Yes, I know," her aunt said. "He followed you! Isn't that
sweet?"

Sweet? It was unbelievable! She calculated the hours in
her head. How had he arrived in London so fast—and why
had he followed her? Abigail tried to will her pulse back
to a normal rate, but that was an impossible task.

"I would like a special dedication on *Orsino*, if you
wouldn't mind," her aunt said as she settled herself on a
corner of the mattress. "He's my favorite!"

"Aunt, where is he?"

Augusta blinked at her as if she were slowitted. "My
dear, you killed him."

Abigail sighed. "Not Orsino. *Nathan.*"

"Oh!" Augusta laughed. "As to that, I have no idea. Butterworth sent him away."

"Away!" Abigail cried.

"Yes, and he didn't even ask my advice, that overbearing, wretched man! I mean Butterworth, of course, not your Mr. Cantrell."

"What did Nathan say?"

Her aunt frowned. "I believe he asked after you, and Butterworth informed him that you were not receiving guests this morning—which, after all, is true. But I still think Butterworth might have consulted with me. The man treats this house as if he were the patriarch."

Having been the butler to the Travers family since Abigail's grandfather's time, Abigail supposed Butterworth probably did feel like a father figure. But Abigail was too distracted to care about the officiousness of Butterworth. "What am I going to do?" she said aloud.

"Do?" Her aunt asked. "About what?"

"About Nathan! Why is he here?"

"That should be obvious. Because you are here."

"But he must know that I was running from him."

Her aunt rapped her on the knee. "Of course he knew— and his instincts were to run after you. Men are just like hounds that way. If something flees, they must pursue it." She winked at Abigail. "In my day, I was quite a capable little fox, or rather vixen. The stories I could tell you!"

Abigail had no doubts about that. "But I am not being coy, I swear it. What shall I do?"

Augusta chuckled. "First, you must have a bath, then food. Then we shall go shopping!"

Abigail looked at her in wonder.

"I took the liberty of looking into your bag, and those brown rags will not do. In order to reject a man who has followed you all the way to London, you must do it in style. Also, your hair needs styling . . . though perhaps it isn't so irregular once it is combed."

"No, it is always irregular," she said, dispirited.

"Well then—that is another project for us." She let out a merry laugh. "I am so glad you came to visit me, Abigail. I feel quite revived."

"It's good to see you, too. We were worried about you when you said that you could not come to the ball.

Though, considering how things turned out, I am glad you were here and not there."

Augusta patted her knee through the coverlet. "I am glad I am able to provide a place of respite for you." She stood, and Abigail felt for a moment that there was something troubled in her aunt's expression . . . though it was hard to tell with her aunt. She might just be thinking of Count Orsino again. "While you are having your bath and dressing, I will compose a letter to your father. I can't decide whether to scold him or reassure him. I would do both, of course, but I am not the writer you are."

Abigail couldn't recommend creative writing to anyone at this point. So far it had only reaped six hundred pounds and a mountain of trouble.

Nathan lifted the lion's head knocker and let it drop, for better or worse. He waited and then felt a touch of exasperation when the same elderly butler who had dismissed him that morning appeared again. The man was tall, slender, and unsmiling. When Nathan stepped forward, his expression looked as if a particularly unappealing beetle were trying to sneak into the house.

"May I help you, sir?"

"I would like to see Miss Wingate. I am sure she expects me."

"Miss Wingate has just returned from a shopping expedition, sir, and is resting. Would you care to leave your card . . . ?"

"I left my card earlier. I could leave cards till doomsday, but that would serve no one's interests, least of all yours."

The man's eyebrows rose. "My interests, sir?"

"Do you want to spend the rest of your days ferrying scraps of paper about?"

The butler, who obviously considered the question an impertinent one, glared at him. "I will inform Miss Travers that you are waiting. If you'll follow me, sir."

At least he had managed to storm the fortress, Nathan thought with some satisfaction, borrowing a phrase from

Lord Fuego. On the trip down, he had managed to get through half of the book Sir Harlan had lent him, in which the charming yet sinister-seeming lord of the title chases a rich widow, who cannot tell if his intentions are entirely honorable.

Nathan himself still was unsure of the lord's intentions, so he could hardly blame the widow for being confused.

He felt a little resentful of Lord Fuego, actually. The man had kept him up reading in bed the night before, squinting by a flickering, smelly candle, his neck crooked uncomfortably in an unfamiliar bed. Nathan was usually of the opinion that one should read in a chair and sleep in a bed, but there he was, irresistibly reading along, curious as to what would happen next after the crafty Lord Fuego had managed to charm all the widow's relatives to join in his scheme.

"Wait here, sir," the butler said, depositing Nathan in a room crowded with furniture and bric-a-brac.

Abigail's aunt seemed fond of nice things, and had a taste for the elaborate. Not a piece of furniture was without some special adornment. Upholstery with tassels, chests with gold inlay, pictures with heavily carved gilt frames. A painting of an unusual but pretty young woman dominated one wall, much as the painting of the peacocks commanded the focus in Sir Harlan's study. The lady in the portrait bore more than a passing resemblance to Sophy . . . and just a little to Abigail as well.

Just then, the door behind him opened, and when he turned, the young lady was standing before him. Only she was no longer young, but on the shady side of fifty. And yet there was something girlish about her still that Nathan could not quite put his finger on.

She came forward. "Ah, Mr. Cantrell. So I will get a look at you after all!"

Nathan bowed, but grew uncomfortable as she inspected him with great curiosity and pleasure from head to toe. "Abigail did not tell me you were so well built!"

He hardly knew how to respond. To his astonishment, he felt a blush rising in his face. "I am much concerned about

Miss Wingate," he said, choosing simply to change the subject altogether.

She waved away his concern. "I would not worry about Abigail! She went shopping today for the first time in an age. She is as happy as a lark, and I myself was quite pleased to be able to spend Sir Harlan's money!"

For obvious reasons, the idea that Abigail would be gadding about town happily shopping while Nathan worried himself sick about her was a little irritating. He had assumed that a young woman running from an engagement would spend more time wallowing in sorrow. Shouldn't she have taken to her bed with a crisis of nerves?

"If I could just speak to her for a few moments."

"She doesn't want to speak to you—and I can well see why!"

Nathan tilted his head. "Why?"

"Because you are—well!" Augusta laughed. "I am sure I never could have rejected you."

She made it sound as if she had practice in this area. Nathan frowned. "But you rejected others?"

"Oh, my yes! A half dozen or more! My mother always said I would rue the day—but then I racked up so many days to rue that she quit bothering to scold me. And of course only Butterworth scolds me these days, but, alas, now for entirely unromantic reasons."

"Butterworth?"

"My butler." A look of fond irritation crossed her face. "The one who shooed you away this morning. Overbearing creature! He obviously thinks I have led a useless, silly life—but I ask you, where would he be if I had married? He might never have received promotion to butler. He could have ended up on the street—or as a lowly footman at one of those large houses! He is lucky that I am so frivolous. Don't you think so, Mr. Cantrell?"

"I . . ." Nathan again found himself casting about for a diplomatic answer.

She sensed his conundrum and giggled. "But of course you would not want to call me frivolous, not when you are trying to win my niece."

The statement was baldy spoken, and true. "Does Abigail know I am here?"

"Oh, yes. I told her straight off."

"And there is no doubt that she will not see me?"

"Not unless you find ambiguity in the words absolutely not." She laughed merrily. "But you are right to keep trying. You must be resolute. Eventually she will have to see you and then . . ." Augusta looked at him and sighed. "Well! Who knows what may happen?"

"Then you are sympathetic to my side in this matter?"

"Oh, my, no! You men have behaved abominably, as usual. Mr. Cantrell—"

"Nathan, please."

She fluttered for a moment before continuing. "Nathan, you are looking at a woman who no man has ever taken seriously." She waved off an interruption he'd had no intention of making. "Oh, to propose to, perhaps! But did they think that I did not know that deep down they thought they would receive a mere ornament, or an amusing sort of flibbertigibbet to have about the house? A woman knows what men think of her, or else she is a true fool, and what man would want a fool?"

Nathan shook his head. He sensed there was some nugget of truth buried in what she was saying, but damn if he could dig it out. "But Abigail must know in what esteem I hold her."

"How?" She laughed. "You have made a complete muddle of the whole business. She thinks you are marrying her because her father blackmailed you into it!"

"If I could just have an opportunity to clarify the matter, though."

"Clarify what matter, Mr. Cantrell?"

Nathan sucked in his breath when he heard Abigail's voice. She stood in the doorway, her dark eyes peered at him from beneath an unfamiliar curled fringe of hair. In fact, after her day in London, she looked altogether different. She had acquired a deep crimson dress unlike those brown rags she usually wore. Nathan was taken aback by the change in her. She seemed sophisticated—discounting the color rising in her cheeks.

"Abigail, if I could speak to you . . ."

"Of course you may." Augusta made a move to slip out of the room, but Abigail stopped her. "Please do not leave, Aunt. Whatever Nathan has to say, he can say in front of you. Mr. Cantrell and I are not on an intimate footing, despite the fact that we might be considered to be erroneously engaged."

"Abigail . . ."

She crossed her arms. "Is that why you are here, perhaps? Did you need to clear up the matter of our ill-fated attachment before you could go along on your fortune-hunting way?"

"I am no fortune hunter," he said. "If you would just let me explain."

She crossed her arms. "Did my father offer you forgiveness of your mortgages and a large sum of money for marrying me?"

Nathan sighed. "Yes."

"Did he not offer the same amount to you were you to choose Violet or Sophy?"

Nathan bit his cheek to keep from wanting to strangle her into silence. "Yes."

She turned to her aunt. "You see? It is just as I said."

Augusta shook her head in disbelief. "You would think Sir Harlan would know he would have to up the ante on Violet!"

Nathan crossed toward Abigail who stood her ground and lifted her chin, as if bracing for a blow. "Abigail, tell me how I can convince you of my sincerity when I say I want nothing more than to marry you."

She bounced slightly on her heels. "Oh, I believe your sincerity. I believe you sincerely hope to save The Willows. If Peacock Hall were endangered, I might feel pressed to go casting about for a rich husband. But I do not feel inclined to be used as a bank note at this time."

"I would never—"

"But just because I am not so inclined," she continued,

"please do not feel that you should not ask Sophy or Violet and cash in on my father's generous bargain. I release you to do so."

"I am not so easily gotten rid of."

Her brows arched. "Marriage to either of my sisters would never be considered easy."

"Abigail, I understand your anger. You are hurt."

"Ha!" she cried.

"You are probably furious that I did not speak to you beforehand, though I tried to explain . . ."

"I am not angry or hurt," she said. "What I am is in a hurry. My aunt and I have a dinner engagement, and I would not like to be late, since our hostess was kind enough to accommodate an extra guest."

In other words, he was being dismissed. Perhaps that was just as well. He wasn't making much headway here. He was still enough of a soldier to understand the benefit of a strategic retreat.

"I will come back tomorrow."

"You will be disappointed," Abigail warned him.

"Not if I am able to see you, at least," he said. "That is never a disappointment. And certainly not when you are looking as lovely as I find you today."

The color in her cheeks almost matched that in her dress, and her eyes seemed to shine with a little of the light he remembered from their encounter in her writing room. That expression was a ray of hope.

Nevertheless, as Nathan descended the steps from her aunt's house, he felt a stab of melancholy. He had hoped to be able to convince her to forgive him today, and start on his return to The Willows. This would take longer than he had thought.

Which meant another lonely night at the inn with Lord Fuego.

Chapter Fourteen

The tall, mysterious man in black jumped from the boat and then, almost as an afterthought, tossed coins at the gondolier. With an arrogant stride, he crossed the rest of the way to the blue door of the Castaldi palazzo and knocked imperiously.

When the decrepit manservant attempted to block the entrance, the menacing gentleman pushed the frightened menial aside and bellowed, "You will announce the arrival of Lord Fuego to your mistress at once, or you will rue the day you dared cross me, old man."

—Lord Fuego's Pursuit

They were becoming old familiars, he and Butterworth. In fact, as Nathan took in that same bald head, that always-puckered brow, that ever-so-slightly downturned mouth, he suspected that he and Butterworth knew each other so well they could finish each other's sentences. By now Nathan could guess what the man was going to say. Their encounters were becoming as predictable and scripted as a children's puppet show, with Butterworth playing the part of an improbably stone-faced Punchinello.

It was an amusing thought, and these past few days had not afforded much amusement. As an experiment, the moment Butterworth opened his mouth, Nathan spoke for him. "Who am I here to see?" he asked, to Butterworth's surprise. The man was accustomed to being the first pup-

pet to speak, and did not seem at all pleased to have his
lines stolen from him.

"Yes, sir. Who are . . ." Butterworth's words trailed off
as he realized repeating the question was futile.

Nathan smiled. "I will give you three guesses."

"There are only two ladies residing in this house, sir,"
Butterworth informed him.

"There! You cannot lose."

The man looked at him warily, obviously wondering
whether five days of rebuffs had unhinged Nathan's senses.
As to that, Nathan could give him a simple answer: Yes. He
had been wandering about London by day, wondering how
his life had come to this—arriving at a doorstep several
times a day to visit a young lady who did not want to see
him, only to be repulsed by her aunt's butler. And these encounters were the highlight of his long days.

Nights he spent reading that blasted book, which he had
been through once and had now started again. He could
see why Sir Harlan wanted him to read it. Fuego really was
a persistent devil. Obstacles only seemed to fire his determination more, and by the time the heroine, a frustrat-
ingly virtuous young lady, relented, she relented body and
soul. Nathan liked the relenting part; it was the pursuing
that was wearing him out.

More specifically, it was the waiting.

Butterworth spoke. "Miss Wingate is—"

"Out?" Nathan guessed before the man could finish.

"No sir," the man said with a disapproving frown.

"Ah, then she is in bed with a headache."

"Just so, sir."

During the time Nathan had been in London, he had
come calling at least twice a day. At each of these visits,
she had either been out, which would indicate an astonishing social whirl for a young lady who knew no one in
town, or suffering from a headache. Lately the headache
excuse had been growing in favor. Nathan was beginning
to become discouraged. Sir Harlan was wrong. Persistence, which had worked for Lord Fuego, was getting him
nowhere.

Nathan had known Abigail was angry. But he had thought their attraction could overcome the contrivances of Sir Harlan that had first brought them together. He thought she felt a real affection towards him. He knew that he was in love with her. He just wanted to get past the last week of disasters and start their life together.

"This headache seems to be one of astounding duration," he told Butterworth. "You might consider calling in the great physicians of the city to make a study of it."

"I will convey your suggestion to the young lady, sir."

"Please do, and add that I hope that she finds being plagued by headache preferable to being plagued by me."

Butterworth bowed. "If I may speak frankly, sir . . ."

"Oh, please do!"

"I often find that the duration of a lady's headache is simply as long as necessary."

Necessary, in this instance, no doubt meant until he left town.

Nathan sighed. He wished there were some other tactic to take, short of scaling the walls to Abigail's bedroom. He had tried asking after Aunt Augusta, but that woman seemed to adhere to a busy social schedule and was never at home to him, either.

"I suppose Miss Travers is out?"

Butterworth nodded. "Yes, sir."

Naturally.

"Paying calls?"

"Miss Gussie has accompanied Lancelot to the park for their usual morning promenade." At Nathan's raised brows, Butterworth's lips flattened even more. "Lancelot is the dog, sir."

Nathan remembered the animal from his one brief entrance into the house. The dog had looked as if it never walked farther than the distance from its rug to its food bowl, but perhaps looks were deceiving.

Nathan smiled at the name Butterworth had used for Aunt Augusta. *Miss Gussie?* It fit, but he would be willing to bet that only Butterworth called her by that diminutive.

She had struck him as a woman who would want to cling to her dignity, just as she clung to her little dog.

A glimmer of an idea, very Fuego-like in nature, began flickering in his mind.

After asking Butterworth to pass along his admittedly futile hopes that Abigail would undergo a speedy recovery from the dual afflictions of head pain and social obligation, Nathan stepped away from the house. An intriguing plan began taking shape; he was surprised he had not thought of it before. It was true that the persistence of Lord Fuego had not gotten Nathan far . . . yet. Perhaps the reason was that he had been imitating only Fuego's persistence, not his cunning. There was one tactic that Fuego scoundrel had used that Nathan had so far not tried.

The relatives.

Nathan spotted his quarry in the distance the next morning as she toddled into the park, the little spaniel waddling officiously at her skirt hem. Augusta's odd mincing walk was due, no doubt, to the height and tightness of her tiny shoes, because her skirts themselves were rather loose and flowing. A shawl draped about her shoulders, and crowning her head was a funny flat straw hat wreathed with flowers and a large plume jutting out the back. As if to admit that the hat was for decorative purposes only, she also held a parasol aloft to blot out the morning sun.

Nathan—well slept, thoroughly prepared, and on the alert—scanned the area, noting the couple of redheaded street urchins tossing a ball (suspiciously new, had anyone cared to take notice) to the side of the path, not far from where Augusta was headed.

Nathan began a casual stroll down the path towards the woman and her dog. When he had almost closed the distance between them, he started to whistle "Rule, Britannia." Just then one of the boys missed a catch and fell at Augusta's feet. Lancelot growled. As planned, the boy reached for the dog. Nathan was poised to lope after the boy and play Galahad to Lancelot.

Unfortunately, he had not counted on Augusta's mothering instinct to be quite so keen.

Seeing the boy trying to snatch her dog, she gasped, snapped her parasol closed, and brought it down on the urchin's head. The boy sprang back, howling.

"For shame!" Augusta screeched at him.

Now the normally dormant Lancelot was barking and had hold of the leg of one of the boy's trousers. The boy attempted to kick him away, which sent Lancelot into a frenzy. He pulled free of Augusta's grasp and bolted off across the green.

Nathan, who had been watching events unfold with the sinking spirits of a man watching his house of cards collapse, suddenly popped back to action when he heard Augusta cry out. Perhaps he could come out a hero yet. He chased after Lancelot, and it should have only taken a moment for him to reach down and scoop the spaniel in his arms. But just as he reached for the beast, Lancelot caught sight of a squirrel and went dashing into a hedge after his prey.

Nathan thrust himself through the greenery, too, and was shocked to observe when he came out the other side that the dog was outpacing him by a good clip.

As he struck down another path leading towards that body of water cutting through the park known as the Serpentine, Lancelot transferred his attention from the squirrel to the swans swimming regally in the water. Before Nathan reached the shore, Lancelot hurled himself at one particularly large black swan and started paddling after him. The dog's sputtering, frantic swimming skills were no match for a cygnet. In fact, he looked wretched and half in danger of drowning.

Nathan plunged in after the dog, expecting a shallow wade, and instead found himself almost hip-deep in mucky water. He splashed toward the gasping little cur and grasped him firmly by the collar. For his pains he received a sharp nip that almost took off his left thumb. He emitted a cry. "Ingrate!"

In reply, Lancelot growled at his rescuer.

Augusta, finally catching up to her pet, stopped abruptly as she recognized Nathan. Her brown eyes snapped open and she took in his dripping-wet appearance in surprise. "Why, Mr. Cantrell!"

He bowed. "Miss Travers. I believe this animal is yours."

"Oh yes!" She took the soaked, wriggling animal gingerly, then set him quickly on the ground, her hand tightly around his leash now. "Thank you so much! I am so grateful to you. Some wretched boys nearly kidnapped Lancelot!"

"I saw the whole incident." Nathan scanned the area to make sure his accomplices had scattered. "Disgraceful!"

"I don't know what the world is coming to," Augusta declared.

"Indeed. But at least I was able to save Lancelot from drowning."

She blinked at him. "Oh, but he wouldn't have drowned. He's quite a good little swimmer! Most spaniels are, you know." She turned her attention to scolding her puppy. "Naughty Lancelot! How many times must I tell you to leave those swans alone?"

As her words sank in, Nathan felt increasingly foolish. And soggy. It served him right for trying to match the cunning of Lord Fuego.

Augusta looked back up at him, her eyes shining. "Oh, but I have never seen so noble a sight as your flinging yourself into the Serpentine after dear Lancie, quite without regard to how ridiculous you looked!" She sympathetically eyed his ruined boots and drenched clothing. "You must allow me to take you up in my carriage and deliver you to your lodgings. Then I hope you shall come to tea at my house this afternoon."

Thus it was that, despite the mishap with the urchins, the dog, and the swans, later that afternoon Nathan, confectioner's box in hand, was able to inform Butterworth that he was calling on Miss Augusta Travers and was expected. He fancied that a brief look off irritation crossed the old servant's face, but the man's only response was, "So I have been informed. Miss Gussie has stepped out for a moment, and asked that you wait for her."

"Is Miss Abigail at home?"

Those flat lips curved up into a satisfied smile. "No, sir. She is out."

"*Out* out?"

"Naturally." And his wide eyes seemed to ask, *Would I lie?* "If you will please follow me, sir."

Nathan was escorted to the salon he had seen on his earlier visit. The room was again empty, and Nathan decided to make himself at home while waiting for the promised tea. This Butterworth delivered in short order, but it was a few minutes before Augusta came bustling in. She greeted him as warmly as if he were a conquering hero.

"Mr. Cantrell, I am so sorry I am late! I do hope Butterworth has taken care of you—Butterworth is my butler, you know."

"Butterworth and I are quite old friends after the past week," Nathan said.

"I am quite put out with him today," Augusta said, then she giggled. "Well! I am quite put out with him every day."

"I admit I thought he rather impertinently called you Miss Gussie."

"Did he! You see then what I must put up with?"

He noticed her eyeing the box in his hand with curiosity. Her eyes shone, and despite himself, he could feel himself being drawn in. There was something about Augusta Travers—she was past her prime, and her mind was definitely a scattershot mechanism, yet he could not miss the liveliness that must have captured many a heart. There was also a self-awareness about her, as if she were a constant source of amusement for herself.

"Would you care for a macaroon?" Nathan proffered the box.

She practically snatched the box out of his hands, then hesitated as if thinking twice. Her hands had frozen midgrab. "But of course they're for Abigail."

"I was simply bringing them to the house. I passed by the shop today . . ." He did not add that he specifically asked the confectioner what candies were the favorites of Miss Travers. "And since Abigail will not see me . . ."

Nathan added, surprising himself by the genuine mourn-
fulness of his tone.

"Abigial *is* being rather cruel, isn't she?" Augusta said,
not at all disapprovingly. "I did not think she had it in her."

Nathan sighed. "It's nothing worse than I deserve. You
put me right on that score, Miss Travers. Tell me, do you
think there is any hope that Abigail will forgive my part in
her father's plot?"

"As to that, Mr. Cantrell, I am not certain. Abigail is a
very particular young lady. While I find her the most
pleasant of my three nieces, there is no denying that she
can be rather hard when crossed."

Nathan's heart sank a little, yet he inched the box a little closer to Augusta's outstretched hands. "Even if I had
someone she cared for on my side . . . ?"

"Hm. I should have to think about that," Augusta said,
her eyes dancing.

"I fear I have misjudged Abigail in many ways," Nathan
said. "Foolishly, because my heart is set on her and no
other."

The older woman blinked her round dark eyes at him.
"Oh! Then you are in love?"

"I am afraid so," he admitted. "Except how can one
judge, when one has never known that feeling before? In
fact, I have sneered at men who . . ." His words broke off.
"Are you sure you would not care for a macaroon?"

Her dark eyes shone with temptation. "Well . . . Abigail
does not seem that fond of sweets. I am sure that she
looked at me quite askance the other evening when I
helped myself to the tiniest second portion of cake."

He dangled the box closer to her. "Then, since you say
Abigail would not be interested . . ."

"It would be terrible to waste them!"

As he sat back with his cup of tea and watched Augusta
choose a treat from the box, he studied the woman's person more closely.

"What a beautiful shawl," he observed.

As a guarantor of warmth, of course, it was useless, for
the lace was lined with an almost transparent linen.

She swallowed a bite of macaroon. "Thank you."

"I believe that is the most exquisite lace I have ever seen in my life." Which was true; not that he had seen a great deal. Or, rather, *noticed* a great deal.

"Are you a connoisseur of fabrics, Mr. Cantrell?" she asked with amusement.

"I wish I were. Or I wish I knew someone who had a good eye for such things. I am new to the subject, but it fascinates me."

She frowned. "Fabrics?"

He shook his head. "No, the production of fabric. When I left the army, I thought I might look into opening a factory."

Her eyes widened. "You don't say!"

"But now . . ." He sighed. "Well, I don't mean to bore you with my problems."

"Oh, but you aren't."

"For some reason, I felt that talk of business would not bore you. You are such a woman of the world. You must have had quite a bit of experience managing on your own."

She straightened. "Very few realize the pressures a woman alone faces in this day and age."

"I cannot presume to know, but I can imagine it is not easy."

"It is not, indeed! And then I have Butterworth calling me Miss Gussie at the age of . . . well, older than I care to admit . . . as if I were trotting around in shorts skirts and rolling a hoop!"

He clucked his tongue. "The name Gussie is all wrong for you. It lacks dignity."

She sucked in her breath. "That is exactly what I think! Augusta is far better."

"Yes, indeed. It makes one think of majesty and grandeur."

"Oh, yes, it fairly reeks of all those things. And yet Butterworth seems to think I have no dignity."

Nathan drew back, as if in disbelief. "Anyone looking at you could tell you are a lady to contend with."

She beamed up at him, so that he thought he had managed to bowl her over. Then he noticed her sharp eyes scrutinizing him more intently. "What were you saying about a factory, Mr. Cantrell?"

"My interest is chiefly in wool," he said. "Fine wool."

"That sounds very practical. Especially coming from the part of the world that you do. It's so sheepy up there."

"The setting is perfect. But conditions have not been entirely favorable for business . . . for me, at least."

She ate half of another sweet before looking at him curiously. "Does Abigail know about this ambition?"

"A little. But I fear it is just another thing she holds against me. She seems to want a man of a more poetic nature."

"Foolish girl!" She shook her plumed head. "But it's the practical ones who always turn out to be the most romantic in the end, you know."

"Well, in my case, practicality is really the only solution to my romantic woes. I must find a way to get myself out of my financial coil on my own, so that Abigail will know that I am no fortune hunter."

Augusta nibbled thoughtfully. As Nathan observed her he felt like a fisherman watching a trout toying around his line. "I would like to hear more about your factory, Mr. Cantrell."

"Please call me Nathan."

"Nathan." She beamed one of her incomparable smiles at him. "And of course you must call me Augusta!"

The warmth in those brown eyes drew him in and he forgot that he had hoped to use a friendship with this charming lady to gain access to Abigail's company. Instead he found himself confiding all his plans and dreams to her as they sat in the little parlor. By the time he had finished his tale, the box of macaroons was quite empty, but his future brimmed with possibilities.

At dinner that evening, Augusta was in more than her usual good humor. As she took a chop from Melinda, the serving girl, she hummed a spirited ditty, and seemed not to notice that the potatoes were boiled beyond having any texture and almost inedible. Her cook's poor skills were usually a reliable topic of conversation, but on this night Augusta did not seem interested in talking, no matter how felicitous her mood. She was in her own world.

Abigail was distressed by her aunt's apparent distract-edness. In the past day, she had found herself starting to feel homesick, and missing the dependable aspects of her days at Peacock Hall—the pleasant monotony of meals (well cooked) and her loose routine of writing, always punctuated by the exasperating yet somehow comforting presence of her sisters.

About the only thing that reminded her of Peacock Hall here in London was the ever-present Nathan. Yet even he had failed to leave a message for her today.

Which was a good thing, she reminded herself. She had told him to leave her alone, and evidently he had taken her at her word.

Besides, she shouldn't be pining for Peacock Hall. She had dreamed of living away from Yorkshire for years, and now she had her opportunity. "I started looking for lodg-ings today."

Her aunt, who was busily aligning her peas into a large A with her fork, looked up suddenly. Her expression made it clear that she was surprised to discover someone at table with her. "What did you say, dear?"

Abigail took a deep breath. Where was her aunt's mind today? "I said I had started looking for lodgings today."

Unfortunately, what she had found had not been promis-ing. The woman with rooms she had heard about through friends of her aunt seemed more desirous of a second up-stairs maid than a lodger. She had even asked Abigail if she wouldn't mind helping her fix her hair from time to time!

Abigail, who never even helped her sisters with their hair—would never be asked to in any case—hurried away from the meeting certain she would have to pay more for lodgings, or take care to dress less like a maid during her next interview.

She had been doing calculations nonstop and had come

up with a rather dispiriting budget. What she had saved would not support a lavish lifestyle. Indeed, she imagined she would only be able to take a few furnished rooms somewhere, with perhaps a little left over to hire a girl to help her occasionally. She would have to be very careful and count every penny. The plan was not ideal—and certainly did not live up to her girlish dream of living in splendid isolation—but with any luck her next book would bring her more money and keep her financially afloat.

She needed to finish *The Prisoner of Raffizzi* soon, or all she would be able to afford would be a flea-ridden closet somewhere.

"Are you sure you want to live alone?" her aunt asked her. "The more I think on it, the more I feel it's not exactly . . . well, proper. I'm sure your father will not approve."

"Of course he won't. He doesn't approve of girls wanting to do anything on their own. It leaves him with less to barter with."

Aunt Augusta laughed, then went back to her peas and her humming.

"I'm sure when I look more I will find a respectable house in a good neighborhood," Abigail continued. "He cannot speak against such a plan, especially since I am not asking him for money."

Her aunt nodded absently and Abigail added, "Though I suppose I will have to confess that I am Georgianna Harcourt to him so that he will know where my money is coming from!"

Augusta looked at her with an unfocused smile.

"Don't you think so, Aunt?"

"Think what?"

"That I should tell my father that I am Georgianna Harcourt."

Her aunt looked stunned. "Why ever would you want to do that?"

Abigail began to wonder if she hadn't been talking to herself the whole time. "Because otherwise he might wonder how I am getting money."

Augusta blurted out a laugh. "Oh yes—perhaps he

would think you had become a notorious woman about town. Wouldn't that be delicious!"

Abigail felt her face redden. "Certainly not."

"It would serve him right for behaving so toadishly to begin with and treating you like a commercial commodity. And having no respect for you! That is so often the problem with men."

"Yes, but . . ." She sighed. "I can't let my father think I have become a courtesan."

Augusta was still chuckling. "I think that would be amusing above all else. I might even direct Nathan to start a whisper to that effect."

"Aunt, do not!" Abigail cried, horrified. Then she frowned. "*Nathan*?"

When had he stopped being Mr. Cantrell to her aunt?

"Oh! I forgot to tell you about this morning's excitement. On our walk, Lancelot was accosted by urchins and got away from me. Then he took a leap into the Serpentine again. I was quite exasperated—you know how he is about those swans!" She frowned. "Or maybe you don't. Anyway, he's mad about them and will paddle after them for an age. But then what do you think?"

Abigail shook her head, unsure where all this was leading.

"Nathan of all people dashed to the rescue! He quite disregarded the ruination of a pair of very nice boots, although I can't say that the rest of his ensemble was much of a loss. But he said it was worth it to restore my dear companion to me!"

"But I thought you said Lancelot could paddle for an age."

"And so he can, but Nathan didn't know that. I thought it quite gallant of him to wade in after Lancie—and considered myself quite fortunate that he happened to be passing by. So I invited him for tea."

"Hmph." Abigail was skeptical that anything Nathan did was ever by accident. And she immediately wondered what had later transpired at the tea between the two. Her aunt looked like the cat that had swallowed the cream. "What did you talk to him about this afternoon? Me?"

Her aunt seemed surprised that she would ask. "Your name came up, naturally."

Naturally! Abigail bristled. She was also bristling to hear more.

"Are you sure you wouldn't like to marry him?" Augusta asked, watching her closely. "He is very handsome."

"He has not behaved handsomely," Abigail volleyed back.

"There is good in him, though."

Abigail's jaw went slack. "How can you say this, Aunt, after he deceived me so?"

Her aunt's brow crazed with light wrinkles as she concentrated on the question. "Of course, it did appear at first that he had deceived you, but perhaps it only *seemed* that way because you were deceived."

"But—" Before she could argue the point, whatever the point was, the words died in her mouth. "*What?*"

"Well, let's consider this logically. You were deceived. But do you know whether Nathan knowingly deceived you? Perhaps it was all Sir Harlan's doing . . ."

"A man does not agree to an engagement scheme such as he entered into unknowingly!" Abigail said hotly. Then she shook her head. "Why are you suddenly calling him Nathan?"

"Because that is the name he asked me to use."

Augusta looked down and started that humming again.

Abigail frowned. "You seem to have gotten quite friendly."

"As I said, Abigail, he seems to have much good in him. I know you don't care for his society, though, so I will try to keep him away from you. I told him you would never forgive him."

"Good!" Abigail attempted to focus her attention on her potatoes, but could not help inquiring, "What did he say to that?"

"He seemed resigned that this might be the case, poor man."

Resigned? He had given up *already*?

Not that she wanted him to persevere, of course. "Poor

man—fiddlesticks! Of course I will not forgive him," Abigail vowed. "How could I?"

Augusta nodded. "It would take an enormous leap of faith on your part, and a great generosity of spirit."

Abigail, silenced, stared at her. Was she implying that Abigail did not possess such generosity?

Though, of course, Abigail had to admit that she did not. Or that if she did, she did not care to extend it to Nathan.

Augusta leaned back and sighed contentedly. "What a lovely dinner!" she said of the completely untouched repast. "I think I shall go to bed early tonight. I have such a busy day ahead tomorrow."

Abigail could not remember anything being said about activities tomorrow. "What are we doing?"

Her aunt shifted uncomfortably. Whatever plans she had made, she had apparently not intended to include Abigail in them. "Oh, dear. I have errands to attend to." As Abigail continued to scrutinize her she added, "Of a personal nature."

"Oh." Abigail sighed. "Well, perhaps I will retire early, too. After the pudding."

Augusta gaped at her. "But there is no pudding."

For some reason, Abigail felt crestfallen. Perhaps because the rest of the meal had been inedible.

"I'm sorry, my dear, but I indulged my sweet tooth so this afternoon that I told Cook not to prepare a dessert."

"Well! That is fine." Abigail aimed a curious look at her. "Where did you have sweets this afternoon?"

"With Nathan. He had a . . ." Her aunt cleared her throat. "It was just a macaroon or two."

Abigail couldn't help drumming her fingers on the table as she watched her aunt sitting there so innocent and happy. So Nathan had rescued her aunt's beloved pet, cadged an invitation to tea, and then plied her full of macaroons and who knows what else . . . probably a lot of hot air.

What was he up to now?

* * *

The church bell from St. Paul's tolled three in the distance, and each gong seemed to escalate Abigail's worry a bit more. Where was Aunt Augusta?

She had been gone all morning.

Of course, Augusta had told her that she would have a busy day, and Abigail had assured her that she would be able to entertain herself for the morning. Yet it still seemed odd that Augusta would be gone this long.

Abigail had intended to go out searching for lodgings today, but her enthusiasm for the endeavor had not taken her farther than the front door, where she had turned back, feeling a slight headache. Odd that she had put Nathan off with headaches for so many days, and yet now, the second day he had not come by, she actually did feel achy. She sensed the hand of divine retribution.

She had tried to work, but her enthusiasm for that was also at low ebb. She assumed this was because she had had such a tiring week, and her life was now at such sixes and sevens. It was difficult to concentrate on Rudolpho and Clara when she had no idea where she would be living a month hence.

Which was all the more reason why she should venture out. Of course, now it was almost too late. Completely at loose ends, she decided to go downstairs and have a cup of tea. She crossed the parlor to ring for Melinda but found herself stopping midway, her heels nearly tripping her as they dug into the carpet before her mind could quite grasp what she had just seen. Surely her eyes deceived her!

But no, there sat Nathan, draped casually across her aunt's sofa. The teacup and saucer balanced on his thigh rattled when he caught sight of her. As if *he* were surprised to see *her*!

"Abigail!" He jumped up, managing the teacup deftly.

Her heart experienced a little fillip. Had it really only been a few days since she had last seen him? Her eyes took him in hungrily, as if it had been an age instead. As if she could detect the subtle differences that the short amount of time had forced on the strong planes of his cheeks. Were those circles under his eyes? Did he seem thinner?

She managed a calm nod. "You seem astonished to find me here," she said. "Maybe you were expecting Queen Charlotte?"

He chuckled. But he did not answer, she noticed. How had he managed to worm his way in?

"Butterworth did not announce you to me," she said.

"Otherwise you would have come dashing down to see me, I suppose." A wry smile played on his lips. "I am glad to see you looking so fit. I was beginning to worry that you might have become a permanent headache victim."

She blushed in spite of herself. Perhaps she should not have told Butterworth to fib for her; it seemed like something Violet would have done. But who didn't make up little excuses when they needed to avoid people?

"I am well today," she replied. "Thank you for your concern."

"I am glad. Truly."

His green eyes met hers and seemed to burn right into her. She shifted her gaze away and tried to will away the quivery feeling in her limbs. She detested that she should go noodle-kneed every time the man smiled at her!

"It surprises me that I did not hear Lancelot barking when you came in," she said. The portly old dog snored obliviously in the corner. "He usually makes more of a fuss."

"We are old friends, Lancelot and I."

She crossed her arms. "Yes, I heard of your adventure yesterday in the Serpentine. How amazing it is that you should have arrived in the park at precisely the opportune moment!"

He grinned slyly. "It was happy timing. I also consider it fortunate that I have a way with dogs."

"And fathers," she added, "and apparently aunts, too." Remembering the missing person in the house, she looked about her, as if Augusta might be crouching beneath a table. "What have you done with Aunt Augusta?"

"Nothing, I assure you. I was to meet her here, but Butterworth informed me she was out—*out* out—and instructed me to wait."

So he had come calling only to see Aunt Augusta. For some reason, this bit of information struck her like a slap.

Not that she cared who Nathan visited.

Come to think of it she *did* care. Clearly she was going a little mad, for why should she care when she had released Nathan to court either of her two sisters—or practically anyone else in the universe?

No, it wasn't that she cared for *him*, she told herself vehemently. It was just that his continued presence reminded her of the whole humiliating interlude with Nathan back in the days before she discovered that she was just being courted as the least of three evils.

Just thinking of her former happiness made a white heat blaze through her. "I would have thought you would be back in Yorkshire by now."

"I had some unfinished business here."

"But you *do* intend to go back?"

"Yes. When my business is finished."

What was this mysterious business? She bit her lip to keep from blurting out the suspicion in her mind.

On second thought, why should she hold her tongue? "I think I know what you are up to," she said.

He laughed. "Do you?"

"Yes, and I don't like it. You are trying to get to me through my aunt."

He kept laughing, which only infuriated her. "Please remember that appearances can be deceiving."

Now it was her turn to laugh, except hers issued from her in the form of a snarl. "How could I forget! Especially when I am staring at a very able deceiver."

His smile disappeared and he looked hurt. He stepped forward, causing her to take a step backwards. "Abigail. Please let me say that I never meant to cause you pain. I thought we were good friends. More than that, actually. Much more. I thought you cared for me as I cared, still do care, for you."

His words, so warmly spoken, rattled her soul. He sounded so sincere, seemed so genuine in his manner. When she looked into his face, she longed to believe him.

She wanted to step into his arms and pretend that everything that had transpired since the ball at Peacock Hall had not happened.

"I truly thought you did care," he continued, "otherwise I never would have gone along with your father. And I could not think that you would see marriage to me as such a terrible thing. Surely you did not want to live the rest of your life in your father's house. Your family there never seemed to properly appreciate you."

As he spoke the words, however, the old hurt in her flared. "So you thought you would simply herd me over to The Willows, like one of those sheep you profess such an interest in?"

"I never thought of you that way."

"And yet you assumed that I would be *so glad* to be proposed to that I would immediately forget the underhanded manner of your courtship. Sheer gratefulness from being spared the life of a spinster would make me leap into your arms!"

"I was presumptuous, I will admit."

She tossed her head back. "More than presumptuous— you showed an arrogance that shocks me still. And now you seem ready to squire my aunt about town in the same fashion, using her for your own purposes. You should be ashamed."

"Abigail, I have no underhanded scheme underway with your aunt. I have learned my lesson on that score, I assure you."

"It is difficult to accept the assurances of one who has lied to you." Not to mention the assurances of one who had been chasing her aunt down in parks and plying her full of sweets.

Nathan came closer to her. Unfortunately, there was no way for her to back out of his way without climbing over a chair. Abigail's heartbeat sped. Was he going to try to kiss her? Would he dare? Before she could find out, she sidestepped out of his path and crossed the carpet. It felt as if they were performing an elaborate minuet.

"Abigail, if there were anything I could do to win back

your trust, I would do it. I hope someday I will have that opportunity."

"That will be difficult, as you will be hundreds of miles away."

His brows arched in question.

"I intend to stay in London indefinitely," she said.

He frowned. "Here, with your aunt?"

"Or on my own."

His mouth dropped open. "Are you mad?"

She laughed. "Possibly."

"But how can you?"

"As opposed to letting myself be whisked away by a man who had struck a financial bargain with my father, you mean?"

His face reddened, and a little muscle in his jaw twitched. "That would be preferable to casting yourself adrift here! How could you even consider it?"

His look was such a mixture of befuddlement and shock that she could not help laughing. "I have my own secrets which I do not choose to divulge to you."

Before he could question this statement, Augusta breezed into the room. When she saw them facing off, she missed the tension entirely and let out a happy sigh. "Ah! So you two are friends again! I *am* glad."

They turned to her in unison, both of them still stiff with irritation with each other.

"Aunt Augusta, I am concerned about you," Abigail declared.

Augusta shot a sidewise glance at Nathan. "Why? I am sorry I was late, but I simply wanted to pick up a hat at the milliners." As if to prove the truth in her words, she held up a box. "Today seemed a special occasion."

Nathan cleared his throat, and Augusta jumped. "Oh! That is . . . I only meant . . . well, who doesn't enjoy having a new bonnet?"

Abigail crossed her arms, feeling more uneasy by the moment. "Should I ring Melinda for some tea?"

Again, glances were exchanged. Nathan shifted. Augusta crossed to Abigail and patted her on the arm. "No, dear.

Nathan and I must dash. But if you don't mind my saying so, you look like you could use some tea. Your pallor is very disturbing today." She frowned at Abigail's face. "Or perhaps it is just the light through the green drapes. I knew I would regret choosing that color!"

Nathan smiled at Augusta. "Shall we go?"

He took the older lady's arm, and with a trill of the fingers from Augusta, the two of them took their leave.

Abigail stood stock still on the carpet. They seemed in a terrible hurry . . . almost as if they had a very important appointment they were in a rush to keep.

No doubt this was a ruse. They probably were hoping that she would follow them and ask to be one of their party.

She would show them. Abigail collapsed into a chair. She would do as her aunt suggested and swill down a few cups of tea. Then she would put the whole annoying business with Nathan behind her. Tomorrow she would continue the search for lodgings. She had a long, exciting life in London stretching ahead of her—one that had absolutely no need of Nathan in it.

No need at all.

She frowned. *Where had Augusta and Nathan gone?*

Chapter Fifteen

Clara grasped the necessity of leaving the castle and this magnetic power Rudolpho held over her. To escape the constant brilliant ray of those green eyes! Yet where could she turn?

All she needed were a few simple rooms of her own. A secluded seaside cottage where she could hide away and overcome these feelings that threatened to overwhelm her soul, these dark yearnings for what could never be hers, this dungeon that was her own heart.

Ah! But lodgings proved shockingly hard to find.
                     —The Prisoner of Raffizzi

The advertisement in the back of the journal had read that a Mrs. Fernheath had rooms to let to a woman of gentle breeding, but either Mrs. Fernheath had mixed emotions about letting out part of her house or a standard of gentility that Abigail had no hope of meeting. The moment Mrs. Fernheath clapped eyes on her, Abigail had felt reluctance oozing out of the woman's every pore.

"From *Yorkshire?*" the woman asked, as if Abigail had introduced herself as a former inhabitant of a far-flung barbarous colony.

When Abigail further explained that she was living with an aunt, the woman's brows had arched strikingly. "Just off Grosvenor Square, you say? *Miss* Travers? I have never heard of her."

Mrs. Fernheath obviously carried a catalog of all the wor-

thies in the British Empire in her head, and had no intention
of renting her musty attic rooms to any upstart pretender like
Abigail.

She left the house discouraged and began to trudge
home under a sky that threatened a summer downpour.
Several blocks from her aunt's house, the sky made good
on its threat. Abigail had neither the energy to run nor the
inclination to be soaked, so she scurried up the stairs to the
first house she came to and hoped the occupants would not
notice the stranger huddled on their stoop.

She was perched there unhappily watching stray fat
droplets winging themselves at her skirts when Nathan
came hurrying along down the street under the cover of an
umbrella. He caught sight of her several feet away, and
when he came abreast of the house she was standing next
to, he stopped and looked up at her.

"What are you doing there?" he asked. He appeared ir-
ritatingly dry.

"I am hovering."

He dashed up the stairs and offered her the protection of
his umbrella. "Allow me to escort you home."

She tilted her head, and asked a question she already
knew the answer to. "I wouldn't be taking you out of your
way?"

He grinned. "Coincidentally, I am on my way to your
aunt's house right now."

She fell in next to him and they descended to the walk-
way together. She knew his talk of coincidence was so
much fiddle-faddle. "You and Aunt Augusta are insepara-
ble now."

"I am an ardent admirer of your aunt."

He used the term ardent in its hyperbolic sense. From
the beginning she had been watching the relationship budding between these two closely, but she had never seen
anything to indicate that anything of a romantic nature was
developing, which would have been shocking in the extreme. Instead, they seemed to be involved in some sort of
conspiracy, and Abigail was fairly certain that it involved
herself. Aunt Augusta had obviously decided to abet

Nathan in his courtship of her, and so in the past days they had been having *tête-à-tête* conferences and secret outings to give Nathan a reason to not-so-coincidentally bump into Abigail.

"It is amazing how a box of macaroons can open doors," Abigail noted.

Not that her aunt was the only one who had a weakness for Nathan's company. Abigail found herself staying close to home to see if he would come, and felt disappointed when she was not included in Nathan and Augusta's plans. Which, she came to be certain, was their perverse way of bringing her around.

The trouble was, it was working.

"Don't forget my valiant rescue of Lancelot from the beak of an angry swan," he added.

"I still find that whole episode suspect."

"You have a suspicious mind—always seeing plots afoot."

She grinned at how true that was; and woe to Georgianna Harcourt if her mind ever changed. "Sometimes there *are* plots afoot, in case you have forgotten."

"In this case, I swear to you nothing nefarious is underway. I have no evil designs on your aunt."

She laughed. "I am confident of that." Then her laughter died. "But tell, me . . . what are you up to?"

He shook his head. "Your aunt does not want me to divulge our plans at the moment."

Naturally. Because Aunt Augusta well knew that Abigail would cry foul at any scheme to bring her and Nathan together.

"I am surprised you have remained so long in town. Isn't your brother still at The Willows?"

"Yes, I got a letter from him this morning."

Abigail's ears perked up. "What did he say? Had he any news of home?" She had received maddeningly little.

"He had visited Peacock Hall and though he gave few details he wrote all there was well. Unfortunately, most of the letter was taken up with a sonnet to Mrs. Willoughby's gooseberry pie."

She nodded. She wondered what her sisters had made of her disappearance. Her father had answered Aunt Augusta's letter, but only said that he hoped Abigail was enjoying her "visit." No mention was made—to Abigail's knowledge—of the ball, or blackmail, or Nathan.

"Actually, I'm not certain if Freddy's skill at poetry is improving, or Mrs. Willoughby's cooking skills are simply inspiring, but it was almost a good poem. I never knew so many words rhymed with lard."

Abigail laughed, and felt happy that she was able to do so. Her foolish behavior of weeks ago, believing Nathan was her own personal Byron, was not so raw anymore. "I should think you would want to return to The Willows."

"I will, just as soon as my business is settled here."

"Still sheep?" she asked.

He nodded. "I have higher hopes, this time."

"I am glad," she said, though she couldn't help wondering if this "business" he referred to wasn't more subterfuge. She wondered if she herself was part of the reason he had not returned home yet.

They came upon a beggar in the street, and though Abigail hurried her footsteps, Nathan stopped and pulled out a coin for the man's outstretched hand. Seeing the grateful look in the man's eyes made her rethink her instinct to hurry past.

"He seemed so young," Abigail said.

"Yes—things are not going well for a lot of men right now," Nathan said. "The army is discharging so many, and back here they find little work."

Abigail had not thought of this problem before. "At home, such things are easier to remain blind to."

Nathan shook his head. "There is the same problem on a smaller scale. That's why I had hoped . . . well, if all goes well, I am hoping to put a few men to work, at least." He spoke a little more about his plans for manufacturing wool near The Willows, but was vague when it came to how he hoped to fund the venture.

"And what about you?" he asked. "Do you still intend to stay in London for good?"

"Yes, in fact I have just returned from looking for lodgings."

His displeasure at this announcement couldn't have been clearer. "I wish you would reconsider."

Abigail's spine stiffened; she did not care to be told what to do, especially now that she was having her first taste of independence. "I forgot that I was supposed to consult you in such matters," she said, her voice dripping with sarcasm.

"You seem to have no one else to consult."

"And I quite enjoy that."

"But you should have an advisor," he said.

"You mean I should have someone telling me not to do what I want," she said. "Never fear, the landlords of London seem to be doing that job. I never knew how hard it would be to find a place to live!"

"Perhaps because your true place is back home?"

She shook her head. "I shall never go back."

"I feel terrible knowing that I am the cause of the estrangement between you and your family."

"There is no estrangement," she assured him. "Well . . . not more than there ever was. I am afraid I was always a black sheep. I longed to leave for years. Discovering my father's scheme simply provided me with the impetus to do so."

"But you will be so far away," he said.

And strangely, those words tugged at her as no others had. A tight knot formed in her throat, and for the rest of the distance to her aunt's house, she was unable to reply. *So far away.* When she had been dreaming of escape in her featherlined room, she had never guessed that once she was free she would look back longingly on Peacock Hall. That so much of her thoughts during the day would be consumed with wondering what was happening in the old home she had been so eager to leave. She was shocked at how much she missed Sophy and Violet. She worried about her father, and whether he was spending too much time alone. She found herself wondering about the servants—Tillie and Patrick and even Peabody.

But mostly, when Nathan said the words *so far away,*

they spoke to a growing realization that who she would most miss would be Nathan when he returned home. Now that her irritation with him had abated somewhat, she had grown accustomed to his presence as an echo of her old life. And she had become even more attracted to his masculine presence, his teasing, the warm admiration in his gaze when he spoke to her.

In other words, his and Augusta's plan had worked. Being around Nathan had made her appreciate him more.

And soon he would be so far away.

A few days later, a discouraged Abigail climbed the stoop to her aunt's house. She had spent another morning in a fruitless pursuit of a place to live.

As she let herself into the hall of the house, she noticed Butterworth with a bottle of champagne and crystal flutes on a tray. It was unusual for her aunt to imbibe spirits in the middle of the day, and she had never seen champagne being served. This curious sight aroused ominous feelings. What was happening?

She halted on the threshold as the merry sound of a bottle being uncorked sounded.

"Is this a private party?" Abigail asked.

Augusta looked up happily. "Abigail! You're just in time to join us."

"Of course, I would need to know what exactly the occasion is that warrants such gaiety."

Augusta's eyes widened. "Come in and we shall tell you. I would have waited for your return, but I had thought you were to spend the day looking for lodgings."

"I fear I might have to find a hollowed out tree in a park somewhere," Abigail said. "Though even then I fear I would have a snobbish squirrel or two to contend with."

Her dilemma was even beginning to creep into her book. Since she was so behind in her writing these days, she supposed that she should be grateful for any inspiration, however unfortunate in nature.

When she glanced at Nathan, she caught him frowning

at her as he always did whenever she mentioned her plans for setting up housekeeping on her own in London.

"Well, never mind, dear. Actually, I am glad you're here. I have the most exciting news for you. You may have noticed that Nathan and I have been out together quite a bit recently, but what you do not know is what we've been doing with our time—although I dare say you may have had your suspicions. We have been consulting my solicitors about forming a business venture!"

Oddly enough, the first feeling that slammed through her as her aunt's words sank in was disappointment. Nathan had not been hanging around the house to be nearer to herself. She had been so sure that this was the reason that she had never even suspected the true nature of his visits with her aunt, even though he had hinted that he had found a solution to his financial problems. How could she have been so wrong?

Perhaps because she had *wanted* him to be coming around for her sake.

The second thing that occurred to her was that Nathan no longer had the need of her or her fortune. Perversely, she felt her spirits plummet at the realization.

She must have been staring slack-jawed at them for a rather long time because her aunt let out a delicate, nervous cough.

Abigail took a deep breath and ordered her thoughts. "How did this partnership come about?"

"It was the afternoon that Nathan rescued poor Lancelot from that nasty swan," Augusta told her. "Nathan just happened to mention his plans for starting a factory and using as many retired soldiers as he could and it struck me as a brilliant idea. He had been hunting for backers in the project for months, but without luck. So, I suggested to Nathan that I could invest in his wool factory," her aunt explained. "I hope you won't be upset, dear—it is a bit of a gamble. But you see, I needed somewhere to keep my money. Otherwise it just slips through my fingers like sand."

Abigail was beginning to feel more and more foolish. "So you are to go into business with Mr. Cantrell?"

"Yes! We just signed all the papers today, and that is why we are now celebrating. Butterworth, hand Abigail a glass!" She lifted her own gleefully. "To the success of The Willows Fine Worsted, Inc."

As they all toasted each other (Butterworth had some-how produced a fourth glass for himself as well), Abigail felt like a soufflé that had just had a fork poked through it—the hot air drained out of her, leaving her feeling de-pleted. All the mystery and excitement of the last two months was over. Nathan and she were both about to em-bark on new lives. New lives apart.

"I can see that you are concerned for you aunt's wel-fare," Nathan said, "but believe me, her money will be se-cure. If the factory succeeds, she will have her investment back and a handsome return. If it does not, you will have a new neighbor, and probably one more congenial to you than I have been."

Abigail hardly knew what to say now.

"You must come out with us tonight, dear," her aunt said, patting her arm. "We are going to the theater. That is to be the true celebration."

Nathan nodded his agreement. "Yes, I hope you will join us."

Abigail smiled numbly and replied that of course she would love to accompany them, revealing nothing of the tumult going on inside her. Nathan no longer needed to marry her and would be returning to Yorkshire soon. She would be remaining here, writing her books and enjoying an independent existence. This was exactly what she had wished for.

Why, then, did she feel so badly when everything was turning out just as she had hoped?

He had hired a carriage that night, and borrowing a page from Lord Fuego, he made sure it was the best that could be had with ready money . . . some of the last ready money he had. He felt a little guilty tossing away pounds on carriages after all his lectures to Freddy about economizing, but he wanted to make an impression on Abigail. And he wanted that impression to say, *I can do without you very well.*

However, I would be happier not having to do without you at all . . .

But if he had expected to impress Abigail with fine carriages, he was doomed to disappointment. The only one he managed to impress was his new business partner. Augusta was all atwitter when he picked up her and her niece. Nathan got the impression that Abigail was merely dragging herself along.

"Was not Butterworth's expression when I told him he was working for a businesswoman priceless?" she exclaimed, slapping Nathan on the arm with her fan once they were installed in the carriage. "You could have knocked the man over with a sneeze! I believe he drank half the bottle of champagne in his shock."

Abigail was looking studiously out the window. What was going on in her head? He wished he knew! He wished they were alone together so that he could take her in his arms and . . .

She turned, catching his glance. Even in the dim light of the carriage, he could see her cheeks stain with red. She looked away again.

"But wouldn't you know," Augusta continued, "the odious man turned sour on me and asked if he should start looking for another position, since our finances were obviously in grave peril. I told him that was an insult to you, Nathan."

"I take it as a joke, not an insult."

"Of course! You are so good-natured. Unlike one man I could mention."

And yet Nathan saw Augusta and Butterworth lasting until the end of their days, locked in domestic combat. He imagined that when the end came for one the other would soon follow, like some husbands and wives he had heard about. They would be unable to function without each other, any more than the front end of a horse could function without its back end.

"And who does he expect would give him a job, I'd like to know!" Augusta said.

Augusta spent the rest of the ride talking along similar lines, discussing Butterworth and his many faults and deficiencies. Every attempt Nathan made to bring Abigail into the conversation fell flat. She still seemed subdued after the revelation of that afternoon—although Nathan had thought she would be relieved to know that he didn't want to marry her for her money.

He did manage to sit next to Abigail in the box at the theater, with Augusta on his right-hand side. During the first act of the play, an amusing piece of farce concerning a man who fakes illness to bring a pair of lovers together, Nathan would look at her for her reaction to what she was seeing. There her guard was let down, and she truly seemed to enjoy herself.

For some reason, that gave him hope.

Augusta was blooming after the first act. She leaned back in her chair and fanned herself happily. "What a pleasure a good play is! I will have to remember what fun I had tonight on Tuesday, when I am stuck at Lady Trammel's for supper."

Nathan and Abigail exchanged frowns.

"Tuesday next?" Abigail asked her aunt.

Augusta chuckled. "No dear, *tomorrow*. I did not tell you about it because I forgot—and Lady Trammel is not the type to accommodate an added guest, alas. Besides, I had no idea . . ." She looked at Nathan and ducked her head. "Well—I simply did not know how long you would be staying, and the excitement of these past days quite rattled the subject of the dinner party right out of my head."

That was not the only thing that had been rattled out of the older woman's head.

"Aunt," Abigail pointed out, "*today* is Tuesday."

The fanning stopped. Augusta's face was a mask of disbelief. "What?"

"Today is Tuesday," Abigail repeated.

Augusta pivoted in shock to Nathan, who reaffirmed that the day was indeed Tuesday.

"Oh, my stars!" she exclaimed when the terrible truth concerning the day of the week finally sank in. She let out a cry of alarm and jumped out of her chair, causing people to swivel towards them and stare. "I must go or else I will be dreadfully late!"

At the prospect of being abandoned alone with Nathan, Abigail protested "But Aunt . . ."

"It is quite all right, dear. Nathan will see you home."

"But how will you get to Lady Trammel's?"

"You must borrow my carriage," Nathan offered.

"Yes," Augusta said, already moving towards the door. "I shall borrow Nathan's carriage. Thank you! There will be plenty of time for it to return here before the end of the last act. I am sure I will be able to beg a ride home from Lady Trammel's with one of the other dinner guests."

"But, Aunt—"

"Don't worry about me, Abigail. I will find a way home. Never fear!"

When Nathan had seen her to the carriage, he returned to the box, where Abigail was perched uncomfortably, overlooking the orchestra.

"I hope you don't feel awkward being alone with me," Nathan told her, at the same time feeling very pleased with the way things were working out. Without Augusta there to chatter the night away, Abigail would have to speak to him. And he knew that if they could just talk to each other, they could find a way back into each other's arms.

"This quite reminds me of the way Father was always maneuvering to get you alone with Violet or Sophy. If this were days of old," Abigail told him with a wry smile, "I would have suspected a plot."

He chuckled, remembering. "What a suspicious mind you had!"

She bit her lip, but there was humor in her eyes as she regarded him. "Oh yes, you are above such schemes, no doubt. You just happened to be in the right place at the time of Lancelot's escape . . . or perhaps even his near-kidnapping?"

He laughed and shook his head. "You make me sound quite the modern-day Machiavelli."

"Oh, no—I meant only to compliment you. You are like a cat that always lands on its feet."

"You have a very different view of my situation than I do. I'll admit I have been lucky and that I am on my feet for the moment, but I see only hard work ahead."

"Not the same as if you had married an heiress?"

The words cut his jovial mood. He would never be able to look on Sir Harlan's bargain without a hint of bitterness that he had felt obliged to take him up on it. "I only ever considered his proposal for Freddy's sake, and to save The Willows."

"Well, you don't have to worry about that now. You can return home in triumph."

"Yes, but it's a rather empty triumph," Nathan said.

"How so?"

He scooted his chair inches closer to hers. "Because I had hoped not to return home alone."

Two rosy dots appeared in her cheeks, and to avoid his eyes, she scanned the crowd.

Something seemed to catch her eye. "I have told you I intend to stay in London," she said.

"Still?"

"Your situation may have changed, but mine has not."

"Yes, but surely you do not really intend to live alone? It's a preposterous idea!"

"It is not—" Her words broke off as she was again distracted by someone in the crowd. "Who is that man?"

"What man?"

"The one down there—staring and waving at us."

He followed her gaze and groaned as the tall blond man started waving frantically. "That's Bentley Fitzhugh. We were in the army together. Quick, look away. The man is an imbecile."

They averted their eyes too late, alas. Bentley started clambering over theater patrons in his quest to get to Nathan and Abigail, but, luckily, the lights went down and the play began again.

Not that Nathan minded visiting with his old friends, but on this night he wanted to take advantage of having Abigail alone. And his memories of Bentley Fitzhugh were not all pleasant. The man fancied himself as something of a ladies' man.

Unfortunately, Bentley was faster getting to the box during the next intermission. "Why Nathan, old man—I didn't know you were in town," he said, speaking to Nathan but never taking his eyes off Abigail. Nathan felt a stab of jealousy. There was no denying that Bentley was handsome. "I thought you were up in . . . where is it?"

"Yorkshire."

"That's it." Bentley smiled more broadly at Abigail. As if the idea of living in Yorkshire was itself amusing.

Nathan reluctantly made introductions, but there was nothing at all reluctant about Bentley's manner in greeting Abigail.

"Charmed!" he exclaimed, bending over her hand in an extravagant fashion that made Nathan want to slap him. He took in the lack of chaperone and shot a sidewise grin at Nathan. "I never knew Nathan had *a friend* in London."

Abigail blushed.

"We are neighbors from home," Nathan said through gritted teeth.

"Are you?" Bentley asked with apparent disbelief. "I would never have taken you for a country girl." He looked pointedly at Abigail's gown, which was in the very latest mode. His glance lingered on the fashionably low décolletage. Nathan ground his teeth.

"And I would never have taken you for a . . ." Abigail's eyes stared glassily at him in a way that made Nathan want to laugh. "What exactly *are* you, Mr. Fitzhugh?"

Bentley laughed. "An admirer of women with wit!"

Abigail and Nathan blinked at him disbelievingly.

Bentley shifted. "What a nice box! Must have cost you a pretty penny, Nate. Mind if I join you for the last act?"

Both Abigail and Nathan began piping objections, but Bentley ignored them and sat down in Nathan's chair. "Thanks—the view's so much better up here, you know."

Nathan resigned himself to this invasion.

Bentley grinned. "My mother is having a little soirée tomorrow night. Nothing too fancy, town's very thin of company right now." He winked at Abigail. "Mother thinks I should be married—tired of her rakish son's ways, don't you know. She's always planning dances and things in hopes of nudging me into matrimony."

Abigail bit her lip. "That is a problem with parents."

"You're both invited, of course. Let my word be your invitation to terpsichorean bliss!"

Nathan rolled his eyes. And yet . . . another evening, another chance. He swore he would do better this time.

"I would be glad to escort Abigail to your mother's."

"Splendid!" Bentley said, taking Abigail's hand again in a move that Nathan found irritating and Abigail obviously found amusing. Still, Nathan worried. If Abigail intended to stay on in London, and Bentley showered her with attention . . .

"I shall look forward to it," Bentley purred.

"I'm so glad you have an engagement," Augusta said. And she truly did seem glad. The smile she sent Abigail suggested an exhausted mother bird watching a fledgling go careening out of the nest. "The Fitzhughs are a very good family—I am sure you will have a gay time," she added, as if to reassure herself about not accompanying Abigail. Augusta had a standing engagement to play cards on Wednesday evenings. "And Bentley Fitzhugh is rather handsome, I think. Dumb as a street lamp, unfortunately, but quite attractive!"

"I was not impressed with him."

"Oh that's right—but then, why would you be? I keep forgetting you have a *tendresse* already."

"No, I do not."

"As you wish, my dear. But I know that Nathan is madly in love with you, and when a man is that handsome and that nice, it is difficult not to return his affection eventually." She laughed. "I believe it is only a matter of time before you're declaring yourself head over heels."

"Oh, Aunt! I'm afraid that you've misunderstood—Nathan does not care for me in that way."

"Fiddlesticks," replied Augusta.

Abigail couldn't help hoping there was some truth to Augusta's beliefs. She wondered . . . *does he really love me? Could it be?* Augusta and Nathan had been so chummy, perhaps he had confided in her.

Oh, but it didn't matter now. It couldn't. She had her pride. "Nathan will be going home soon, and I intend to stay here." As always, that notion caused a tightening sensation in her chest.

Her aunt smiled. "That's right. Nathan might have left today, in fact . . . if someone had not kept him."

Abigail tried not to hope too hard that she was the reason he had decided to stay, as her aunt clearly wanted her to believe. No matter if it was the next day or the next week, he would return home, and become consumed with his business concerns, and forget all about her.

"If I were twenty years younger, I would try to finagle a proposal out of the man myself." Augusta sighed. "Of course, whether I would accept the proposal once I had done the finagling is another matter entirely . . ."

Abigail marveled at her aunt. Such was Augusta's whimsy, apparently, that she could not even be nailed down to accepting proposals she had only hypothetically won.

"As far as I am concerned, you would be welcome to do as you pleased with Mr. Cantrell," Abigail said, though with far less conviction than she would have been able to muster a few days ago. "I have no immediate intention of marrying, so all this talk is nothing but folly."

Augusta laughed breezily. "No doubt, no doubt. Well, in any case, when you find these lodgings you are so set on, I suggest you get yourself a nice puppy, like my Lancelot. He has been an endless comfort to me. Better than a husband, I always say."

Abigail cast a skeptical eye at the mound of fur on his

tasseled pillow. A husband certainly couldn't snore any louder.

Nathan called for her again in a hired carriage, and she tried to keep her aunt's mad ideas at bay as they sat together in the dark, almost touching, and listened to the soft grind of the wheels against the pavement. Nathan was not in love with her. Preposterous!

And yet, when she cut a glance sideways at him, his green eyes smoldered at her through the semidarkness, quickening her pulse. She suddenly felt awkward, vulnerable almost, as she had never felt with a man since . . . well, since shivering in that pond with Nathan during their first encounter.

Oh, why hadn't Augusta begged off her card game? She had sent her maid along to serve as chaperone, but Melinda was as quiet as a mouse. Abigail sorely missed her aunt's talkative presence. When it came time for Sophy to come up to London, Abigail would have to remember to advise her father that perhaps Aunt Augusta was not the most watchful of women. In fact, they would need a chaperone for the chaperone or else Sophy would be in no end of trouble.

And yet Abigail could not deny that a small part of her was thrilled to have Nathan almost all to herself. Once they arrived at the party they would be almost entirely on their own.

However, when they arrived at the hulking Fitzhugh residence—a newer home near Regent's Park—she realized to her dismay that they would not be so alone as she had hoped. Bentley Fitzhugh would see to that.

He was on top of them the moment they stepped foot inside the cavernous new ballroom of Fitzhugh House, which was ornamented liberally with gold; plaster putti darted about the moldings high above them. The family had an obvious love of the baroque.

Or perhaps it was simply a love of extravagance.

Nathan was greeted by at least a dozen of his old comrades in arms, and Abigail was not surprised by how warmly they all seemed to regard him. However, she was surprised that this approval extended towards herself. She was swept into one dance and then another by newly retired young soldiers, all still bearing the dash of victory.

Meanwhile, Nathan was borne off to smoke and reminisce before they had even had a chance to dance, leaving her to feel more alone still. How hollow her aunt's assurances of his affection rang now! Her appeal was apparently running a distant second place to the lure of tobacco.

So much for his being in love with her!

Nathan thought he would explode if he had to listen to more chatter about "the old days on the peninsula" while out of the corner of his eye he watched Abigail being whisked ever farther away from him. Yet all his old colleagues were eager to have his ear and told the same story.

Since leaving the army, they felt at loose ends. And not a few were in the market for an eligible wife.

Even Bentley, who could have scraped gold off the walls of this very ballroom, cried poor.

"Glad to see you looking so well, Nate," he said. "Glad to see someone is, at any rate."

"Aren't you?" Nate asked, sensing the answer would be in the negative. "I am sorry to hear it."

And he felt ever more indebted to Aunt Augusta for her backing of his business.

"Why do you think I have agreed with my mother to start hunting for a bride? The Fitzhugh coffers need replenishing," Bentley complained. His eyes followed Abigail about the room. "You say Miss Wingate is . . . ?"

"From Yorkshire. Her father was a merchant."

He had expected the word merchant to frighten Bentley, but instead the man perked up even more. "Nothing wrong with that—so long as he got rich."

Nathan shrugged noncommitally. "I couldn't say exactly."

"Of course, if she were *too* rich that would be no good, either. Just look at Miss Plimpton."

"Who?"

"Minerva Plimpton, the ale heiress," Bentley said, pointing to a swarm of coats surrounding a chair.

Nathan could only assume that all these coats were obscuring the heiress herself. "I have heard of her."

"'Course you have! She is one of the richest women in England . . . but one can't get near her. A fox pursued by too many hounds." He snorted and elbowed Nathan sharply. "And none of us are quite the dogs we used to be, eh what?"

Nathan forced his lips into something like a smile. He turned around to see Abigail—still dancing. He would have gladly strangled her partner.

"But one doesn't need a Miss Plimpton to solve one's problems," Bentley said, fairly licking his lips as he followed Nathan's gaze to Abigail. "Just a fairly charming girl with a middling fortune—correctly managed—would suit me."

Now Nathan found himself wanting to strangle his host.

"Excuse me," he growled.

He pushed away and marched towards Abigail and some nitwit about to escort her onto the dance floor to join the other couples as the orchestra struck up a waltz. No one did anything but waltz anymore, he thought peevishly.

He saw that Abigail's would-be partner was Wilfred Douglas. No doubt Wilfred had jockeyed unsuccessfully for Miss Plimpton, too! Nathan was suddenly disgusted with it all, and the terrible thing was, he had been no different. No wonder Abigail had been repulsed by the manner in which her father had promised her hand . . . this barter that men and women went through to secure family fortunes and property and simply please the expectations of their elders *was* unseemly. He had always thought so . . . until those few weeks when he had been looking at the matter in the light of his own circumstances. But now the light was shining on Bentley and Wilfred and God-only-knows-who-else pursuing Abigail after he returned to Yorkshire.

He grasped Abigail's hand. In fact, he nearly yanked her off her feet. "Miss Wingate, I believe this is our dance."

Wilfred looked offended, and laughed nervously. "Afraid you're out there, Nate. Fact is, I am to dance this one with Miss Wingate—"

"I think you'll find you mistake the matter," Nathan said, dragging Abigail into his arms.

She stared up at him as if he had lost his mind. "Have you gone mad?"

"I always look forward to these dances," he explained, "but I forget how difficult it is to secure the partner of one's choice."

Her brows arched at him. "So you simply choose to commandeer your dance partners now, like a ballroom highwayman?"

"Only because I have something very important to say to you."

Her gaze softened. "What is it?"

"I do not think you should stay here."

Her eyes widened in mock alarm. "Here? Am I in danger of social contamination? My aunt assured me that the Fitzhughs were a well-regarded family."

He should have known that she would attempt to make light of his advice. "Here, in London."

She appeared astonished. "You are telling me to go home?"

"I am saying that would be the wisest course."

Her jaw tightened as she stared at him. Neither one of them was moving with any feeling. Their feet were as close to being immobile as those of dancers could ever be. "Why?"

"Because a young woman alone in London is not safe."

"From whom?"

"Men of low character, charlatans, fortune hunters."

She stared at him for another long moment and then pushed away, her arms akimbo. "And you think those do not exist in Yorkshire?"

He remained silent.

"Believe me, they do! I have come dangerously close to them." She turned and churned furiously toward the punch bowl.

He followed her. He had made a mess of things, as usual. "Abigail, forgive me," he said when he had caught up to her. "I only meant to protect you."

"I see." Her jaw was now clenched so tight her cheek twitched. "You have only my best interests at heart now. No doubt, since you have allied yourself with my aunt, you look on my future with brotherly concern."

"Never that," he whispered.

Her eyes glistened, and she lifted her chin. "Aunt Augusta has also been advising me. She told me I should forget husbands and find myself a dog."

"Preferably one with better breath than Lancelot," Nathan snapped.

Abigail could not help but smile. "Lancelot's breath is better than that of some of the men I have danced with tonight."

Nathan chuckled.

Abigail laughed with him. "What made you suddenly care so for my future?"

"I have cared about your future since we first met."

Her lips pursed. "But what made you charge across the dance floor and risk the wrath of Mr. Douglas?"

"I happened to be watching the lascivious look in our friend Bentley's eye as he watched you . . . and asked about your father's fortunes."

She fanned herself. "Ah, I see."

"He was pointing out Minerva Plimpton to me."

"The ale heiress?" Abigail asked with interest. "Is she here?"

"Here, but plagued by fortune hunters."

He pointed to a pack of men surrounding someone near the dance floor. A tiara of diamonds and emeralds was the only evidence of Miss Plimpton, and yet Abigail eyed that bit of tiara as reverently as if she were watching a queen. Then a bubble of laughter burst forth from the crowd—Miss Plimpton's voice, apparently—followed by a dutiful echo of answering masculine laughter from the throng around her.

Abigail's lips turned up, and she eyed Nathan with

mirth. "Ah! I can see why you were worried for me. Just the fate every girl dreads—being surrounded by an adoring hoard."

"Be serious," Nathan said. "You would not want men pursuing you for your money."

"How well you would know the extent to which I would dislike it!" she shot back.

He took the justified barb like a man. "That is why I felt I should warn you."

She laughed. "Thank you for your consideration! But I regret to inform you that times have changed since your escapade with my father. I would now enjoy being fortune-hunted immensely. Especially when it came time to tell the hunters that I have no money."

He stopped, frowning. "No money?"

She shook her head. "No, not really. Or, not that much. Nothing that would draw throngs of admirers, I am afraid."

"But when you said you would live independently . . . I thought your father . . ."

She laughed. "Father would give me nothing now. Nor would I ask. His only interest was in grandchildren, you know—not my comfort."

"Oh, but . . ." Nathan shook his head, confused. "Then how in the deuce do you propose to live in London?"

"Ah! That is my secret." She twinkled at him mysteriously, then laughed at his expression. "You look completely confounded. Don't tell me you are about to abandon me in the middle of this ball!"

"No . . ."

She slipped her arm through his. "Good, because I should like to finish our dance."

He led her out onto the floor again, but his feet felt sluggish.

She smiled up at him. She was moving as breezily as a butterfly around a boulder. "Is something bothering you, Nathan?"

"Yes. I don't understand you."

"What is there to understand?" She grinned at him. "I feel free. That is all. And now I know that my biggest fear should be becoming Miss Plimpton, when Miss Plimpton seems as if she doesn't have a care in the world."

"I would not like to think of you all alone here, without sufficient means . . ."

"I have means," she said, cutting him off. "Sufficient. Barely."

"But—"

She tilted her head. "I am not doing anything against the law. I simply have my own savings, that is all. Would you like to go over my accounts?"

He drew back. "I did not mean to presume . . ."

"To tell me what to do?" She asked, smiling. "I should hope not. Because from now on I intend to do just as I please."

And that was a troubling notion.

On the other hand, as he caught the wicked glint in her eye, he decided it was a very appealing notion, as well. He only hoped he figured prominently in what pleased Abigail.

Chapter Sixteen

All was lost.

Fuego knew now that Leticia, that pearl of great price, would never be his. All his efforts, his machinations, his cunning, had been for naught. Now all there was to do was bid his love goodbye.

And yet his cunning was not yet at an end. In parting, he took the damsel's hand, caressing the soft white tenderness of her bare skin, and lifted it gently to his lips. "Farewell, signorina. We will never meet again, except perhaps in my dreams. For try as hard as I may, I shall never forget you. Never. But a gentleman knows when he must accept the fact that he will forever remain heartbroken."

Her lips parted. Her eyes shone. She shivered exquisitely.

And in that triumphant moment, he knew she would be his after all.

—Lord Fuego's Pursuit

Augusta noisily pursued the last bit of strawberry preserves out of the china jam pot with a silver spoon. Then she examined the small pile she had managed to amass on her toast with a depressed frown. "I do believe Butterworth is in the kitchen rationing again."

Abigail eyed her aunt's plate sympathetically. "Perhaps they have not been putting enough out since I have been here." She worried once again that she had disrupted her aunt's comfortable routines.

"Oh, no—do not blame yourself," Augusta said. Then she laughed. "Blame Butterworth. I always do."

Abigail smiled.

"Perhaps he will be in a better humor when I return from Bath," her aunt remarked.

"Butterworth does not accompany you?"

"No, thank heavens! He is off to visit his sister in Devon. His *older* sister, if you can believe it."

Abigail wondered if she would be off visiting her sisters when she reached the butler's advanced age. The thought filled her with a sentimental hope for the future; she could picture herself, Sophy, and Violet toddling along the seashore arm in arm.

Then it occurred to her that she and her sisters had *never* been fond of walking arm in arm, and she felt a bit ridiculous.

"Devon will be nice this time of year," she said.

"Yes, I dare say," Augusta said, taking a bite of her toast. "Anywhere is better than London right now."

Abigail frowned at her own breakfast as an unanticipated feeling of despair washed over her.

Augusta sympathetically squeezed Abigail's arm with a sticky-fingered hand. "How thoughtless of me. I'm sure you will be very happy here . . . so long as you stay indoors and out of the heat and dust."

Abigail nodded. "I will be fine."

"Of course you will." Her aunt pursed her lips. "Except you haven't found a place to live yet, have you?"

Abigail's spirits sank a little further. "No."

Augusta gave her another pat. "No matter! You can always stay here. Why not?" She frowned as the answer to her own question occurred to her. "Oh, dear. That won't be very comfortable for you, since I am closing up the house and giving the servants leave . . ."

"I will be fine," Abigail reiterated with more confidence than she felt.

"Naturally you will." Augusta sighed. "I wish I could take you with me to Bath. You would have such a good time! But of course I am to be a guest of Lady Cranbrook, and she barely tolerates my bringing along Lancelot."

In other words, the dog was looking forward to superior accommodations than Abigail was likely to enjoy herself in the upcoming month.

"You may stay here without servants, of course. Though it would be very inconvenient for you."

"I will manage somehow," she assured Augusta. "Thank you for the offer. I hope I will not have to camp amidst your dustcovers, but it helps to have that option."

"Oh, you make it sound very rustic and thrilling!" Augusta said admiringly. "It almost makes me want to forego Lady Cranbrook's, though of course I must go. And if I were staying, I daresay Butterworth would cancel his trip to his sister, so it wouldn't be rustic or thrilling then, would it?"

"Of course you must go to Bath, Aunt."

Butterworth entered the room with the morning post. Abigail hoped for a letter, but received none. Though she tried to hide her disappointment, she couldn't help looking longingly at the little pile next to Augusta, who tried rather self-consciously to ignore it.

"Who have you heard from?" Abigail asked, trying to put her relative at ease about her embarrassment of correspondence riches.

"Oh, just the usual . . ." Her aunt flipped through the assortment of envelopes and then hesitated over one. "What's this?"

She broke the seal on the envelope and read the missive smiling. "Why, it's from Nathan. He wants to take us on an outing this afternoon. How thoughtful of the boy!"

Abigail's spirits suddenly brightened. "This afternoon?"

"He apologizes for the scant notice, but hopes we will come with him to Burlington House to view Lord Elgin's marbles." Nothing could have pleased Augusta more. "Of course, I will have to hurry back so as to ready myself in time to attend the Llewlynns' card party."

Even the prospect of a short visit with Nathan buoyed Abigail's spirits. And perhaps he would have an idea for an evening activity. They had enjoyed themselves on a recent trip to the opera, during which they had successfully evaded Bentley Fitzhugh.

"At any rate, I should not like to miss an opportunity to enjoy Nathan's company," her aunt continued. "Heaven only knows how much longer he will be around."

The words were like a dousing of cold water. Abigail, who had been considering which frock she should wear that afternoon, focused on her aunt. "Has he said anything about leaving?"

"No, but of course he must." Augusta laughed gustily. "The boy needs to get to work, or I shall never see a return on my investment."

Abigail knew Nathan had to go home. She had been bracing herself for this moment . . . though perhaps she had not been bracing herself strongly enough. Since their walk in the rain, they had become increasingly comfortable in each other's company. She found herself looking forward to their lively discussions of everyday life in London, and hearing Nathan's views on current events, which she was somewhat surprised to learn closely matched her own. He was a soldier who must have seen some horrifying sights, yet he was not at all hardened by such experiences. He was surprisingly gentle and full of compassion for those less fortunate than he.

There were only two things that made her uncomfortable in Nathan's company. The first was that he so obviously disapproved of her staying on in London. For a man who had a female business associate, he was disappointingly conventional in his views of how Abigail should live her life. She had not confessed to him that she was a businesswoman, too, in her own way. His snide comments about lady authors had not been forgotten. She saw no reason to hold herself up to his ridicule.

The other source of discomfort was harder to put her finger on. Or, rather, it was more difficult for her to admit. She found Nathan so agreeable, and their views were so compatible—and he was the most handsome man Abigail had ever had for a friend. She was attracted to him as she had never been to any man. It had seemed that he found her pleasing, too. And yet . . .

He had not kissed her.

Had not even tried, since the ball at Peacock Hall.

It was maddening, frustrating. Once he had accompanied her home from the park at dusk, and she had been sure he would find an opportunity to take her in his arms. Yet he had not.

Riding home alone from the opera the other evening in the carriage had provided them all the seclusion that such an intimate embrace required, but did Nathan pursue this opportunity? Of course not. Instead of taking advantage of the romantic situation, he spent it speaking, tensely, of the chances for rain on the morrow. Towards the end of the drive, he had taken her hand once, leading her to hope—until she realized that he had only been reaching for the glove she had accidentally dropped on the seat between them.

The horrible thing about his adherence to a strict gentlemanly code was that the longer he went without taking liberties, the more she wished he would. She felt depraved, and yet the more time dragged on with a complete absence of a physical expression of love from him, the more time she spent each day *thinking* about such a thing.

Why didn't he kiss her, damn it?

He certainly had not been so reticent back at Peacock Hall. As she lay in bed at night, she often trembled as she remembered their passionate encounter on the sofa in her study. Could he possibly have forgotten? Could he have failed to notice that she had responded to his touch like a well-tuned instrument responds to a fine musician's hand?

Of course she understood that back in those days he had ulterior motives for wooing her. Yet he had sworn that he cared for her even then. He swore that he cared more for her now. All of this swearing—and not a single kiss.

"Are you all right, my dear?"

Abigail's gaze, which had been glued to an embroidered peony on the tablecloth, now rose and focused on her aunt's concerned expression.

"Your face is all rosy," her aunt pointed out.

Abigail cleared her throat. "I am fine . . . just lost in thought."

"Love thoughts, I'll be bound!" her aunt said, giggling as Abigail's color no doubt deepened to yet a darker shade of red. "Those are the best kind."

"I am not in love."

"Well . . . one does not have to be *in love* to have thoughts of love."

"Aunt!" Abigail cried, mortified.

Her aunt chuckled. "You youngsters are such prim creatures these days. The time of my youth was a more earthy era."

The comment made Abigail happy she lived now. Though in her heart of hearts, she wouldn't mind a world that didn't condemn a person for behaving a little wantonly on occasion.

If one was lucky enough to ever have such an occasion . . .

"Would you like me to beg off this afternoon so that you and Nathan could have some time alone?"

"No, of course not."

Her aunt studied her. "One needs to take advantage of time, you know."

Abigail lifted her chin. "If you are suggesting that I go chasing after Nathan, that is something I will never do. I will be sorry to see him leave London, but I have always known that he was going."

"You are admirably stoic," her aunt said, taking a sip of coffee. "You shall get along famously with yourself in the years to come."

Her aunt's tone was so flattering, it was some moments before Abigail realized that getting along with oneself famously was just another way of saying that she was likely to spend the rest of her life in loneliness.

For the life of him, Nathan could not keep his mind on the antiquities before him. Not when Abigail was standing right by his side. He was going out of his mind with wanting her, but since he had muffed everything so badly back at Peacock Hall, he was attempting restraint. So far he had succeeded admirably.

The trouble was, he was fed up with restraint. Restraint was keeping him awake nights, and making him daydream while he should have been thinking about all the work he had ahead of him. He would go mad if he showed one more day of restraint.

And now one more day was all he had.

What could he do? As Sir Harlan had once liberally said, these were not the dark ages where you could drag your bride to the altar against her will. Nor was it that wonderful other world of Lord Fuego, where a man could scheme his way into a young woman's heart. (God knows, Nathan had tried.) He was going to have to resort to good old-fashioned honesty, and a little pleading.

But where? When? He had to tell Abigail that he was leaving London, and that he wanted to take her back with him, but he didn't particularly feel like having an intimate conversation in the middle of a cultural outing. Nor did he particularly relish the idea of speaking in front of Augusta, who was for once taking seriously her duty as chaperone and sticking to them like glue.

"It gives one pause to see things of such beauty and of such age, doesn't it?" Abigail whispered as she stared at one of the Elgin marbles.

"What?" Nathan had been standing in their midst for quite a while now, and hardly had noted them. He tried to snap back to attention. "Oh, yes. They're . . . quite something."

Abigail's lips were parted in admiration. For the marbles, unfortunately. She gazed on the pilfered Parthenon frieze with open-mouthed wonder.

"Seeing something so beautiful, so old, makes one realize how insignificant we are, doesn't it?" Abigail rhapsodized on. "These pieces will be here forever, yet we are here for such a short time."

"Let us hope we are only here a short time," Augusta

said. "I should hate to end on display like one of those Egyptian mummies at the British Museum."

As Abigail rolled her eyes in exasperation at her aunt, Nathan lifted his hand to his mouth to cover a smile.

Augusta blinked at them. "Well, would either of you enjoy being propped up that way, spending all eternity in rags? Heaven knows I am not an overly vain woman, but I would find being gawked at in such a state of dishabille most unpleasant."

"You should make sure and put a codicil in your last will and testament," Abigail advised her, "so that you don't end up in a museum."

"I just might do it." Augusta sighed. "Though I wouldn't mind my likeness being in a portrait gallery."

They walked on in silence among the ancient statuary. It wasn't that Nathan didn't appreciate art, but he felt pressed for time. Once they left Burlington House, there was a possibility that Abigail would slip away from him forever.

"I think I would like some air," Abigail said.

Augusta nodded her approval of that plan. "That is a good idea. Nathan can accompany you. I just want to go and have another look at the first piece. One of the soldiers looks just like dear Gerald Frobisher, to whom I was engaged in the season of 1789."

"Your Aunt Augusta has a very personal approach to art," Nathan remarked as that lady hurried off to the indicated marble.

Abigail fanned herself to counter the still afternoon torpor taking hold of the city. "She is a very dear woman."

"I feel that, too," Nathan said. "I owe her a debt, and not just a monetary one."

"Her new venture has brought her happiness. I think she looks forward to visiting her new friends and telling them she is a businesswoman."

Nathan sighed. "There is much work to do."

"But that's to the good, isn't it?" Abigail asked. "You must be very happy about your prospects now."

"I am indeed. However, I'm not so happy about leaving London."

The fanning stopped. "When do you return to Yorkshire?"

"Tomorrow."

Her lips parted. "Tomorrow!" she exclaimed. "But why so soon?"

"I have been away too long already," he said. "I want to go home and tell Freddy the good news in person. He has been very unsettled by the prospect of having to leave Cambridge. I may now spare him that worry at least."

"I am glad about that," Abigail said. "He is such an engaging young man."

"Yes."

Abigail let out her breath in a puff. "Tomorrow."

She sounded as if she was unhappy at the prospect of his going, which perversely made him feel hopeful. "That was my reason for inviting you and your aunt out today. I wanted a chance to bid you farewell in person."

"Ah, I should have known that where you are concerned, there is always an ulterior motive."

She was jesting, but the remark still made him wince uncomfortably. He stepped forward. "Before I go, I hope you will say you have forgiven me any unhappiness I may have caused you."

"Oh, yes. I absolve you." She smiled stiffly. "You may return to The Willows with a clear conscience."

"It is more than I deserve."

"Very likely," she agreed.

They stood awkwardly while she squinted into the distance and he tried to read her thoughts. He had no luck there. Her expression had turned impassive. "I shall miss London," he said. "I will miss these times we have had together here."

Her fan snapped open again. "Yes, London is a very agreeable place, for all its problems. There is no end of things to do here. I have always dreamed of living here."

He frowned, remembering her pleasure in the theater, the opera, and the museums. He had not considered this before. When she spoke of not wanting to return home, he had thought she had meant she wanted to stay away from Peacock Hall because of her father. He had never thought she might simply prefer London to the country.

"And yet you have not spent much time here before now."

"No, I never had the opportunity," she said. "Or rather, I did, but it . . . hmm, never worked out. Now that I have sampled a taste of city life . . ."

Nathan nodded. He, too, enjoyed London. But he also loved The Willows, and the simpler pace in the country.

"What time do you leave tomorrow?" she asked him.

"Early."

"Of course," she said. "Well!"

He cleared his throat to speak, but she interrupted him before he had the opportunity to make his declaration. "I wish you all the best in your endeavors," she said.

It sounded like the closing of a business letter. "Abigail, I would not like to think this is the end of our friendship."

"Indeed no! I am certain I shall hear all about you through my aunt, with whom you will no doubt be in frequent correspondence."

"Would it be presumptuous for me to ask permission to write to you as well?"

"You would be most welcome to. I will have Aunt Augusta forward my address to you. When I have one."

He shook his head. "I am uneasy about leaving you here."

"Come, let us not pull caps on that issue any more. I am staying, and that is the end of it."

"You are headstrong," he said, feeling as dispirited now as he had been hopeful just moments before.

She laughed. "I shall take that as a parting compliment."

She seemed very light-hearted about parting; indeed, her good humor took the wind out of his sails and left him luffing in the still afternoon heat. He was pulling out a handkerchief to mop his brow when Augusta came practically skipping out of the outbuilding housing the marbles. Even though now both Nathan and Abigail were staring at her, she yoo-hooed at them loudly.

"Magnificent!" she called out as she approached. "Weren't all those Greeks quite divinely handsome!"

"Nathan is leaving tomorrow," Abigail blurted out.

Augusta came to a stop, frowning. "Oh—so suddenly?"

"Yes, I must go home."

She linked arms with him. "Of course, you're right. You must go home and make us pots of money. Perhaps I will take a jaunt into Yorkshire soon."

"I hope you may be right about the successfulness of our business venture," Nathan said. "And I hope that we will meet again soon."

"Of course we will," Augusta said. "I have no doubt of it."

Nathan shot a quick glance at Abigail, but she was looking away from him.

Nor were the ladies forthcoming with any invitation for this, his last, evening. As the carriage came to a stop before Augusta's house, he felt foolish for wanting to linger, but knew he could not part from Abigail without some last gesture.

Suddenly, he remembered Lord Fuego. "I must say farewell, then, and let you go. But I will miss you, Abigail. I shall not forget you."

He took her hand in his, and then lifted it to his lips.

Her lips parted, and for a moment he felt hope rising in him.

But she let her arm drop without speaking again.

"What a shame Nathan has to leave so soon!" Augusta exclaimed later that evening as she was waiting for her carriage to take her to dinner and cards at the Llewlynns'.

Abigail had been invited to accompany her aunt, but had begged off at the last minute. She did not feel capable of smiling and chattering through a sociable evening. Not now.

"I was hoping to enjoy his company some more," Augusta said.

"But you are about to leave for Bath," Abigail pointed out.

Augusta went still, and her brow puckered, as if this thought had never occurred to her before. "You are right. Well, then I suppose it is just as well that he return home and start making money."

Abigail did not point out that *she* was not going to Bath and might have enjoyed his company, too.

Her hand still burned from where he had kissed it. And her cheeks burned every time she thought of his parting words.

Augusta chuckled. "You know, when I came out of the museum today, I was half expecting to find you two engaged!"

"You can't be serious," Abigail said.

"Why do you think I invented the ruse about wanting to take a last look at that Gerald look-alike sculpture? Heaven knows I had my fill of him when I was engaged to him."

"You were very convincing in your desire to remain behind."

Augusta smiled wistfully. "Perhaps I should have gone on the stage instead of becoming a woolen mill investress. At any rate, I was almost certain Nathan would screw up his courage and ask you to be his." She looked inquisitively at Abigail. "He didn't, did he?"

"He did not even make an attempt!" Abigail blurted out in frustration. "He said he wanted to say good-bye and ask my forgiveness."

"Whatever for?"

"For lying to me at Peacock Hall."

"That, still?" Augusta laughed. "I thought you two had buried that hatchet long ago."

"It was no small thing, Aunt. His behavior bespoke a dishonesty that I found devastating."

Augusta clucked at her. "You would never have found it devastating if you didn't love Nathan to begin with."

"Love him!"

"Certainly. If it had been another man—Bentley Fitzhugh, say—who had schemed with your father, you would have despised him, but let the matter drop. Because it was

Nathan, you had to get yourself in a monumental dither and run halfway across the country to flee him. And when he followed, you had to pretend that you hadn't wanted him to, when it's as plain as the nose on your face that you were pleased beyond all measure that he pursued you."

Abigail was speechless. "But he only came to secure his business prospects. Now that you have rescued him, he is leaving me."

"He wasn't looking for a backer when he first came hoofing after you. He only turned to me when he found nothing but discouragement from you, and it was my idea that we go into partnership together. Why, look at the way he kissed your hand, and that pretty parting speech he made! So romantic."

Yes, it had been that, and unexpected. Abigail had been so surprised, and so aware of her aunt standing right next to them, that she hadn't known how to respond.

"A man can't go on chasing a girl forever, you know. Those Gothics you write are fiction, in case you have forgotten."

Abigail frowned. "My mind is clear on that subject."

"And in any case, you cannot expect Nathan to behave like a storybook hero when you are giving him no help whatsoever."

"What do you mean?"

"I mean, here you are torn to ribbons by the prospect of his leaving, but did it occur to you to tell him so?"

"Of course not!" Abigail said, practically sputtering. "I would never!"

"Why not?" Augusta said. "Not everyone is as adept at reading your mind as I am. I could tell this afternoon that Nathan was flummoxed by your indifferent behavior."

"I told him I would miss his company."

"And . . . ?"

Abigail lifted her arms helplessly. "What else *could* I say?"

Augusta laughed. "Well! If I have to tell you, perhaps there *is* nothing more you had to say. These things usually happen naturally between lovers. And I would not call you an inarticulate person."

"Do you mean I should have . . ." Abigail practically gulped. ". . . told him I love him?"

"That would have been rather bold," Augusta admitted, then winked. "On the other hand, boldness often reaps beautiful rewards."

All at once, Abigail felt foolish for having been so reticent. A growing panic built in her chest. "What should I do now?"

"Do? There is nothing to do—the man leaves tomorrow. You will have to hope you can flirt more advantageously in letters than you do in person, which is probable, now that I think on it—you are a talent with your pen."

"And a muddlehead in real life!" she groaned, sinking back against the sofa. She absently gave the snoring Lancelot a pat, which elicited a sleepy growl. This made her doubt if she would find much solace in taking her aunt's advice and getting a dog of her own.

"Now, now," Augusta said, flitting over to give her a quick, bracing hug. "Do not fall into a fit of blue-devils over this. Tomorrow we shall spend the morning having a lark together, and you will forget all about having let the love of your life get away." Her aunt frowned suddenly. "Oh, no. I have an appointment with my dressmaker. Well! Maybe in the afternoon."

"You have tea with Lady Binkman tomorrow afternoon."

Her aunt's brow pinched. "Do I? Oh my word . . . and I can't invite you along there to cheer you up, because Lady Binkman is so tedious, poor thing. Ever since she started having tooth trouble she can talk of nothing but her gums."

"It is all right, Aunt Augusta. I am certain I will survive. I have so much to do myself . . ."

"Quite right!" Her aunt said, hopping up. "That is the spirit. And now I *must go*, or else no one will invite me to dinner anymore. And then I would be completely at Cook's mercy!"

She flitted out of the house in a flurry of worrying that

she had forgotten her reticule and her new Norwich shawl, only to return for a different bracelet to go with her ensemble. All in all, Abigail considered it a miracle that her aunt ever made it anywhere.

Abigail continued to lie on the sofa, brooding, until the maid came to turn down the lamps. "Oh, Miss Abigail! I forgot all about you!"

"That's all right, Melinda," she said. "You may extinguish the lights and retire for the evening. I am going up to my room to read."

The woman looked relieved. "All right, miss, if you're sure."

Abigail reiterated her intentions. And to make good her assurances, she headed upstairs. But no sooner had she shut herself in her room than she decided that she would not be able to stay there. The four walls felt claustrophobic, and she could not see turning in early and tossing in bed half the night, thinking of Nathan. That would be agony.

In a split second, she made the decision.

Or, rather, she made no decision at all, but acted solely on instinct. As her aunt said, she was not a timid person. Why was she behaving that way with Nathan? Why hadn't she been more clear in telling him how she felt about him?

True, it was not something a young lady was supposed to do, but those conventions of modesty were things she had always scorned in her heroines. And look at her sisters! They never hesitated to let their feelings show, and no matter what she thought of their manners, there was no denying they were better than she at getting what they wanted.

And what Abigail wanted was Nathan.

That thought left her stupefied. Could it really be as simple as that?

And if it was that simple, did she dare to follow the dictates of her heart?

Quickly, before she could give herself the opportunity to think twice, she grabbed her cloak and slipped out of the house. She could hardly believe what she was doing. But her feet felt as if they were moving on their own. She headed towards the other side of the square, where Nathan's hotel was. It was not a large hostelry, but a smaller, more intimate house. Her heart pounded as she turned onto the street. How would she find Nathan? What if he wasn't even there? And if he was there, what would she say to him?

The manager of the hotel looked up at her in surprise as she walked in. She pulled down the hood of her cloak. "I am here to see Mr. Nathan Cantrell. It is a matter of some urgency."

The man eyed her skeptically, and Abigail felt her face coloring. "I am his cousin from Yorkshire, and I have an important message for him."

His eyes took in her rather plain cloak and bonnet, her uncurled hair, and slowly he did seem to reach the conclusion that she did not have the makings of a prostitute. Or perhaps he merely thought that if she were a fallen woman, she was one to be pitied. "This way, miss."

When Nathan opened the door to his room, he exclaimed. "Abigail!"

"Cousin Nathan," she replied.

His face registered not a moment of confusion. "Please come in." He pulled her across the threshold and thanked the clerk before shutting the door.

Alone in his room, she felt the blood rising to her cheeks. Coming to a man's hotel room! She had never thought she could be so brazen. And yet she felt so relieved to be here, to have this second chance. If only she could speak; her heart was pounding in her chest, and her throat was so dry that she could hardly make herself form words.

"I had to come," she said, noting that he was still holding onto her sleeve. The heat from his touch radiated up her arm.

"I am glad you did," he said. "I was miserable."

"Me too!"

He chuckled. "We have quite an effect on each other, don't we?"

She wanted to laugh, but couldn't. She still felt so breath-less, so anxious. "Nathan, I wanted to tell you that I . . . well, perhaps I gave the wrong impression this afternoon. Perhaps you thought that I didn't care."

"And do you?"

"Yes! A great deal!" Tears sprang to her eyes, but they were tears of relief to be finally saying what had been em-bedded in her heart for weeks.

He pulled her to him and held her tight, kissing the crown of her head softly as he whispered, "Abigail, Abi-gail."

She had always lamented the ordinariness of her first name, but now, as Nathan whispered it over and over in her ear, it sounded like the sweetest song. The warmth of his breath, the huskiness in his voice, sent a shiver down her spine. He brought his hand to her chin and tipped her face up to his. "You must know that I have been in love with you from the start."

Her lips parted. "The *start?*"

"The moment I saw you in the pond. My water sprite!"

"Oh—that wretched afternoon."

He shook his head. "It was a beautiful day, and our meeting is one of my fondest memories."

She tilted her head. "The memory of watching me choke?"

He grinned. "No, the memory of you rising out of the water in your clinging shift."

She blushed frantically, but she did not pull away when he lowered his lips to hers. The warmth of his mouth was delicious. In fact she could taste a hint of brandy, it was an intoxicating, masculine flavor that caused a shudder of longing to course through her. He pressed his lips harder, then shocked her by beginning an exploration of her mouth with his tongue.

What was even more amazing was that she responded in kind, and Nathan let out a soft groan.

"Perhaps you should not have come, after all," he said after they had kissed so long she was sagging against him, limp with longing.

She blinked up at him, seeing him only through the haze of her own desire. His words caused a small panic in her. Did he not want her? "Why?"

"Because you have to leave again, and that will make parting all the harder."

Her body screamed at the idea of parting at all. In fact, she didn't see how she would even be able to find the strength to push away from his chest. "Why must I leave?"

"Because . . ." He stopped, gulping, and she could feel a tension seize his entire body.

Boldly, she pressed closer to him, shocking herself. "After all, in the eyes of all those attending Father's ball, we *are* engaged."

He groaned. "I am going home tomorrow."

She grinned. "Let's not worry about tomorrow when we have tonight." She angled her lips up for another kiss.

And he obliged her. Apparently, her Nathan was no saint. He could be tempted, and tempt him she did. Unversed in the ways of the flesh though she was, she found that she instinctively knew how to move against him in order to break down whatever resistance he was putting up against her. Never in her life had she expected that she would have the opportunity to act the part of seductress, and yet here she was, shamelessly offering herself to a man.

But what a man! Every stroke of his hand on her arms, up and down her back made her thrill deliciously. She was playing with fire, she knew. Knew it because she could feel a coiled strength in him, like a panther getting ready to pounce, but making sure he had his prey sized up well beforehand.

He was doing all his sizing up by touch. As they kissed, he leaned her back against the closed door, so he could explore her. And he apparently intended to explore every inch of her. She gasped as he brought one finger down the line of her jaw, down her throat, to the neckline of her dress. Moments later, those same fingers deftly began to work their way through buttons and laces, so that he had her overdress off and puddling around her ankles. He traced her breast, which was nearly exposed through the thinner material of her shift.

Abigail gasped, both from the pleasure and the shock of the sharp sensual surge that rushed through her. Then he pushed the thin cloth to the side and touched his lips to her breast, causing her to let out a cry of pure delight. This was undiluted pleasure. Her eyes opened wide, and as she looked over the top of his head cradled against her chest, she noted the bed with the covers turned down.

And she knew without a solitary doubt that in another few moments she would be in that bed. In fact, she longed to be there.

What had happened to her? All her life, she had been so proper. Could she throw away a lifetime of propriety in just an instant?

Nathan moved to her other breast and suckled the tight yearning bud.

Oh, yes—she could!

Nathan undid her light corset and pulled her shift up and over her head, so that she stood shivering before him practically naked. He let out a low groan. "I should not have done that," he said.

"Why?"

"Because now I will not be able to keep myself from making love to you."

At the sight of those green eyes that had been in her dreams so often feasting on her nude form, she gulped. "I don't want you to stop."

His hands tightened on her arms and when he spoke, his voice was very nearly a growl. "If I possess you, I will never be able to let you go. I don't care if I have to drag you back kicking and screaming to The Willows with me."

Drag her back? She nearly laughed. Right now she was prepared to follow wherever he might wish to lead her. He would have to beat her away with a stick.

She could hear her own heart pounding as she confessed, "I want to be with you always."

He looked into her eyes, and in the next moment, he lifted her against him as if she weighed no more than a feather. He carried her to the bed and laid her gently on the mattress. She felt a delightful shudder of anticipation moving through her. And a sudden fear. She closed her eyes against the sudden, intense wave of anxiety that swept through her. *What was she doing?*

As she lay there, she felt movement on the mattress next to her, and heard a soft rustling of clothing being removed, the muffled thump of shoes landing on floor. She swallowed.

"Abigail . . ."

She fluttered her eyes open. Candlelight flickered across that magnificent torso that she remembered from their swim. The muscled chest, the light dusting of hair, and lower . . .

She swallowed again. Oh, heaven! It hadn't looked like *that* when they were at the pond. As her eyes remained fixed on the magnificence of him, she felt a hitch in her chest resulting from a combination of pure lust and panic.

He bent down, and began kissing his way down her body, making a thorough exploration of her with his mouth. Everywhere his lips touched her bare flesh, it felt like a small fire being set. Soon her worries were doused, replaced by sheer longing. She bit her lip as he traveled down past her breast, flicking his tongue around her belly button, then her abdomen, to her thighs.

He spread her legs and then lightly placed his tongue against the soft flesh there, and she let out a sharp cry, half expecting him to do the gentlemanly thing and release her until she was able to catch her breath again. But apparently the laws of gentlemanly conduct no longer applied, because her persistent, gentle suitor was now a relentless purveyor of sweet torment. Heat built inside her until she felt she was going to burst. She began rocking then almost bucking against him so that she thought she would die of shame, yet she couldn't stop herself. Her response only goaded him to further stoke the flame building in her.

The sudden intensity of it, the overwhelming desire roaring inside her, caught her unawares. It was as if her whole body were spiraling out of her control. She held on as long as she could, but for a few moments the world seemed to crash away from her, leaving her on a plane of sheer undiluted bliss.

When she opened her eyes, panting, Nathan was hovering over her, his eyes gleaming. His body lay against hers. The shaft of his manhood pressed against that most tender area he had just been ministering to. "I love you," he whispered, pressing against her, entering her, opening her.

A fierce burning pain caused her to bite her lip, and he bent down to kiss her. They lay still for a few moments, joined as only a man and woman could be. When the pain receded, she felt in awe of how much she had surrendered to him, and how easily it had been done. Now she wanted to give him even more.

She moved against him tentatively, and he responded in kind, leaving her awestruck at the sensation. She had never known a man could be so strong, or so gentle.

Afterward, Abigail belatedly insisted on modesty, and they lay entwined beneath the sheets. Nathan did not complain. He rained kisses on her, and she snuggled contentedly against him. He had never felt so exhausted, so sated, so happy.

So *lucky*.

He felt like a man who had just escaped from the gallows. Before Abigail had arrived, he had been more depressed than he could ever remember. He was stumped for ideas of how to win Abigail's regard. And then the very object of his desire had knocked on his door.

Had offered herself to him.

"The hotel manager is not going to believe you are my cousin," he said, chuckling with amusement. "Not when I try to smuggle you out with your clothes wrinkled and your hair so wonderfully mussed."

She laughed and shook her head. "I barely had him convinced of my respectability to begin with."

"I'm afraid we are neither of us very good actors."

"Unlike Aunt Augusta."

He pulled back to look into her eyes. "What do you mean?"

"Aunt Augusta told me tonight that she had not wished to remain behind looking at the friezes in Burlington House. She just wanted to give us a few moments of privacy."

Nathan smiled. "Have I ever told you how much I adore your aunt?"

"Yes, you might say she is the patroness of our romance. It makes me quite nervous about my sister Sophy's future career in London. I worry she will need a much more vigilant chaperone."

"For Sophy, a steel trap would about do the trick."

Abigail dissolved into nervous laughter.

Nathan kissed her reassuringly. "Do not worry. My advice would simply be to keep your sister away from Georgianna Harcourt."

Abigail went still. *"What?"*

"You know, that writer whose books your father was reading. Specifically, I would keep Sophy away from men who read such stuff."

"Why?"

He bent down and kissed her again. "Your aunt isn't the only patron of our relationship. I'd say more than half our thanks should go to a devilish fellow named Lord Fuego."

Chapter Seventeen

Oh, the agony! To have been tricked thus . . . and by such a blackguard as he. The man who had ruined her family, seduced her sister . . . and now herself! Leticia looked out over the high precipice to the jagged, sea-struck rocks below. Never in all her tragedy-filled life had she known such woe. What in the name of heaven was she going to do?

—*Lord Fuego's Pursuit*

"Is something wrong?" Nathan asked her. "You look pale."

"What did you say?"

"I said you look pale."

"No, before that."

Nathan squinted at her as if he didn't understand the question. "Let me get you some water."

"Did you say Lord Fuego?"

Nathan paused midway to the water carafe on the dresser. That he was stark naked only made Abigail's mind feel all the more flustered. "Yes."

She gaped at him, stupefied. She could hardly credit what he was saying. "Could you possibly mean Lord Fuego from a book by the title of *Lord Fuego's Pursuit*?"

Nathan pointed to a worn volume sitting on the bedside table, which she had not noticed before. *Her* book! "Your father gave me a copy of the book before I came to London, and I've read the silly thing twice."

Silly!

He chuckled. "Sir Harlan told me I could do worse than pattern myself after that Lord Fuego character." Grinning at her, he added, "And I must say, it worked rather well."

Her stomach did a flip. But not from desire, though she could still look into his eyes and feel her insides quicken with wanting him. But washing over that desire was a wave of troubling uneasiness. All the events of the past days played back in her mind, this time with ironic clarity. The way he had followed her—nothing so suspicious there! And that he had charmed her aunt. Then, on this very day, he had kissed her hand and given her a pretty speech that made her heart melt.

But of course it had. She had penned the script herself!

Abigail groaned and fell back against the pillows.

Nathan hurried to her side again. "Darling, what's the matter?"

She stiffened. "Nothing is the matter. I see everything very clearly now. Only *don't* call me darling."

He looked at her as if she had gone mad. And perhaps she had. Her mind felt as if it were reeling. She kept writing the plots for her own seduction. And now. . . .

Now she truly had been seduced!

She was a fallen woman, like poor Leticia. That unfortunate young lady had ended up hurling herself off a cliff.

Luckily there were no cliffs in London. Though she supposed she could make do with a bridge if her mind deteriorated any further.

Nathan reached for her and she hopped away, taking the sheet with her and winding it around herself to protect her modesty, such as it was. "I must go," she announced.

And oh, Lord! What a mess getting out of here was going to be. She looked at her pile of rumpled clothes and groaned at the thought of having to skirt through the lobby of the hotel. And what if she woke up the house when she returned home? How on earth would she explain her absence to Aunt Augusta?

Perhaps her aunt wouldn't be home yet . . .

"Did I say something wrong?" Nathan asked, confounded by her sudden skittishness.

And why shouldn't he be confused! Moments before she had been throwing herself at him. Practically begging him to make love to her. She remembered what he had done to her in that very bed, how enthusiastically she had reacted, and shuddered. "No . . . I simply must go. If my aunt discovers me missing, she will worry."

The excuse sounded hollow, since they both knew that her aunt was unlikely to discover her missing before morning.

"I am sorry I ever mentioned Lord Fuego," he said. "I assumed it would appeal to your sense of humor."

She had been pulling on her dress, and now stopped. "Why?"

"Because . . ." He shook his head. "Well, never mind. Let us not allow a silly thing like a Georgianna Harcourt book to come between us."

Silly! "It cannot help but come between us!"

He frowned. "But why?"

"Because *I* am Georgianna Harcourt!"

The room went so completely still that her statement reverberated around the four walls in the absence of any other noise or rustle of movement.

"*You?*" Nathan's eyes were unblinking and owlish as he stared at her. "*You* wrote *Lord Fuego's Pursuit?*"

"And *Count Orsino's Betrothal*, and *The Scarlet Veil* . . . and others. I am one of those silly lady scribblers whose books you so enjoy deriding."

"I don't believe it!" he muttered.

"I have been Georgianna Harcourt for four years. It has been my secret all this time, but only Aunt Augusta knows of it . . . and now you."

He shook his head. "Then your family's believing that you were invalidish was just a ruse to allow you more time to yourself in your study?"

"Yes." She muttered, ducking her head. Then Nathan laughed, and the sound of his laughter raised her hackles. "I do not see what you could find funny in this situation."

"Do you not?" he asked. "I think you were rather clever to have pulled it off."

She looked up. Clever was better than silly, at least.

"Clever enough to be undermined by my own creations not once, but twice!"

"But naturally I did not know you were the creator of Lord Fuego."

"No—you probably had no idea what an awful lady scribbler looked like!"

His grinned rather sheepishly at the reminder of his earlier remarks. "Hmm, I did make some disparaging remarks, didn't I?"

"Yes! When we were at The Willows together, those comments about the writers of Gothic novels hit closer to home than you ever could have dreamed! Your criticism went directly to the source."

A look of understanding appeared in his eyes, as if a great mystery had been solved. "But I did not know. I wouldn't have said anything to offend you for all the world."

"You were obviously speaking your mind."

"Well . . . but that was before I had read anything you had written. I have now read through Lord Fuego twice."

"Naturally," she said with a sniff. "You needed to memorize your lines."

"Not at all," he said. "I found it a very diverting story."

"And instructive, no doubt. You must congratulate yourself. Patterning yourself after Lord Fuego worked beyond all imagining."

He shook his head. "You are wrong. I was only joking when I said we owed our love to a book. What we just shared was very real."

Her hands flew as she buttoned and laced her dress as hurriedly as possible. She must have been mad coming here. Now that she looked back on it, she had acted like a woman possessed, or bewitched. And that is how she felt. As if she had been under some kind of spell.

But now the spell was broken. It had to be.

Nathan was pulling on his own clothes now, too. The two of them might have been in a race to see who could be dressed first.

"What difference does it make, anyway?" he asked.

She snorted as she stepped into her shoes, which were scattered several feet apart from each other. How had that happened? "It makes all the difference in the world. You have been dealing false with me from the start. How could I ever trust you now?"

"After what we have been through, how could you not?"

She looked into his green eyes and felt heat rising to her cheeks. "Because you tricked me."

"How?"

Her jaw clamped shut and she searched for her gloves.

"Perhaps I did behave a bit like Fuego at times, but my motives were pure. I did it because I love you." He crossed to her.

Drat, he had managed to get dressed before her. As she was about to dart out of his path, he stopped her by catching her arm and pulling her to him. "Did I trick you into coming to my rooms tonight?"

Her face burned, and her mouth felt dry. "I came out of my own accord . . . but for my own reasons."

"Ah! Did love bring you here?"

"No," she insisted, trying to draw away from him. With no success. "I came for purposes . . . of . . . well, of literary curiosity."

He eyed her skeptically. "Was literary curiosity the reason you put your arms around me?"

She attempted to swallow past the lump in her throat. If only his voice weren't quite so deep, so resonant. It seemed to vibrate through her, making her own words seem like thin, flimsy things. "Yes."

"I see. And when you kissed me . . . that was simply research for a future book?"

"I . . ." She was about to say that she had not kissed him—that it had been the other way around. But now that she thought about it, she could not say positively that this was the case. Those moments when he had taken her in his arms were all a blur to her now. And there was no denying that she had acted very brazenly.

She could not think clearly. Especially when he was holding her. When she could smell the wonderful male scent of him. When she looked up at his lips and wished only that they were pressed against hers again.

"And if I kissed you now, would that help you in your future endeavors?" he asked, bringing his mouth down to cover hers.

Again that wondrous feeling enveloped her, and she could not resist sinking against him and reveling in the magnificent sensuality of his expert kiss. She had never dreamed she could feel such powerful need just by a mere touch of skin to skin. But the way Nathan made her feel was beyond anything she had ever imagined.

She could understand now why women could be so bird-witted when it came to love. And though she had written more than her fair share of unfortunate females who had come to grief because of their weakness for men, particularly bad ones, she had never dreamed that *she* could ever be in a comparable situation to the Claras, Fionas, and Leticias of the world. Yet here she was. In the arms of a man she did not entirely trust, excusing his actions as long as they could continue their current pleasurable activity.

Because more than anything else, she wanted to shuck all these clothes that they had just put on again, and jump back into that bed.

And never leave it.

She moaned and pushed away from him. "I must go now."

His eyes were twinkling as he looked down at her. "Had enough research?"

She lifted her chin, not deigning to dignify his teasing with an answer. "I will just get my cloak and be gone."

"I will take you back to Augusta's."

At that suggestion, she let out a horrified squeak. "But you cannot!"

"Do you think I would let you walk through the dark streets after midnight?" he asked. He waggled his brows at her. "Even Lord Fuego would not have done that."

Perhaps under the circumstances mentioning that ficti-tious person was not the most diplomatic move on his part, yet she could not help but smile.

And relent.

After all, she did not relish walking the streets alone.

Abigail thought she would die of mortification crossing through the hotel lobby, but the tired clerk was so sleepy that he barely noticed their passing. The streets they passed through were mostly deserted, so that she now only had to worry about entering her aunt's house unnoticed. How would she explain if questioned? How could she explain without fibbing? She wanted to consult with Nathan, who was striding silently next to her. Yet after she had accused him of dealing underhandedly with her, she did not feel entirely comfortable asking him to help her concoct a plausible lie to tell Aunt Augusta.

She still held out the hope that her aunt would not have returned to the house yet, or if she had, was already in bed and so sound asleep that she would not hear Abigail unlocking the door.

That hope was dashed the moment Nathan escorted her up the steps to her aunt's house. Before Abigail could even reach for her key, the door was thrown wide, not by Butterworth or Melinda, but by Aunt Augusta herself. The lights from inside the house threw a bright glare on Abigail and Nathan as they stood guiltily at the threshold.

At least, Abigail felt guilty. Nathan looked very calm. As if it was perfectly natural to be escorting Abigail home on foot in the wee hours of the morning.

But Augusta only looked at them with relief. "Oh, thank heavens you're back! It's been a madhouse here!"

"I am so sorry, Aunt Augusta. I was at loose ends this evening . . . and then I remembered that Nathan was leaving tomorrow . . ."

To her surprise, her aunt did not seem to be the least bit interested in her explanations. "Yes, yes—of course! Please come in. You too, Nathan! I have the most awful news!"

The words trembled through Abigail, and all at once she took note of the fact that the hall behind her aunt was illuminated as if it were still evening. Lamps Melinda had turned down hours before were shining brightly again. At the foot of the stairs, Abigail noticed there lay a man's hat and coat next to a small valise. That coat looked very familiar, but she couldn't think. . . .

She and Nathan exchanged anxious looks and followed her aunt into the parlor. The fear in Augusta's eyes seemed more ominous now.

"Aunt Augusta, what is wrong?"

"I'll tell you what is wrong! A crime has been committed!"

At the sound of the deep, familiar, yet wholly unexpected voice, Abigail swerved. Sir Harlan, looking less than his usual genial self, was standing next to the fireplace.

The sight of him nearly stopped her heart. *What was he doing here?* She could not help cringing before him, as if she had committed the crime he spoke of. She could hardly look him in the eye, fearing he would read her thoughts . . . and know what she had been doing all evening. Of all the times for her father to have come up to London!

"What crime?" Nathan asked. *He* didn't look guilty.

"Some dastard has kidnapped Garrick and Mrs. Siddons!" Sir Harlan bellowed in outrage.

Augusta looked at the group assembled in her parlor. "Is it not incredible? One week poor Lancelot was nearly snatched in the park, and now this—a birdnapping! What is the world coming to?"

"There was a note delivered to the house two nights ago," Sir Harlan said, ignoring his sister-in-law's interruption. "It said if I ever want to see my birds again, I am to raise five thousand guineas, cash, and await further instructions. So I rode to London directly and will meet with my bankers tomorrow. With any luck, I can be on my way back to Yorkshire by noon tomorrow."

"But, Father, who would do such a thing?"

"I don't know, some sadistic bastard." Sir Harlan eyed them with anguish. "Do you think they'll harm my birds?"

Both Abigail and Nathan were speechless.

As horrible as Sir Harlan's predicament was, Abigail could not help feeling thankful that the birdnapping had distracted her relatives from asking awkward questions . . . such as where she had been this evening. No one seemed the least bit curious about her disappearance at all, in fact.

She had not spoken to her father since the night of the ball, and yet she could tell that incident was far from his thoughts, too.

"Now, I am sure they will be fine, Sir Harlan," Augusta said. "You must try to put the worry from your mind. I have put the kettle on for tea. And perhaps we could have some toast and jam."

Abigail's stomach was in such a knot she did not think she could bear to swallow anything. "I for one must start packing."

Her aunt's eyes bulged. "Are you leaving?"

"I will accompany Father home tomorrow. Maybe I'll be able to help him in some way."

"As to that, Abigail," Sir Harlan said, "I don't have my carriage with me. I rode with just Old Hal accompanying me."

"Old Hal!" she exclaimed. "Was he well enough to come all this way?"

"He complains incessantly about that shoulder, but he would not hear of my traveling alone. It was either Hal with his bad shoulder or Peabody, and can you see Peabody riding *ventre à terre*?"

Abigail and Nathan both had to smile at such an image.

Her aunt looked pleased. "There! You see? There can be no call for you to leave tomorrow. If you won't have some tea, perhaps you should retire. It is dreadfully late, you know."

"I don't know if I shall be able to sleep tonight." Not with the tumult going on inside her. What would she and Nathan do now? They had not mentioned specific plans . . .

Her father nodded. "It is hard to think of rest when the fate of my birds is so insecure."

"Well, you both must try to sleep, for tomorrow will be a long day," Nathan said. His eyes were warm with understanding as he looked at Abigail. "You are coming home with me. I will hire a carriage, and Sir Harlan and Old Hal can ride along with us."

"That's very kind of you, Nathan, my boy. I don't mind telling you that it will ease my mind to be traveling with another man since I'll have all that cash on me. And you are a soldier, to top it all off."

At that moment, Abigail could have thrown her arms around Nathan and kissed him in front of everyone. Instead, she tried to convey her thanks silently, with her eyes. She thought she saw an acknowledgement of her gratitude in the warm look he returned her. Before she could even speak, he was headed for the door.

"Are you sure you wouldn't like some tea and bread? I just found the most wonderful orange marmalade that Butterworth has been hiding from me!" her aunt chirped after him.

"No, thank you," Nathan replied. He turned to Sir Harlan. "I will be back in the morning and will be ready to accompany you by noon, sir."

He bade them good night and hurried out.

"How lucky that he was with you so that he could help iron out all these difficulties!" her aunt exclaimed when he was gone. "How did you two happen to be out this late?"

She eyed Abigail expectantly.

Abigail fought a blush . . . unsuccessfully. She was sure her aunt, at least, could see everything that had happened to her, written in her face. "We were saying good-bye before he left on the morrow, and . . ." She abandoned the attempt at explanation. "It has been quite a whirlwind of an evening."

"I see." Augusta evidently decided to take pity on Abigail and continued, "My evening was quite eventful, as well. What with Sir Harlan arriving and not knowing where you were. *And* I lost seven and a half pounds at whist!"

She then guided Sir Harlan to the kitchen, leaving Abigail standing in the parlor ruminating over the earlier part of the evening. If only all she had lost this evening had been a few hands of cards!

*** * ***

The only carriage he was able to procure that morning was a more bare-bones affair than Nathan would have preferred. It was decidedly not designed with luxury in mind, but it was a solid carriage, and it would serve in this emergency. Best of all, the team that he hired was made up of magnificent animals. He was going to hate parting with them.

He had been concerned about what Abigail would think about the older phaeton, but he might have saved himself the worry. She barely spared their mode of transportation a glance, and stood by impatiently as her aunt loaded them down with food hampers, cushions, and lap robes that would surely be unnecessary in the heat of August. She was in as much of a hurry to be on their way as Sir Harlan, who had been pacing the hall since returning from his trip to the bank.

Abigail kissed her aunt good-bye, surprising Nathan and no doubt even herself by shedding a few tears. Somehow, even the sight of tears that he had not caused made him ache inside. Seeing Abigail hurting in any way was unacceptable to him.

Even though he was driving far faster than he should have, it seemed to take them forever to get outside of London and onto a clearer road. He found himself muttering curses at the many holes and slower carts on the road.

"At this rate we'll never make it out of town."

Abigail frowned. "I understand my father's worry, but why are you in such a hurry?"

"I don't know. I guess hearing about the chaos at Peacock Hall makes me wonder what has been going on at The Willows in my absence. To tell the truth, when I saw your father I half expected he was bringing news of Freddy."

"How much trouble could such a young man get into in a few short weeks?"

"You don't know Freddy. He had already managed to offend the staff by likening the billiards room to a French garrett. I thought Mrs. Willoughby was going to give notice!"

Abigail smiled. "Why would Freddy want to be living in a garrett?"

"To get him in the spirit of his proposed career as the next Lord Byron."

Abigail giggled.

Nathan admonished her. "Laugh all you want, my girl. But will you think it's so funny when I tell you that he has settled on Sophy to be his very own Lady Caroline Lamb?"

Abigail began to laugh so hard that tears began to stream down her face. When she could finally speak, she remarked, "Actually, it's usually Sophy who drives the men insane for love of her rather than the other way about." Then she had a thought. "So it's Sophy who must be the muse he wrote of in that dreadful poem."

"What poem?"

"The one I mistakenly thought you had written about me."

He shook his head. "Did you really think I had written you a poem?"

She smiled ruefully and Nathan was grateful to see that their spat of the night before, the controversy over Lord Fuego, seemed to be well behind them. Abigail was not looking at him as if he had somehow wormed his way into her affections under false pretenses. "Yes, I thought briefly that we were fellow scribblers!"

He winced at the reminder. "Abigail . . . what I said about Georgianna Harcourt . . . I had no idea I was insulting you."

She folded her arms. "Of course you did not. But why should you not say how you feel?"

"Because in the main I was speaking out of ignorance. It is no mystery why I read *Lord Fuego's Pursuit* twice through in a matter of days. It was an entertaining story, and well done."

"For what it is, you mean," she added.

"What is the matter with that?"

She frowned, but said nothing.

"So you thought I was a poet," he mused.

"Yes. A bad one."

He laughed. "Well, I can say with some certainty that were I ever to choose to write poetry, I would most likely make a hash of it. I am not gifted that way. Ability with words is a talent I admire."

She sent him an amused stare. "Even in a silly lady scribbler?"

"I will be your most ardent follower now."

She turned away and stared at their progress down the rutted road for a moment. As Nathan looked ahead to Sir Harlan riding alongside the groom, he continued, "Of course, I shall have to vie for that position with your father. He is already a Georgianna Harcourt enthusiast, and he doesn't yet know that he is responsible for her very existence."

Abigail harrumphed. "That might squelch his enthusiasm rather than enhance it. He has never been very supportive of his daughters. Look at last night—he was all concern for his peafowl, and not the least worried about where I had been."

"Luckily for us both," Nathan said. "Or else I would have had a shotgun to my back."

Her cheeks went deliciously pink.

"He is gruff, I'll grant you, but good at heart."

"So you think I should forgive him for attempting to auction me off like a prize at a charity bazaar?"

Nathan thought for a moment before speaking. It was never easy to counsel anyone on their own familial relations. Heaven knows he had fallen short as both a son and a brother. But he did not like to see Abigail estranged from her old life. "Speaking from experience, it is difficult sometimes to see past a father's shortcomings. I was angry at my father for gambling away all the Cantrell money— still am angry, if I think too long on it—but my anger temporarily made me forget what a gentle, kindhearted person he was, and how much he truly did love me."

Abigail bit her lip.

"What strikes me about your father," Nathan went on,

"is how much he is guided by his desire to see his family continue. I think he misses your mother greatly. Did you hear him say that he had started reading your books after her death?"

She nodded. "Yes, he did say that. I never thought about it, but he must have been very lonely."

"That is what I thought."

"And there I sat under the same roof as he, lonely in my own way." She shook her head. "Neither of us helped each other."

"Ah, but Georgianna Harcourt did," he said.

Slowly, she nodded. "Yes, I suppose she did."

At dusk, Nathan stopped at an inn in the small old market town of Barnsley. Their group had debated driving through the night, but Nathan did not feel it was safe or desirable, especially when they were traveling with such a sum of cash. Unfortunately, by the time they had agreed on the necessity of stopping, their choice of accommodation was limited.

Indeed, there was no choice at all.

The proprietor of the Parrot and Thistle, which contained neither parrots nor thistles as far as Nathan could tell, seemed awed to be hosting such a refined party. He referred to Abigail as "the lady," and apologized for the fact that his wife had died six years ago and that there was no other woman on the premises to see to her comfort. Abigail was led to the best room, a simple affair, yet cozy enough to satisfy her. Nathan and Sir Harlan were assigned to a tiny room that usually housed the boots. That unfortunate boy would now have to put up in the stables with the ever-complaining Hal.

When they asked about food, the proprietor appeared mortified. "There are some cold meats and bread," the man said. "I had not expected travelers this evening."

"Meat and bread will do very well, thank you," Abigail said, feeling sorry for the awed man.

"We have ale . . . though of course the lady won't be drinkin' that."

Abigail looked disappointed.

"I should be glad for some ale," Nathan said.

Sir Harlan also perked up at this prospect. "Sometimes it's these out-of-the-way places that have the best brews."

Indeed, after sampling the amber concoction placed before him, Sir Harlan pronounced himself well satisfied with their location. "Excellent. Now I would love some of that bread and meat you spoke of."

The man, who had been attentively serving Abigail, looked up almost as if he had forgotten about the men's existence. "Oh, will you be wantin' somp'n, too, sirs?"

"Just whatever is left over after you have seen to the lady," Nathan remarked dryly.

The proprietor grumbled. "I'll see what I can do."

Impatient to stretch his legs after his day of riding, Sir Harlan got up to inspect the public room.

"I never knew one would be treated so well in such a tiny place," Abigail said to Nathan when they were alone. "I should have become a traveler much sooner."

"You do seem to be receiving royal treatment here."

Her eyes twinkled with humor. "From now on you may call me 'your majesty.' "

Nathan lowered his voice to a husky whisper. "I would prefer simply to call you 'my love.' "

Abigail looked worriedly over to the door Sir Harlan had disappeared through. Hearing his voice talking to his unfortunate groom, she smiled. Then she had to stifle a yawn. "I shall sleep like a log tonight."

"And yet you were the one who did not want to stop."

She bowed. "I cede to your superior wisdom. You were right and I was wrong."

"How magnanimous of you to admit it!"

"Not particularly. After all, I will not be closeted in an attic room tonight. I fear I must warn you that my father has been known to snore. It will be a miracle if you are able to sleep a wink."

"I am not so concerned about my rest as that of our horses." Nathan worried for a moment. "I checked earlier, and there will be no hiring a fresh team at this stop. We'll have to change at the next fair-sized village."

One of her brows arched in amusement. "You might consider bedding down with the horses if you are so concerned. You would have more room to move around in and no snoring to contend with."

He laughed, then touched her hand discreetly. He knew he should avoid temptation, but he could not help himself. "There is only one other bed I would prefer this evening."

Her cheeks turned pink. "How romantic that you should prefer my company to that of the horses!"

"And to that of your father, as well," he reminded her.

"Any more flattery and I might grow quite conceited."

Her sarcasm brought a smile to his lips. "I think you are enjoying yourself more than you would ever admit."

"Oh yes—how often does one get cold mutton *and* compliments such as being compared favorably to a horse as a bed partner?"

He laughed. When he spoke, he kept his voice low. "And if you were by chance to find a poor refugee sneaking into your chamber tonight, would you turn him out?"

She eyed him. "You wouldn't dare!"

"Or do you save your brazen behavior for the better hostelries?"

"I save it for when my father is not present!" She shook her head. "I should never have visited you at your hotel at night. It was wrong."

"I disagree. I wish that you would do so more often."

"Barge into men's hotel rooms?"

He nearly choked on his ale. "No. Just mine."

"Well! I will certainly not be doing so tonight. I intend to enjoy a good night's rest tonight. After all, I didn't get much last night."

He squeezed her hand. "Abigail, I hope that you have forgiven me. Have you?"

"Forgiven you for what?"

"For the words I said about your books. For the mix-up about Lord Fuego."

She thought for a moment. "Perhaps I did overreact last night."

"Then you have forgiven me?"

"They say that imitation is the sincerest form of flattery. In that light, you did Fuego a great honor."

He had meant to keep serious discussions for a time when their lives were calmer. He wanted the atmosphere to be perfect. A greasy oaken table, over a platter of cold meat, was not the greatest setting to make a declaration of love. Yet he could not help himself.

"Abigail, every word I spoke last night was true. When we get all this kidnapping business sorted out, I intend to speak to your father."

To his great relief, she did not question his motives, or remind him that he had once been in cahoots with her father.

To his sorrow, she did not seem at all encouraging, either.

"We should wait to see what tomorrow brings. There may be no time. My father will no doubt be very busy."

Nathan sat back. "Yes. We have got to discover what happened to those birds. It is ridiculous for him to pay out a fortune for their ransom."

She shook her head. "Do you think we can find them?"

"We must. And when I find the joker responsible for this prank, I promise you I will deal with him severely."

She took a thoughtful sip of tea. She seemed altogether calmer on this subject than Nathan felt himself. "What I don't understand is who could have thought of doing such a thing. How many people know that my father would be susceptible to such a scheme?"

Nathan rolled his eyes. "The whole neighborhood knows how Sir Harlan dotes on those birds."

"Yes, there is a deal of talk in small towns." Abigail looked pensive.

"Uh-oh, what's running through that pretty head of yours now?" Nathan asked.

She eyed Nathan evenly. "I was just thinking of the scandal that our behavior of the other evening would cause, if it were to become known."

"There will be no scandal because we're going to be married before anyone has a chance to make up talk. After all, we are already engaged."

She tilted her head and looked at him questionably.

"Well, the neighborhood *thinks* we're engaged," he admitted.

And he intended to clear up the exact nature of their relationship at the first available opportunity.

Chapter Eighteen

Clara could not stop her heart from racing as Rudolpho took her trembling hands in his. These were the hands that had thrilled her to her core . . . and yet the same hands whose deeds had ruined the lives of so many. And yet! Even his worst deed had to be measured against the fact that he had found the father she had thought she had lost as a wee babe, and rescued him from a cold, dank dungeon.

How could she not love such a man?

— The Prisoner of Raffizzi

The following morning Nathan pulled the carriage into the driveway of the Black Swan outside of Leeds to arrange for a change of horses. As he turned to follow Abigail and Sir Harlan inside to a private parlor to wait while the new team was being prepared, he noticed a dilapidated old coach to the side of the yard. Then he saw a familiar gray head speaking to another one of the Swan's grooms.

It was John Willoughby!

Nathan hurried over to the man. "Willoughby, what are you doing here?"

The old servant turned to him and seemed to sag with relief. "Master Nathan, if you ain't a sight for sore eyes, I don't know what is. We've missed you at The Willows these weeks, I can tell you that."

Those words did not comfort Nathan. "Have you got Freddy with you?"

"Ach, no it's not Master Freddy I be hauling all over

the countryside, but that Mrs. Treacher from Peacock Hall and her snooty manservant."

"Violet?" Nathan asked, surprised.

"Ay!" The old man spat.

Why would Violet and Peabody have commandeered his coach, Nathan wondered with a sinking feeling. He turned and hurried towards the inn, hoping to find out.

Inside a veritable Wingate family reunion was occurring. Quick hugs were exchanged, and even Peabody seemed inordinately glad to be laying eyes on Abigail, and even Sir Harlan, again.

"It's about time you returned," Violet was saying. "As you can see, once again it has been left for me to solve this family's problems."

"But what are you and Peabody doing here?" Abigail asked, speaking the question on all of their minds.

"Well you might ask!" Peabody exclaimed, as he and Violet exchanged exasperated glances.

"That odious groom from The Willows insisted on stopping here to rest his horses for a bit," Violet said. "I don't see why he couldn't have chosen a more fashionable inn to stop at."

"I didn't mean why are you at this place in particular, but rather what are you doing on the road at all?"

"Oh. I forgot you all don't know what has happened since Father went haring off to London." Violet gathered herself for a moment, as if bracing herself against unpleasantness. Peabody stood by her with a fan and a glass of water, ready to provide assistance as needed. "After that chaotic morning, I noticed that Sophy was spending a lot of time away from home riding. It made me rather suspicious of what she was up to—you know I always said we were going to have trouble with her. So I sent Peabody out to follow her, and you'll never guess what he discovered!"

"What?"

"Sophy and that Freddy Cantrell were the kidnappers!"

To the astonished looks of those assembled, Peabody nodded briskly. "It's true! They were keeping Garrick and

Mrs. Siddons in an abandoned shed on Lord Overmeer's property."

Sir Harlan gasped, obviously thinking of his birds, not Sophy. "A shed!"

Violet put her hands on her hips. She *was* more concerned about Sophy—and the reputation of the Wingate family in general. "Can you believe it? Our sister out tending livestock with a male neighbor *unchaperoned*! And her riding habit was filthy when Peabody brought her back to the house. As you can imagine, I gave her a terrible scold."

It was unclear whether the scold had centered more on the illegality of kidnapping, the impropriety of being alone with Freddy, or the soiled state of her clothing.

"I sent Sophy to her room without dinner last night," Violet said, "but she must have sneaked a message to Freddy somehow. This morning I found this on her pillow." She handed Abigail a note.

> *Violet,*
> *After your cruel treatment of me, I am left with the only alternative of flying with my partner in crime. Speak of this to no one.*
> *Sophy*
> *P.S. Please tell Tillie to tend to my velvet riding habit.*

"Of course, the peacocks were missing again. After all this, Peabody and I hurried over to The Willows, hoping to stop the two idiots from whatever mischief they were now intent on, but we just missed them. So we discussed it with Nathan's housekeeper, and she had Willoughby get out the carriage and we set out in pursuit. We ran into some men on horseback who spotted a wagon with a covered cage in the back headed this way . . . and here we are."

"Has anyone asked the owner here if he's seen them?" Nathan asked.

Sir Harlan went running off to do this and returned a few minutes later discouraged.

"We missed them." His face was drawn and tired.

"But they *were* here?" Abigail asked.

"When I described them to the owner, he said that they had been here an hour ago. He served them beef pies and cider."

"Good heavens!" Violet cried, although Abigail was unsure whether her distress stemmed from the fact that her sister had so narrowly escaped her pursuit or from her being seen in a public house eating a beef pie.

"Can we be sure this was Sophy?"

"From my description of her, he seemed confident that it was she," Sir Harlan said. "He said that the young man and woman he had served had bickered throughout the meal, and that the girl had gotten up after finishing and stomped off in a huff."

Abigail bit her lip. "That might be Sophy . . ."

"She is so overly emotional," Violet said, "and she wouldn't think twice about making a scene."

"Yes, but she's practical enough not to have stomped off *before* she had finished her pie," Abigail said.

"That is what I thought," Sir Harlan agreed. "We must comb this area for further sight of them."

They all stared at each other, unsure how to go on. Nathan met Abigail's worried gaze. He didn't know what had gotten into his brother's head. He only knew that when he next saw him, he would give him a good throttling.

It did not help that Nathan had hardly slept at all the night before. Abby's father did indeed snore. So Nathan had burned a candle most of the night, reading a book that had fallen out of Sir Harlan's bag. It was another Georgianna Harcourt . . . an author he had a much keener interest in now.

Everyone was arguing about what route they should now take. Should the groups split up and cover more ground or stay together? In the middle of this turmoil, Sir Harlan looked out the window, worriedly.

"I hope that young puppy of a brother of yours is treating my animals right. If I had to lose them, I would have sold Garrick and Mrs. Siddons to Clatsop. At least then I would know that they were being kept in the manner to which they are accustomed. But of course, I'd as soon sell my own children!"

Abigail snorted. "Perhaps if the earl had offered to pay you in grandchildren instead of a few hundred pounds . . ."

Nathan stepped forward before an argument could begin. "The Earl of Clatsop offered you hundreds of pounds for your birds?"

"'Course he did!" Sir Harlan boasted. "Said they were some of the best specimens in all the land."

Nathan hesitated. If what he suspected were true, he felt sure Sophy and Freddy would return to their respective houses soon. But if he were wrong, they might be wasting precious time.

"I believe I know where we can find Sophy and Freddy," he announced.

"Where?" Abigail asked eagerly.

"At the Earl of Clatsop's."

Sir Harlan frowned. "What would they be doing there?"

"Their kidnapping plot was foiled, so they are attempting to sell the birds."

Sir Harlan looked too stunned to speak.

For a moment, Abigail stared at Nathan as if he had gone insane on them. "What would that solve?"

Nathan shook his head. "This is my fault. I had told Freddy of our financial woes, and he was very disturbed by them. He knew of my efforts to try to save the place . . ." He looked at Abigail self-consciously. "Well, he knew that I was trying to solve the problem. But while I was in London, I did not tell him that a solution had been reached because I wanted to inform him in person. No doubt he tried to take matters into his own hands."

"By kidnapping my birds?"

"Yes," Abigail said, obviously understanding it all now. "And when Peabody caught them, they decided to sell them to Clatsop for ready cash."

Sir Harlan chewed his lip. "Hadn't thought of that."

Violet chimed in, "That is a very interesting plan from Freddy's point of view, but why on earth would Sophy go along with such a scheme?"

Abigail grunted. "Because she is capricious, and always afraid that life is passing her by. She probably thought that this would be a grand adventure."

"Exactly," Nathan said. "Together they probably convinced themselves that they were doing a wonderful thing by saving The Willows."

"But the price they'll receive for the pair won't be nearly enough, so what good would that do?"

Nathan sighed. "My brother doesn't know the particulars of our financial situation and he has no concept of money, anyway. Perhaps he thought it would make a start in paying off our debt." He turned to Sir Harlan. "I am mortified by his behavior. I cannot begin to apologize to you for my brother's actions, except by saying that I will do everything in my power to return Sophy and your peacocks to you."

"You needn't do anymore, my boy. In fact, the rest of you might as well toddle on home," Sir Harlan said. "I will go to the earl's now and find out myself if what you say is true."

"I'm sure it is!" Abigail said. "What else could they be doing with two peacocks in a wagon?"

"What indeed!" Violet, who was suddenly very keen on the conversation now that the earl was involved, put a sympathetic hand on her father's sleeve. "Father, you cannot make such a journey alone. It would be too much of a strain for you. *I* will accompany you."

"I haven't time to spare," Sir Harlan said. "I must inform the earl that the birds are not for sale before it is too late."

Violet looked panicky. "I will not slow you down! I can ride in the phaeton with Abby and Nathan. Peabody will ride standing up on the back."

Everyone turned to look at how Peabody was accepting this plan. He made a manful attempt to appear undismayed.

"By God, the whole world is going to descend upon that poor earl. We might as well take your carriage, Nathan, and be a little more comfortable. I am saddle-sore from so much riding, anyway," Sir Harlan muttered as he stomped away to order the carriage brought around.

Peabody looked much relieved to know that he would be traveling in the comparative comfort of the carriage.

Nathan turned to Abigail. "You must be very tired already after our long journey. There is no reason why you should accompany us to the earl's. I am sure we could rent you a room where you could wait until our return."

She smiled up at him. "I need to go to protect Sophy from Father's wrath. Violet would be useless in this matter."

Nathan laughed. "I cannot argue with you there. Nor can I deny that the trip will be more bearable if you are with us."

She tilted her head and eyed him thoughtfully. "I am very impressed by your powers of deduction," she said. "You solved the mystery of Freddy and Sophy abducting the birds very quickly."

"Ah! I am an old hand at plots like these now. I have been trained by a master."

Her eyebrows arched. "How do you mean?"

"Because several aspects of the theft bear a striking resemblance to the story of *The Diamonds of Torrento*."

Abigail's lips parted in surprise and wonder. Nathan would have liked to kiss those lips just then.

"I merely substituted the peacocks for the heirloom diamonds of that story," he explained.

"You are right! But how . . . ?"

"Your father," he explained. "It seems in the midst of his worry over his peacocks' kidnapping, he still found time to pack a Georgianna Harcourt novel."

"I might have known," Abigail said.

"I have enjoyed it immensely, thus far."

She crossed her arms. "You have not finished?"

"Reading was slow-going last night. It was hard to concentrate, imagining you in your room down the hall."

Abby ignored this provocative comment. "I hope Sophy comes to a better end than poor Marguerite in *Diamonds*!"

He shook his head. "You seem to favor grim endings for

your damsels. I would say you have a surprisingly dark turn of mind."

"Only in fiction," she said, laughing. "In life there is nothing I like more than a happy ending. But maybe I will imagine a happier ending for the book I'm writing now."

"I hope Sophy and Freddy will have one. And Garrick and Mrs. Siddons, too."

But it was actually their own future he worried about more.

Violet was having a hard time suppressing her excitement as they traveled ever closer to Clatsop Castle. She was dressed in her best traveling dress and had found the time at the inn to redo her hair in a more attractive manner. Clearly she had no intention of arriving on the earl's doorstep in anything less than pristine condition.

And now she perched on her seat in the carriage, as giddy as a girl going on her first picnic. Her normally pale cheeks were brightened by a high rosy color.

Sir Harlan slumped on the seat next to her, his own pallor a disturbing shade of green. The man did not look at all well. Probably he should have ridden next to the carriage, despite his saddle sores. Abigail had almost suggested it, but then she was afraid if she had, that Nathan would also feel obliged to ride, and she selfishly wanted his company in the carriage herself.

"How much longer?" Violet asked, as impatient as a child.

"Not far."

"I hope Peabody is keeping an eye on my box."

Though Violet had prepared hastily for the journey to parts unknown that morning, she had not failed to have Tillie toss into a traveling trunk every item in her possession that might come in handy no matter what circumstances she found herself in. Her wardrobe for runaway-chasing included her best evening gown, nightclothes, a change of traveling clothes, a riding habit, and all the accoutrements, including shoes, hats, and jewelry, to complete these ensembles.

"What is there to see to?" Abigail asked. "It's strapped down on the roof."

The trunk weighed down the roof of the carriage, and was being watched over by a more than customarily anxious Peabody now that they were heading for the earl's residence. Both man and mistress realized that they were being presented with their best opportunity to gain a toehold into the peerage. Indeed, with the contents of Violet's trunks, they could practically move right in to Clatsop Castle.

Violet sent Abigail an even stare. "The straps could break. It could slip off."

"More likely the infernal trunk will cave in the roof of the carriage and crush us all!" Sir Harlan said with a moan. "A fine state of affairs that will be."

"Are you feeling well, Father?" Abigail asked.

"'Course not! How am I to feel well when I've had my second daughter run off in two weeks, and with a bird-kidnapper?"

Abigail felt chastened. She had felt so angry when she left Peacock Hall after the ball, she had not considered the fact that her father might harbor concern for her welfare. She leaned forward to comfort her green-hued parent. "I returned safely, Father. I am sure Sophy will, too."

"But what about Garrick and Mrs. Siddons?" Sir Harlan shook his head. "All I wanted, all I've ever wanted, was a home full of family, a few creature comforts, and my birds. Not too much to ask for, one wouldn't think. But when I go about trying to secure a grandchild or two, what happens? Disaster! You get uppity and flee for London, Sophy runs off with a criminal, stealing my poor birds in the bargain. Now they may be sold!"

"Don't worry, Father," Violet told him. She was practically wriggling with anticipation. "All your problems might be solved in one blow today. You shall be reunited with your birds, and I might get my earl, and then you shall have your grandchild."

Sir Harlan shook his head. "I wouldn't be too sure of Clatsop—he is a man set in his ways."

"But once he sees how beautifully his house might be set off by a wife . . ." She smiled. "Well! I have heard that Clatsop Castle rests amid wondrous natural beauty." Her tone seemed to indicate that wondrous natural beauty of her own presence there could only enhance the landscape. She bit her lip thoughtfully, considering her future home. "I wonder how many rooms the castle has. These old residences sometimes do not have all the modern conveniences, like ballrooms."

Abigail chuckled. "I have never heard a ballroom described as a convenience."

Her sister blinked at her. "If you are having a ball and you don't have one, it is certainly very *in*convenient."

It was sometimes difficult to argue with Violet's logic, Abigail admitted to herself.

Nathan cleared his throat, and Abigail looked up at him, noticing a change in his manner. He wasn't looking at her—in fact, he was very studiously *not* looking at her—but instead faced Sir Harlan. "Sir, I would like you to know that, however the events of today turn out, your efforts will not have been in vain."

"What's that?" Sir Harlan asked, rousing himself a little.

Nathan smiled at Abigail, then turned back to her father. "I respectfully request permission for your daughter's hand in marriage."

Violet gasped. Even Abigail, who was not entirely surprised by the statement, felt her heart jolt violently.

Her father squinted at him. "Which daughter might you be asking for?"

Nathan seemed surprised by the question. "Abigail."

The older man's eyes bugged. "What? That again? She already bolted from you once!"

Nathan took Abigail's hand. "I have reason to believe that she would not run away a second time."

Her father leveled a curious gaze on her. "What do you say to all of this? You seemed sure enough the night of the ball that you wouldn't have him."

Abigail had to blush. "As to that, Father, I have had a change of heart."

"Well!" Sir Harlan barked out a laugh. "This is a spot of good news."

"Then you would agree?" Nathan asked. "I have to tell you, sir, that I am now in a position to repay the mortgages . . . eventually. So I do not expect our original arrangement to stand."

"Well, well, I congratulate you. How did you do it?"

"Abigail's Aunt Augusta has invested in my woolen mill."

Sir Harlan's jaw dropped. "What? You talked Augusta Travers into putting her money into something as practical as that?"

"Augusta has more facets to her than people give her credit for."

"My, my," Sir Harlan mused. He winked at Abigail, then turned back to Nathan. "Took my advice, did you, and patterned yourself after that Fuego character?"

Nathan and Abigail exchanged amused glances, and at his unspoken inquiry, Abigail gave Nathan a nod. "Unfortunately, it almost put a period to my hopes when Abigail realized that I was using Fuego as a role model."

"Why?"

"Because she is the author of *Lord Fuego's Pursuit.*"

Sir Harlan nearly fell off the seat. Then he made Nathan repeat the news.

"But why did you not tell me?" he thundered at Abigail.

"Because I thought you would believe it a waste of a girl's time," she said. "You always said you hated literate females."

"But to have Georgianna Harcourt living under my own roof!" he bellowed. "I certainly don't disapprove of literate females who make money!"

She laughed and sent Nathan a relieved look. And now that she thought about it, she did feel a little foolish for not having told her family before. It felt dishonest now to have kept her secret for so long.

Even Violet was impressed. "Just imagine! A talent like

writing—when one is a success—can be an entrée into society all its own. You could have a salon in London."

Abigail squeezed Nathan's hand again. "Fortunately, I won't have time. I will have a home in Yorkshire instead."

Violet looked appalled that anyone would make such a choice, but obviously held her tongue on the subject in response to the celebratory mood taking hold in the carriage. "And just think, Father," she said, "by this evening, perhaps you'll have even more to celebrate."

Another engagement, was the obvious insinuation.

They rode the rest of the way in a merrier frame of mind, then stopped in the ancient village of Clatsop for directions to the earl's place. It was fortunate that they had them, too, because it was unlikely they ever would have found it without specific instructions. Indeed, if they had driven right past the place, it was doubtful that they would have realized it. Clatsop Castle was not what they had expected.

The building, which looked more like a tiny crumbling fortress than an actual castle, was made of a sickening yellow-gray stone that was almost black in places. It had a moldering, crumbly look that might have seemed interesting in a ruin; in an inhabited house it was rather alarming. Abigail thought that if someone knocked too hard on the front door, the whole thing might collapse into a heap.

One look was all it took to realize that there would not be a ballroom. At best, there might be a communal hall with a still extant Saxon fire pit.

"Oh!" Violet couldn't help exclaiming.

"Clatsop has always bragged of his home's antiquity," Sir Harlan said. "I can see why, now."

"That pile is not antique, it's medieval!" Violet exclaimed. "One would almost expect dogs and pigs to be rooting around the entrance."

And as a matter of fact, as they drove closer, a decided stench rose to the nostrils of the carriage's occupants, almost as if there were a barnyard in the driveway.

"What is that smell?" Violet exclaimed, lifting her handkerchief to her nose.

"Birds," Sir Harlan said. He alone did not seem disturbed by the odor.

"Oh!" Violet was practically hyperventilating.

"The earl was telling me that he has just built a new dovecote," Sir Harlan announced.

"At least the birds have some modern conveniences," Abigail said.

As soon as the carriage came to a stop, the old earl came running out of his door. In fact, he outpaced the doorman who was coming to open the carriage doors.

"Wingate!" the earl cried by way of greeting. In fact he nearly fell upon his old acquaintance with relief. "Thank God you've come! I thought you would never get here."

"You were expecting us?" Sir Harlan asked.

The earl was caught short. "I sent you a note. Your daughter is here."

"I never received a note—we must have missed your messenger."

"I sent my man as soon as ever I could," the earl explained. "Your daughter and young Cantrell have done nothing but argue since they arrived here with your peacocks."

At the mention of Garrick and his mate, Sir Harlan looked as if he might faint for joy. "Are they all right, then?"

"Oh, yes. Quite well. And to answer the question that is surely on your mind . . . I gave your daughter no money for them."

Sir Harlan sagged in relief. "They were taken without my permission."

"I feared as much." The earl sighed. "I had hoped . . . but it seemed too good to be true."

By this time, the carriage was emptied. Nathan and Abigail stood half-listening to the conversation, and yet at the same time looking out for Freddy and Sophy. Peabody had come down from the top of the carriage and was supporting a clearly distraught Violet. The two of them clung to each other in their hour of disillusionment. Clatsop Castle was obviously a far, far cry from the shining refuge that they had imagined. Indeed, both servant and mistress eye-balled the castle and its environs with gazes that clearly said they would just as soon move into a pig wallow.

"Unfortunately," the earl went on, oblivious to the emotions that were passing between the Wingate butler and the woman who could have been his for the asking before she saw his relic of a home, "as soon as I told your daughter and her friend that I would not purchase the birds from them, the arguing began in earnest. I feared that there might be violence, which I do not have to tell you was very disturbing to my fiancée."

Abigail gasped. "Are you engaged, sir?"

The old man blushed red to the roots of his nonexistent hair. "Indeed, I am. In fact, I was hoping to give Sir Harlan's pair of birds to Miss Mudge as an engagement gift."

At the mention of her old rival from the Wingate ball, Violet could not help letting out a snort. But this time her disdain for the woman also had a healthy dose of pity in it. "Miss Mudge? Is she your betrothed?"

He nodded. "Yes, since last week. I suppose I have to thank you, Wingate, for bringing us together. We renewed an old acquaintance at the ball, where I discovered that I could not like to spend the rest of my life without her."

Nathan and Abigail locked gazes. Though the earl and Miss Mudge were not the most romantic pair, hearing of a happy romance was always welcome to those who were also in love.

Just then, Sophy and Freddy descended the steps of the castle. Sophy practically threw herself at Sir Harlan. "Oh, Father! I am so sorry—and so unhappy!"

Sir Harlan, whom everyone had expected to have a fit when finally face-to-face with the runaways, instead astonished them by giving Sophy a fatherly pat on the shoulder. "There—it's over now. As long as Garrick and Mrs. Siddons are all right."

"Then you aren't angry?" Sophy said, tilting her head to study him, to make sure.

"Not permanently so," Sir Harlan assured her.

"Because it was all Freddy's idea!" Sophy blurted out, glaring at her partner in crime.

Freddy sent a startled look to Sir Harlan, then glared at Sophy. "That ransom note was *your* brilliant notion," he pointed out.

She jutted out her chin. "You took it up quickly enough."

"Yes, and I dropped it as soon as I realized what a stir we were causing." He turned to Sir Harlan. "It's true, sir, I would never have taken money from you for kidnapping the birds. But Sophy sent me a note that she was going to sell them to the earl. So I followed her and when I caught up to the wagon I couldn't persuade her to return home. So I decided to accompany her here and wait for you to come for her."

She lifted her chin and appealed to her audience. "You see what I had to put up with! And listen to him placing the blame on me."

"And who was the one who would not stop talking about the peacocks and how much they were worth, I'd like to know," Freddy reminded her.

She bridled defensively. "Only because you seemed so dejected!" She angled her gaze back up to Sir Harlan. "Oh, Father, couldn't you simply tear up those silly mortgages and let the Cantrells have their stupid old house? I'm sure there will be no end to the disagreeableness until *someone* gets his way."

If Freddy and Sophy had been ten years younger, they might have stuck their tongues out at each other. As it was, Sophy just sent him a withering gaze, which he returned full force.

"As it happens," Sir Harlan announced, "all the disagreeableness, as you call it, is at an end right now. I will tear up the mortgages."

Freddy gasped. "Oh, sir—thank you."

Sir Harlan brayed, "Not for your sake, you kidnapping young fiend! I will forgive the debt as a wedding present for my daughter."

The younger Cantrell's head appeared to be spinning. "B-but we're not getting married! I can assure you that nothing of an untoward nature has ever occurred between myself and Sophy—"

"I know that," Sir Harlan said.

Freddy squinted. "Did someone ask for Violet's hand, then?"

Nathan cuffed him on the arm. "*Abigail* is to be your sister-in-law, you young dolt!"

Freddy gaped at her. "What? But she rejected you at the ball!"

Abigail laughed, and so did the rest of them.

"We obviously have some catching up to do," Nathan told his brother.

When the catching up was done, and the party had returned to Peacock Hall, Abigail and Nathan found a moment of privacy in her study. Nathan looked around the place nervously. He would never get used to the effect of all those feathers applied to the walls.

"I hope you do not expect to replicate this feathered effect at The Willows."

She chuckled. "I am certain I can live with that disappointment."

He tugged her to him. "I promise there will be other compensations."

Her heart pounded. Would a lifetime spent looking at his face be enough? She doubted it. "Of that, I have no doubt," she purred back at him.

He pushed her onto the sofa where they had shared such a memorable embrace that summer afternoon, and he kissed her long and hard. Kissed her until her toes curled and her insides simmered with desire. She cuddled happily against his chest, pleased with the notion that he belonged to her now. She had never considered herself an acquisitive soul, but now that she had acquired a lover, she was quite happy with him.

Nathan sighed. "So this is where the creation of all your books has taken place."

She nodded. "Except the last book has been going rather slowly."

"Why?"

She shrugged. "I have been distracted. And every time I sat down to my desk, my hero started looking more and more like a certain neighbor I ran across one day at Lord Overmeer's pond."

"No, really?" His brows rose playfully. "A handsome fellow?"

"I suppose some might find him so."

"Charming?"

She hesitated. "Rather rude, I thought. It took a while for me to appreciate his provoking manner."

"And now?" he asked, drawing her even closer.

Try as she might, she could not even pretend indifference. "Now I am quite fond of him."

He smiled. "Abigail, I love you."

"And I love you," she answered, moments before he bent to bestow the sweetest of kisses on her lips.

Epilogue

From the top of the windswept hill, Clara looked back fondly towards Raffizzi Castle. She could hardly believe the terror that this view had once struck in her. What had once been a prison to her now was her heart's refuge. Where once she dreaded the arrival of its master, now she longed for his return with impatience.

Suddenly she caught sight of a man on a black steed approaching at a gallop. The rider dismounted just as Clara threw herself into his arms.

"Carissima Clara, how I have missed you!" Rudolpho exclaimed.

"And I you, my husband. I hope that your trip was successful?"

He smiled at her happily. "Yes, soon we will see the arrival of the new winepress. With any luck it will be here in time for the fall harvest."

"That is not the only new arrival we can expect at the end of summer, my love!" As Clara looked lovingly into her husband's face, his magnetic green eyes shone even brighter at the implication of her words. Then he enfolded her in his arms and they kissed as if it were for the first time.

—The Prisoner of Raffizzi

Sir Harlan closed the pages of the marble-backed book with satisfaction. By heavens, that was her best one yet! He wondered when he could look forward to seeing

Abby and Nathan. He supposed they would need at least a day to recover from their trip to the sheep auction in Scotland. He'd bet his eyeteeth that he was about to realize his dream of seeing his first grandchild come this September. He wasn't Georgianna Harcourt's father for nothing.

The older man picked up the glass of Madeira resting on the side table, looked up with pride at the picture of Garrick and Mrs. Siddons, then gazed wistfully towards the portrait of his wife and gave a toast. "To Clara and Rudolpho and, more importantly—to Count Orsino!"

ABOUT THE AUTHOR

His Chosen Bride is Alexandra Bassett's first novel. She is currently working on her second, which will be published in July 2006. Alexandra loves hearing from readers and you may write to her c/o Zebra Books. Please include a self-addressed stamped envelope if you wish a reply.